QUEEN OF STORMS AND SILENCE

CRESCENT QUEENS

BOOK THREE

TRICIA MEYERS

"The end is never the end. It's always the the beginning of something."
—— Kate Lord Brown, The Perfume Garden

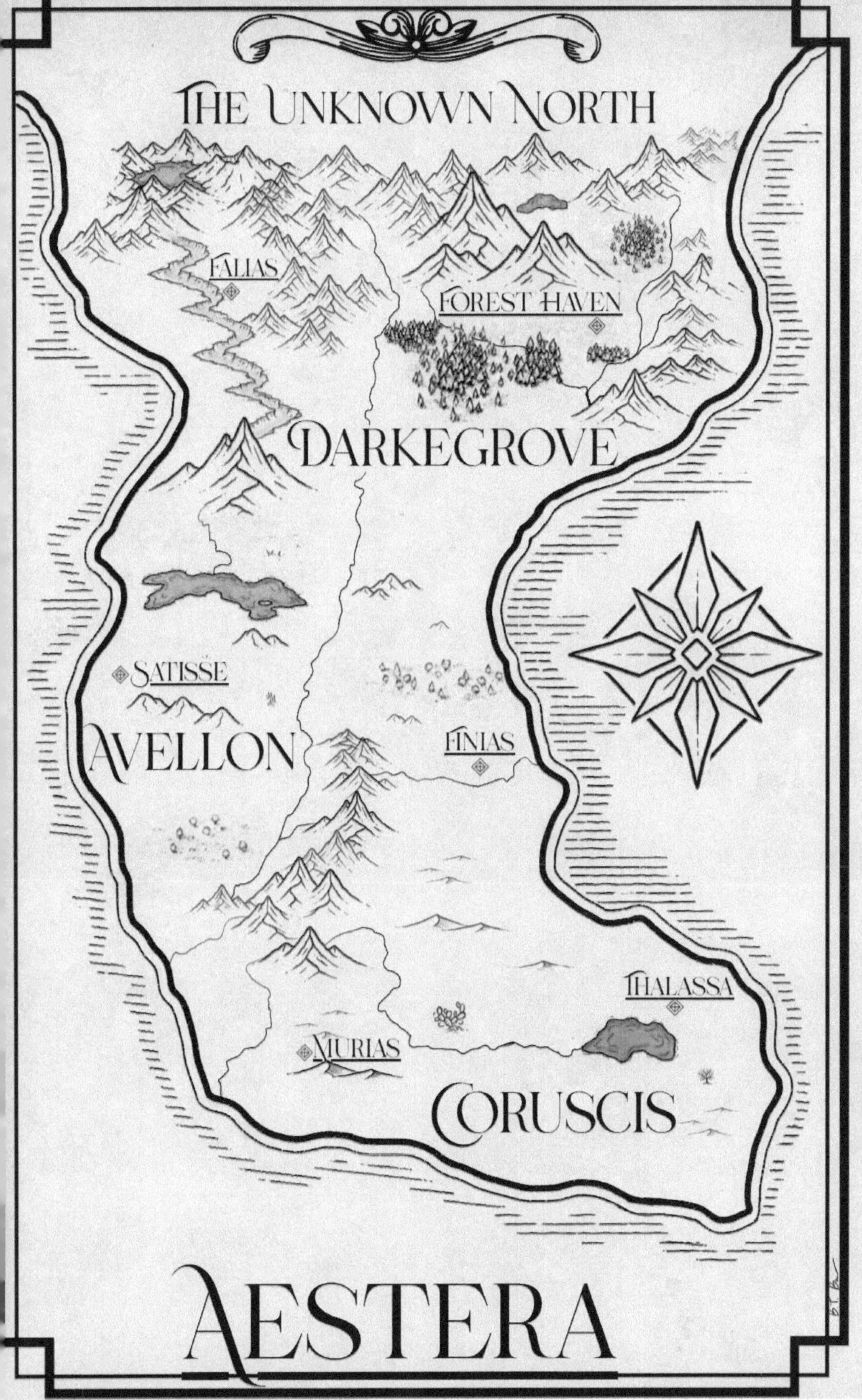

THE UNKNOWN NORTH
FALIAS
FOREST HAVEN
DARKEGROVE
SATISSE
AVELLON
FINIAS
THALASSA
MURIAS
CORUSCIS
AESTERA

Content Warnings

Please review these content warnings before reading.

- violence
- explicit sex
- blood play
- on-page death
- the death of a parent
- torture
- strong language
- sexual threats/threats of SA
- PTSD/panic attacks
- thoughts of self harm

Pronunciation Guide

Evelyn- eve-lin
    Aurelia- or-ell-ee-uh
    Naia - n-eye-uh
    Damian- day-me-uhn
    Damla- dam-luh
    Lir- leer
    Endri- in-dree
    Suri- sir-ee
    Maren- mare-in
    Zayan Hidar - zay-uhn hee-dar
    Callan- cal-en
    Leysa- ley-za
    Valerian- vuh-lair-ee-in
    Cathal- cuh-hall
    Aelius- ay-lee-us
    Vallyse- vuh-leese
    Sybella- sigh-bell-uh
    Eyla- a-luh
    Brida- bree-duh
    Kore- cor-ee

Amias- ay-mee-us
Gorias- gore-ee-us
Avellon- ah-vell-on
Coruscis- cor-oo-sis
Finias- fin-ee-us
Paradisus- pair-uh-dee-soos
Kavala- kuh-vahl-uh
Xanthos- zan-those
Livorno- live-ore-no
Paralia - puh-rah-lee-uh
Zale- z-ail
Valora- vuh-lore-uh
Cordelia- core-deal-ee-uh
Hadrian- hay-dree-uhn
Lucienne- loo-see-in
Celio- say-lee-oh
Risa- ree-sah
Vivien- viv-ee-in
Silas- sigh-luss
Colette- c-ohl-ette
Sidra- sid-ruh
Cordis- core-diss

Relevant Members of the Pantheon

Macaria - Goddess of Death and Destiny - (muh-car-ee-uh)
Keithia- Goddess of Life and Earth - (ki-thee-uh)
Helie - Goddess of the Sun and Healing - (ey-lee)
Araceli - Goddess of the Night Sky and Prophecy - (air-uh-sell-ee)
Astraia - Goddess of Judgement and Justice - (uh-stray-uh)
Lir- God of the Sea and Storms - (leer)
Endri- Genderfluid God of Dreams and Inspiration - (in-dree)
Vidar- God of Silence and Restraint - (vee-dar)

PROLOGUE

They gathered in the secret place, the last one hidden from her view. Not even the prayers of their human children could reach them here. Fear was thick, heavy as iron as it weighed down upon each of the gathered gods. All of them were here, he noted, scanning the crowded vestibule. The upper level was just as full, he could tell, from the many faces he saw looking down from the balcony above.

"Lir."

He turned then, to face Araceli. The goddess of the night sky and prophecy, as mad as she was lovely, was one of the few who had chosen to get personally involved in the war that threatened them all, thanks to her daughter's involvement.

"You've made some of us very nervous," he said, the corner of his lips tugging upward.

He didn't personally count himself as one of those number, but then, he was always more intemperate than the others. He hadn't yet decided if he would become involved, despite the push from Keithia and Helie. That determined duo had been on his ass from the beginning to offer the cauldron bearer his boon. Perhaps, if she proved herself up to the task, he would.

"Time is running out," Araceli stated, her gaze distant and voice soft.

Prophets, he thought with mild disdain, as she continued. "The girl with the heart of thunder must be claimed. All will be lost...all will be lost..."

Lir rolled his eyes and turned his gaze back to the gathered gods. All eyes were on the center of the room, where the god of sight had opened a viewing pool. Images of the war played across the still water. Sword clashed against sword as the battle raged, before shifting to the hilltop where Helie's chosen was changed, drawing her first breath as a newly created fae.

Light, pure and deadly, erupted from the sword bearer minutes later, decimating the Void's army.

To his surprise, Lir felt the first stirring of hope in their success. Perhaps these mortal women would rise to the challenge laid at their feet by fate. Perhaps, he thought, it was time for him to meet his own chosen in person and determine for himself if she was what they needed.

CHAPTER 1

As she did every morning, the Queen of Coruscis took her breakfast on the eastern terrace, overlooking the sandy shores of the Silver Strand. The section of beach that ranged from just below the cliff face, marking the border her kingdom shared with Avellon, all the way to the tide pools at Leukiros earned its name thanks to the stunning white sand that made up the coastline.

Bare feet against the marble announced her younger sister's arrival just as Naia popped a fat grape into her mouth.

"What's that look for?" Maren asked, referring to the arched expression Naia greeted her with.

"You should tell the Prince of Avellon to be quieter if he's going to be sneaking about," she said as if discussing the weather.

Secrets were a tool to be wielded, to be used to gain an advantage over a situation or a person. Her younger sister had usually taken a different stance, but judging from the blond she saw sneaking out of her sister's chambers in the wee hours of the morning, perhaps Maren's opinion had changed.

Maren's mouth fell open, then closed again quickly. Her warm almond eyes, identical to Naia's own in shape, less so in color as Maren's were a soft brown and Naia's neared black, drifted to the sea beyond. "I should've known you'd figure it out," she sighed.

"How long has that been going on?" Naia asked idly, snagging a piece of bacon from the tray between them.

Maren shrugged lightly. "Awhile."

The crashing of the waves beyond filled the silence between them for the span of a few heartbeats. Maren brushed her dark wavy hair back from her face, and a familiar pang of jealousy swept through Naia.

She was beautiful, in a soft, delicate sort of way that Naia would never achieve. Her perfectly straight hair was lovely, but paired with her more striking, angular features it tended to make her look more threatening than alluring.

Not that I should care, Naia thought. She had no desire to be alluring, necessarily, but having the ability to be so when the mood struck her would have been nice.

"Does he make you happy?" she asked finally. In her mind, it was the only question that mattered. Political ramifications aside, if Maren was happy, Naia was happy. Their mother would likely disagree, but Naia hardly cared. Damla's opinions on politics ceased to carry weight the moment she passed the crown to her daughter only weeks ago.

The soft smile that graced Maren's face was answer enough, but her sister replied, "Yes, he does." The matter was settled then, for Naia. If Aelius Vallyse made Maren happy, then she would accept it. If he hurt her...well, then Naia would end him, treaty be damned.

"Good," Naia said, nodding her thanks as a servant placed a pair of letters on the breakfast table. The evergreen seal of Darkegrove along the back caused her brow to raise. With a thoughtful hum, she swiftly read through the contents. Shock and no small amount of sympathy washed over her.

The second was scooped up instantly and torn open. This one, from her own personal spies, held the more interesting information between the two and had her eyes widening further at each word written across the page.

"What is it?" Maren asked, finally beginning to pick at a bit of the fruit before her.

Naia laughed, dropping the letters to the table. "Evelyn Darrow has just taken the throne of Darkegrove."

Maren blinked. "She's chosen a husband?"

Naia shook her head. That backward tradition had never made sense to the people of Coruscis, whose throne had been occupied by women for three generations now. To say she was impressed to see the princess she'd always thought of as little more than a pretty head with little inside of it actually take a stand was an understatement.

The news of her mother was a pity. Though she hadn't known the former queen very well, she was sure Damla would take the news poorly. She could sympathize with the pain of losing a parent at least, and now Evelyn had lost two in such a short time.

"No," Naia replied, tossing her long braid over her shoulder. For at least the third time this morning alone, she contemplated cutting it short. Braiding it made her lengthy hair easier to deal with but it was still in her way more often than she would like. "She took the throne herself. Her mother, Riona, has been murdered too."

Maren gaped, dropping a piece of melon back onto her plate with a thunk. "She killed her mother for the throne?" she whispered, horrified.

"Gods, no," Naia replied, waving a hand. "The spies report that more than one attempt was made on Evelyn's life in an attempt to stop her from taking the throne." Maren frowned, muttering a curse. "Before, and after," Naia continued. "They murdered her mother to try to stop her."

Maren looked as if she was going to be ill. As an emissary, it was hardly unusual for her to be privy to some of the more deadly political games played on their continent, and those of their neighbors far to the south and east, but this sort of thing had never happened so close to home.

"Mother is going to be devastated," Maren remarked, leaning back into her chair with a sigh. "I think she was rather fond of Riona Darrow."

Naia gave no response as she rose from her chair and strode to the balcony. Her heart longed to be out there, on the sea. She hadn't been sailing in years, not since their father...

Her gaze snagged on the darkening sky far on the horizon. Clouds like that could only mean one thing. A nasty brute of a storm would be here soon, with thrashing rain and lightning whipping across the sky.

She couldn't wait.

Turning to Maren with a grin, she said, "A storm is brewing; we should prepare."

Chapter 2

From her place on her bed, Naia watched as the sea roiled and raged. Thunder crashed outside as rain battered the window. *The sea is angry tonight*, she mused. Her father had always been good at predicting the moods of the sea and had ensured his daughters understood them to a degree as well.

Things change swiftly on sea or sand, he would say. *And neither are forgiving.*

The words echoed in her mind, though the exact timbre of his voice had been forgotten over the nearly ten years since he'd been gone.

At fifteen, she thought of her father as invincible, hardly capable of being taken by something so common as a shipwreck. A frustrated sigh escaped her as she rolled onto her side, still watching the sea. Despite having taken her favorite person from her, she still loved it.

Ocean water ran through her veins, inherited from him more than her mother.

A quiet rap at the door announced her mother's arrival. "Come in," she called. It was early yet, too early for her to be going to bed, and if Damla was here, there was likely some crisis she needed to attend to.

"Napping?" her mother asked, judgment etched in her tone.

"Of course not," Naia replied, sitting up. At only forty-nine, her mother still looked young enough to pass as her sister. The former queen carried herself with exquisite poise and grace, and, Naia thought, had learned how to look down her nose at you from birth. "Is there something wrong?"

"Are you ill?" Damla asked, gaze raking over her daughter, ignoring Naia's question.

Here we go. "No Mother, I am not," she sighed. "Although I do believe a headache is beginning to come on." Rising from her bed, Naia went to stand by the window, turning her back on her mother, something she knew would piss her off. "What do you need?"

She could feel Damla bristle behind her. The corner of her lips tugged upward slightly. It wasn't that she disliked her mother, it was just that annoying her was so very amusing at times.

"I just wanted to tell you myself about what has happened in Darkegrove."

Naia spun to face her mother, brow raising. "Something else has happened?"

Her spies had been quiet since Riona's death and Eve's coronation. Either there was little to report, or something had happened to them. With the treaty in place, the former was most likely, but a nagging in the back of her mind warneding her something was amiss.

Damla glanced past Naia to the raging sea, her gaze darkening ever so slightly.

Unlike her daughter, she hated the ocean for what it had taken from her.

"There has been some kind of attack. Reports are murky, but it seems Queen Evelyn has disappeared."

Naia inhaled sharply. Her mind raced with the possibilities of who could be behind something like this. Had those set on barring her from the throne become so bold as to attack a reigning queen?

"Okay," she replied, moving past her mother to leave the room.

"Where are you going?"

"To see to our defenses," Naia replied without looking back. "And to prepare to send aid, if we're asked. She needs to be found."

～

No call for aid was received from Darkegrove, and the silence unnerved Naia more than anything. Where Eve Darrow had gone remained a mystery, but the spies had managed to uncover some information about who had taken her kingdom. Strange soldiers, dressed in livery that didn't match any of the known kingdoms they'd encountered, had assumed control of Stoneweald.

The streets of Forest Haven were quiet, they said, and the few citizens who ventured out of their homes were too frightened of the ever-watching conquerors patrolling the city to say much. It was a wonder, they'd explained, that they had been able to make it in and out undetected. The only bit of interesting information they'd been able to find was from a maid inside the castle, who had managed to get word to her brother, a blacksmith in Forest Haven.

These strange soldiers were searching for something–and most troubling of all, they didn't seem human.

How they could be anything but, Naia had no idea. The only nonhuman creatures that could move and look like men were fae, and they had been gone for centuries. The maid simply could not have been thinking clearly. Fear and stress could certainly cause the mind to play tricks, and there were certainly advantages to making oneself seem more dangerous than you truly are.

Clouds still blocked the sun as she stepped outside into the courtyard, days after Eve's disappearance. As much as she relished the stormy season, this particular band of storms seemed to hang around longer than most, and even she enjoyed the sunshine from time to time.

With an irritable sigh, she glanced skyward. "You can go away now," she muttered.

"Talking to the sky, sister?" Maren teased, seated on the edge of the turquoise fountain. The water bubbled gently beneath Maren's idle fingers as they skimmed the surface.

Naia rolled her eyes and dropped into a nearby chair. Her fingers skimmed the broad flat surface of a plant, and she wrinkled her nose. "Just getting a bit tired of the clouds."

"It'll pass," Maren replied lightly. "Any word from Darkegrove?"

"You know there hasn't been," Naia said. Maren had her own spies and often knew things at the same time, or before, Naia herself did. Her ability to navigate secrets and collect information made her invaluable as an emissary.

Maren shifted so she faced Naia fully. "It seemed rude not to ask." She paused a beat before asking, "What's bothering you?"

Dropping her hand, she leaned back in her seat, face skyward as she closed her eyes.

Truthfully, there wasn't a rational answer to that. Something felt unsettled, restless, within her. Perhaps it was the strange events unfolding in Darkegrove causing her to feel ill at ease, or perhaps it was something else entirely.

"I feel..." She sighed, waving a hand idly. Speaking about her feelings was not something she was skilled at. "Unmoored."

Maren hummed thoughtfully. The slide of silk against porcelain told her that Maren had moved, but she didn't bother to look. "Keep your eyes closed," Maren said from right behind her.

Anytime Naia felt anxious, unsure of herself or her path, Maren was there, ready to ease her nerves. Maren's fingers slowly unbraided Naia's hair, letting it fall freely behind the chair. Since they were girls, she had used this trick to ground and calm her sister when the worst of her temper flared or her restless nature threatened to cause damage that couldn't be undone.

"You," Maren said, voice low and calm, running her fingers through her sister's hair gently, "are light," she continued, massaging Naia's scalp gently. "And free and wild as the sky. A storm cloud, roving across the seas." Slowly, she began to rebraid Naia's hair, nearly putting her to sleep with the comforting sensation. "Where are you going to go?"

Naia's thoughts drifted to the sea. In her mind, it was calm, the waves gentle and rolling. The salty breeze kissed her skin as she drifted. "To the east," she whispered. "I want to see the dragons."

Maren laughed quietly. That was typically her answer. "Are you going to ride a dragon?"

"Gods no," Naia laughed. "I have no desire to get eaten."

Finished with the braid now, Maren gave a gentle tug on Naia's hair before moving to stand in front of her. "Don't let it get to you," she said as Naia straightened. "All of the uncertainty. Everything will be fine." At

Naia's raised brow, she added, "Or it won't. Either way, you'll navigate it."

Offering her sister a smile, Naia nodded. "Alright, know-it-all, I have real work to do. Go play with your princeling or something," she said, waving a hand.

"Maybe you should find one of your own," Maren teased as she left, wiggling her eyebrows suggestively. "Might relieve some of your stress at least."

"Oh, get out before I have you thrown in the dungeon you menace," Naia tossed back, smiling despite herself.

CHAPTER 3

I t was with stress relief in mind that she padded through the
corridors of Evertide two nights later. They had agreed to stop
these secret meetings at night, but sleep had refused to come, her
mind racing with the possible threat that loomed on the horizon, the
worry over a kidnapped, or assassinated, queen.

If one queen could be taken, why not another?

Especially concerning was the lack of information she'd been able to
find. Her spies either vanished or came back with nothing to report.
Frustrated, she dismissed the thought as she neared the familiar door at
the end of the hall. Summoning a smile, she lifted her hand and knocked
twice, softly to avoid being heard by his neighbors.

It took several heartbeats for the door to open, but when it did, she
inhaled sharply.

Zayan was shirtless, wearing only loose linen pants that hung low
around his hips, leaving the sharp vee of his lower abdomen on perfect
display. His bronze skin glistened, the dark curls across his chest still
damp from bathing. A single, thick, dark brow rose over his rust-
brown eyes as he leaned against the doorframe with one arm above his
head.

"I thought you said we were done?"

Naia shrugged lightly even as heat began to pool between her legs. "I changed my mind," she said simply.

The corner of his mouth twitched upward as he turned, allowing her entry to his room. "How may I serve, Highness?"

Naia stepped inside, dropping the dressing gown she wore to the floor the moment his door clicked shut behind her. "I can think of one or two ways–" she began, only to be interrupted as he lifted her by the waist. Her legs wound around his hips as his mouth claimed hers in an intense kiss.

Wood scraped her bare back as he pressed her gently against the closed door, drawing a gasp from her parted lips. His lips were a brand against her skin as he kissed a trail down the column of her neck, claiming her nipple with his mouth.

Desire flooded her veins like wildfire as his hips ground against hers, and he straightened, dragging a hand down the side of her ribs to grip her hip. "Tell me what you need, my queen."

"Fuck me," she whispered, nails digging into his shoulder, adding emphasis to her demand. He obliged instantly, yanking his pants down in one moment, and entering her in one swift movement in the next, drawing a gasp from Naia.

Wordlessly, he moved his hips against hers, a steady pace that did little more than scratch a proverbial itch. Dipping her own hand between them, she circled her clit with two fingers, in time with his movements. Pleasure rocketed through her in bright, electric jolts, and within moments she came undone, clenching and unclenching around him rhythmically as he found his own release with hers.

Pinned between Zayan and the door, she lay her head against his shoulder. *Just stress relief,* she thought. *Nothing more.*

Slowly pulling himself out of and away from her, Zayan retrieved her gown and held it out for her. "I had a feeling we weren't really done," he said with a grin.

Naia rolled her eyes. Gods he was sexy, but he was irritatingly arrogant.

"That was the last time," she said, yanking the dressing gown back on. "I mean it this time."

"Alright," he replied with a smirk. "But if you change your mind..."

"I won't," she declared, turning for the door. "Not again," she added more for her own benefit than his.

~

The next morning at breakfast, she idly picked at her fruit, mentally cursing her abysmal choice of lovers. It wasn't like she couldn't have found someone more exciting, someone she could actually connect to on a deeper level, but the truth was that she was afraid. Zayan was decent in bed, usually, and completely uninterested in what he could gain from her.

He had enough money of his own to rival even her own family, and with his connections, was welcomed at nearly every capital city on the known continents.

She felt nothing for him, only attraction and the enjoyment of what he could offer her in the bedroom, and some measure of a friendship.

And that was just fine with her.

And yet here I am, feeling unsatisfied, she thought irritably.

"Did Zayan not do the job?" Maren teased as she took her place at the table. It was no surprise that Maren knew about their meeting. She knew everything that happened inside this castle, always had.

Keeping her gaze on the calm sea beyond the balcony, Naia sighed. "It was...fine."

"Ouch," Maren replied, shaking her head. "You should find someone better."

She didn't respond to that. Most would see only the crown or the Colvari fortune when they looked at Naia. Finding someone else that would ask for nothing more than *her* was an impossible task.

"Have your spies found anything out?" she asked, knowing Maren would understand both her need for a change in subject and exactly what she was referring to.

"No," she replied between bites of her own breakfast. "But there is something else."

Naia turned to Maren then, brow raised. "What?"

"Aldrich Vallyse has taken ill," she replied, staring down at her plate. "Aurelia is going to be crowned soon."

Naia sighed. That would mean that Aelius would likely be spending less time gallivanting as he pleased. His sister would need his help, and the shift in power would require him to be present, to keep things in Avellon stable. "I'm sorry."

"It's fine," Maren replied lightly, finally looking up. "I'll be going to Avellon at some point anyway, to meet with the new queen formally."

"Of course," Naia replied with a grin, ignoring the dread that crawled up her spine. She had no idea why, but something inside her sounded the alarm. She looked back out to the sea, half expecting to see another storm creeping in, but found only a sunny sky above gently rolling waves.

Something is coming, the tiny voice of intuition whispered. *Something terrible is coming.*

Chapter 4

The day-to-day tasks of ruling a kingdom as vast as Coruscis were dreadfully dull, but also entirely necessary. Without approval from someone within Evertide, too many important things would simply grind to a halt, including the official caravans that ventured into the desert to trade with the nomadic groups calling the vast expanses of the Shimmering Strand home. Their numbers had dwindled in the past century or two, according to records, but the exact explanation for their decline was a mystery that none of her ancestors had solved.

Thanks to the harsh environment of the central part of her kingdom, a vast majority of the population called the coastlines home. All along the Shimmering Strand, cities and towns graced shorelines and small islands. Ships, primarily from Southwind shipyard out of Atrani, just south of Thalassa, were a lifeline for Coruscis. So when Naia found herself staring at the latest report, a leaden weight settled on her chest.

The shipyard was struggling to keep up with demand. It relied heavily on timber from Darkegrove, and with the recent turmoil there, trade lines had all but dried up. They could get by, according to the report, for a few more months on what they had, but something would need to be worked out, and soon.

It would have to be Avellon then, she sighed, setting the report to the side. There was little to no indication of a resolution being reached in Darkegrove. Eve was still missing, and no new power had yet laid claim.

I'll write to Aurelia or Hemera, then, she thought, only to pause as a servant stepped inside, another missive in his outstretched hand.

"From Queen Evelyn of Darkegrove," he said, brow raised slightly. Dismissing him with quiet thanks, Naia waited until she was alone to open the carefully folded envelope.

Sure enough, the seal was that of Darkegrove, to her surprise. Perhaps the letter had been sent before the fall of Stoneweald, she pondered, or perhaps the wayward queen, whom all had begun to assume dead, had miraculously returned.

The idea made her snort. Naia didn't believe in miracles.

She scanned the letter once, then twice, before slipping it into a drawer. Her gaze shifted to the fountain that bubbled merrily nearby. Despite the warmth and sunshine of her office, the cheer that the various potted plants brought her, fear, ice cold and sharp as a knife, settled in her gut. Eve's letter warned of a great evil that loomed over them all, of gods and fae returning–of things that could not possibly be true.

A tiny voice inside screamed in warning, but Naia ignored it. Rising from her chair, she started for the door.

"Have the beach cleared," she said to the servant who waited in the hallway. "I'm going for a swim."

The ocean would clear her mind of this nonsense. Whomever sent that letter, whether Eve or someone who had somehow managed to get their hands on her seal, they lied. There was no way these lost gods had returned, no way the fae had either. She didn't believe in miracles, and she believed in the gods even less.

Fae had once called these lands home, she could accept that as a proven fact. But the gods were nothing more than imagination. The way ancient people sought to understand the unexplainable. Weather that frightened them would be an angry god, or a farmer's poor luck could be a curse, for example.

The gods simply didn't exist, and as far as Naia was concerned, Eve Darrow was dead or insane.

CHAPTER 5

There had been little need for the beach to be cleared, she realized, as she stepped up to the water's edge. The sky above had darkened ominously as yet another storm approached, and from the looks of it, was going to be a nasty one. By now, the servants would be drawing shutters closed at Evertide and preparing the castle for the beating from the wind and rain.

Waves crashed angrily against the shoreline, warning her to stay out of the water. The looming storm brought with it dangerous currents that would easily take her out to sea, never to be seen again. She would have only the sea air and the edge of electricity on the air to soothe her nerves then, she realized with a sigh. Her gaze scanned the horizon, vast and seemingly without end, toward the east, where dragons still reigned and–

Naia blinked in surprise.

For the span of a blink, she could have sworn she saw a dark head among the roiling waves, turned toward her as if watching. But that was impossible. She took a step forward, hoping to catch another glimpse of whatever it was she had seen. Because while it couldn't possibly have been a person, she certainly had seen *something*.

"I don't think it's the best time for a swim, beloved," Zayan called from behind her.

Turning, she offered a slight smile. "I thought I saw someone out there."

"That's impossible," he replied, echoing her thoughts. "It was probably just driftwood." Coming to a stop beside her, he trailed his fingertips down her arm, despite the presence of her guards.

The possession in his gaze and the sheer audacity of the gesture had her stepping back. The waves lapped at her ankles as she frowned at him. They were done. She'd made that clear, hadn't she?

"Zayan," she said firmly but soothingly. "I meant what I said." She cast a glance toward the nearby guards, out of earshot but close enough to watch what unfolded. "You want more than I can give you."

"Only you?" he countered.

Their affair had carried on for nearly a year now, and for at least half that he'd been pushing for more. More than the purely physical relationship she'd been perfectly clear she wanted.

His insistence on making their relationship more had been why she'd decided to break things off. Maren's spies had picked up on the whispers, the rumors that he would be the king, not consort, but king.

She could hardly act on rumors alone, especially as there was no proof they originated with him, but her gut told her it was time to walk away. As his jaw tightened ever so slightly, she could see it darkening his brown eyes. Ambition. Brief, but there.

"I told you I'm done," she replied, with less gentleness than before. "Walk me back?"

The expression lasted only for a moment, swiftly replaced with a grin. "As my Queen commands," he replied smoothly, bowing before extending his arm for her to take.

She ignored his outstretched arm, offering him a pointed look as she began to stride toward the castle. A single brow rose in response, but Zayan said nothing as he fell into step beside her.

"Your mother is well?" she asked, not bothering to look at him as they walked.

"She is. King Xanthos' court is treating her quite well," he replied, referring to the king of Kavala, the northernmost kingdom in Laestros.

"Though she misses Coruscis, she finds the jungles quite pleasing. She was gifted a pet monkey by one of the trade princes," he laughed, the sound as practiced and smooth as everything he did. "Have you ever seen one?"

"A monkey or a trade prince?" she asked, glancing sideways at him, wondering where exactly he was going with this. The trade princes of Kavala were well known, of course. Each of them commanded their own small fleet of ships and boasted fortunes that could rival true royalty in most places.

Spices, silks, and even flesh; each of the trades fell under the command of one of the princes. It was a practice limited to Laestros but there had been stirrings amongst the wealthier merchants in recent years, some calls for the practice to be adopted by Coruscis; something Naia would never agree to. Almost all of the princes had reputations that spoke of cruelty, and many suspected Xanthos himself had become little more than a figurehead, forever bowing to the demands of the princes.

She would never allow such a thing to happen here.

"Such strange little creatures," he replied with a light laugh. "The monkeys, I mean." Pausing a beat, he added, "But on the subject of trade princes, I thought perhaps–"

"No," Naia said flatly, turning to face him. They'd reached the terrace now, just as the first crash of thunder echoed over the sea. "Coruscis will have no trade princes," she stated, shaking her head.

"Of course," he replied smoothly. "I only ask because I was approached by an investor interested in helping to establish the practice here. Coruscis would benefit, and we could work the arrangement in such a way as to keep them from having any power here. Perhaps your eventual king consort might see the advantage of the partnership one day." He shrugged, glancing skyward at the oncoming storm.

Naia sighed, tossing her braided hair over her shoulder lightly. "I'll give it some thought," she conceded if only to shut him up, already knowing she would say no. To allow the trade princes into Coruscis would be to invite their corruption as well, and that was something she would never allow to happen.

Casting a glance toward the guards, who remained a respectful distance away, Zayan leaned slightly closer, lowering his voice. "Will you come see me tonight?" His grin was one of invitation and seductive promise. At her flat stare, he raised his hands in surrender. "I had to try, for old times sake."

Temper flaring, she said nothing as they strode inside, parting ways in the entry hall, as she went to find the one person whose advice she could count on.

Chapter 6

"I've asked my contacts in the city," Maren said by way of greeting, plopping down onto the settee across from Naia. "I'm told Lord Hidar has, in fact, been spending a rather large amount of time with a visitor from the south. One who spends extravagantly and whose business dealings are rather...secretive."

Naia frowned. A trade prince had been dealing in her city, under her nose, and she'd been unaware? A conversation would need to be had with the harbormaster, she told herself.

"And?"

"And," Maren continued with a sigh. "It seems as though he has been overheard by some of the serving girls at his favorite tavern promising to establish connections between this southerner and Coruscis; thanks to his close friendship with the queen. He was smart enough to avoid explicitly stating how he intended to ensure this agreement, but..." She let the words trail off, allowing Naia to draw the obvious conclusion.

"He expects to be king."

Maren hummed thoughtfully, leaning back and tilting her head skyward to watch the rain pelting the glass above. The interior garden had been added to Evertide by some ancestor or another, many years after the western wing of the castle had been built.

The domed glass above protected the royals from rain, with vents to allow cool sea air for relief from the summer heat while still offering them the opportunity to relax in what felt like an outdoor space. As with many of the other living spaces, potted plants and lovely bubbling fountains were in abundance, adding to the illusion they were in a lush oasis rather than within the walls of a castle.

"If you like, I am sure an invitation to Livorno could be forthcoming if you think Lord Hidar would be interested."

She could feel her sister's gaze as Maren waited for her reply to the thinly veiled threat. Livorno, the sister empire to Venustus, was a dangerous place, especially for foreigners who held themselves as more important than others, as Zayan did.

"I don't think that will be necessary. But perhaps he can be convinced to go and see to his mother in Kavala," Naia replied, turning her gaze skyward at the first crack of thunder overhead. "For the sake of our long friendship, I will allow him one chance to correct his course."

When she returned her attention to Maren, who looked rather unconvinced, she grinned. "And if he refuses, then we will ensure he receives a warm welcome in Livorno."

The promise of violence that laced Naia's words drew a raised brow from Maren who inclined her head to look the queen over a moment. "Grandmother would be proud of the queen you've become, I think."

Their maternal grandmother had been a fair and well-beloved ruler during her time but had also developed quite a reputation as merciless where her enemies were concerned. She had not tolerated disrespect and any threat to her rule, or the safety of her kingdom, was dealt with swiftly, and in some minds, brutally. Naia wasn't certain she wanted to live up to that particular legacy, but being known as one who would defend what was hers with ferocity held some appeal.

"Mm." Naia didn't voice her true thoughts, the ones that had a small voice whispering in her mind. That voice sounded an awful lot like their mother's, and whispered words of judgment. She'd clearly made a mistake with Zayan. What other mistakes might she make?

Despite what she'd always believed, it was clear enough now that

Zayan saw himself becoming king consort; and siring an heir on her no doubt. The very idea left a bitter taste in her mouth.

He had proven to be ambitious, and ambition in a man who had so rarely been told no was a dangerous thing. Tradition would have prevented him from claiming any real power within Coruscis, but tradition, Eve Darrow had so recently proven, was a fickle and fragile thing.

A crash of thunder rattled the glass dome, and she rose from her seat, casting another glance at the fish in the fountain. "Go ahead and reach out to your connections in Kavala, and Livorno, in case the invitations become necessary. I would like it done swiftly if we're correct."

If the madness in Eve's letter was to be believed, the world was quickly changing, and if that was the case, she needed to be prepared for whatever may come. Any threat to her rule could not be tolerated, and her relationship with Zayan was proving to be dangerous.

"At once," Maren replied, following Naia as she made her way back into the castle proper. "And the welcome, should he travel to Livorno," she began, pausing to smile at a guard as they passed. "How elaborate a party shall we plan?"

Naia considered for a moment before replying. The Hidar family was formidable, and making enemies of them would be counter-intuitive. "Something small, I think. Just enough to get the point across."

Offering her sister a brief curtsy, Maren headed off to handle the preparations as instructed. If Zayan reacted to her rejection the way they feared, well, Gods help the man.

Chapter 7

"I have decided it's time for you to visit your mother in Kavala," Naia said by way of greeting as she stepped into Zayan's dimly lit chambers.

He smiled, bemused, striding toward her confidently, his long legs closing the distance between them quickly. She had taken no more than a few steps into the room, remaining close to the door, and the guards who waited outside.

Lifting a hand to touch the side of her face, he purred, "And leave your side?"

Naia sighed. She hated repeating herself. "We're finished, you will never touch me again. Is that clear?"

He fell silent, stopping just beyond arm's reach of her. "This is not funny, Naia."

The use of her name, spilling so casually from his lips, only made her more resolute. He'd never taken the liberty, even in their most intimate moments, using pet names instead. It had been an unspoken agreement between them.

Yet another line he was crossing.

"You have not been given leave to use my given name, Lord Hidar." She narrowed her eyes at him and closed the short distance between them, the movement feline in its grace. "And I am most serious. You will be leaving Coruscis tonight, on a ship bound for either Kavala, or Livorno, your choice. You'll be greeted on the docks by your new hosts upon your arrival at whichever destination you choose. I suggest you choose wisely."

"You're going to regret this," Zayan seethed, voice low. His eyes had gone dark, all pretense of the amused playboy vanishing in a moment.

His threat didn't frighten Naia in the least. They were the empty words of a frightened man who recognized he had fallen short of his reach for power. "You overstepped, Zayan," the queen replied coolly.

His eyes flared at her words, some poisonous retort ready on his tongue, she was sure.

Before he could give voice to whatever thought he had, securing himself a most unpleasant welcome upon landing on the shores of Livorno, she interrupted. "Pray you do not find yourself within the bounds of my kingdom again," she said, tone deadly, emphasizing the fact that Coruscis would never be his. "On pain of death."

Turning her attention to the door, and the guards who waited in the hall, Naia ignored the strangled cry of anger that erupted from the man she'd called lover. "He is to remain under guard until he is safely aboard the ship of his choosing. Both are waiting at the southern docks. Do not let him out of your sight until the ship is well on its way."

The guards bowed as she swept from the room, leaving him stunned and sputtering.

Having removed one threat to her kingdom, it was time for her to turn her attention to the greater one that supposedly loomed over them all. Eve Darrow's letters, hidden away in her desk, required her attention once more, but this was tomorrow's problem, and she was exhausted.

It was late, well beyond midnight by the time she made her way into her bed, after changing swiftly into a light nightdress. The night would be cooler after the storm they'd had, but she preferred it that way anyway. It was unbearably hot some nights and near frigid others, but her wardrobe never changed. Cool nights were when she slept best, and with the sea breeze blowing in from her open terrace doors, carrying in the sweet scent of the ocean beyond, she knew she would sleep like a babe.

Within minutes, a dream like no other claimed her.

She found herself standing on an unfamiliar shoreline. The churning of the waves was utterly foreign to her, as was the black sand that shifted beneath her feet as she walked, striding toward two figures who seemed to be waiting, watching her expectantly.

"So this is her," the taller of the two remarked, his gaze sweeping over her, leaving her chilled. She wore only the thin nightdress, with her hair braided back, just as she'd been when she'd fallen asleep.

The man, dressed in loose-fitting midnight blue breeches that hung low on his hips and nothing else, folded his arms across his thin but muscular, bare chest and gave her a rather unimpressed stare.

"I suppose you'll do," he sighed. His hair, as dark and nearly as long as hers, fell freely past his shoulders, the ends grazing his biceps. Dark, angular eyes observed her closely as she looked from him to the person standing to his right.

"As if you have a choice," the other stranger remarked idly. Dressed in all white, they also wore loose-fitting breeches, this time paired with a matching tunic that covered their larger frame. Silver hoops adorned their ears, and stark white hair framed a round face with bright, crystal blue eyes. "You cannot undo what has already been done."

The other snorted in response, his expression saying he could damn well try. "Well, girl, speak," he ordered.

Naia could do nothing more than blink.

What an odd dream.

"Not entirely a dream, I'm afraid," the one clad in white said, startling her.

"It has to be," Naia replied matter of factly. That the strange person in white, currently standing in the dreamscape her mind had created, had apparently read her mind left her utterly unfazed.

The shirtless man muttered something under his breath, though she could only make out the last two words, and not very clearly. She could have sworn he'd said, "...mortal minds" but that made no sense. What else could they...

Eve's letter came racing back to the forefront of her mind like a tidal wave. "Oh," she blinked.

"And there it is," the man remarked, rolling his eyes.

"Patience, Lir," the other said placidly.

"You're gods."

The one who was apparently the more relaxed of the two offered a half smile. "This is Lir, God of Sea and Storm. I am Endri. Dreams and inspiration are my domain."

"Before you say it," Lir cut in. "Yes, we were gone, but now we have returned. Please get over your confusion now, as we have little time."

Endri made a tutting sound, but Naia ignored them entirely as she glared at Lir.

"I'm well aware, thank you." Her gaze slid between the two as she straightened. "What do you want?"

The corner of Lir's lips turned upward briefly as if amused, but the expression was gone as quickly as it had appeared, replaced with a flat, unreadable expression. "What we want is for you to retrieve your cauldron and save the damned world, girl."

Endri released a long-suffering sigh, and Naia expected them to intervene again, but they said instead, "Our time is up. Someone is trying to wake her."

"What are you–" Naia began, before blinking awake, as a cool wet nose bumped against her own. She was greeted by a mass of unruly orange fur and wide, green eyes staring directly into her own. Loud, raspy purring rumbled through her as Suri settled herself contentedly on Naia's chest. "Good morning to you too, you little beast."

Mindful of the claws that grabbed onto her nightdress, Naia carefully removed the fluffy monster from her chest and deposited her beside her on the bed. Suri, as dignified as any queen, made her displeasure known with a swish of her tail in Naia's direction before plopping right onto her pillow.

With a scratch behind Suri's ears to appease her, Naia turned her gaze to the windows across the room, the ones with the best view of the ocean. The earliest rays of the sun were just beginning to peak over the horizon.

Leave it to a cat to wake me so early, she thought, dragging herself out of bed.

The strange encounter in her dream hung over her like a fog, clear enough to recall the conversation and the strange beings within, but with a hazy quality that kept the more minute details just out of reach.

It had merely been the strangest dream of her life, probably brought on by Eve's warnings, she told herself.

But what if it hadn't been?

The possibility nagged at her mind as she donned her dressing gown, seafoam green with delicate shell embroidery at the hem, and rang the bell for her maid. She wouldn't, couldn't, let go of the strange encounter until she decided whether or not to believe the claims the queen of Darkegrove had made, and what the strangers in her dream had declared.

What was this cauldron they mentioned?

Why would she, of all people, be destined to save the world?

She had little interest in heroics, especially those that involved long-lost gods and great danger. Coruscis was where her attention needed to remain. Where her destiny lay. Her kingdom, and its people, faced enough challenges to keep her occupied for a lifetime.

Moving through the palace as if pulled by an invisible thread, with Suri in her wake, she found herself in the office, greeting the terrace guards with a light nod.

Her thoughts still dwelled on all that had been claimed by Eve, and now the strange, haunting, dream.

Had the dream merely been because of the outlandish claims Eve had made or....

No, she thought, shaking her head as she sank into her chair. *It cannot be true.*

And yet...

Irritated, she yanked open the desk drawer containing Eve's letters, plucking them from where they had been hidden away before turning to another drawer, the one holding letters from long ago, when two princesses wrote to one another in hopes of connecting before taking their respective thrones.

Holding the newest letter up toward the lantern light, alongside one of the letters from their teenage years, she examined her name across the envelopes. There was the same sharp point of the 'N,' the same swirling, elegant 'a' swishing below the 'i,' and most telling of all, the tiny star above the 'i.' Perhaps a childhood habit Eve had never quite broken, or perhaps a way for her to show Naia that the dire warnings enclosed within had, in fact, been penned by Eve's own hand.

Her heart thundered.

So it was true, then. Or, at least Eve believed it be so.

Perhaps the world *was* in danger, and she was one of a few destined to save them all from some horrible demise. With a long sigh and trembling fingers, she returned the letters to their place, hidden in her drawer. Her gaze drifted to the bubbling fountain where Suri perched, watching the fish swimming within.

Even if it's true, she thought, *how would I even know where to look for this cauldron?*

Rising from her chair, she wandered the room, letting her fingers drift over each of the many plants she passed, thoughts consumed with this supposedly world-saving item her family had apparently held onto for generations. She could recall no such item, unless...

A thud, soon followed by a single shout outside the terrace doors, had her starting, and Naia spun to see what had caused the commotion. She could do little more than watch in bewilderment as first one guard, then another fell to the ground, lifeless.

Surprise or some other irrational thought had her moving toward the terrace door. Suri's low growl startled her back to reality, but by the time she realized her hand had found its grip on the polished handle of the terrace door, it was over.

Each of the four guards, the most elite of their protectors, was dead; and now perched on the wrought iron railing of her terrace, the single man responsible watched her with cold, dark eyes.

"Do not scream, Queen of Coruscis, or it will be the last sound that pretty mouth of yours makes."

Chapter 8

Naia snorted in response to the stranger's threat. She knew she was in danger and, of course, knew that her life was likely over. But she'd be damned if she'd let a threat like that cow her into submission.

She wouldn't scream, wouldn't risk the lives of the other guards who would surely rush to save her. After how swiftly and easily he'd dispatched the four men on her terrace, it would have been a waste of the lives of good men and women.

So instead, she turned, intent on snatching the pair of daggers that lay just behind the small potted plant on the edge of her desk.

The one that rested inside a cauldron with three legs. Naia didn't dare let her gaze linger too long on the plant, or the cauldron that contained it. The one she'd only just realized moments before was very likely the very same one the gods had claimed she'd need.

Had they given her any idea how to use it, what its powers might be, perhaps she could have used it to save her own life. But she had been left ignorant, facing her own death thanks to that ignorance.

Her fingers barely had time to graze the edge of the desk before two strong arms wrapped around her like iron bands. He held her, one arm around her lower belly, the other crushing her breasts, as he pulled her backward against his chest. The stranger's grip was unforgiving, as cruel as his eyes had been, as he held her so tightly she could scarcely draw breath.

"That was very foolish," he breathed against her ear. "But I'll give you credit for your bravery. Stifle that urge, the one that tells you to fight. It will not serve you well where we're going."

A fierce hiss echoed through the room as a mass of orange fur launched itself at her attacker. Surprise had him loosening his grip, but only slightly. The arm across her belly vanished for a moment, only long enough to toss Suri off of him with more care than he was currently showing her with his bruising grip. The cat landed on her feet with a yowl and lowered herself to the ground, still hissing ferociously but not moving to attack again.

Alarm raced through her mind as his arm clamped across her waist again, and she struggled against him. Futile or not, the instinct to save her own life, and that of her cat, was not one she could ignore. He was larger than her, easily double her weight, from what she had observed, a mass of muscle and a well-trained warrior, as indicated by how swiftly he'd dispatched her guards. Fast too, impossibly so.

Fae.

"No!"

Her mind raced, searching for something in her memory of Eve's letters to help her escape this situation, even as she kicked and writhed. Both arms remained pinned to her sides, so moving was nearly impossible.

She couldn't draw enough breath to scream any louder than a whisper. Maybe she could escape from wherever he took her. Naia knew these sands and seas better than nearly anyone, certainly better than some fae monster from another kingdom.

A strange sort of wind began to whip around them as he chuckled, the sound vibrating through her body. "The cat will live, but I would stop all that wiggling if I were you, and close your eyes."

Darkness spread quickly at the edge of her vision, and she stilled.

"What?" Her gaze darted frantically around them, trying and failing to make sense of what was happening. Had his grip tightened around her so much now that she was going to pass out? She could still breathe, not deeply but enough to remain conscious, she'd assumed.

She hadn't closed her eyes. She hadn't passed out; they were falling into impossible emptiness.

Finally, she screamed, sheer terror dragging the sound from her lips, an unwilling captor as much as she herself was. The sound had been hoarse, barely audible over the thrumming sound in her own ears. Wind, panic, or something else entirely, she wasn't sure. But before she could decide, they were still again.

Within the span of a blink, she found herself staring not at the plant-laden office nor the empty black space of wherever they'd just been, but at the unending desert–and a pair of men who watched her with triumphant eyes.

"You did it, Damian," the one closest said, his tone full of surprise and congratulations, as her captor finally released his too-tight grip on her.

She fell into the sand as he approached, the rough texture threatened to rub her knees raw, even through the thin fabric of the nightgown and dressing gown she hadn't bothered to change from this morning. Her hands curled into fists as tears threatened.

Naia's gaze remained on the ground in front of her, and then the tips of the man's boots as he came to stand directly in front of her. She knew without looking that her captor, Damian she now knew, remained in place behind her.

"You doubted me, Lukus?" Damian asked in a tone that had the other man keeping his mouth shut, as he dropped down to a crouch before Naia.

Lukus' rough fingers gripped her chin tightly, yanking her face upward to force her to look at him. "Hm," he remarked, attempting to yank her head to the side, staring at her ears of all things. "Your timing is good, Damian. She'll be pleased."

Naia had no idea who 'She' was and frankly did not intend to stick around long enough to find out. She gripped the sand in her hand tighter, ready to fling it into Lukus' eyes the very moment the opportunity presented itself. She was fast, not as fast as a fae but maybe, with the element of surprise on her sid, and the sand in his eyes slowing him down a little, she could snatch the knife at his hip and slit her own throat before they could stop her.

The Queen of Coruscis would die before she would be used as a pawn in whatever scheme these fae bastards had planned.

"She didn't say the little human had to remain untouched did She?" The third one inquired, turning the fire in Naia's belly to ice in an instant. Nausea washed over her in waves.

No. No. No.

Her gaze met Lukus', his pale green eyes shining with such hunger that she nearly vomited on his boots. "Now there's a thought," he replied. "We haven't had–"

Without warning, she was yanked free of Lukus' grip, pulled upright by the unforgiving grip of Damian's hand on her upper arm. Jerking as hard as she could, she pulled her arm free of his hand. She knew he'd allowed it, but that did nothing to dampen her hatred of him. Lukus turned a sharp stare to Damian, but his attention shifted back to Naia within a moment.

"I would rather fucking die," she snarled, dragging her gaze from one of them to the next, "than be touched by a fae beast. If you so much as try it, whatever mistress you answer to will find her prize to be nothing more than a corpse, and something tells me that wouldn't serve her purpose very well."

The other two burst into laughter, but Damian, observing her with what might have been an impressed stare, remained silent.

Lukus rose to his feet and folded his arms across his stout form. Greasy-looking brown hair danced in front of his pocked face as he regarded her a moment, lips curved into a cruel grin as he took a step closer. His breath was hot, smelling of decay and whatever poor beast he'd eaten for lunch, as he threatened, "You're not a queen here, bitch. If we want it, we will take it, and there is not a gods damned–"

"You won't lay a hand on her," Damian interjected icily.

Three pairs of eyes turned to stare at him incredulously.

"But Damian," the thin, red-haired one who'd initially suggested her rape, whined. "It's been a long time, and surely She won't mind if we have a little fun before–"

"I said no," Damian said again, and for a moment, Naia could have sworn the temperature in the desert dropped several degrees as if an icy wind had blasted across the sand-baked sands. Indeed, her tawny skin had gone goose-pimpled, despite the hot temperature that had Damian's compatriots sweating, especially the redhead in the back who gulped audibly.

She would have laughed had the situation been anything other than this.

"You don't get to deny us what we want, Damian," Lukus grumbled. "You aren't in charge."

As the men argued over her fate, Naia scanned the encampment. Three tents had been erected in a semi-circle around a large fire pit. Small cooking pots lay scattered to the side of it, as well as a barrel of what she assumed was water. There was little else in the camp, save, she realized with utter dread, a cage. One just large enough to fit an adult woman, adorned with chains ending with shackles.

Fuck that.

She'd been so focused on the cage, and what it meant, she'd missed the near brawl that had broken out beside her. Lukus, a couple of inches shorter than Damian but no less muscular, had moved to stand nearly nose-to-nose with her captor turned somewhat savior.

Here was her chance, she still had the sand in her hands, and they were distracted. She didn't need to move far. Lukus was less than an arm's length away now. Slowly she opened one hand, letting the sand fall to the ground. Keeping silent, she let her gaze shift to the third man, the slimy redhead who had begun this argument in the first place. Blessedly, he wasn't looking at her, his rapt attention was locked on the two men who argued over her as if she were little more than a bleeding steak dangled in front of starving dogs.

Her outstretched hand moved slowly, cautiously, as she reached for Lukus' knife.

She could be dead before they realized what she was up to.

"Back up, Lukus," Damian warned.

"Fuck you, Damian," Lukus retorted.

Damian chuckled quietly, the sound devoid of any actual humor as he lifted a hand to stroke his beard, sending a chill down her spine. "Then you can explain to Her why the Queen of Coruscis is damaged, or," he added, gaze flitting to Naia, "dead as she seems so intent on being. Watch your knife, Lukus. Fucking idiot."

The element of surprise lost, Naia let out a furious shriek, tossing the sand in the general direction of the two closest men before making a desperate scramble for the knife.

It was as futile as she'd expected, with Damian pulling her back once again before she could reach the knife, this time with more gentleness than he'd shown before.

"Fuck," Lukus griped, already pale skin turning pallid. "I didn't realize..."

"Nobody touches her," Damian ordered, and this time nobody argued. "Unless you want to risk Her wrath."

One look at Damian's expression, with his jaw set, the lack of sweat beading on his bronze skin, and the hard stare in his dark brown eyes, and Naia knew her one chance at taking her fate into her own hands had just been lost.

Whoever this mysterious woman was, she held enough control over these men to make them afraid of allowing Naia to be lost, or damaged, in any way; that knowledge alone frightened her more than any of their threats.

CHAPTER 9

Within minutes, Naia found herself inside the cage. Her wrists, thankfully, were left free of the shackles she'd spotted before, a small blessing she hoped would be to her advantage.

Damian had said nothing as he'd gripped her wrist tightly and all but dragged her across the loose sand before tossing her roughly into the nearly carriage-sized cage sat atop two large slats in place of wheels.

She'd seen similar designs amongst the desert-dwelling people of her kingdom, the slats of wood designed to skate easily over the sands, making travel less troublesome.

Did that mean they weren't going to be traveling the way Damian had? Using whatever fae magic he obviously possessed to hurtle her through bleak nothingness only to arrive, well, wherever they were.

Sighing, she settled into the center of the cage. One tentative touch of the metal bars told her they were scorching hot. Not at all surprising given that the fae men hadn't bothered to cover the metal with so much as a piece of fabric. If she leaned against these before they'd cooled, she was sure she'd be left with angry red welts for days. Her gaze skimmed the vast expanse and found nothing. As far as she could see, in every direction, there lay only sand.

Without landmarks to guide her, it was impossible to be sure which part of the desert they were in. There were none of the ancient temples that spotted the desert, no encampments, no oasis or sign of the sea to give even so much as a hint to their location.

Running, she now realized, might be as good an option as the knife had been. Sure, it would be slower, and they very well might catch her before she succeeded, but if she couldn't get her hands on a weapon, it may be her only choice.

"Still considering suicide?"

Damian's voice caught her off guard, drifting from several feet to her right. He'd taken up a position just outside his tent, seated on a faded blue mat, fiddling with a strip of leather.

Lukus didn't bother to look up from his place by the fire, she noted, attention sliding to where he was cooking something over the fire.

Turning back to Damian, she sneered, "Not that I have the chance now."

He shrugged in response, lifting his hands to tie his long black hair at the nape of his neck with the leather. "If I didn't need you alive, I'd help you die myself."

"How very altruistic of you," she snapped back. Not that she understood why. She wanted to die. To be free of this situation rather than face whatever terrible thing waited for her, when they decided to deliver her to this mysterious *She* they all seemed to fear so much. "Who are you taking me to anyway?"

At that, Damian smirked. In this light, his dark eyes seemed lighter somehow, shifting into different shades of brown versus the almost deep black they'd seemed to be before; though they remained as cold and calculating. "Your friend from the North didn't bother to tell you that?"

She didn't answer. Naia simply met his stare with one of his own, expression flat. There was nothing on this earth that could force her to show him what she felt. She would gnash her teeth and snarl, fierce as any beast, and show him every bit of the rage she felt. Her screams of rage would echo across the sands for eternity. She would haunt him, her ghost following in his footsteps as close as a shadow, if she could manage such a thing after her death. Fury would be her mask, and she would wear it well.

But the hurt and fear? She would never allow them to see that.

Taking her silence as an answer enough, Damian turned to eye his companion closely for a moment, and they fell into an uneasy silence.

"How long until we leave?" she asked, glancing upward. If they were out here long enough and they failed to cover the cage, perhaps the sun would do the job for her.

"Have somewhere to be, bitch?" Lukus finally spoke, rising from his place and sauntering toward her. "I'm getting sick of hearing your fucking voice. Shut up."

Naia tilted her head and snorted. "Do you think me so weak that a simple word would hurt me?" Letting her gaze fall lower, to what she knew men were most sensitive about. "Or perhaps you're just that *small* of a man."

A snarl of rage, alongside a burst of laughter from Damian, sounded as Lukus launched himself at the cage, gripping the bars tightly before releasing the scorching metal with a hiss. "You'll regret that smart mouth of yours, *bitch*," he threatened.

"Now, now, Lukus, don't go making threats you know you can't keep," Damian said idly, though his eyes carried no small degree of malice as she and Lukus both turned to look at him.

"Fuck you, too," Lukus spat at him before retreating to his own tent.

If there had been a door to slam, she thought, he would have done so with the same petulance of a child throwing a tantrum.

"Keep provoking him, and you might just get your wish after all, Thunderheart," Damian warned, rising from his seat as he dragged a hand through his thick beard. "Though I doubt it would be as swift and painless as you'd hope."

She said nothing as he disappeared into the tent. Her heart indeed thundered in her chest, and the roaring in her ears rivaled the fiercest ocean waves. Within the span of a few heartbeats, Damian returned, dragging a long tapestry behind him. To her chagrin, he draped it over the top of the cage, shielding her from the harsh rays of the sun.

Suppressing the sigh of relief she felt, she narrowed her eyes at him. "And will you be staying awake all night to ensure I don't?"

Without even an ounce of emotion, he replied, "Like I said, I need you alive."

CHAPTER 10

B y nightfall, Naia was ready to pull her own hair out, if for no other reason than to give her something to do. She had tried to engage Damian in conversation, both in an attempt to entertain herself until the inevitable happened and she could once again attempt to take her fate into her own hands, and to perhaps learn more about where they were, where they were headed; or who *She* was.

Tapping her bare foot against the cool metal of the bar in a rhythm that barely resembled the tune playing on repeat in her mind, she let out a frustrated growl. Naia knew she was going to die, but she didn't have to die bored and ignorant.

"Stop," Damian grumbled from his mat just outside of his tent. His eyes had fallen closed sometime in the last few moments, she noted.

Despite her words of bravado earlier, she truly did fear what would happen if Lukus decided to carry out his threat from earlier in the day. Death was something she desired for no other reason than to thwart whatever plan these fae bastards had for her, and because what waited for her at the hands of men like Lukus was worse than death.

"Make me," she shot back, without thought.

In the blink of an eye, he was there, forearm halfway through the gap in the bar, and his hand gripped around her ankle. He squeezed hard, just shy of the point of pain. Her yelp of surprise went ignored as his gaze met hers.

"Do not presume to have power here, Queen of Coruscis."

Naia narrowed her eyes and leaned forward slightly. "Fuck. You."

To her shock, the corner of his lips twitched upward. "Do not test me, Thunderheart."

She snorted and moved to tug her foot away, only for him to squeeze harder. "Let go," she ordered, and to her surprise, he did. Pulling her legs close, knees resting against her chest, she peered at her ankle.

From what she could see in the dim light, only the faintest remnants of his handprint marred her skin, fading quickly already, strange considering her skin felt so hot where he'd touched her.

Probably some strange fae magic at work, she decided. "Why do you call me that?"

Tilting his head, he looked at her, and for a moment she thought he'd walk away. She wasn't so desperate for conversation now, not when his touch had left her feeling like she'd been burned.

"Thunderheart," he began, shrugging. "Fitting for a weak, human queen, baring her teeth and raging at things so far beyond herself. A simple human trying to fight against the inevitable."

Naia blinked. "Pretty words," she remarked. "But what does that even mean? Who is She?"

With one last assessing glance her way, Damian turned back to his mat, lowering himself onto it with a sigh. "If it will quiet your tongue, I will tell you what I can."

No longer bored, and hopefully soon to be more enlightened, Naia scooted closer, leaning her head against the bars gently, and gestured for him to continue. The dressing gown she'd taken to using as a blanket of sorts shifted against her skin, the whisper of fabric the only sound in the heavy silence as she waited for him to speak.

"She is darkness, the destroyer. She is the end of all things, and She is forever unending." His voice fell lower with each uttered word, dark eyes scanning the surrounding desert as if afraid She might appear at any moment.

The hair at the back of her neck rose slightly, skin prickling. Ancient instinct, born at the dawn of all time, when humans and fae first sprang to life, told her without question that she was being watched; by someone other than the fae male who had gone very, very still.

Surely it's just the eerie way he said those titles, Naia lied to herself, even as she slowly straightened. Dragging her gaze from Damian, she turned to scan the sands herself. At first, there was nothing, just darkness in every direction. The dim glow of the dying campfire barely illuminated their camp, much less the vast expanses beyond.

Nothing, she chided herself suddenly. But then, a small voice whispered in her mind, Why was Damian reacting so strangely? Turning to peek at the fae, she found that he had risen, so silently she hadn't noticed. Jaw tense, he continued to stare into the darkness, and for several seconds she could do nothing but stare.

He was the largest man she'd ever seen, taller than most and with more muscles than any one man needed, but somehow also agile and graceful in a way she could only dream of being.

Fearsome, the word sprang forth in her mind, the perfect way to describe the imposing man who stood before her.

Fearsome, and yet...when he spoke, she could swear she heard the tiniest bit of fear edging into his tone.

"Go back to your hiding place," he warned, voice raised so that it carried out into the darkness with ease. "You will find only death at Her hands, if you linger."

Her other captors stepped out into the night, alarmingly well-armed and staring into the direction in which Damian had been speaking.

"We move," Damian barked at the others suddenly. "Now. Emil, go join the others, tell them we saw—" He paused, casting a glance toward her cage, but falling short of meeting her stare. "Tell them what we've seen. Lukus, we will take the queen to the third camp."

"Shouldn't we just take her to the others now?" Emil questioned, still staring out into the darkness.

"No," Damian snapped. "Our orders were clear. You know where we are to bring her. Until we're told otherwise, we will follow the plan. This...interference changes nothing."

"What's happening?" Naia demanded, head spinning. They were speaking so quickly, and saying nothing that held any meaning for her.

Wary of whomever, whatever, they'd all sensed watching them in the desert. "Where are we going?"

Her demands for answers went utterly ignored, even as Emil vanished into thin air, giving her a start. She managed to stifle the undignified yelp of surprise that threatened to bubble up, but only barely.

Damian, with Lukus close on his heels, strode to the cage, sliding the heavy bolts free with surprising speed.

"If they find us again," Lukus said finally, as Damian grabbed hold of Naia's arm, tugging her out, not ungently. "We should take the bitch directly to Her."

"Maybe," Damian replied.

Her feet had no sooner hit the cool sand before he was tugging her into what would have appeared a lover's embrace under different circumstances, her back pressed firmly against his chest, his arms wrapped tightly around her. "In case you decide running might be a good idea," he whispered. Ignoring the way her skin warmed at the sensation of his breath against the shell of her ear, Naia snapped her head backward, connecting with his cheek most satisfyingly.

"Thunderheart," he chuckled, to her dismay.

As they plunged once more into darkness and wind, Naia could have sworn she heard the distant sound of thunder crashing.

CHAPTER 11

Camp three, as it turned out, was yet another remote location in what appeared to be the middle of nowhere. They were to stay only the night, Damian informed her. There were no tents here, and no cages either. Only the bank of a large lake, a soft grassy place to lie down in her increasingly dirty nightdress. For the first time, she had some inkling of where they were and her gaze turned toward what she guessed to be the northeast, toward home.

So close, yet still impossibly far. The thought had her heart aching.

"We're moving again in the morning," Damian stated, as she lowered herself onto the grass near the clear water. Casting a glance over her gown, he frowned slightly. "We'll feed you then, in case you're planning to starve yourself to death," he added, before striding to the water's edge.

Lukus, hovering nearby, snorted.

Ignoring him, Damian tugged a waterskin from his belt and filled it before bringing it back to her. "Drink," he ordered, thrusting it in her direction.

She was inclined to say no. Three days without water should kill her, if she recalled, but one look in his eyes told her he was not above holding her down and forcing her to drink, if necessary.

With a frustrated snarl, she yanked the waterskin from his hand and drank deeply before all but throwing it back at him. She wouldn't dare let him see how grateful she actually was, how much the cool water soothed the burning of her throat.

"Good girl," he smirked, dropping to sit beside her.

"Fuck you."

With the sunrise, he took her in his arms once again, this time less tightly than before, and dragged her into that strange darkness once more. As Damian released her, Naia could do little but stare at the massive ruin before them.

"Where are we?" she asked, not bothering to hide the awe in her voice. Though she had traveled into the desert to visit with the leaders of the nomadic communities on occasion and knew, from historical records, where most of the important fae ruins lay, she'd never heard of a structure quite like this.

Even in ruins, it was massive on a scale the likes of which she had never seen. Towers, with the tops lying shattered on the sand below, nearly encircled the central building. What would have once been a domed ceiling, with more than half of it missing, graced the center, and two massive arched doorways marked the entrance.

The doors were long since gone, as were the windows that surely would have once been stunning sights, dotted along the rounded building and towers.

The trio moved in silence, Lukus leading with Naia following behind, gaze shifting this way and that to take it all in, and Damian just behind her. As they reached the main building, a vision flashed in her mind, the bright sun gleaming off turquoise windows, bits of silver painted glass in the shape of a spiral adorning the center of each. Without thought, as they passed she raised her hand to touch the place where the glass would have been in an empty window.

She could all but feel the warmth of it beneath her finger as she traced the spiral shape in the empty air. A sadness so visceral, and inexplicable, it brought a tear to her eye. Longing like she'd never known had her swallowing hard.

"What's wrong with you?" Damian asked, drawing her attention from the melancholy that had overtaken her.

Snapping back to reality, she shook the feeling away and shrugged. "It must have been beautiful once," she remarked.

He said nothing for a moment, another of his unreadable expressions passing over stony features. "Yes."

Before she could ask more about it, what purpose this place had served, who had called it home–because surely someone had called a place this large home once–Lukus shouted for Damian.

"If we camp here, all of the entrances are visible," Lukus began, gesturing toward a massive open area in the center of the domed building.

Aside from the crumbling remains of the ceiling lying in chunks around the circular room, it was barrn. Arched spaces lined the walls between the windows, most of them empty. A few bits of colored tile still graced what little of the ceiling remained, indicating that there had once been some type of adornment there, but unlike her vision of the windows, she couldn't picture what would have been there during the building's prime.

The conversation between her captors continued as she found herself drifting around the room, feeling as much a ghost as those who had once walked these halls. Fallen stone under her feet went largely unnoticed as she continued her stroll, moving farther and farther from the center, finding herself drawn to one of the few partially intact mosaics. Bits of blue in varying shades, all of them faded and chipped, lined the bottom, with pale golds rising above them.

It was so similar in design to the mosaics along the walls at Evertide that she knew without doubt it was a stream running between two mounds of sand being depicted, with what appeared to be a woman's feet crossing it. Most of the tiles making up her body and face, as well as the scene behind her, had fallen away, leaving only scant traces of what appeared to be a castle, and flowing dark hair.

Who had this woman been? Someone of great importance, she

assumed, to be immortalized in a place that obviously held significance once.

How sad, she thought, *for the sands of time to wipe away someone whom people had been so intent on remembering. Will I be forgotten like she has been?*

A glint of something sparkling on the floor in the morning light caught her eye, and she knelt to see more. Sweeping away the light coating of sand, she found herself looking into the eyes that no doubt belonged to the faceless woman of the mosaic. Even through the ravages of time, she could make out elegant shades of brown, a ring of gold around the pupils, the glint of which had caught her attention in the first place.

Delicately, she began to lift the piece from the floor, eager to get another look, to see the rest of the face, still hidden beneath the sand–

"Where the fuck do you think you're going?" Lukus snarled from right behind her, startling her enough that she dropped the fragile artwork onto the ground, cracking it in two.

She barely had time to register the sorrow she felt at the loss of something so beautiful and important, as he roughly grabbed her arm, yanking her to stand.

"I asked you a question, bitch," he spat in her face before shoving her hard against the wall.

Pain lanced through her back as her spine connected with some sharp bit of stone protruding from the wall. Without thought, she swung at him, fist connecting with his jaw in a most satisfying way.

"Bastard!" she shouted, anger overriding her pain for the moment.

His hand wrapped around her throat, cutting off not only her words but her air. Stars sprang to life in the corners of her eyes as her vision dimmed. She'd wanted to die, to escape whatever they'd had planned for her, but instinct took over and she fought; clawing at his arms with her nails, kicking her feet as hard as she could, though she had no idea what parts of him she connected with.

Time passed slowly, every second a lifetime, as she began to fade.

Here, she would die alongside the long-forgotten woman whose face she'd longed to glimpse if only to give her a single moment more of remembrance. As the last of the fight left her, she let her eyes fall closed, and she tried to recall the faces of those she most wanted to see before she crossed into the Otherworld. Her mother and father, Maren, even little Suri.

Finally, the mysterious brown eyes with golden rings. Maybe in death, she would learn who the woman was, and why she felt so drawn to her.

Without warning, the pressure against her throat vanished, and she fell to her knees. Her eyes flew open as she sucked in precious air, expecting to see Lukus standing over her, only to find him in a heap across the room amidst the rubble of a portion of the ceiling.

Damian knelt in front of her, eyeing her warily, but saying nothing before standing and crossing to Lukus.

The latter stumbled to his feet, expression murderous. "I will kill you," Lukus screamed at Damian, pulling both arms back and flinging them toward him. The air around them thrummed as red mist poured from Lukus' hands, weaving its way toward Damian, who, to her shock, merely smirked, as the strange mist wreathed around his throat.

"You're more of a fool than I thought," Damian stated flatly. "And that is a rather impressive feat, Lukus."

As he spoke, the mist dissipated into nothing. A shiver that had less to do with the scene playing out before her and more the sudden drop in temperature, coursed down her spine.

Lukus screamed with rage and frustration. "Fucking Samach bastard," he shouted as he tackled Damian.

She rose to her feet, throat and back screaming in agony with the movement. But this was her opportunity. If there were a way to escape into the desert, perhaps they wouldn't find her, or maybe she could find a high enough point from which to jump or a sharp stone.

Damian could clearly handle himself against Lukus, and knowing that eased the tiny amount of guilt she felt leaving while they fought after he'd saved her.

The pair fell to the ground in a heap of muscle and rage. Punches were thrown and dodged, and for a moment, Lukus managed to pin Damian on the ground, all but stopping her pounding heart. He was hardly a savior given his reasons for rescuing her, but Damian was the preferable captor; and if Lukus killed Damian and managed to capture her again...

The thought was barely finished before she was snagging a stone from the ground and charging at them. Focused entirely on his impending victory, or perhaps simply dismissing her as a threat, Lukus didn't bother to turn as she raised her arms and bashed the back of his head with the rock.

It did little damage, though it was enough to distract him, giving Damian enough of an advantage to flip Lukus off of him before yanking a strange wooden knife free from his belt and stabbing Lukus in the thigh. Certainly not a killing blow, but a painful one judging from the yowl that escaped Lukus from his prone position.

Turning to Naia with pitch-dark eyes ringed in gold, Damian grabbed both of her hands, twisting just hard enough to force her to release the rock.

Here was the fae monster she'd expected, staring at her with deadly intent, blood coating his hands and arms. She should have taken the time to run, to escape. Why had she been so damn foolish to stop and save him?

"Are you going to kill me now?" she croaked hoarsely. She felt no fear, instead, she was resigned, cold in the way of one accepting their fate.

"Your life was not his to claim, nor is it mine," he replied darkly, dropping her hands abruptly. Turning to Lukus, who still lay whimpering on the ground, he added, "And you will pay for your treason."

She turned away as he yanked the knife free of Lukus' leg, unable to stomach any more brutality. Only the deafening silence as Lukus' screaming stopped told her it was over.

Dragging her attention back to the man who had threatened to brutalize, and had nearly succeeded in killing her, she found that she felt nothing when her gaze landed on his unseeing eyes, staring accusingly at Damian, who had gone utterly still beside her.

"You're going to take me to Her?" she whispered, wincing at the pain in her throat.

"Stop talking," he ordered quietly. Turning away from her.

There was no fight left in her, too much pain in her throat to argue further, so instead she simply moved around the lifeless body of her attacker to the spot where she'd dropped the tile depicting the strange eyes of the ancient woman. She could feel his gaze on her back as she sifted through the sand where it had fallen to retrieve the largest piece that remained, a single eye, staring back at her through the ages.

Holding it in her palm, she made a silent promise to remember, for as long as she could, what she was willing to fight and to die for.

Chapter 12

The next camp was another ruin, another secret place not marked on any map that Naia had ever seen. Far less grand, but stunning in its own way. A handful of small buildings formed a near-perfect circle. To her surprise, most buildings had at least one wall standing, with one still boasting a roof.

It was within that building that Damian declared they would be sleeping.

"How long will we stay here?" Naia asked. Her thumb idly grazed the shard still clutched in her palm. He hadn't bothered to take it to her surprise, but she supposed it would hardly be a useful weapon anyway.

"Until it's time to move."

His flat tone annoyed her almost as much as the lack of answer.

Turning, she scanned the space with curiosity. Had the open space once been divided into rooms or had the occupants simply shared one large space? Had it been a home? A store? There was no way to tell for certain with no furniture or markings to identify it.

"Was this a fae town? Or human?" When he remained silent, she turned to look back at him, only to find him staring at her. "What?" she asked, brow raised.

"It was a fae town," he answered finally, turning to look out at the rest of the town. "A small but prosperous one."

"Here? This far into the desert?"

Turning back to her, he gave her an exasperated stare. "You forget we had magic, Queen of Coruscis."

"Naia."

Exasperation turned to what she could have sworn was surprise. Now it was his turn to ask, "What?"

"You keep calling me by anything but my name; Thunderheart, Queen of Coruscis, Human," she explained, dropping to sit on the sand that had laid claim to the interior of the building. "My name is Naia. If you're going to kill me, I want you to remember that." Staring up at him, she paused. "Say my name aloud. Commit it to memory."

For several heartbeats, he met her gaze evenly. "Yours is a name I will never forget," he said finally.

Irritation flared, and she opened her mouth to speak, only to stop short as he knelt in front of her, dark eyes still locked on her own as he bound her hands slowly.

"Naia. Human Queen of Coruscis. Thunderheart."

Her heart indeed thundered in her chest. Her bravado wavered, if only for a moment, before she nodded once. "Good."

THE SANDSTORM SWEPT IN SO POWERFULLY AND SUDDENLY, that even Damian seemed wary. Thankfully, despite having carried little with them in their flight away from whomever, or whatever, had been watching them in the dark that night at the first camp, Damian had at least kept a singular pack with a large enough blanket for them to both take shelter in.

What he'd failed to bring, however, were rations. Something Naia's stomach reminded her of as it grumbled and ached. Damian turned his attention from the raging winds and sand to Naia.

"Humans are so fragile," he remarked, frowning.

Snorting, Naia frowned right back at him. "Fae don't need to eat."

Damian rolled his eyes. "Of course we do. But we can go longer without it."

"It's hardly my fault you forgot you were taking a human captive, and that she would need to eat."

He stared back at her, expression flat. "Then perhaps you'll get your wish after all."

Naia's cheeks heated. "Maybe I will."

To her surprise, Damian chuckled. "I will go and fetch you something when the storm passes."

Naia turned away from him, eyeing the rippling fabric, just visible thanks to the dimmed sunlight, almost entirely blocked by the raging sand. She wouldn't let him see the gratitude in her eyes. Death was better than the fate that awaited her, she was certain, but starving to death was hardly what she'd had in mind. "So you can keep me alive for Her."

It wasn't a question, simply a statement of irrefutable fact. This being he feared, and worshipped, waited for her. Images of herself chained to a strange altar flashed in her mind.

Would She kill Naia slowly? Would She drain the life from her quickly? Or would She keep Naia alive, a living trophy to announce her victory?

When he didn't answer, Naia let the tears fall silently, her back to him, and sent a silent, rage-laden prayer to the gods who had abandoned them all.

CHAPTER 13

By nightfall, the storm had passed, and true to his word, Damian had vanished. He'd left her alone, but not before fastening her to a boulder with a bit of chain.

Of course he'd remembered that over food, she thought irritably.

In the near flat expanse of the desert, the night sky overhead was an endless blanket of stars. He'd been gone long enough for her to count and name nearly every constellation she could spot while lying on the blanket in one of the sections of the building without a roof.

"The maidens," she whispered to herself, raised finger tracing the invisible line connecting the stars into a pattern that resembled four women, huddled together. In her other hand, her thumb grazed the piece of tile. One of the more difficult to identify, as the pattern was large and only visible on the clearest of nights.

"Finally he leaves," a sardonic male voice said suddenly.

Naia jolted to a sitting position immediately to find Lir standing a few feet away. His long dark hair danced on the light breeze, angular eyes looking her over as the corner of his mouth dipped into a frown. "I expected more."

"More what?" she asked, anger blooming in her chest.

"Just...more," he replied, waving a hand in her direction. "You plead for death, rather than fight."

"So help me," she all but shouted in return, shifting so that she was on her hands and knees. Rather than a supplicant, she looked a predator, ready to launch herself at prey. "Fucking do something. Unchain me. Free me from this fucking fae bastard."

Lir tilted his head, glancing over his shoulder. "He returns." Turning his attention back to her, he leaned forward ever so slightly. "You want my help? Earn it."

He vanished in an instant, leaving Naia to do little more than scream in frustration and rage, yanking at the chain that bound her. She'd been resigned, for now at least, to being a prisoner. But to have a god arrive, not to save her but to taunt her? That was more than she could bear.

Tears of anger, grief, and rage stung her sunburnt cheeks.

Earn it? How did he expect her to do that? She had fought and raged and defied. Had done everything she could to get away.

Naia would rather die than allow Her to achieve whatever end she had in mind for her.

But it was not enough to please the asshole of a god apparently responsible for her. What more could she–

"Scream all you like, Thunderheart, there's nobody around to hear you," Damian said by way of greeting as he appeared nearly exactly where Lir had stood, in a whoosh of darkness.

"Fuck you."

Raising a brow, Damian strode toward her, a small sack in his hands. "Such foul language from a Queen."

She wanted to show him just how foul her language could be, but the scent of fresh bread wafting from the sack he carried had the words dying on her tongue, and her stomach growling loudly.

"I brought bread, dried meats, fruit, and what I'm told is a delicious wine from Avellon," he said, moving to sit beside her on the blanket. She waited, still as a stone, as he unwrapped the food and passed her a chunk of bread.

Without so much as a thank you, she immediately began to eat; careful to keep her pace slow to avoid purging it all because she ate too quickly. "Avellonian wine is okay," she remarked, lifting her gaze to his. "But Kavalan is better."

"I've never been to Kavala," he replied, tugging a knife from his belt. As he began to slice an apple, she paused. In order to find fruit that fresh, he had to have traveled a good distance. Apples were a rarity in Coruscis, almost entirely imported from Avellon. To have them in the desert communities was almost unheard of.

"How far are you able to travel with that...," she searched for the words to describe the whirl of darkness and wind that carried him from one place to another. Finding none, she settled on a whooshing sound and a wave of her hand to illustrate her point.

"Pacing," he supplied. "As far as I like. It helps if I've been there before, but it isn't necessary."

"Anywhere?" she asked, unable to keep the awe from her tone. To travel that freely, to see every corner of the world...that would be an amazing gift. She'd longed to travel for so long; had grown up on her father's tales of his younger days, spent sailing to distant lands. He hadn't been tethered to Coruscis by the burden of being born royalty as she had.

"Yes," Damian said. "They have dragons in the east," he added, passing her a sliver of apple. "Have you heard?"

"My father once went to Anguis to see them. He said they're almost extinct."

Damian nodded in agreement. "Not quite."

They fell into silence then as they ate. Naia's thoughts on dragons, her father, and traveling to distant lands. Anything to distract her from Lir's words that still echoed in her mind.

Earn it.

"Will others be coming?" she asked after they'd had their fill and the rest of the food was packed away.

Damian watched her a moment, something unreadable passing over his features. "No."

"Then we're going to them?"

A muscle in his jaw feathered. "No."

Naia frowned in confusion. "Is She coming here?" she asked, sliding her hand beneath her thigh to tug the bit of tile free from where she'd hidden it while eating. "Then this is where I'm going to die."

To her surprise, Damian growled. "Have you gone soft so soon? Are you ready to roll over, offer your throat to the wolves?" Leaning closer, he wrapped his hand around her throat and squeezed gently. "Where is that thunder now?"

With his hand still around her throat, Naia struck. Her hand flew before she could consider the consequences, and punched him squarely in the face. She hadn't accounted for the tile, still clasped in her hand, that sliced through her palm with the impact.

Her knuckles ached. She hadn't punched anyone since childhood when she'd found the son of some Lord or another harassing a serving girl.

His hand never left her throat, and yet it didn't tighten either. Even as he chuckled menacingly, leaning so close that their noses nearly touched. "There she is," he whispered, brown eyes deepening to a near black. "Thunderheart."

Something in her roared as they gazed at one another; a silent battle between them raging almost as powerfully as the one within her. When his thumb slid across her skin, slowly, purposefully, her mind emptied. The tile fell from her hand, landing unheard onto the sand as she lifted her bloodied hand to touch his cheek. Red smears marked the trail of her touch, from cheekbone down to his full beard, to his own throat.

Damian's eyes never left hers, even as he swallowed hard beneath her touch.

She had never felt so powerful, so in control, despite the chain that remained wrapped around her ankle. Sliding her hand to the back of his neck, Naia let herself act on the screaming instinct within her.

CHAPTER 14

There would be no tenderness, no whispered words of endearment here; only heat. Rising to his knees, Damian pulled Naia with him as he yanked her filthy nightgown upward and over her head, leaving her kneeling in only her undergarments, breasts bared to him.

His hands gripped her backside, yanking her close without warning. With a shocked gasp, Naia let herself be pulled into him, gripping the back of his neck hard enough to leave marks with her fingernails and a trail of blood from her palm. With one hand still on her ass, Damian pulled his breeches just low enough to free himself.

Lips and teeth and tongues collided in a frenzy. Her uninjured hand dipped low to wrap around what she was delighted to find was an impressive cock. One stroke of his length had his breath shuddering and his grip on her ass tightening. In the span of a blink, she found herself turned around, with the chain clanking loudly as it was stretched tight.

Naia hardly noticed the increase in pressure on her ankle.

Her back was pressed against his chest, one hand at her throat and the other on her abdomen, holding her close. His cock pressed between her ass cheeks had her thighs slick with need.

"Do you want me to fuck that pretty pussy of yours, Thunderheart?" he breathed hoarsely against her ear.

Naia nodded, swallowing hard.

"Say it out loud," he ordered.

"Yes," she whispered. "Fuck me."

His tongue flicked her earlobe gently. "Good girl."

Sliding his hand from her throat, he wrapped her long hair around his hand and pushed her down on all fours before ripping the final barrier between them away. The hand that had been around her hips moved to stroke her clit and she shuddered a breath. Slow, methodical circles brought her to the brink of climax but before release found her, he pulled away.

Sand scraped her palm, irritating the cut further, but the pain was little more than a distant memory. Anything before him, before this, was forgotten.

All Naia could feel was this moment, as if the rest of the world had ceased to exist.

"What—"

Her words were cut short as he entered her in one hard stroke, drawing a cry of surprise and utter wanton desire from her.

"Now come for me, Naia."

Her name on his lips was her undoing. He released her hair, sliding both hands along the sides of her ribs, coming to a stop on her hips. She crashed around him, tightening and releasing over and over as he moved until his breathing came in ragged sighs, and he once again gripped her throat, pulling her gently until her back met his chest again, his cock still inside her.

"Again," he ordered, squeezing her throat gently, free hand sliding over her clit as he slammed against her ass, deeper inside of her than she would have thought possible in this position.

She couldn't think, could barely breathe, from the dizzying heights he took her to. When orgasm ripped through her again, she came apart in sobbing breaths. Pressing gently against her lower abdomen, he held her still as he came. Chests heaving, they remained there, intertwined, until finally he released her, rocking back to pull his breeches up.

Still on her knees, Naia looked toward her nightgown, discarded on the sand, and frowned. She could hardly put that on again, and on top of that, she no longer had undergarments to wear.

"Here," he said hoarsely, and she turned to find him holding out his own shirt for her to wear.

"Thanks," she replied, quietly.

As she dressed, the reality of what had just happened hit her. She'd just fucked the man who wanted to turn her over to some nightmare goddess.

No—she'd asked him to fuck her.

The distinction between the two had shame and anger flooding her cheeks, and she turned to glare at him. "I need to clean up," she said finally, glancing at the blood caked on her palm. There was sand in the wound that would need to be washed away, not to mention the evidence of what they'd just done, still slick between her legs.

He walked behind her, disappearing from her view. She hadn't bothered to watch him, instead letting her gaze turn to the desert. A million thoughts raced through her mind, emotions swarming. Surprise at her behavior, and confusion. But not shame, she realized. No, there was no shame in her choice.

The chain rattled and tugged on her ankle, then suddenly the weight of it was gone. He tugged her upward and before she could turn to question it, the familiar wind and darkness began to sweep them up. When they once more settled onto solid ground, Naia was shocked to find herself standing on a familiar shoreline. Far from home, but one she had seen before many times.

"You brought me to Paralia."

"You've been here?" he asked, as she strode toward the sea.

She didn't answer until she was ankle-deep in the surf. "Here," Naia said, peeling the shirt off again. She needed to bathe, and she could hardly do that wearing what she assumed was the last piece of clean, well mostly clean at least, clothing between them.

Damian followed her into the water, and took the shirt from her outstretched hand wordlessly. He was waiting for her reply, and for a moment, she considered leaving him to wonder.

Something had shifted between them; so palpable she could feel it washing against her almost as intensely as the waves. Wading further into the sea, she let the cool saltwater wash away the physical evidence of her choice.

"I've been here a few times," she explained finally. With a hiss of pain, she dipped her injured palm into the water. The salt stung, but perhaps she needed the reminder of what was really happening. A bit of pain to drag her back into reality. "That tile really–"

Guilt finally rose to the surface, and she spun to look at him. Waves crashed against her back but she remained firm, feet lodged in the sand. "We have to go back."

Damian's brow rose. "Why?"

"I left something behind."

For a long moment, he simply stared at her, expression inscrutable. The only sounds were the lapping waves and the roaring in her ears. How could she have forgotten? A promise had been made to the woman in the tile. One bout of sex and she'd forgotten entirely, if only for a moment.

"This?" Damian said finally, reaching into his pocket and producing the broken tile.

"You knew." The words were as much accusation as statement. "Give it back."

"Why is it so important to you?" he asked, eyeing the shard a moment before dragging his gaze back to her.

Naia swayed with the surf as it crashed into her over and over. Every moment that passed, the sand beneath her washed away with the ebb and flow of the tides. How could she even begin to explain the connection she felt with the unknown woman she'd seen depicted in the temple?

"It just is."

"That isn't an answer," Damian countered, turning the tile over in his hand, eyes on her face.

Tense silence fell over them once again, each breath emphasized by the crashing of the waves. Would he keep it, toss it away into the waves? When he delivered Naia to Her, would he keep it as a trophy?

"I thought she should be remembered, even if it's only for what little time I have left," she said finally, only truth in her words. She knew she was going to die. Maybe, if she was lucky, he would carry that piece of both women with him for the rest of his long, long life.

He turned his attention to the tile, eyeing it thoughtfully. "She was fae," he said after a moment. "And she was lost a very long time ago."

"Let's go," he ordered, holding the shirt out for her.

Naia strode toward him on legs as unstable as the sand beneath her feet. "Is it time?"

He only watched in silence as she dressed again.

Left in a shirt that fell just to her thighs, she glanced back at the sea. "What will She do to me?"

Again, he didn't answer. Naia wanted to rage at him, to curse his silence, but the sensation of his fingertips at the nape of her neck stopped her short. Damian had moved, so swiftly and silently that she hadn't noticed.

"It's time to go," he said, voice gruff. No sooner had his arm wound around her midsection than the darkness enveloped them both, carrying Naia away to her fate.

Chapter 15

Night fell shortly after they arrived at the next camp. Yet another crumbling ruin lost to time and sand. Something in her chest ached at the thought of so much being lost.

"What was this place?" she asked, spinning in a circle. The room was wide, open to the sky above, despite most of the walls remaining. Bits of blue tile still clung to the stone in a few places, but there were no faces staring back at her this time.

"A smaller temple," Damian replied.

"Who did they worship here?" Naia asked, settling onto a fallen pillar. The night sky above shone brilliantly. Her gaze turned upward, searching for a familiar constellation.

Damian moved toward her, and she tensed. She'd given her body to him, had claimed his in truth, but she didn't trust him. He still intended to turn her over to a monster.

"A goddess whose name has been erased from history," he replied vaguely.

"Why are we moving so much? Don't you have some sort of schedule?" she demanded, not bothering to keep the disdain from her tone as she lowered her gaze. "I'm sure She must be impatient."

Damian's expression darkened, but rather than answer, he held his hand out, the bit of tile between his fingers. "Take it."

Slowly, she did just that. Her gaze dropped from Damian's face to the eye in the tile. No words of thanks were offered, and she didn't bother to raise her gaze to his again. Her thumb swept over what remained of the woman's face, brushing away the dried blood.

I'm sorry I couldn't give us both more time, she thought.

Shaking her head, she cursed her foolishness. This woman was long dead, as Naia would soon be. Why she was holding onto such sentiment over her, Naia would never understand.

"I could slice my wrists with this," she said finally, still not looking at Damian. "I doubt you could stop me in time."

"I know," he replied flatly.

"So why didn't you keep it from me?"

"Because you won't."

Naia sighed, dropping her hand to her lap and turning her attention to him. From this vantage point, sitting and staring up at him, he was imposing. Looming above her like death itself; dark eyes shadowed, almost haunted, against a backdrop of endless stars.

"How much longer?"

Damian stared at her a moment. "Not long." Turning his gaze skyward, he frowned. "Get some sleep."

"Fuck you," she said halfheartedly, even as she moved to lay on her back on the soft sand beside the pillar. When had those words lost the fire they'd carried so many times before?

When he had no reply for that, Naia returned her attention to the night sky above. The maidens were there, she noted, gaze roaming. There was the shepherd, the bear, the crow. One by one, she counted and named each of the constellations and stars she knew the names of until she drifted off into sleep.

The sound of birds awoke her several hours later.

Birds.

There were few that traveled deep into the desert, she remembered, as she slowly opened her eyes. So why—

What greeted Naia was hardly the endless expanse of sand she'd expected, but the rolling sea. Had he moved her while she slept?

"You're awake," Damian said by way of greeting.

Sitting up slowly, on a narrow blanket that had been laid beneath her, Naia turned to find him seated on a piece of driftwood near her feet.

Feet which were now wearing sandals, tied around the ankles–and those were loose, billowing pants she was wearing, and a proper fitted shirt. Lifting a hand to the hem of the teal shirt, she frowned.

"You moved me...and you dressed me in my sleep?" she asked incredulously.

"You're a very heavy sleeper," he replied as if it were the most obvious thing in the world. "And that other shirt was barely covering your ass."

Rolling her eyes, Naia turned her attention to the campfire nearby, and what looked to be a steaming plate of eggs and fish, like it had been set out to wait for her.

"You cooked."

"How observant."

Narrowing her eyes, she shot him a look that quite clearly said 'fuck you.' "Why? How?"

Damian sighed the way a parent would with a particularly exasperating toddler. "Just...eat."

Hunger outweighed her curiosity, so she did just that, scooping the eggs and fish together with what turned out to be freshly baked flatbread. "Where did you get this?"

"There's a village nearby," he said. Pinning her with a stare, he added, "You'd never outrun me. If you tried to hide from me there, I'd be forced to kill anyone who got in my way."

He was right, she knew, so rather than respond to that, she turned away from him, watching the rolling sea. "It's going to storm."

Damian scoffed. "It's a cloudless day."

Between bites, she replied, "I can tell by the waves. A storm is coming."

They fell into silence, with only the sound of the lapping waves and calling birds to break it. The energy between them was as real a thing as the sand beneath her feet. Solid, but ever-shifting. Unable to bear the weight of her own emotions any longer, she turned to him.

"Tell me something about yourself."

Damian rose a brow at her, lips curling downward. A rare display of emotion. "Why?"

Setting the plate to the side, she twisted to face him, crossing her arms. Her gaze darted to the rolling sea briefly as she considered her response. She could hardly tell him the truth. Barely wanted to admit it to herself.

"I need the distraction," she replied finally, turning to look at him again. The truth, but not all of it.

He shrugged, turning back to his own breakfast, and began to eat again.

Naia frowned. So he wouldn't answer then. Fine, she thought, rolling her eyes and resuming her silent study of the sea. She wouldn't press the matter. It's not as if she truly wanted to get to know him anyway, and if he wouldn't indulge her, then she simply wouldn't speak to him.

"I don't like to talk about myself," he said, tone emotionless as always. "But, I suppose if you have questions, I will answer them. Within reason."

She didn't turn to look at him, knowing somehow that if she did, he would simply stop speaking again. "Do you have any siblings?"

When he didn't respond for several seconds, she finally turned, finding his gaze locked on the sea, dark and cold. "Ask something else, Thunderheart."

The words were quiet, and hard as stone, sending a chill up her spine. Only old wounds, big ones, earned that type of cold. "Okay then," she sighed. "Tell me something else then. Something mundane. Do you prefer the mountains? The sea? The desert? Where do you most like to be?"

"This is a ridiculous question."

"Well, you didn't want to talk about your family. Indulge me."

Damian scoffed, but acquiesced. "The desert."

"Why?" Dipping her hand to the sand, she let it fall from one palm to the other, over and over in an idle motion. Just something to keep her hands busy. An old habit she'd shared with her father.

His gaze lowered to her hand, and he watched as the sand fell, replying a moment later. "It's the emptiness, the quiet, I suppose." His attention never leaving her hands, he asked, "Tell me about your family."

Frowning, she watched him watching her. For a moment she considered refusing to answer, as he had. "I have a sister I adore and a mother who is...difficult. There is little else to say about them."

"I know all about Maren and Damla," he replied. She stiffened, hackles raising at the use of their names, barely resisting the urge to toss the sand in his eyes. He must have noted the shift in her posture or the way her fingers twitched as the sand fell from one hand to the other because he smirked as he added, "I did my research before I claimed you, Queen of Coruscis. I'm not stupid."

"I have nothing else to say about them," she snapped back.

"Tell me about your father," he pressed on.

If the use of her mother and sister's names made her angry, the use of her father's made her cold. Time, she'd been told countless times, dulled the pain of grief, but it remained. Buried, perhaps, enough that she could sometimes go days without its sting, but always there. Dropping the sand to the ground she shook her head.

"No."

He gaze lifted to hers, dark eyes narrowing slightly. "You were close?"

Naia stiffened. A dozen curses danced on her tongue, but she kept her lips pressed together. Reining them in, for the moment at least. Silently she nodded, one sharp movement to answer his question.

"His death must have hurt you."

The wound she'd worked hard to keep closed ripped open, and she no longer had the restraint to hold her tongue. "Fuck. You. Of course we were close. When he died," she snapped. "I lost them both. I lost–" She jerked her head to the sea, dropping her hands helplessly to the sand. The sea that had taken him. "I lost too much."

His hand brushed hers, sending a jolt across her skin. Jerking her hand away, she turned to glare at him. "I don't want to speak of him again."

Damian nodded. "I understand loss, Thunderheart. Now rest. We have a long day ahead of us."

~

By midday, the sky had turned a deep shade of gray, and the wind howled across the sea. Damian reached for Naia's hand, and with a wistful glance, she said a silent goodbye to the raging ocean, wondering if this would be the last time she saw it.

Darkness enveloped them, and soon they found themselves in a familiar place.

"Wait here," Damian commanded, just inside the door of the ruined temple. The very place she'd felt so strangely connected to. For a moment, she could have sworn the tile in her hand warmed.

"Where are you–"

Naia gagged. As if someone had left a feast to decay; the scent of rotting flesh and molding fruit assaulted her nose.

Lukus.

She's nearly forgotten the man Damian had killed to save her life. Guilt washed over her. Not guilt over his death, never that, but guilt for leaving his corpse here–for desecrating this once sacred space. She hoped whomever this place had belonged to would forgive her from the next world.

Ignoring Damian's command for her to wait, Naia strode inside. She didn't want to see what remained of Lukus, so she turned away as she entered the grand space, moving to the opposite wall from where the fight had occurred. Sliding her thumb over the tile in her palm, she let her gaze roam over the few bits of remaining tilework.

Would Maren commission a mosaic such as these in her memory?

Her sister and mother would be left to wonder what had happened to her after her disappearance. Damla would lock herself away, drown in her own grief and ignore Maren's pain, much as she had when their father had died.

In contrast to their mother, Maren would rage, would never stop looking for Naia, or at the least an answer for what happened to her. Maren would–

Naia froze, chest aching. No. Maren would be dead, Damla, her people. From Eve's dire warnings, the intervention of long-absent gods and the evil she could all but feel emanating from Lukus when he spoke of Her, she knew.

If She succeeded, the world would plunge into darkness.

"I told you to wait."

Damian's cool tone sounded to her right, and she turned to face him. A sort of weariness she'd never known had settled over her. "She will kill them all, once She has me, won't She?"

"Who?"

Naia stared at him, too tired to levy insults now. "Everyone."

Damian fell silent, meeting her gaze as dispassionately as he had so many times before. "Yes."

His simple reply awoke something within her and drew her back from the precipice of her despair. "Then why are you helping Her? Explain it to me," she ordered, closing the distance between them and shoving him hard with the palm of her free hand flat against his chest. "Do you have nothing in this world that you care for? Are you so alone, so empty of emotion that you would stand by—no, *help Her* destroy everything?"

Damian didn't resist as she shoved again, merely stepping back with each push. A muscle in his jaw feathered and he met her gaze, eyes darkening. "You know nothing of what I love, what I have lost. What matters to me."

"Then tell me!" Naia screamed, furious tears falling from her eyes. "Tell me why!"

"No," he replied, voice low.

"Let me die."

"No."

For the first time, she could have sworn there was some emotion there. Something she didn't care to try to identify. She turned away from him, eyes burning. Squeezing the tile, careful not to slice her palm again, she let the tears fall.

There was nothing more to say; only one last chance to save them all.

Chapter 16

They made their camp in a smaller room of the main circular space. She hadn't spoken a word to Damian since their argument. Hadn't asked what had become of Lukus' remains, or why he wanted to camp elsewhere this time. None of it mattered. She had one last chance to stop this, one plea to make before she was forced to do what he had declared she wouldn't.

In silence, Damian had spread blankets atop the sand and bits of rubble, sparing her only the occasional cryptic look. Looks which she utterly ignored. Night had fallen fully by then, and she lay back staring up at the stars. It had become a habit, naming and counting the constellations. As before, the maidens, the bear, the crow, all those so familiar greeted her again and sang ancient lullabies that had her drifting swiftly into sleep.

~

"Hello again," the white-haired child said sweetly, offering Naia a soft smile. They stood on a beach, like the first dream; only now she was alone with an ethereal girl of no more than ten dressed in flowing robes of white. "I hoped I would have another chance to speak with you, Naia Colvari, Queen of Coruscis."

"Endri?" she guessed, tilting her head.

The girl smiled, inclining her head once. White robes fluttered on a phantom breeze, giving the god an utterly eerie appearance. "If my chosen form is disturbing, I can choose something that will put you more at ease. Though I must warn you, I believe our time to be short."

"That isn't necessary," Naia replied, turning her gaze to the sea. Unlike last time, the sea in this dreamscape had gone still. The wrongness of it sent a chill down her spine. "Where is Lir? I need to speak with him."

Earn it. The memory echoed in her mind.

"He is...occupied elsewhere," Endri replied softly. "I have come with a bit of guidance. I hope you will take it to heart."

Dragging her attention away from the eerie sea, Naia folded her arms across her chest. She too had been clothed in robes, she realized, as beads scratched against her skin. Turquoise swirls adorned the pale grey robes in whirling patterns.

"What is it?" she asked, lifting her gaze.

Endri smiled patiently. "Only this," the god replied. "When the Darkness comes, do not be afraid to reach out your hand. The girl with the heart of thunder needn't be alone."

"What does–"

Naia jolted upward. The shore had vanished, replaced once more by the ruins, and the night sky above.

The girl with the heart of thunder.

Thunderheart.

Damn the gods and their cryptic words. Scoffing, Naia dragged a hand through her hair, fingers snagging on tangles, and then...

She stilled, scanning the darkness silently. Something had changed. The moonlight above illuminated most of the ruined room, but there were shadows so deep that she could make out nothing within.

"Are you here?" she whispered.

Perhaps She had finally come to lay claim to her prize.

Only silence answered her in the darkness. Naia's heart pounded in her chest.

Had Damian abandoned her here for his mistress to claim?

"Hello?" she whispered again into the darkness. But it wasn't fear that drove her, it was anger. Snatching the tile from the sand, Naia rose to her feet. "You will not claim me," she stated, pressing the sharpest part of the tile to her wrist. "I'll die first."

Movement from behind her had her spinning, and Naia's heart dropped to her feet as she came face to face with the last person she expected.

"Hello, beloved," Zayan grinned menacingly.

CHAPTER 17

Zayan Hidar should have been halfway across the world by now, not standing in the farthest reaches of the desert, staring at her like he knew exactly how he was going to end her life. The term of endearment made her skin crawl and fury like lightning skittering through her veins. There was only one reason why he would be here now, only one way it would be possible.

"How are you here, Zayan?" she demanded coldly. Where was Damian?

Not that she needed him to save her, but the fact that he'd abandoned her to die like this?

That pissed her off.

Zayan lifted his hand to his chest, pouting in a feigned display of hurt. "You wound me. I'm told you've taken that fae bastard as your lover. Do you intend to make him your consort as well?" He tutted quietly, eyes narrowing. "I could have given you so much more, Naia."

Seething, Naia straightened, hazarding a step toward him. She had no weapon, but by the looks of his casual dress, in simple linen pants and an unbuttoned shirt, neither did he. He was muscled but not a fighter, and not nearly as large as Damian.

I can take him, if I have to. Maybe.

"You've lost the right to use my name," she shot back. "Should I have had them remove your tongue before you were exiled?"

"And you're not my queen anymore, bitch," he spat, beginning to move toward her. Slow, graceful, like a snake in the sand, waiting for the right moment to strike. "I serve another now. She who is darkness. Pure power in its rawest form. Everything you could only hope to be. And She wants you dead."

Naia launched herself at him before he could utter another word. Before he could use his size to his advantage. If he got her down, she knew without a doubt she would lose. Her screams echoed off of the crumbling walls, fury, pain, and fear in their most primal state. Death would be on her terms, and if he wanted to claim her life, then he would have to earn it.

Her body collided with his, hard enough to knock them both to the ground. What might have once appeared as an intimate moment between lovers, was now a battle with the highest of stakes. Raising the shard of tile above her head, she brought it down hard, aiming for his eyes.

Cries of pain and anger erupted from him as the first blow landed, then the second, before he managed to grab hold of her wrists, twisting hard enough to force her to drop the tile. Wrenching her arms painfully, he slammed her sideways, attempting to pin her to the ground as he rolled.

Blood dripped onto her face from vicious gashes across his cheeks and forehead. She'd missed, but she'd damn well done significant damage to the face she'd once thought handsome.

The moment he hovered above her, Naia brought her knee up, nailing him in the groin as hard as she could. The grunt of pain had satisfaction warming her veins, and she spat in his face. Twisting and kicking, she continued struggling to free her wrists from his grasp to no avail.

"Be still, beloved," he ground out, lowering his face to within an inch of her own. "This will be so much easier on the both of us if you do."

"Fuck. You," she spat, headbutting him squarely in the nose.

Screaming in pain once more, he released one wrist. "Fucking whore. I should have killed you in Thalassa."

Naia didn't bother to answer him, instead punching at the crook of his elbow in an attempt to free her other wrist. If she could just—-

The thought fell away as his free hand closed around her throat, followed by the other. Tighter and tighter he squeezed. She fought; kicking and clawing until her nails sliced his arms and his face. She fought for what felt like an eternity. Above her, Zayan's eyes were wild, filled with a cold hatred she hadn't thought him capable of–and as she faded away, Naia could have sworn she heard the sound of someone screaming her name.

CHAPTER 18

Stark, endless white greeted Naia as her eyes fluttered open. Standing, not lying, with cool stone beneath her bare feet rather than warm sand. A few feet away, Lir stood, watching her expectantly.

A strange, bittersweet, relief flooded her. She hadn't wanted to die, but if Lir refused to help in some way, maybe this was the next best option. Her death would, hopefully, spare the lives of everyone she loved. Would end the nightmare unfolding, with her at the center; trapped and unable to escape.

"Well, here we are," he said by way of greeting, irritation dripping from his every word.

"It's over."

The god of storm and sea rolled his eyes. "Not quite," he retorted, flipping his long black hair over his shoulder. "You have a choice to make."

"I'm actually allowed a choice in any of this?" she snapped back.

Lir stepped closer, lightning flashing in his eyes. "Watch your tone, mortal."

Narrowing her own, Naia countered, "Or you'll kill me?"

Shifting her gaze away from him, she took in the room.

No, a tunnel, she corrected herself. A long, empty tunnel.

"I'm already dead."

When she turned back to him, Naia found Lir frowning at her, an impatient adult weary of dealing with a petulant child. "But you needn't stay that way."

Confusion swept over her. She was dead. The matter was settled. With Naia dead, Her plans were thwarted.

"Did you truly believe it would be so simple to end this?" he asked incredulously. "If your life was the cost of saving this world, saving our lives, you would have been dead long ago."

"I don't understand." His callously spoken words made her feel foolish, insignificant. What was the point of it all?

"Your fellow queens were offered the same choice," he continued as if she hadn't spoken. *Arrogant bastard.* "Remain dead, hope that all will not be lost and that the others can succeed without you. Doubtful," he remarked, brow raised. "Or you can make the wise decision, and step up as they did. Lay claim to your true power and live to fight."

"What does that even mean, my 'true power'? What decision?"

In her letters, Eve had never spoken of a choice; only explaining that the fae had returned, that some great evil threatened them all. She had spoken of a war to come, of the cauldron and the gods. Had warned that the three queens of Aestera were destined to defeat Her.

"The life-blessed one did not tell you. Humans," he laughed humorlessly. "She is fae, as is the sun-blessed Queen of Avellon. Human no more," he explained. "The three of you were born to wield the artifacts, to bear the burden of saving us all."

"She told me about the cauldron, but I don't have it."

"It would do you no good, without being fae." Waving a hand, he added, "It is safe anyway. The location of the artifact is of no importance at the moment. As I said, you have a choice to make."

Naia considered it for a moment. "Stay dead, or become fae," she replied flatly.

"Well?" Lir prompted impatiently.

"We'll be able to kill her if I change?"

"Perhaps," he shrugged. "If my sisters are correct, and you truly do have a heart of thunder."

"Then do it."

CHAPTER 19

Lightning lashed her veins as Lir took her hand in his. The back of her hand, through her fingertips burned; the pain like nothing else she had ever known. A scream erupted from her lips, and she squeezed her eyes closed, reminding herself that it would be fleeting; worth it for the chance to end Her existence.

To save her sister, her mother, from whatever this monster had in store.

As the pain subsided, she opened her eyes once more to find pale morning light above. Her body lay cradled in a pair of strong arms, her head resting against a broad chest. Damian held her close, making no sound despite his chest heaving with every ragged breath, his heartbeat pounding in her ear.

"Fuck," she groaned, attempting to wiggle free of his grasp.

"Naia," he breathed, releasing her. He'd been sitting, she realized, on the edge of a large chunk of stone, cradling her lifeless form.

But why?

Her body, her new body, felt strange, not entirely her own, as she slid from his lap to kneel in the sand before him. He simply watched, staring at her with near-black eyes. Remaining utterly still, he didn't speak, barely even breathed. Waiting, she realized, for her to explain.

"She sent him to kill me. I guess She got tired of waiting for you," she bit out sarcastically.

His gaze dropped to her hand, hanging limply at her side, something akin to alarm flashing in his eyes before he turned his attention to her once more. He continued to stare, breath still ragged.

"Say something," she ordered, squirming beneath his stare.

"I–" he began, stopping abruptly as he dropped to kneel before her. "You're fae."

"Apparently."

"Lir?" he asked, voice low.

"That ass? Yes." She turned her gaze toward the sky, not lightened with the early morning light. "Where is Zayan?"

"Who?"

"The man who...killed...me," she explained, the words strange and sour on her tongue. Jumping to her feet with a speed that made her head spin, she looked around for him; or his corpse she assumed, now that Damian was here.

Finding nothing, she spun to stare down at him. "Where is he?"

"I found you alone," he replied, jaw tensing. "I would have gone to look, but I couldn't leave you."

"We have to find him. I'm going to kill him with my own bare hands."

Damian stood then, closing the distance between them with a single step. To her shock, his hand came to rest on the side of her cheek, callused skin sliding against her own. "His blood will be yours."

She could do little more than blink, heart racing. "Damian," she warned quietly. Unsure what was happening; why he was touching her like this. Sure they'd fucked, but that had simply been a moment of heat and lust, hadn't it? A need for release.

Something in the back of her mind, a voice that sounded an awful lot like her own, laughed. *Stupid girl,* it snickered.

"I thought you were dead," he began.

"That was your goal, ultimately, though I'm sure She–"

He squeezed her face gently. "Shut up."

Naia bristled at his tone. "You don't–"

He ignored her, stopping her short as his other hand came to rest on her face. "I thought you were dead. Something snapped. I saw you, lifeless; bruised and broken." He swallowed hard then. "I was prepared to hunt him to every corner of this world. The sands would be forever stained by the blood of whoever had done this to you."

"But you wanted me to die. By Her hand."

He nodded once. "I did."

"What changed?" she whispered, scarcely believing what she was hearing.

"You" he replied fiercely. "Your courage, your fire. You never stop fighting. You were prepared to die, to kill. The way you raged at the gods, against Her. It's you, Thunderheart, and I will never allow this to happen to you again."

When his thumb slid across her cheek, she felt as though her heart might leap from her chest. "Damian," she breathed, unsure how to respond. Nothing could have prepared for this...this declaration. Her captor had become her protector somehow. She couldn't name the storm of emotions that swam through her. That small voice still snickered in the back of her mind; as if it knew some secret she didn't.

"We need to go," he said, clearing his throat and dropping his hands from her cheeks. "She knows where we are, and I doubt She'll be content with his account of things. She'll want to see your body herself."

She followed his gaze as it dropped to her hand. Bolts of lightning, in a deep blue, rose from her middle finger and up the back of her hand, coming to a stop at her wrist. Lir's mark, she assumed. A symbol of whatever gift the god had bestowed on her.

A faint sparkle in the sand caught her eye. The tile, the ancient eyes that seemed to watch her every move. Gingerly she brushed the sand away from the ancient woman's image.

We've come a long way together these last few days, she said to the long-lost woman. *And we'll be together a little longer.*

Rising to her feet, she reached for his hand, and let him drag her into darkness and wind once more.

Chapter 20

Light rippled off of the clear water of the oasis as she dropped his hand. "I need to bathe," she said, gaze drifting to the blood still caked on her hands from her attempts to save her own life.

Without waiting for his reply, she began to slip free of her clothing. He'd seen enough of her body to dispel any shame she might feel in revealing her nude form to him now. Had touched her in ways that had driven her mad, had laid claim to her body in the most primal of ways.

Damian remained silent, still behind her, as she waded into the warm water of the pool.

She wanted every trace of Zayan off of her, needed to cleanse every place on her body he had ever touched. She'd known him to be capricious, selfish even, but had somehow been blind to the true nature he hid beneath that mask. But cruel enough to murder? That surprised her.

Whether his actions had been his own, or some influence by Her, she didn't know, and supposed it didn't matter now. The man she had once called lover, and friend, was gone. Replaced by a monster she didn't recognize.

"We can't keep running," Naia called out to Damian as she sank back into the water, the familiar, comforting, feeling of weightlessness one only found in water easing some bruised part of her soul.

Turning, she found him seated on the shoreline, watching her closely. "I need to go home, and then find Eve and Aurelia. We have to be together to finish this."

"There's someplace else we need to go first."

"What could possibly be more important?" she asked, before slipping beneath the water to soak her hair. When she rose to the surface once more she added, "Where?"

Rather than answer, he posed a question of his own. "What do you know of the prophecy that started all of this?"

Naia shrugged. Eve hadn't spoken of a prophecy in her letter. "Nothing."

Sighing, he dragged a hand through his dark hair. "When the gods touch the crescent once more, the lost children will return and herald a new age."

She considered the words a moment, applying what she knew now to the cryptic message. "Touching the crescent," she began, lifting her tattooed hand. "I assume that means this." Brushing her hands down her arms she strode closer to him, bare breasts rising above the surface of the water. "The lost children would be the fae. I know they've returned. Eve told me in her letter. Falias, right?"

Damian nodded. "Yes, but it isn't just Falias. With the second queen's rise, Finias returned."

She exhaled slowly as realization dawned. "Of course. Aurelia is fae now. Finias is the kingdom in Avellon?"

"Yes." He shifted, gaze drifting to the expanse of sand beyond her. "Now that you've been changed, Murias should have returned as well." Returning his attention to her face, he added, "We'll need them."

It made sense, of course, the need for the aid of all three fae kingdoms. But her very being screamed for her to race to her cauldron, to Eve and Aurelia. "I need to get to the cauldron before she finds it, Damian. And they need my help."

"I know. But this has to be done."

Something in his tone had her wavering. "Did you know someone there?"

"Yes," he replied carefully.

"Someone important," she prodded, wading through the water toward him. She narrowed her eyes, coming to a stop in front of him.

The corner of his lips tipped upward, eyes darkening. "You're jealous."

"No," she lied.

She was within arms reach of him now, her body screaming for him to reach out and touch her. To grab her hips, pull her close. To erase every memory of Zayan's hands on her and replace them with memories of his.

"Liar," he grinned as he answered the silent call of her body. Grabbing her hips, he urged her closer as he lay back against the sand, pulling her down until she was kneeling above his face.

"What are you doing?" she gasped, eyes wide, even as heat pooled between her thighs.

"What I've been dreaming about for days," he replied, easing her downward until she hovered just above his lips. "Say you want it."

Breathlessly, she nodded.

Oh, she wanted it.

Wanted to feel his tongue against the most intimate parts of her. To let him devour, to leave her shaking and sobbing for breath. To make her forget her name, forget every awful thing that had happened to her over the last few days.

"Out loud," he commanded, squeezing her thighs.

"I want it," she said, gripping his hands with her own.

With a smirk, he pulled her lower and slid his tongue languidly over her, teasing. Unable to stop herself, she arched her back, grinding against his tongue wantonly, drawing a dark chuckle from him that reverberated through her, sending lightning through her veins.

"I'm just getting started, Thunderheart," he whispered against her.

She said nothing, simply looking down at him with narrowed eyes dancing with silent challenge.

A challenge he threw himself into meeting.

His tongue darted against her clit, swirling, with just enough pressure to draw a gasp from Naia's lips. Her very skin was aflame, mind consumed with thoughts of him as he held her fast, feasting on her. His thumbs dug into the soft flesh of her thighs, hard, but she ignored it.

Perhaps he'd leave bruises later, a fleeting mark to remind her of this moment.

His teeth scraped against her clit, dancing along the line between pleasure and pain as his tongue swirled just within her entrance. She was rising higher, arching back with her gaze skyward. It was more than she could have dreamt. It was everything. She whimpered as he pulled away.

"Come for me, Thunderheart."

With another swipe of his tongue against her clit, she came undone. Wave after wave crested through her, drawing a cry from her lips as she rode his tongue. Weightless and spent, she rose on her knees, rolling to the side and off of his face, crashing into the sand. There was no consideration for where exactly that sand might end up, that was a problem for later, and she doubted she had the ability to walk at this point anyway.

Turning to look at him, she found him sitting up, staring in that quiet way of his again. "In a thousand lifetimes, I could never tire of tasting you."

"Too bad we only have now," she laughed.

He gave no reply to that, turning away from her as he said, "It's time to go."

CHAPTER 21

The midday sun greeted them as Damian returned Naia to the exact place he'd claimed her days before. She could find no sign of what had happened to her within the office. The fountain bubbled merrily. The desk remained perfectly in order, as if she'd simply gotten up and walked away.

Frowning, she hazarded a single step inside. Other than the bodies of the guards, long since removed she was sure, had the violence that had touched this place even left a mark?

"You know you can't alert them, Thunderheart," Damian warned quietly from behind her.

"I know, you'll kill them," she replied bitterly. Her gaze swept the room, and when she found no guards or staff within, she sighed with relief.

"Mm," he hummed noncommittedly.

Or would he? She wondered. Now that things had shifted between them, what would he do if she screamed? Would he kill his way through her guards or would he let himself be taken?

More importantly– what would *she* do if they were found?

The image of Damian chained, bound like she had been, her prisoner now, flashed in her mind. Her heart galloped at the idea of it. With fear, with the dark satisfaction, thanks to the last dregs of her hatred of him that clung to the darkest corners of her soul.

"What are you thinking about?" Damian asked, shadowing her as she strode toward her desk; the last place she'd seen her cauldron.

"Nothing," she said, waving him off.

The gods blessed artifact had been turned into a flower pot some years back, after a maid had found it hidden away in a closet. Forgotten about years ago, it seemed. How many generations of her family had passed since it had been hidden here? She wondered.

Naia stopped dead in her tracks. "No. No, no, no," she muttered lurching for the desk and shoving Eve's letters to the side frantically.

"What's wrong?" he asked, coming to her side.

"It's gone. It's fucking gone," she barked. Whipping around to face him, Naia's heart sank to her feet. "It was here when you took me, and now it's gone."

Damian's expression hardened, and he opened his mouth to reply but snapped it closed again. "Someone's coming. Small. Female. Alone."

"My sister, or my mother," she replied, turning to face the doorway. "Maybe a maid."

With a hint of surprise, he added, "And a cat?"

Joy brightened the darkness that had settled over her, and she started for the door. "Maren." Though it had only been days, there was nobody she wanted to see more. "I–"

Damian seized her arm, stopping her short. Naia spun to face him, yanking her arm free. "You can't tell her anything."

Naia scoffed, just as the door began to swing open. "She'll have noticed I was abducted," she snapped back. Turning to the door, Naia's eyes met Maren's and a choked sob sounded from the latter.

Dancing around her ankles, Suri meowed grumpily, as if to say *'where the hell have you been'*. Relief washed over her that her little would-be savior hadn't been hurt.

"I thought you were dead," Maren gushed as she rushed to Naia, and the sisters enveloped one another in a fierce hug.

Naia, tears flowing down her cheeks, pulled back after a moment. "I know and I'll explain everything, but I need to ask you a strange question first. That old metal pot I had on my desk, where did it go?"

Maren's teary gaze slid from Naia to Damian, and her lips pressed together. "Did you endanger my sister, or did you save her?" she asked tightly, as if she hadn't heard Naia's question.

"Both," Damian replied in a flat tone. "In equal measure."

For a moment she looked as though she might beat Damian to death with her bare hands, but to Naia's surprise, Maren's attention returned to her. "The cauldron is with Eve and Lia. I assume your fae friend here has filled you in."

Naia could do little more than stare for the span of a heartbeat. As soft as she was, Maren had always been strong, fierce as a sandcat and quick witted. It was of no real surprise that she would uncover the truth of what was happening and take it in her stride.

"Okay," Naia began, turning to glance at Damian. "Where are they now?"

"Near Serona," Maren replied, taking Naia's hands in her own. "I know you have to go," she said, gaze flicking to Damian once again. "But when you've finished saving the world, I want to know everything."

"Promise," Naia replied, giving her sister's hands a squeeze. A small bump against her leg had her attention shifting to Suri, currently winding her way between their legs. "And I'll be sure to make up for all the snuggles you're owed."

Suri let out a meow that might have been acceptance or curse, either as likely as the other.

"Hurry," Maren said, releasing Naia's hands. "They've been searching for you. They need you now."

Wrapping her arms around Maren's shoulders in another brief hug, Naia lowered her voice to a whisper. "I love you."

Maren nodded against her cheek. "I love you too."

Holding back tears, Naia backed into Damian's waiting arms. "Oh," she said, as the darkness began to gather. "If Zayan shows up, don't hesitate to remove his head from his fucking body."

CHAPTER 22

"It still feels wrong," Naia said, as they appeared before the tallest gates she had ever laid eyes on. Glistening white, almost too bright to look at beneath the full desert sun. "Not going to Eve and Lia now. I need that cauldron. I can feel it in my bones."

"You do," Damian conceded, releasing her from his arms. "But this is important, I promise. We won't have time to do it if we wait."

Something inside her bristled at the idea, but she was willing to hear him out, for now. If this took more than a few hours she would find a way to get to them. "This could be another attempt to kill me, or turn me over to Her," she pointed out as they began to walk.

Damian cast a sidelong glance at her. "Is that what you think this is?"

She considered it a moment. Part of her wanted to snap back that yes, it could very well be. He had kidnapped her and threatened her. Chained her. Had planned to deliver her to the greatest evil to walk this world.

And yet...

She knew with unyielding clarity that she was safe with him.

As if by magic, the gates swung open. "This is Murias?" she asked, as they passed through. Beneath their feet, sand turned to sandstone.

Palms lined the wide street just inside the gates, and within a few steps a wondrous city was revealed. Low buildings with domed roofs spread as far as she could see. In the distance, a palace of enormous size, with the same domed roof; the only building to reach two stories.

To one side, in a small square filled with market stalls, shoppers packed nearly shoulder to shoulder passed beneath a wide, canvas canopy no doubt intended to protect both patrons and wares alike from the punishing sun above. Opposite the market, to her left, a group of what had to be students read from texts, while an older male supervised.

Damian inclined his head, "This is Paradisus, the capital city."

It was so utterly normal that the scene could have taken place as easily in Thalassa. Simply people living their lives, unaware of what transpired elsewhere in the desert.

Fae, she corrected herself. These were fae. It had been one thing to meet the three fae males who had taken her, to spend these days with Damian, but to see so many...

The arrival of new people, a human at that, caused enough of a stir that many paused to turn and appraise them. Only the approach of a small contingent of men and women in copper-colored tunics tucked into matching, loose-fitting pants–with deadly sharp curved swords at their hips; led by a striking woman with long, curly dark hair had them turning away.

"The queen," Damian explained, voice low. "Cilla Valessos."

Naia nodded, and let her gaze sweep over the approaching queen. The queen whose less than pleased expression lay fixed on Damian.

As Cilla and her guard stopped several feet away from them, the entire square seemed to fall into silence. "You were told never to step foot inside my city again, Damian."

Naia's gaze slid to Damian, eyes wide. He had failed to mention that bit of important information when insisting they come here. "What?" she demanded in a harsh whisper.

"Then you know I wouldn't be here if it weren't important, Aunt."

Naia blinked again. She'd expected a lost lover, or friend maybe. To find that he had family here wouldn't have been entirely shocking, but his relation to the queen surprised her.

"I know why you're here," Cilla replied calmly. "The human queen," she began, drawing Naia's attention once more.

Lifting her chin slightly, she met Cilla's eyes, warm, elegant brown, angular eyes set in a heart-shaped face. If she were closer, Naia wondered, would she see gold lining the pupils? It took only the span of a heartbeat for shock to course through Naia's veins, recognition sweeping her.

She had seen those very eyes so many times and had spoken to them in desperation.

"Well, formerly human," Cilla corrected. Lifting a hand she signaled a guard to step closer. "We've been waiting." To her guard, she turned and said, "Go and tell the king they've arrived."

"I know you," Naia blurted finally, earning sharp looks from Damian and Cilla. "It's you," she said, lifting her hand to reveal the broken tile within; the beautiful eyes of a woman long forgotten. "I found this at the temple in the desert," she explained, turning to Damian. "She's the woman in the mosaic?"

"You took her there?" Cilla asked, surprised.

"It's not–"

"Not here," Cilla interjected. "Queen of Coruscis, may I call you Naia?"

Turning back to her, Naia's lips twitched downward. She disliked the refusal to give her a clear answer, but she acquiesced, lowering her hand and tucking the tile safely in her grasp again. "If I may call you Cilla," she replied. "So that we are on equal footing."

Cilla grinned. "Then allow me to properly welcome you to my home, Naia. I have much to tell you."

CHAPTER 23

Like the halls of Evertide, the castle the royals of Murias called home was a masterwork of smooth stone, tile mosaics, and sweeping windows. Swaths of fabric designed to shield the interior from the harsh desert sun had been pulled low, blocking the view beyond to Naia's disappointment.

The main difference between the two lay in the theming of their artwork. Where Evertide's mosaics and paintings depicted the sea as well as the sands, Murias' artists seemed fixated entirely on the oasis the city-kingdom had been built around, and the desert surrounding it.

"We can't stay," Naia said, as Cilla led them down a long hallway lined with paintings depicting various fae men and women. Most bore a resemblance to Cilla. "I need to find the others."

"I know," Cilla replied. "We're prepared to help you with that. Finias and Falias are already with them, and we were warned by the gods to be ready for your rise."

"Lir?"

Cilla snorted. "No, not him." Casting a glance over her shoulder, she added. "You'll find that there are few blessed by that one. I serve Alessia."

Naia frowned. "I'm not familiar."

"War and strategic thinking," Cilla said with a sharp grin. "You've got spark and fury. I have a mind for strategy and war."

As they approached their destination, a simple wooden door, flung wide to reveal a small library, Damian added, "Zale is blessed by Alessia's mate, Ashur. His domain is wisdom and rule."

"A perfect match," Cilla proclaimed.

"Bragging again, my love?" a gentle male voice called from within.

Naia's awestruck gaze swept the room. Shelves lined every wall, stacked full of books. Some were old and weathered, others appearing as if they'd been freshly bound. Faint sunlight from slanted openings in the dome roof above was the only illumination.

Turning, Naia found herself facing the king of Murias. Like Damian, he was tall, but that was where the familial similarities ended.

Perhaps Cilla is the one he shared blood with then.

Zale's jaw was sharp, cheekbones high, giving him an arrogant appearance. One that didn't quite match the softness of his light brown eyes.

"Better for it to be dark than risk them catching fire," he explained, noting the gaze she'd cast upward. "Damian," he added, shifting his attention to his nephew. His tone, Naia noted, was considerably softer than Cilla's had been, with a clear fondness shining in his gentle eyes.

"Uncle," Damian replied, his usual flat tone wavering slightly.

"We are in a hurry..." Naia prompted. Though she could see the reunion was a difficult one, there was little time. If She found them...

Cilla cleared her throat lightly. "They went to *the* temple, Zale. I thought it best if we explain. She believes the mosaic was me."

"You?" Zale laughed softly. "I'm afraid you're mistaken there," he said, turning his gaze to Naia. "I will try to keep the tale brief, but I must insist you rest before you join the others. The path ahead is dark, and not a short one. You may think you're writing the end of this story, but I can assure you, it is far from over."

Naia frowned, tensing. "We were told if we gathered the artifacts we could stop Her."

"And you can," Cilla said, moving to her husband's side. "But it is far from a simple task, and it will not be won in a single battle."

Zale nodded. "The enemy you face is ancient. Cunning. She will not make it easy for you, even with all your gifts."

"I expected as much," Naia replied, irritation lining her words. "And I appreciate the warning, but I need to find them."

Cilla started to argue, only to be calmed by her husband's hand on her arm. "We understand," he replied smoothly. "Would you like to hear the tale at least?"

Naia's gaze shifted to her fist, still closed around the bit of tile that had become something of a lifeline for her. Part of her wanted to refuse, to insist they leave now that the fae rulers were aware of her rise, of the battle to come. But she had been dedicated to ensuring this woman was remembered–and she clearly had been.

How could she possibly walk away without knowing now?

With a sigh, she placed it gently on the desk between them. "Tell me who she was."

A few minutes later, Naia found herself seated across from the desk in a sturdy wooden chair, Damian at her side. Cilla had perched herself on the arm of Zale's chair, like a watchful bird, as he began to launch into the tale of this ancient woman and the temple Damian had taken her to.

"Her name has been lost to time," Zale said regretfully. But Naia didn't miss the quick glance he shot in Damian's direction. "But her story is one that we," he said, glancing at Cilla, "will ensure is never lost."

"It seems it already has been, given the state of the temple," Naia remarked, earning a reproachful scoff from Cilla.

"That was not our doing," the fae queen shot back.

Damian stiffened beside her.

"That," Zale interjected smoothly. "Was done long ago; and not part of this particular tale."

Rolling her eyes a bit, Naia cast a glance at Damian, who frowned at her. "Apologies."

As if there had been no interruption at all, Zale continued. "You know your role as Bearer, yes?"

Naia nodded once, shifting in her seat impatiently as she turned her attention back to the king and queen. "I do."

"You're not the first," he explained. "A very long time ago, there were others. The original Bearers. Women of great strength. Fae born. Blessed from birth by the very gods who created each of the artifacts." Zale leaned closer, bracing himself on the desk with his elbows. Gentle brown eyes lightened with excitement as he spoke. "The artifacts were created for these women specifically, you see. With their gifts in mind."

"We don't know that part for certain, love," Cilla said quietly, placing a hand on his back.

Zale shrugged. "That's what some of the oldest tales claim at least. But what we do know for certain, is that every time the artifacts come into play, the Bearers are reborn."

"Reborn." Naia's tone was flat, at odds with the thundering of her heart. "You're saying that I'm some ancient woman reincarnated," she began, gaze dropping to the stone tile on the table. "And she was?"

"She," Zale said, as he took the tile into his hands reverently, "was a Cauldron Bearer. Perhaps the first, or only one of many. As is much of the story, that part is unclear," he added, gaze flicking to hers.

"How do you know she held the cauldron?"

At that, Cilla smiled, replying, "Because she was my ancestor. Through my mother's line, many generations removed."

Zale nodded. "The rest of the mosaic depicted water, yes? She was crossing a stream in the desert?"

Naia thought back to the temple, the remains of the mosaic. Bile rose in the back of her throat as another memory, forever intertwined with the lovely artwork, flashed in her mind. Lukus' hands around her throat, the sharp pain of the stone in her back.

The sensation of a warm, broad hand closing over her own had her turning to meet Damian's dark eyes. Danger lurked there, in the endless depths of his near-black eyes, but not for her. Never again for her, she knew; even if she didn't understand why.

"Yes," she said, clearing her throat as she turned away from him. Ignoring the thundering of her heart. "Most of it was gone, but I saw her feet, stepping over a stream in the desert."

Zale grinned. "Just as I remembered," he said pleasantly. "The cauldron, you see, it grants you whatever you need most. It hears your call.

Yours alone, mind you. Only the Bearer knows exactly how it works, but the few recorded texts on the matter claim it's like–"

"It grants wishes," she said flatly. "Really?"

"Not exactly," Zale shook his head. "More accurately, it offers aid. The mosaic you saw tells the story of this woman, this ancient queen. Disaster had struck Aestera, the details are once again unclear, but what the temple tells us is that she brought life back to the ancient people."

Naia listened with interest, but also with impatience. "While I am glad she's remembered as a hero," she began gaze dropping to the tile. *You weren't forgotten.* "I don't understand why it was so important for me to hear the story now."

"You need to know how it works," Damian replied, pulling his hand away from hers finally.

"It's time she had the whole truth, Damian," Cilla said quietly.

Naia turned to him with confusion. Of course he held secrets, they hadn't exactly poured their hearts out to one another these last few days; but Cilla's tone made it clear whatever this one was, it was huge–and greatly important.

Damian's expression darkened, eyes filling with some emotion she couldn't name. "It isn't simply the Bearers who are reborn," he began slowly. "But there are those who are...guardians of a sort. Destined to protect the Bearers–in every lifetime."

"Twin hearts who beat in time with another, echoing across space to find their match in every way, usually mates," Zale explained. "Most are unaware of this."

"Mates," Naia repeated, head spinning. "You're saying they're literally born to be the lover of the Bearer?"

"No," Cilla interjected. "Not always. Some could simply be a friend or even a sibling. They are simply there to support the Bearer, to help them in whatever way they can. Despite typically being utterly unaware of this fate." She shrugged then, casting a glance toward Damian. "Others may even come into the Bearer's life in more....unexpected ways."

Naia spun to face Damian fully. "You're not saying–"

"That's not possible," he replied flatly, glaring at Cilla and Zale.

"You've known this whole time," she accused. Ignoring the presence of Cilla and Zale entirely, she added, "You fucked me because of this."

Damian met her gaze with his own, anger banking in those dark eyes. "Absolutely not. I only knew the story, and that I was somehow connected to it. I knew nothing about the guardians, or the...rest. When I joined Vidar's order and met him for the first time, I was told of the connection in only the most general sense. He didn't—all he would say is that I had an old soul, and a lesson to learn. When the gods abandoned us, I was angry, so angry. I had given my life to something I believed in only to be abandoned, left without a role to fulfill. So when she arrived..speaking of an order, of a purpose..."

An icy wave washed over her, leaving her trembling with rage and something akin to grief. "You should have told me," she said with deadly calm. "You should have fucking told me." She didn't bother to wait for his reply as she abruptly rose from her chair. "I would like to sleep, and then I would like to leave. As soon as possible."

Cilla, casting a knowing glance at her husband, nodded and rose. "Of course, follow me."

As she stepped out the door, he replied flatly, "I know."

CHAPTER 24

Naia tossed in her temporary bed. Hours had passed since the confrontation in the library, and she couldn't get Damian's face out of her mind. Reincarnated. They had been born to enter each other's lives.

What an introduction, she thought bitterly.

The gods certainly had a perverse sense of humor.

What about how they had been beginning to feel about one another? Attraction certainly, but friendship as well, strangely enough. Had the gods engineered that to ensure their victory?

A glance toward the terrace doors told her the sun would be rising soon and with it, the fight of her life. Cilla had assured her that Murias' army was ready and would march with the dawn. Damian would take her to Eve and Lia. Their armies had been located swiftly, using some fae magic or perhaps just good scouting. She hadn't been informed of the details.

Naia grumbled and dragged herself from the bed slowly before more angry thoughts could take hold, keeping her there to seethe in her bitterness.

At least this would be over soon. Lir had warned the battle would likely not be swiftly won, but Naia was pissed and had powers now.

Lifting her hand, she examined the new tattoo. Not that she knew how to use them, exactly. Cilla had agreed to give her a brief explanation, at least. Her own gifts were entirely different, but she knew enough about how fae gifts in general worked to give some general advice.

Fresh clothing had been laid out for her before she'd arrived in the room, and Naia dressed as quickly as possible. She was pulling on the pair of impossibly comfortable leather boots when a soft knock at the door sounded.

Expecting Cilla, or a servant perhaps, she straightened and called out, "Come in."

Pulling her hair to one side, she swiftly began to braid it, assuming it was now time for them to depart. Her hands stilled as Damian stepped in.

"Is it time?" she asked coolly, unwilling to show him even an ounce of emotion. Anger and betrayal roiled within her like a storm, but she'd be damned if she'd show him how it continued to affect her.

"Almost," he replied quietly. "Naia–"

"Stop." There was no need for discussion, for apologies. She had no desire to hear what he had to say. He had been her captor, they had formed an...alliance; and had sought release from one another in a tense situation.

That's it.

She should never have expected honesty from him. Had no real right to do so. It was utter foolishness to trust him, simply because he made her come.

"No," he countered, anger seeping into his tone finally, as he stepped closer.

"No?" she snorted, wrapping a leather band around the end of the braid and rising to her feet. "I have nothing to say to you. Nothing." Spinning on her heel, she yanked the bag that had been prepared for her from the ground. Water and a few other essentials in case they were needed.

"Then shut up and listen."

She whirled on him, closing the distance in quick, angry steps. "You have no right–"

"For once just stop fighting," he shouted, "and listen."

Naia's eyes widened, and she lifted her hand to slap him, only for him to grab her wrist before she could make contact. A frustrated cry sounded from her, and she yanked her hand away.

"My feelings for you," he said, voice lower, "are mine. Do you hear me? I lied to you, yes. You can be angry about that all you fucking want, but tell me what you would have done in my position. You challenged everything I thought I believed in. With your infuriatingly unbendable will, with your spirit, your wit." His gaze dropped to her mouth and back to her eyes, his own darkened with emotion. "You changed me. And I hate you for it."

Something in Naia's chest ached, brief and utterly ignored. "Well, the feeling is mutual."

"I'm not done."

"I am." Brushing past him, she made her way toward the door.

"I love you," he called out from behind her.

"I don't care," she lied.

~

Damian found her in the courtyard minutes later, with Cilla, Zale, and the commander of their armies. A burly man with a thick, dark beard, and a no-nonsense air about him. Esker, she'd been told, when they were introduced, just before Damian's arrival.

"We're nearly prepared. Our scouts know where they are, and we'll pace to them shortly." His dark gaze swept to Naia and Damian. "I'm told Her forces have been spotted as well, marching on our allies. Time is short, you should go."

Naia nodded her understanding, casting a wary glance at Damian. "Let's go then." Turning to Cilla and Zale, she offered a half smile. "Thank you for your hospitality, and I suppose I'll see you there." Cilla would be joining her armies, with Zale remaining behind to see to Murias' defenses, should the worst happen.

"Best of luck," Cilla replied, turning a pointed glance on her nephew.

There was no reply to that, none that wouldn't be utterly rude on her part, so Naia nodded and reached for Damian's hand in silence. Within moments the now familiar darkness and wind overtook them, pulling them through the world to meet the other queens on the battlefield.

CHAPTER 25

Darkness danced across the sky, an impossibly large storm of unfathomable magnitude. Ahead of her, the familiar forms of Eve and Lia, hand in hand, stood atop a dune watching, waiting. Alongside them, a group of men and women she didn't recognize...and, strangely enough, a bear.

She had no time to question it, not with the darkness swiftly approaching. Without a word, she stepped to Eve's side, earning a surprised glance from their companions. Lia and Eve, however, remained focused on the darkness. Naia watched in shock as pure light erupted from Lia's outstretched hand, pressing back against the darkness.

Still, the darkness approached, slowing but not stopping.

Slipping her hand into Eve's, Naia let her power rise from the depths of her soul, adding her strength to theirs, as Cilla had shown her.

Lia's light pulsed, bolstered by the boost of power from Naia.

Lightning crackled through Lia's light, spearing toward the darkness. The final push had Her recoiling, withdrawing finally, in little more than the blink of an eye. A wail of frustration sounded from across the desert, a primal sound of rage and perhaps a little fear.

Something within Naia shrank away from the sound, bone-deep recognition flaring to life within her. From her side, she heard the gasp of surprise as Eve turned to Naia, whose gaze met Lia's evenly.

"Where is my cauldron?" Naia asked.

CHAPTER 26

Within minutes of Her retreat, her forces below foundered. Those at the back retreated, leaving their comrades to fall at the front lines, slaughtered by the combined armies below. Finally, Eve and Lia whirled to face her fully.

"What happened to you?" they said in near unison.

The others gathered and watched in cautious silence; even the bear seemed to listen, as he shifted closer to Lia's side, pressing against her as if to guard her. A swift glance around them ended with her gaze landing on Damian, who remained a few feet away, separate from the group, and very, very still.

"I was taken," Naia began, turning back to Lia and Eve. "Kidnapped from Evertide and held captive by a group of three fae that served Her." She paused, considering her next words carefully. If she told them now that Damian had taken her, she had little doubt the fearsome group of fae, she'd noted their pointed ears and made an educated guess, would turn on him. Emotions were still high, the energy in the air all but crackled with barely contained violence. "He saved me."

She could feel the tension radiating from Damian ease, but she didn't turn to look at him.

"We were worried," Lia said gently. "But I think I speak for all of us when I say that your arrival couldn't have been better timed. Kore would have claimed us all, if you hadn't arrived."

Naia frowned. "Her name is Kore?"

"Yes," Eve supplied. "An ancient goddess of sorts."

"I've been told about her, but never her name," Naia explained, before repeating her earlier question. "Where is my cauldron?'

Eve cast a glance toward the dark-haired man standing closest to her. The one who hovered close, watching Eve with an expression she could describe as nothing short of utter devotion. With a nod from the redheaded queen, he vanished into a whirl of darkness.

"We kept it safe," Eve replied. "Waiting for you."

Mere moments passed before the man returned, carefully cradling the cauldron, turned flowerpot, in his hands. As the weight of the cool metal pot settled into her hands, a sizzle of power raced through her palms and a sense of completion washed over her.

With an amused smirk, Naia eyed the cauldron. "You left the plant?"

"That plant created an interesting turn of events," Eve laughed. "Have you been told how the artifacts work, how only we can wield our own?"

Naia nodded, and Eve continued.

"I was touching the plant, cursing my goddess, and wishing she would answer my call," she explained. "And suddenly she was there. It seems the cauldron, with the plant inside it, granted my wish. The plant allowed me to connect with it."

Naia could do little more than blink. "Strange."

"Very," Eve agreed.

"I'm sure you're both very tired," Lia prompted. "We should regroup." An air of anxiety flowed through her seemingly simple words, and she cast a nervous glance to the battlefield below.

Her brother, Naia realized. Aelius. Turning her gaze below, she scanned the armies they'd gathered. There among them, she saw the standard of her own kingdom. "Maren sent aid."

"Yes," Lia replied. "We're very grateful."

Naia smiled. "Of course," she said pride swelling. She would never have doubted Maren's willingness to help, even if the cause seemed all but hopeless. "Lead the way."

～

THEY GATHERED INSIDE THE JOINT COMMAND TENT, SWIFTLY erected with the nearby encampment. Aelius had joined the three queens, along with the dark-haired male clearly in love with Eve, and a silver-eyed female who hovered nearby Lia.

Damian had followed as well, remaining as separate from the group as space would allow.

"I think some introductions are in order," Eve said, as soon as they were all settled into chairs surrounding a low, round table. Each of their artifacts, a sword, a crown, and her cauldron, rested atop it. "This is Callan, my mate, and king of Falias," she said, turning a proud smile on the man to her side. "Beside Lia is her mate, Bella, she's..."

"A demi-goddess," Lia supplied, taking Bella's hand in her own. "Daughter of the goddess of the moon and prophecy." Her tight smile warned Naia away from making any disrespectful remarks toward the woman, so she offered a polite dip of her chin.

Damian, only now cautiously lowering himself in the chair beside Naia, cast a glance at her. How would she introduce him? The question was clear enough in his gaze.

"This is Damian," she began slowly, with trepidation. "He's...well it's complicated." Lifting her chin, she took a steady breath and steeled her spine for their reactions. "He is the one who kidnapped me," she said. Rushing to add, "But then he saved me. As I said, it's complicated."

Eve's lips pressed into a thin, tight line. Beside her Callan stiffened, gaze turning murderous. Lia, for her part, looked little more than shocked, and Bella...she looked utterly unsurprised for reasons Naia couldn't understand.

"He took you," Eve repeated, tone matching the stony resolve in her eyes, as she turned her attention on Damian. "He's the reason we didn't have your help, the reason you were in danger to begin with?."

The ground beneath their feet began to rumble, and Naia blinked in surprise. Across from her, Callan placed a hand on Eve's thigh. "Calm, dove."

Slowly, the trembling abated, and Eve breathed deeply. "Tell us everything."

So she did; recounting every detail, except for the most intimate. Those she would keep for herself. The group fell into cautious silence, no doubt weighing the facts and forming their own opinions on whether or not to trust Damian.

"How do we know you won't betray us?" Callan asked, arm stretched across Eve, hand resting on her thigh. It might've been simply the casual touch of a lover, had his jaw not been so tightly set.

"Because of her," Damian said calmly.

Naia could feel his gaze on her cheek, so palpable that it made her skin sizzle.

Bella shifted in her seat, reaching for Lia's hand suddenly. "Thunder crashes against silence, and the way forward is open," she said quietly. "He will never turn against her. Not now."

Lia and Eve turned toward one another, some unspoken understanding passing between them as if they'd heard the strange words before.

"I don't understand," Naia said, shifting uncomfortably.

Thunder and silence.

A small voice whispered in her mind, *Yes, you do.*

"He is the silence to your thunder," Bella replied as if it were the most obvious thing in the world. "Your mate, your protector. His heart beats in time with your own."

Naia's attention jerked to Damian, and they stared at one another in silence. "We're aware of the reincarnation thing. That he was born to be my guardian, in this and every lifetime." Turning back, she leveled her gaze on Callan. "As I suspect you are for her," she added, pointing toward Eve.

"What?" Eve demanded, gaze shifting to Callan, who looked equally confused.

"We're the reincarnated souls of the original bearers," Naia explained.

"We know that," Lia said gently. "But we've never heard of these guardians."

Naia sighed. So many secrets and histories lost to time. It made her head spin. "There were guardians, appointed by the gods to aid and protect the Bearers. Their souls are entwined with ours, in different ways each lifetime. I was told they can surface as lovers, siblings, friends." Casting a glance at Damian, she added, "Enemies turned reluctant allies."

Bella and Lia shared a look, but neither spoke.

"Mates," Eve smiled, leaning into Callan.

"So it seems," Naia replied dryly. Desperate to shift the conversation away from anything that alluded to her relationship with Damian, she said, "So we've won the day, but not the war. What do we do now?"

Chapter 27

"They'll be coming back," Callan said, eyeing the map that had been spread on the table between them. The artifacts had been moved to a low table just feet away; still well within reach of their Bearers. "But I would wager we have time to regroup, let our soldiers eat and rest, and tend to our wounded. Normally I would suggest taking the fight to her, but we've no idea where she's gone, now that they've paced, and I don't want to lose our strength by searching for her."

"The shifters are on guard, watching from the sky and sand for any sign of their approach," Eve supplied.

"Shifters?" Naia asked, frowning.

"Fae blessed by the goddess of wild things and the hunt. They can change into animals at will," Damian offered, earning a hard look from Naia.

She still had little desire to speak to him, though she knew the time was fast approaching. They would need to work out their differences, at least enough to be civil again, for the sake of their world if nothing else.

"I see," she replied. "What is your gift, Damian, I only saw it once, when Lukus..."

Damian cast a glance toward the others, tensing. "I am Samach," he said slowly. Someone gasped, though Naia didn't bother to look to see who. "I have the gift of silence. I can stifle the magic of other fae." Turning toward Eve and Lia, he added, "But my gifts don't work on you, if you have your artifacts."

"We know," Lia said with a smile. "We learned that during the last battle."

"I need to practice," Naia said, turning to the others. "Aside from what we did earlier, I've never used my magic. It's still so new."

Eve nodded, glancing toward the cauldron. "You should take that with you. I think you'll be surprised by what it can do."

Callan rose then, followed by the rest of the group. "I'll meet with Aelius, Brida, and the other commanders to make sure we're prepared when the time comes. I recommend staying outside of the camp to practice, in case you lose control. But I wouldn't go far."

"That makes sense," Naia agreed, moving to take the cauldron. Another small shock raced through her as she took it in her hands.

Curious, she thought.

"I'm going with you," Damian announced, moving to her side.

"No. I'll go alone," Naia argued, hackles raised.

"I think we should all go find Aelius...or something," Bella suggested, leading the rest of the group to shuffle out awkwardly.

Damian glanced over his shoulder before continuing. "Absolutely not. You can refuse me all you want in every other way, Naia, but I will not stop protecting you."

"I don't need your protection."

"Don't be a stubborn fool," he snapped back. "You may well be the most fearsome creature to walk these sands, but even you cannot face what comes for us alone. What would you do if her scouts found you alone? You can't outrun them. You haven't mastered your powers yet. You can't pace; as far as we know. So tell me, Thunderheart. What would you do?"

She couldn't argue with the logic of his words. She needed someone with her, but surely there was another fae who could go with her, someone who could take her away immediately if danger arose. Someone who she wasn't furious with. "I'll take someone else."

"If you try that, I'll kill them," he replied darkly. "I'm going with you."

Eyes widening and temper flaring, she opened her mouth, only to close it again. The look in his eyes told her he damn well meant it, and there was no point in arguing further.

Weighing the importance of standing her ground out of her anger against potentially starting a war with their allies, she conceded. "Fine. But you only touch me when absolutely necessary. And you don't speak to me at all."

Damian rolled his eyes and grabbed her by the upper arm. "By your command, Queen of Coruscis."

~

NAIA TUGGED HERSELF FREE OF DAMIAN'S GRASP. THE DUNE below offered a perfect view of the armies below, of the commotion erupting as soldiers dressed in the copper standard of Murias appeared out of thin air.

"Should we go back and make introductions?" she asked, no small amount of disappointment in her tone.

"No," he replied. "Cilla knows the queen of Finias, and I would assume she's at least heard of Callan Thorne."

Biting her tongue to silence the questions she wanted to ask, Naia turned focusing her attention on the task at hand. "I don't think I'm ready for you, just yet," she murmured, carefully placing the cauldron at her feet. Rolling her shoulders, Naia called on the ancient power residing in the depths of her very soul.

Lightning and wind, storm and sea.

Saltwater flowed through her veins.

Thunder in her heart.

Lifting a hand toward the sky, she commanded it to obey. And obey it did.

The clear blue sky above them darkened in a near instant. Not the endless, empty black darkness Kore had commanded, but clouds in shades of grey, with purple and blue streaks flashing within them. Her gaze fixed on a random dune in the distance; she pointed and willed the storm to obey once again.

With half a thought, the lightning struck with such force it rattled the sands.

"Gods above," Damian murmured, awestruck. "You've mastered it already. That, or you've got tremendous power."

She ignored him instead turning her attention to the other part of her gift. There was no sea here to command, so she lifted her eyes skyward and called upon the only water available.

Within moments, a torrent of rain fell upon them, soaking Naia and Damian both. Chin still lifted, she let it fall, and fall, and fall.

Let the tears fall. The rage, hurt, and fear that had haunted her every moment were released in a flood. She screamed, the sound all but drowned out by a massive clap of thunder.

Her life had been overturned, a boat capsized on a stormy sea. She'd lost her life. Her throne. No fae could sit atop the throne of Thalassa. Of course, she'd made the decision to accept Lir's bargain, but had it really been a choice? Death or to save the world; at the expense of her human existence; there was only the illusion of choice in that moment.

Her mother, her sister, all that she held dear would wither and die, as she remained young. How long was a fae life anyway? She wondered. How many centuries would pass, left with only her grief and fading memories of those she'd loved?

"Thunderheart," Damian called, above the roar of the rain and the crashing of thunder. "Let it go. You've got to let it go."

And him. She jerked her attention to the man who had started it all.

"You did this," she accused. "You took it all from me."

"I was part of it."

She took a step closer. He remained where he stood, letting her approach despite the trepidation in his gaze. "You took me."

"If I hadn't, you still would have ended up here. Or you would have died. If it hadn't been me, it simply would have been another monster."

She shook her head, denying the truth of his words.

"You know it's true, Thunderheart."

For a long moment, she simply stared at him, the storm raging above and within her heart. He wasn't to blame, not entirely at least. Kore had done this. Had taken so much from all of them. Kore, and the gods, who had damned them with this 'blessing.' Where had their choice in any of this been?

"You're going to drown them," he warned, gesturing toward the camp below.

Dragging her gaze away, she saw it then. Water streamed into the camp, wind whipping at tents as soldiers ran about trying to secure them. They didn't deserve this. Her heart still ached, still raged, but she willed the storm to calm as she turned back to him.

"I've lost everything," she sobbed.

"I know," he said gently. "But you'll find a way."

She shook her head again, brushing soaked tendrils back from her face. "How?"

"By being you," he replied with certainty. "By being the strongest person I've ever known. You're too brave, too fierce, to be conquered by this."

"I hate you."

"I know," he nodded, eyes darkening.

"And I love you," she added, shaking her head as if to deny the truth.

Shock, and perhaps a touch of hope, colored his features as he watched her carefully, as if she were an asp, prepared to strike. "Naia..."

"Shut up," she ordered, closing the distance and taking his face in her hands, claiming his lips in a kiss that was all ferocity and hunger. No tenderness lay between them, only raw emotion. Anger, and hatred, and love, all at once, a tempest within her.

Thunder crashed above as they came together. Body to body, heart to heart, one ancient soul connecting with the other. His hands wound into her sodden hair, holding her close as if afraid to let her wash away with the storm she'd called.

Though the rain no longer fell, the clouds above remained, thunder and lightning reigned above, a raging tempest that mirrored every anguished beat of her heart.

She pictured the tent that had been erected for her use. She hadn't seen it yet but knew the location, quite near Eve and Lia's, within a short walk of the command tent.

Naia thought of the long walk, from this lonely hill to the tent.

How long would it take her to lead him back there, to strip free of their wet clothes? She wished for the power to move them in an instant like he had so many times.

She felt Damian's shoulders stiffen, felt him pull away, and opened her eyes to find them swirling through darkness one moment and then standing beneath a wide canopy the next.

"You moved us?"

"No, Thunderheart, you did."

Jerking her attention back to him, she balked. "What?"

"I told you, you're more powerful than you know," he grinned, taking her face between his hands and pulling her closer.

She allowed the kiss, reveled in it, but only for a moment. "The cauldron!" she gasped, shoving him away lightly. *How could I be so reckless? So easily distracted.*

"I'll go get it," he said, vanishing into nothing.

Relieved she dropped onto a cushioned chair to wait. It should take no more than seconds for him to return, she knew, but each passed like a small eternity. Heartbeat after heartbeat she waited, and yet, he didn't return.

With a sudden intensity that had her gasping, hand flying to her chest, her heart ached.

Worry, she thought, *and stress.*

Minutes passed and still, no Damian.

Wracking her brain, she recounted the moment she'd inadvertently paced them to the tent.

"Okay," she whispered to nobody. "I want to be on the dune. I want to go to my cauldron." She willed it, picturing the place she longed to be.

Nothing.

No darkness overtook her, no sweeping wind.

Frustrated, she screamed.

Storming out of the tent she ran for the command tent. If she couldn't get herself there, she'd have Callan take her. Or someone else. *Anyone* else.

Within, she found only Lia's twin and a tall, brown-skinned female;

both of whom looked up from the map between them, staring at her with surprise.

"Naia?" Aelius questioned. "Is something wrong?"

"I need someone to pace me to the dune. Something's wrong."

The pair shared a glance. Naia speared the woman, with telltale pointed ears and amber-brown eyes, with a stare. "You. Can you take me?"

She shook her head gently. "I cannot, but I'll get you someone who can," she replied before striding out of the tent.

Turning her attention on Aelius once more, the pair of royals stared at one another for a single, tense moment. "I love her, you know," he said.

She needed no clarification as to who he referred to. "I know. She loves you too."

The corner of his lips tipped upward. "If we survive this, I intend to marry her."

"That will complicate things."

He frowned then. "Why?"

"She'll be the queen of Coruscis," Naia replied. "And I suspect you'll be taking your sister's throne."

Aelius fell silent, a shadow passing over his features. "I'd give it up for her," he said quietly.

Naia didn't reply to that, simply nodding.

To be so loved was a gift. One that she wanted dearly for her beloved sister. If they survived, and he held true to his word, Maren would be loved and treasured for the rest of her life. It was nearly enough to ease the hurt of living a nearly immortal life without her.

The woman soon returned, with fae male in tow. "I'm Valerian," he said, with an easy smile. "Where do you need me to take you?"

THE INSTANT NAIA'S BOOTS TOUCHED THE SAND, SHE KNEW something was wrong. Spinning in a slow circle, she found her cauldron, exactly where she'd left it.

Relief washed over her, followed swiftly by concern. It was safe, but where was Damian?

"Shit," Valerian's voice sounded behind her.

She turned to find him several feet away, staring down at...

No. No no no no.

The words were a cascade of screaming in her mind as she snatched the cauldron from its place and ran to where Valerian stood, staring down at Damian's lifeless form, face down in the sand. Thunder raged above, echoing the roaring in her ears, as she dropped her head to his shoulder and screamed.

CHAPTER 28

Straightening, Naia wiped the tears from her face with the back of her hand and inhaled slowly. "Okay," she sighed. "I can fix this. I can–"

"We have to go," Valerian said, gently placing a hand on her shoulder. "They're coming."

She knew he meant to pace her back to safety, but she couldn't leave him here. Not when she could fix this. Lifting her gaze, she saw the figures approaching. Men dressed in ivory, with masks covering their features. Men with bows raised, arrows nocked.

They did this.

Wind whipped the dune brutally, sand lashing her skin with only a small cushion of air protecting her eyes.

Wordlessly, she screamed, a tempest of anguish, hatred, and pain. The fracturing of her heart and soul. She released it all upon them. Lightning speared the sand in a near-perfect circle around Valerian, Naia, and Damian protectively.

Still more lightning erupted from her chest and speared toward the men, sending them flying backward onto the sand; dead. Though their deaths made her feel nothing, she quieted, dropping her gaze to Damian and the cauldron beside her. "I can fix this," she said hoarsely.

"Naia," Valerian said cautiously, dropping to the sand beside her. "We need to go back. He's gone, we should give him peace–"

"No!" she shouted, head whipping toward him. Lightning flashed in her veins, along her skin. "Do. Not. Touch. Us."

Each word was punctuated with a crash of thunder above, and Valerian rocked back on his heels. "We're too exposed here," he cautioned. "We should go back to camp, where you can do what you need to do safely."

She considered it a moment. There was wisdom in his warning, certainly. "If anyone tries to stop me or to take him from me, I will kill them," she warned. "Anyone."

Nodding his acceptance, he held out a hand for her, allowing her to make the decision. The lightning abated finally, and as she released her storm, Naia sighed. "You'll have to take my arm," she said flatly. "I need to take the cauldron, and...him."

"I'll get him," Valerian offered, easing closer. "If you'll let me."

Naia nodded. She wouldn't be able to lift him, especially now that he was–

She couldn't allow herself to even think the word.

"Take the arrows–" she choked. "Take them out first."

Offering a sympathetic glance, Valerian waited for Naia to turn away before doing just that.

The horrible sound of the arrows being pulled free from Damian's back would haunt her for a lifetime. Along with the image of him, lifeless; lost to her forever. He should never have been there. Not alone. Her stupidity had led him to the dune to retrieve something she never should have forgotten in the first place. This was her fault, and she was going to fix it.

"Okay," Valerian said finally, drawing her attention back to him. Standing, he had Damian over his shoulder, in the way a soldier would carry a wounded compatriot off of the battlefield.

To be healed.

As *she* would heal *him*.

Dragging the cauldron along with her, she rose to her feet and took Valerian's hand, allowing herself to be taken back to the camp. A flurry of activity had already spread by the time they arrived in the sand just outside Naia's tent.

"What happened up there?" Callan roared, as he swiftly approached, with several others in his wake.

Naia didn't bother to look at him to see who accompanied him, to even hear Valerian's quiet response.

"Put him on the bed," she ordered quietly.

Valerian hesitated a moment, earning a sharp look from Naia.

"You agreed."

With resignation in his eyes, he nodded and did as she asked, laying Damian gently on the bed. His glance beyond her told her the others had followed, but they remained silent. Or perhaps, she had simply gone deaf to the world.

Falling to her knees beside the bed, Naia cradled Damian's too-pale face with her palms. "You can't leave me. I won't let you," she whispered hoarsely, pressing her face to his cool cheek. "I'll hate you for it. But I'm going to fix it."

Rubbing her thumb across one cheek and pressing her lips to the other, she nodded before finally rocking back on her heels to look at those who'd followed her into the tent.

Callan, Eve, Lia, Bella. The blonde man and dark-haired woman who had been there when she arrived. She didn't know, didn't care, what their names were. Valerian stood closest, sympathy radiating off of him in waves.

Each of them watched her in uncomfortable silence.

She hated the pity on their faces, the way they watched her as if she were some fragile thing about to break.

Swiping at the tears with the palm of her hand, she shook her head. "I'm going to fucking fix it."

Eve stepped closer, reaching back for Callan's hand as she did. "Naia," she began slowly. "He's gone...I don't think–"

"I don't care what you think," Naia screamed. "If you try to stop me, I will fucking kill you."

Shadows slithered across the floor of the tent, winding their way toward her. A low growl sounded from Callan.

"Stop," Eve said, jerking her attention to her mate. "She won't hurt me."

Naia ignored the exchange, instead turning her attention to the cauldron resting on the ground beside her. "I'm going to fix it. I'm going to save him," she repeated.

Naia took the cauldron in her hands and reached for the power within it.

CHAPTER 29

"Hello Bearer," an eerily childlike voice said. "*You call upon me at last.*"

"Bring him back," Naia ordered without preamble. Had she not been so far beyond rational thought, she might have found it unnerving. Might have questioned the fact that her cauldron was sentient. But she was as a cloud to the land now, far above and beyond such things.

"*I cannot,*" the cauldron replied, as if it speaking of the weather. "*Ask me for something else.*"

"You are mine to command. Bound to grant me whatever I most need," she shot back with desperation.

The cauldron sighed, with childlike boredom. "Life and death are not my domain. Ask me for rain to water drought-ravaged crops, ask me for fire to vanquish those that threaten you, for a lover to please you. These are the things I can bring you. Ask me for something else, or let me return to my rest, Bearer."

Naia screamed in frustration. "What use are you?! Help me!"

The cauldron remained silent for a moment, before replying carefully, "There is one thing..."

"Tell me, damn it!"

"I can bring you to the one who can help, the one who commands death," the cauldron said hesitantly. *"But she may yet refuse you."*

"I don't care. Take me to her. Now."

"As you wish."

There was no darkness, no ethereal wind, to carry her to the place the cauldron had spoken of. To the domain of death.

In the span of a heartbeat, Naia found herself seated on a lush, ebony couch in a room of endless black marble; directly across from a young woman on a matching chair, dressed in silk, with a veil covering the upper half of her face. Painted red lips curved in a patient smile. There was no doubt in Naia's mind as to who sat across from her. Only one could carry the air of stillness, of peace, that she did.

"What can I do for you, dear?" the goddess of death purred.

"Bring him back," Naia said emotionlessly; drained.

The veiled goddess tipped her head sideways. Beneath the veil, Naia suspected, she watched closely. "Why should I?"

Naia stiffened, hands curling into fists at her side. She waited, prepared for the lightning to soar through her veins, but nothing happened.

"Oh, you'll find your gifts are beyond your reach here," the goddess said, pointedly turning her attention to the cauldron, settled beside Naia's feet. "Wise little thing, you are."

"Bring him back," Naia repeated. If her powers didn't work here, then she would have to use the next best thing: bargaining. "Or I leave."

"Leave, dear?" the goddess' attention slowly shifted back to Naia. Her tone remained light, as easy as if they merely discussed the weather.

"I will walk away, and never help you defeat Kore."

The goddess hissed. "Do not speak that name here."

"Do you want Her dead?"

Macaria didn't respond to that, merely pressing her lips together thoughtfully.

"This is my price. His life, to save all of yours."

The only indication of Macaria's surprise was the stiffening of her shoulders. Naia grinned cruelly. "I suspected. You abandon your children for centuries, and then expect us to believe you've come simply to save us all? This is equally about your survival, perhaps even more so. If you want my help, you will pay my price."

"Who are you to demand such things of the gods?" Lir's voice thundered suddenly, as he appeared in a flash, behind Macaria.

"The only hope you have," Naia shot back, gaze shifting to the god. She was beyond caring about her own safety now. Had she retained her sense of self-preservation, she might've been more mindful of her tone, more tactful with her request.

A small, broken part of her hoped they would strike her down, if only so she could see him again, to beg his forgiveness for what she'd caused.

"A question first," Macaria intoned in that eerily soft way of hers. "Why do you want him back so badly that would be willing to sacrifice the world?"

"Who cares–" Lir interrupted, only to be silenced with Macaria's raised hand.

"I would like to know why we're being put in this position."

Naia bristled at the question, fury lashing through her veins. "Just do it."

Macaria's lips curved upward. "Answer my question, and we will consider it."

Fists balled at her side, Naia barely contained the sharp retort that danced on her tongue. She had pushed her luck as far as she dared, and one glance at Lir's thunderous expression told her that any further insolence would not be well tolerated.

"Truthfully," Naia began through gritted teeth. "I love him."

"Is that all?" Macaria asked, smirking as if she held some secret behind that veil of hers.

Confusion and a storm of other emotions swirled within Naia. She knew there was something more between them. A tiny voice in the back of her mind whispered a word she didn't want to acknowledge.

Let us survive this, then I'll worry about that.

Without waiting for Naia's reply, Macaria turned, tilting her head to look up at Lir, who in turn shifted his attention to meet her veiled gaze. Unspoken words hung between them in the silence. For several moments, Naia thought they meant to refuse her, and the broken part of her soul screamed anew.

Suddenly the goddess of death turned back, a small smile gracing her lips. "Done," she said quietly.

"Go," Lir said bitterly. "Wield your heart of thunder and win our war. We've paid your price."

"But how do I–" Naia began. From one blink to the next, she was thrown back, back to her position by the bed, with Damian in front of her. As still as he had been before. Her chest cracked. "Liars!" she screamed.

Sobbing, she dropped her head to the bed. She would find a way to kill them all for this betrayal. Thunder cracked overhead, and men shouted outside. She would rain down hell upon the gods; and would walk away from Aestera forever. Let Her claim them all. Maren. She would take Maren and run. She would–

"You're going to scare the shit out of the humans, Thunderheart," Damian croaked.

Naia's heart stopped. She jerked her head upward to find him watching her through heavy-lidded eyes. A thousand emotions she would never be able to name, even with the many endless years ahead of her, coursed through her veins at once. The thunder quieted, as did the shouts.

Every other person in the tent was forgotten about entirely, and for that moment, only the two of them existed. Her heartbeat steadied, and, to her shock, she could hear his matching the beat of her own. A lifeline, connecting them. Something she would never tire of hearing, this assurance that he remained.

"I told you I would fix it," she breathed.

His hand found the back of her head, pulling her closer so that their foreheads touched. The quiet sound of the others shuffling out finally registered, though she didn't bother to look. Slowly breaking the contact, Naia rose and moved to straddle him on the bed.

Damian's brow rose sharply. "I just died, Naia, I might need a little time to recover before you mount me–"

"Shut up," she shot back, halfheartedly. Laying her head against his chest, she wound her arms around him and listened.

Thump, thump. Thump, thump. Thump, Thump.
The most beautiful sound Naia Colvari had ever heard.

CHAPTER 30

DAMIAN

For three days, shifter scouts took to the air day and night, searching the sands for signs of their approach, signs of where they could have gone, reporting only endless desert. His Thunderheart still hadn't grown used to the fae who could turn into animals at a moments notice.

Especially after an incident involving a feline shifter that she'd mistaken for a large housecat. Neither Naia nor the shifter had left the exchange with much of their dignity intact, he was afraid.

She had hardly left Damian's side, in the days since his temporary death. Fear the gods may yet betray them haunted her every moment, no matter how many times he and the others assured her all was well, that Macaria, at least, would not betray her agreements.

He'd never say it aloud, but he relished it; this closeness, as much as he feared losing her again.

What he felt for Naia was a tempest, unyielding, a sudden storm within him that he knew would never end. It encompassed him, dominating his every thought, every action. He'd meant it when he told Naia whatever fate the gods had woven between them had nothing to do with how he felt for her, his Thunderheart.

Damian had come so close to losing Naia, thanks to his own resentment-fueled actions, and he would never admit how much it had frightened him.

He could never admit to her that a man who had served silence faithfully for most of his life, had been a soldier, prepared to meet his death one day with dignity, was terrified of dying; if only because it meant existence without her in it.

For so long he had served in silence, never feeling, never *wanting* to feel. Every emotion had been stifled, every desire.

Now, with Naia, it was as if those parts of his soul that he'd walled away were finally breaking free after so many years. His fierce little queen was tearing down decades upon decades of granite walls within him as if they were little more than sand caught in the winds of her storm.

"Are you well?" Cilla called after them, as each of the leaders went their separate ways, late in the afternoon. Regular meetings were held with the three queens and their closest advisors, many including the fae rulers from Murias, Finias, and Falias as well; with Callan standing as representative of his own kingdom. After hearing what happened to Damian, Cilla's attitude toward her nephew had shifted, in a subtle yet noticeable way. Worry often clouded her eyes, and even, perhaps, a touch of guilt.

Shielding her eyes from the sun with the shawl around her head, she offered Damian, and then Naia, a tight smile. "We haven't spoken since..."

"My death," Damian supplied flatly, casting a small glance toward Naia, who watched in silence.

"Yes," Cilla said, frowning. "Are there any...ill effects?"

Damian laughed mirthlessly, shaking his head. "No, Aunt. I am well."

He turned, taking Naia by the hand to leave. "We should–"

"Damian, wait!"

Naia squeezed his hand, hard, and he sighed. Message received. Hear her out, Naia's eyes ordered. Shocked that she hadn't spoken the words aloud, he rolled his eyes at her, earning a sharp zap of electricity in his palm.

"Ouch," he grumbled, and she offered him a sweet smile.

Cilla came to a stop a couple of feet away from the couple, expression wary. "I think we should talk about all of it. The reasons why I exiled you, the—"

"I know why," he interrupted sharply, losing his patience. "I have no desire to go over this again."

"There are things—"

"I don't care, Cilla," he warned. "Drop it."

Naia frowned at him. "I would like to know what happened."

Sighing, he turned his gaze to Naia. If she wanted something, she would get it, he knew. That determined gleam in her eye told him this was not a subject she was likely to drop.

"It's not—"

"You deserve the truth, Damian," Cilla said gently, surprising him enough that he stopped arguing.

"What did you do?" Naia asked, narrowing her eyes at Cilla.

Cilla pressed her lips together. "I would prefer to have this discussion in private."

"Well as I'm outnumbered," he snorted. "Let's go talk."

Cilla followed them in silence, an air of anxiety radiating off of her. Naia, for her part, seemed on edge. Her heartbeat remained steady, but storm clouds gathered in her eyes. If Cilla so much as spoke out of turn, he had little doubt Naia would handle it in a way that his aunt would not enjoy.

Once inside the tent, they each took seats around the small table reserved for Naia and Damian's meals. Naia, perched on the edge of her seat, pinned Cilla with a stare. "You had something to say to him."

Damian's heart gave a squeeze. This fierce, gorgeous woman; this woman who he had hurt, was now his most ardent defender. He would never tire of trying to make up to her what had been done, would never stop proving what he felt for her was *him*; not some ancient soul bound by the gods. He knew, and wondered if she did, they were mates. He had heard every beat of her heart since her rebirth, but the knowledge of that weighed on him.

Would she bolt if she knew?

"I did," Cilla replied, tone sharp. Clearly Naia's tone was beginning to wear his aunt's nerves, but frankly, he cared little. There was no love lost between them, not after what had happened all those years ago. "You wanted to know what happened, so allow me to start there." Cilla shifted in her seat. "Damian's mother is my younger sister, Valora."

Damian's mood darkened at mention of his mother's name. Her face flashed in his mind's eye. Soft features, and a bright smile. Her laughter like bells in the wind. The look of terror as she told him to run. Jaw set, he stifled the painful memory and waited for his aunt to continue.

"She died, when Damian was thirteen–"

"Skip ahead. I don't want to talk about that."

Naia turned her gaze on him then. It wasn't sympathy that shone in her eyes, but a fierce look of love.

Nodding, Cilla pressed on. "In the years after he came to live with us, he grew restless," she said. "He was often in trouble, getting drunk in the seediest parts of the city, stumbling in with low women."

"I was grieving!" he shot back. "You all pretended everything was fine, she was gone, and I was alone."

Cilla shook her head. "You were never alone, I–"

"Ignored me entirely," he interjected, leaning back in his chair and fixing her with a stare daring her to contradict him. Naia placed a hand on his thigh, leaning back in her own chair.

His aunt shook her head, looking to the floor dejectedly. "I suppose there is some truth in that."

"So what caused you to banish him?" Naia demanded. "Surely the rebellious acts of a grieving teenager didn't rise to that level."

"You're right," Damian said darkly. "Tell her why."

Cilla looked up then, sighing warily. "His mother, my sister...She had been with Zale before we were married. Zale is...Zale is Damian's true father." Biting her lower lip, she quickly added. "The only reason he isn't acknowledged as such is for his safety. Zale's reign has been challenged in the past, for reasons I won't get into now. We thought it best–"

"Liar. It was done to ensure your children would inherit. Despite me telling you repeatedly that I have no interest in it."

"I had to protect all of you," she hissed. "My children as well as you, Damian. If you had only–"

"If I had agreed to take the vows?" he snapped back, sarcasm dripping from his every word. His mind turned to the past, to the angry teenage boy who wanted nothing more than to find a home with the only family he had left. Cilla's voice echoed in his mind, the words spoken so many years ago...

"If you will only accept the vows of Faron, Damian, we can put this all to rest."

"But I don't want it, Aunt Cilla. It...I would never be allowed to marry, to have children, to live my own life!" Damian's heart pounded. He knew what was coming next.

"It is non-negotiable, Damian," she replied, tone icy. "Take the vows, or leave Murias forever."

"You're my family..I–I- I have nowhere else to go."

Cilla straightened, eyes hardening. "Then make the right choice."

"What does Uncle say–"

"He is in agreement." Cilla's eyes darted to the nearby guards. "Make your decision. Now."

Defiance flared within him. Even then, he had been steely in his resolve. If this was what his life would be like here in Murias, sworn to a god, to a life of service that he did not believe in; one that would take away the freedom to choose, then he would find another way. "I will not take the vows."

"What vows?" Naia's voice drew him from the memory, and he turned to meet her curious gaze. Cilla, wisely, remained silent.

"To Faron, the god of service and humility. Like Vidar, he has requirements of those who serve in his name. You must give up all worldly possessions, renounce your titles and your family. Never marry, never have children. Your life, however long it may be, is spent in destitution, serving others." His bitter gaze shifted to his aunt, who avoided his gaze. "It is a noble calling, for those who choose it. A prison for those who are pushed into it unwillingly."

Thunder crashed overhead, and one look into Naia's gorgeous face told him his Thunderheart was very quickly losing her temper.

Sure enough, her gaze shifted slowly, so slowly, to Cilla. "You tried to force a grieving teenage boy into that?" Every word was laced with promised violence.

"It was a long time ago," Damian said, taking Naia's hand into his own. "And we can hardly afford the war that would surely come if you murder the Queen of Murias, Thunderheart."

Naia laughed darkly. "Then perhaps it's best if we end this meeting now."

"I would like to say one more thing," Cilla said calmly.

Brave, if not a little foolish.

"One thing," Damian replied, thumb drifting over the back of Naia's hand to calm her.

"I thought you should know that Zale..." she began, sighing, and looking down at her hands, folded neatly in her lap. "He never knew. He still has no idea why you left, or that I banished you."

Something in Damian's chest cracked. Centuries of practiced control kept his emotions from taking over, and settled the rage and grief that threatened to overtake him.

"It doesn't matter," he said, in the flat tone he had used for so many years—the voice of a Samach. "We're done here."

With only a small, regretful glance in his direction, Cilla left, leaving Naia and Damian in weighted silence.

CHAPTER 31

L ying in the dark, with Damian breathing steadily beside her, Naia seethed. Cilla's words, the actions she'd taken against a grieving child, burned in her mind.

What would Damian have become if he hadn't been forced into the desert to fend for himself?

He'd explained his survival, how he met with a band of pilgrims heading to the temple of Vidar, deep within the desert. At their peak, the fae of Murias spread across the sands widely, with settlements built around varying oases like Paradisus had been. He spent weeks living on the streets, with little money to survive, the only kindness Cilla had bestowed on him—a small bag of coin, enough only to feed him for a month or two.

When the money ran out, desperation had him seeking refuge and aid from the temple, and with bitterness and hurt in his heart, he made vows to serve the god of silence and restraint.

And now, she thought, turning to look at him in the moonlight shining from the opening in the tent above, he was here. Perhaps all that hurt, the grief, had led them here, to find one another. Would he take it all back, if it meant a happier life for his younger self, she wondered.

Naia's fingertips grazed his cheek, just above his thick beard, and he murmured something in his sleep that she couldn't quite make out, shifting closer to her.

Would she take back every moment of pain and fear that led them to find each other?

She hesitated, Lukus' face flashing in her mind.

No. Laying her palm against his cheeks she smiled. She would live it all again, to fall into this man. Her feelings for him, while complicated, were something she would never give up. Naia could no longer imagine a life where he didn't exist, in some way or another.

If he had remained in Murias, as prince or as servant, she would be dead now. The Void would have claimed them all by now.

The steady beat of his heart sounded in her ears, a reminder of life, of love. Her hand drifted to his shoulder, down his bicep, fingers gliding over taut muscle. Slipping closer to him, she let her hand roam over his shirtless back, down to the waistband of his linen pants.

"What are you doing, Thunderheart?" he asked sleepily, eyes still closed.

Leaning closer, she nipped his earlobe. "Exploring," she breathed against his ear.

She could feel his smile against her collarbone. "And what are you hoping to find?"

His voice was low, thick with desire, as his teeth grazed the sensitive skin of her neck, followed by a gentle kiss.

"Mm," she replied with a soft laugh. Her hands dipped below the waistband, moving to palm his thick length, delighted to find him already hard for her. "I think I just found it."

His breath hitched. "Fuck, Naia."

Her only reply was a breathy laugh as she let her fingers slide from the base to the sensitive tip. "Oh yes," she replied, shifting so that their lips nearly touched. "I found exactly what I was looking for."

Damian's lips crashed against hers, claiming her in a fierce kiss. In an instant, he gripped her hips, flipping her so that she lay flat on her front, her cheek resting against the pillows. With his knees on either side of her thighs, he looked her over, hunger in his darkened eyes.

"I wasn't done," she teased, smirking up at him.

He leaned down, breath warm against her ear. "And I'm just getting started." An electric shiver danced down her spine, and dampness pooled between her thighs.

Rough hands slid under the light tunic she'd worn to bed, before ripping it in two without warning. Her heart pounded in her chest. "I liked that shirt," she said breathlessly.

"You'll like this more," he promised darkly.

His hands roamed over her exposed back. A single finger drifted from the base of her neck, coming to a stop just above her her ass, barely covered by silk undergarments. Since they'd had no clothing, Lia had kindly gifted her several outfits.

The queen of Avellon had fine, and expensive, tastes.

Damian hooked his fingers in the waistband and began to pull them down slowly, rocking backward out of her view as he lowered them to her thighs. A hiss of appreciation sounded from behind her. "You have the most perfect ass," he growled.

Something in her belly coiled tight, her skin heating at his words. She wondered if he knew the impact his words had on her.

Leaning down, he kissed her spine, between her shoulder blades gently, breathing against her skin, "I can hear your heartbeat, how it thunders for me." Sitting back, he gripped her hips, raising them until she was on her knees, face still resting on the bed. "Are you wet for me, Thunderheart?"

Words turned to dust on her tongue as his hand slid around her hips, fingers sliding against her slit. A small cry escaped her lips and she turned her face to the pillow. Surrounded by so many others with fae hearing, she was desperate to keep quiet.

"So wet," he said approvingly. His thumb grazed her clit, and she moaned his name into the pillow. With a husky laugh, he slipped a single finger inside her as his thumb worked in excruciatingly slow circles.

Tension built in her lower belly, coiling and rising. A wave of pleasure ready to crash. Just as he brought her to that edge, Damian pulled his hand away, leaving her whimpering with need. The bed shifted as he lowered himself to whisper in her ear, "Not just yet, Thunderheart."

"Damian," she breathed, turning her head to the side again. "Please."

Her need for him was a tangible thing, a living flame within her. The absence of his hands on her skin, of him inside of her, was almost painful. Bucking, she sought his touch and was rewarded with a firm grip on her hips.

"What do you want, what do you need, Thunderheart?" he asked, voice low, as his thumbs slid over her skin, fingers pressing firmly into her hips.

"You," she sighed.

Leaning closer, his hardness pressed against her ass, and she whimpered again with the need for him. "What do you need, Naia?" he repeated.

"You," she said again, adding. "Inside of me."

"Good girl," he laughed, removing one hand from her hips.

The tip of his cock pressed against her entrance, teasing.

"Damian," she ground out, frustrated. The tightness in her belly, the heat in her core, driving her mad.

Without a word, he entered her in one, slow, thrust; and she came undone, screaming his name into the pillow. The orgasm left her breathless, her veins on fire as the wave crested and broke, her core tightening and releasing over and over until she was utterly spent. He hummed approvingly behind her.

She cried out, turning to the pillow once more, hands gripping the sheets. It was all the motivation he needed as he pulled back, before pushing into her once more. With every thrust the tempo rose, and she moved her hips to meet his rhythm. His name was a prayer, a plea on her lips.

One hand gripped her hip, the other slid down her back to fist her long hair. Another orgasm built, faster and harder than the first. She felt him tense behind her, as he whispered, "Come for me, Thunderheart."

And she did. Sobbing his name into the pillow as he released her hair to hold her hip again. He went still behind her as they came together, his cock pulsing inside her along with her inner core.

"Gods, you're perfect," he groaned.

Utterly spent, she fell onto the bed. Her breathing was ragged, her limbs feeling like little more than jelly. He'd wrung every ounce of pleasure from her possible, and left her weightless, content.

His arms came around her waist, pulling her on her side, back to his chest. The hard length of him pressed against her backside, and she laughed, even as her blood heated.

"Already?"

His answering chuckled reverberated through her. "I'll never get enough of you, Thunderheart."

Wordlessly, she rolled to face him, pressing her lips to his in silent demand, and as he pressed her back onto the bed, she sent silent thanks to the tides of fate for bringing them together.

CHAPTER 32

The soft sound of gentle waves crashing greeted Naia as she stepped onto the now familiar shore of her dreamscape–the place where Endri and Lir had first approached her. Now, she was alone and at peace. Naia had fallen asleep in Damian's arms, content, sated, and utterly in love. They were on the brink of war, disaster looming on the not-so-distant horizon, but with him, she could find those small moments of respite.

The sand shifted beneath her feet, a soft smile gracing her features, as she walked along the ethereal shore. A gentle breeze lifted her hair, sending the white robes she wore dancing on the phantom wind. It was utter serenity here, she could–

With a sudden flash, a white-haired woman stood before her, terror etched into her face. "Bearer! She comes! You must find–"

From one shocked blink to the next, the beach vanished entirely, leaving Naia in utter darkness. Floating...or falling, she couldn't be sure. With nothing beneath her feet, no light to show her which way was up or down. No sound. Utter emptiness.

Terror seized her heart. Endri's panic-stricken warning echoed in her mind.

She comes!

With Endri's disappearance, the dreamscape had also vanished. Were the two linked? Naia had no idea, and could only guess at the workings of the gods. What frightened her the most was the absolute terror in Endri's eyes. The god she had only ever seen calm, poised, had been panic-stricken.

Wake up, wake up, Naia chanted in her mind. She needed to warn the others.

Jolting awake, she lay still for a moment, processing what had just happened, before shaking Damian awake.

"We need to–"

A scream erupted from somewhere in the camp, somewhere not far.

Leaping from the bed, Naia sprinted out of the tent in only Damian's tunic and her undergarments; utterly disregarding his shouts for her to wait.

Across from her Eve emerged from her own tent as swiftly, green eyes widened. To her side, Lia followed only a heartbeat later, looking every bit as frightened as Naia felt.

"Did you see?" Naia all but shouted, as guards converged on them, and their respective mates stepped out of their tents.

The three queens stepped into the space between them, coming together in a small circle of sorts.

"I saw a man with white hair and pale skin," Eve said, taking a deep breath. "He warned me, She's coming."

Lia tugged her silken robe around her slender frame tightly. "Same, but I saw a child."

Naia let her eyes fall closed for a moment before explaining. "Endri, the god of dreams. I've spoken to them a few times, they take many forms."

A thoughtful hum sounded from Lia as Eve dragged a hand through her disheveled red curls. "Did you fall into darkness after?"

The other two queens nodded at once.

"I think..." Lia began quietly. "I think they've been taken. Did you see how frightened they were? I wonder if our dreams–if they simply vanished because Endri was captured," she said, glancing at Naia for confirmation.

"I thought the same, but how would that even happen?"

Lia looked over her shoulder to the pale woman with long dark hair who hovered just outside her tent. "Bella," she called, waiting for the woman to approach before continuing. "The gods are in hiding, but we think Endri has been captured."

Bella's silver-grey eyes widened. "I don't see how. Where they are–" she paused, frowning. "Unless…"

"Unless what?" Naia demanded impatiently, earning a sharp look from Lia.

"Endri is more involved with humans than most," Bella explained, unfazed by Naia's tone. "They often visit with dreamers, enjoying discussions with mortals that the mortal often doesn't remember."

"So what you're saying is, Kore waited until Endri was visiting a dreamer, and she took them?" Naia frowned.

Why would the god take that risk? Why not remain in safety with the others? Of all the idiotic…

"What would happen to the dreamer?" Lia breathed.

Bella offered Lia a soft look, placing a hand on her folded arm. "Likely just what happened to you, but without knowing who…" She left the rest unspoken.

They would likely never know whose dream Endri had been taken from, but it mattered little to Naia. "We need to talk to the gods. We don't know–"

Shouts sounded from the western edge of the camp, and within moments a large hawk flew directly to them, landing mere feet from Eve. With a flash of light, the hawk changed, becoming a brown-skinned woman with bouncing curls. Her eyes were hard as she met Eve's gaze.

"Leysa? What's happening?" Eve asked, frowning.

"Something is approaching from the west."

"She's here?" Lia asked, taking Bella's hand in hers.

Leysa turned to the blonde-haired queen, shaking her head. "No, this is something else…it's like…" She paused, considering her words. "I know this sounds strange but it looks like a group of mountain cats. They're all black, shadowy."

"How can you even see them in the dark?" Naia asked. She felt his approach then, Damian, coming to stand at her side.

"Shifter eyes," Leysa replied, meeting Naia's gaze with a half grin. "We can see very well in the dark, better than any other fae."

"Shadow cats?" Damian asked.

Callan stepped up then, wrapping a protective arm around Eve's waist. "She *is* the Void," he explained gravely. "She can likely create anything out of that darkness."

"Fuck," Naia breathed, casting a glance at Damian, whose expression mirrored her own thoughts. A captured god, and a primordial goddess who could apparently create demonic cat creatures from nothing.

"We deal with this," Damian said. "And then we'll decide what to do about Endri." When each of the others nodded in agreement, he added, "We'd better get ready."

Callan looked to Leysa. "Go back to the shifters, have them ready. Get another to help you warn the other commanders." Looking at Lia, he added, "We don't know what it'll take to kill these things, but I'm willing to bet your light will do it."

Lia's lips pressed together. "I'll be ready."

Naia's heart pounded. With fear, but also anticipation. "Let's show this bitch what's coming for her."

CHAPTER 33

Cool, dry wind swept over them as Naia and the other queens arrived on the western edge of the camp. The alarm had been raised throughout the gathered armies, with shifter eyes on every side of them, in case the approaching beasts were little more than a distraction. But the only reported sighting came from where they stood, facing the west, toward Murias.

Naia peered into the darkness. With her new fae vision she could see farther than she ever would've hoped to as a human, and yet, she saw nothing. No movement, no eyes looking back.

"Have they gone?" Lia asked, glancing toward the bear at her side, who huffed in response.

"Was that a yes or a no?" Naia remarked, unable to keep the sarcasm from slipping into her tone.

The bear turned to her with an unimpressed stare, huffing again.

"They're still out there," Leysa, thankfully in her fae form, said from behind them. "You'll see them in a moment."

True to Leysa's word, within a few seconds Naia began to make out six shapes in the distance. Somehow darker than the night itself, they were indeed feline in shape, but larger than any she'd seen before.

Devoid of any discernible color, save for their crimson eyes, they approached at a rapid pace.

"We can't let them get too close," Eve said from beside her, lifting a hand. Naia watched with equal parts admiration and shock, as a wall of stone erupted from the ground in front of the beasts. "That should–"

Her words were cut short as the creatures simply passed through the wall, materializing on their side as if it had been made of little more than sand.

A ripple of fear washed over Naia, who called upon her own gifts. A violent crash of thunder rattled the ground as she called upon the storm. Lightning struck each of the six approaching monsters, and Naia watched with satisfaction as they stumbled, falling to the ground—

Only to get back up again, and resume their rapid approach.

Naia's heart fell to her feet. Turning to her left, her gaze landed on Lia. "It has to be you," she whispered.

Lia's eyes met hers, and she nodded once. Lifting a hand, Lia turned to face the oncoming beasts, so close now that even their human soldiers could see them, judging from the string of curses sounding from behind Naia.

Light, pure and unrelenting, erupted from Lia's outstretched palm; a serpentine wave of sunlight against the darkness, almost liquid in its movement. As Lia's light reached them, the creatures howled, in terror or pain. The beasts halted, skidding across the sand in a desperate attempt to avoid her magic.

Four managed to stop in time, but the two that didn't found themselves skidding into the light turned to dust the moment they touched it.

Shouts of victory sounded behind the queens.

But Naia remained focused on the remaining beasts.

Lia's light flowed toward them as the queen turned her attention, but they were fast, faster than their companions had been, deftly avoiding it.

A frustrated growl sounded from Lia as they danced and prowled, avoiding the light.

"Here," Naia said, shifting closer and taking Lia's hand in hers. "Let's do it together."

Lia glanced toward her offering a brief smile in thanks.

Raising her free hand, Naia let her power flow into Lia and felt Lia do the same in return.

Lightning arced within Lia's light, and her light flared bright, doubling in speed. The beasts had nowhere to go, nowhere to run. From Naia's outstretched hand, lightning flew with a warm light that danced along each bolt–and when it speared one of the remaining beasts, it howled before vanishing into dust.

Relief washed over Naia like a cresting wave as she watched the remaining beasts turn into nothingness when Naia and Lia's power swept over them. This time, when shouts of victory rang out, Naia allowed herself to smile.

"She'll be back," Damian remarked from behind her. "This was a test."

"I know," Naia said, turning to face him as the other two queens stepped away with their mates, in quiet conversations. Conversations Naia knew were likely similar to the one she was having with her own mate.

"I think," Damian added, as they turned away from the darkness, "that you've given her good reason to be very afraid."

Callan stepped around Eve, his gaze moving between Naia and Damian. "The shifters are going to double the watch, in case she tries anything else tonight."

"She's testing our defenses," Damian said. "It won't be long until she finds a weak point and a real attack comes."

"I agree," Callan said, sighing. "And there's the matter of Endri."

Naia frowned. How were they to find a missing god? Endri's capture had been for a reason, a damned good one, she would wager, given that Kore had waited until now to do so.

"Let's move to the command tent and talk," Damian suggested.

Shortly after, they met in the command tent near the center of camp.

Gathered around the large table dominating the space in the round tent, a tense silence fell over the group, whichhad been joined by several other leaders. Too many faces, too many names she didn't know. Naia's gaze swept over the gathered fae and one human with chestnut hair who stood at Eve's side.

"I fear with Endri...taken," the white-haired fae queen began, struggling to get the word out. "That we will no longer be able to keep Kore from our dreams."

"Likely the very reason they were taken then," Eve agreed.

"Mm," the fae queen said, her striking gaze, one eye gold, the other blue, sweeping over those gathered. "We are all in more danger now."

Callan let out a frustrated growl, and Damian shifted slightly closer to Naia's side.

"Then we sleep in shifts," Callan said, glancing at Eve. "We've seen what she's capable of in our dreams. One person in each tent must remain awake, at minimum."

Aelius stepped up, folding his arms across his gold-armored chest. He'd been the only one of them able to don armor before the attack, or perhaps, Naia considered, he'd already been awake and dressed when it had occurred. "We'll pass the word through the soldiers' camps. They'll take shifts."

Damian sighed, interjecting, "She'll target the three of you."

Eve, Naia, and Lia glanced at one another in turn. "She already has," Eve replied. "I think it's most likely she'll come for one of you two next."

"Perhaps," the white-haired fae queen murmured.

"So," the human woman at Eve's side began, glancing at each of the fae in turn. "What happens if she does target one of the rest of us? It took two of you to save Eve. If she decides to go after a human, it would take us a long time to reach one of you. What then?"

It was Leysa who answered, saying, "I'll have shifters spread throughout each camp. If she attacks, they'll be able to go for help faster than anyone else."

Seemingly satisfied, the human woman nodded.

Naia's head spun. They had gone from fear to victory and back again in such a short span. Truthfully, she hadn't had time to fully consider the magnitude of Endri's absence. To hear it spelled out so clearly now, it was far worse than she'd initially considered. She hadn't yet heard the full story of what happened to Eve when Kore had invaded her dream, but from the haunted expression on Eve's face, it must have been harrowing.

"They won't come if we call, will they?" she asked, knowing the answer even as the words left her mouth.

Callan shook his head, exchanging a glance with the white-haired fae queen. "No. We're on our own."

CHAPTER 34

Naia lay in bed, listening to the soft sounds of a war camp at rest. Guards sharing quiet conversation outside, torches and braziers crackled, and the occasional flap of wings above. Bird shifters had been assigned patrols, in shifts, in case of another attack, and she noted, glancing at the large wolf lying by the entrance to their makeshift home, to each of the royals' tents. Prepared to alert the others, should Kore make her way into their dreams.

"You should be sleeping, Thunderheart," Damian uttered quietly, pulling her closer with his arm draped across her abdomen.

"I know," she sighed. "It's difficult when you know a real monster may be invading your nightmares if you do."

The idea of it, of being attacked when you were at your most vulnerable, utterly unable to defend yourself, was terrifying. A threat in the waking world, something she could face with her bare hands, a blade, or her lightning–that she could manage with little fear. But this? This was something else entirely.

Without Endri, would Lir appear, she wondered? Would she have the chance to once again demand his aid? Something told her no; and she had to admit that even if he did deign to speak to her, after their last encounter his answer would likely be a resounding no, issued in the most sarcastic tone possible.

"What about Maren?" she frowned, heart stuttering. "You don't think she'd go after our families?"

Damian pressed a kiss to her shoulder, left bare by the oversized tunic that had slipped down. "It is a possibility, but I would wager she is focused entirely on you three, after what you did when we arrived. We sent help to Thalassa and Satisse though, just in case."

Naia nodded. There was little else to say. Anything more would be a pointless worry. There was little to be done but hope they could keep Kore's attention on them, and hope that when the time came they could defeat the bitch once and for all.

"It's coming soon," she whispered. "The end of this. Can you feel it?"

Damian didn't reply at first, going still in the darkness. "I feel it."

The wolf shifter by the entrance whined, drawing Naia's attention. He stood alert, listening to something that not even her fae ears could pick up.

After a moment, he settled, lowering himself to the ground again. No danger, then.

"Try to sleep, Naia," Damian ordered gently. "I'll be here if she comes for you."

With a sigh, she rolled to her side, pressing her back against his solid chest, and closed her eyes. As before, she found herself floating in nothingness. No sound, no sight, no smell. Even in a dreamscape, the total absence of her senses was unnerving.

A whisper sounded in the darkness.

Naia couldn't be sure if the voice was that of a man or a woman. Perhaps neither, she considered, as it neared. There was something preternatural about it, ancient and beyond her understanding.

"Bearer," the voice whispered, a female, she could now recognize as it drew nearer. "So long have I waited to lay eyes on one of you again." The disembodied voice giggled, girlish; but with a manic undertone that set her nerves on edge.

"What are you?" Naia demanded, turning her head this way and that. With no floor beneath her, she couldn't quite turn her body, not that she would be able to see in this darkness anyway.

The voice giggled again. "Is it a floor you want?"

Without warning, Naia fell, her feet colliding with something hard with so much force that she stumbled forward, landing on her hands and knees. She winced but held her tongue for a moment, considering her reply carefully. Fear had her heart drumming in her chest. Surely Damian would hear her heartbeat, feel her fear, and wake her from this nightmare.

"Are you Kore?"

The thing in the darkness hissed. Sudden movement in the darkness brushed by her, nearly close enough to graze her arm.

"That isn't very nice," the voice whined.

Something shifted in the darkness ahead of her. Though she couldn't see what waited for her there, she could feel it. A weight, like holding your breath too long, settled in her chest.

"Then tell me who you are," she snapped, regretting her tone the moment the words left her lips.

The being giggled again. "I forgot how fiery you are. Perhaps Aden would have suited you as well as Lir."

She had no idea who Aden was, only assuming he was another of the forgotten gods.

"He is," the being replied, clearly reading her thoughts. "The ruler of fire and passion," they explained. "And a little bit of an ass, if I do say so myself. But then, brothers often are."

"You're a god, then?"

"God*ess*," she corrected, sounding mildly bored. "Do you want to see me?"

Naia considered saying no, but with fear of offending this mysterious goddess, held her tongue. She'd pressed her luck once, with Macaria and Lir, driven to do so out of desperation and love. Lost in this dreamscape with only a mysterious goddess to save, or punish her, she would do what she must to survive.

"Please."

Slowly, a greyish light formed just above her head, barely illuminating the darkness before her, and the strange goddess stepped out of the gloom, just enough to be seen clearly.

The petite woman was draped in two panels of white gauzy fabric that fell from either shoulder before meeting at her navel, cinched with a silver belt in the shape of a serpent. Beneath the sheer fabric, her breasts were on full display, her feet bare.

"Oh, you're so much prettier this time," the goddess announced with manic glee, bouncing on the balls of her feet as she clapped her hands together once.

Naia's lips twitched downward.

"I'm Erys," the goddess began, spinning on her toes to start a slow circle around Naia, fingers twirling in her unkempt black curls. "Chaos and destruction."

Her heart sank to her stomach as Erys continued dancing in circles around Naia. "Are you here to kill me?"

From behind her, Erys giggled again. "I haven't decided yet, silly. That's why I've come to see you for myself." She sighed, stepping back into view. "Aden wants me to help them, to help you little fae." Waving a hand, she added, "Humans too I suppose."

Naia swallowed hard. "And what do you want?"

Dark curls fell over her shoulder as Erys tipped her head sideways. "Well," she began before rushing toward Naia, stopping just shy of colliding with her. "Helping *Her* would be more interesting."

Fear was ice in her veins. Naia opened her mouth to speak but the words turned to ash on her tongue. What could she possibly say or do? Thought escaped her, replaced only by dread.

Erys' pale grey eyes swept over Naia, from head to toe. If she sensed Naia's fear or heard her thoughts, she gave no indication. "So pretty. Hedone would have fun with you. Though I suppose she takes her pleasure with just about anyone," she breathed, voice barely above a whisper.

Naia's throat went dry, even as a hint of irritation flared in the back of her mind. She opened her mouth to speak again, only to be silenced as Erys placed a single slender finger on her lips.

"No, no," Erys cooed. "Wait your turn."

The goddess dragged a pointed fingernail down Naia's chin to her throat, stopping only when she reached the center of Naia's chest. Looking down, Naia found herself clad in a loose gown made of layers and layers of grey fabric in every shade of a stormcloud.

Erys tittered once before continuing. "I think…"

Naia lifted her gaze to Erys' wide, frenzied eyes. She could do little more than blink as Erys leaned forward without warning, pressing a chaste peck on Naia's lips.

"…that you should wake up little Bearer," the goddess cackled.

Naia awoke with a start, jerking to a sitting position.

"Damian," she all but shouted. "We have a fucking problem."

CHAPTER 35

"Who?" Eve frowned, glancing at Callan.

Naia settled into the chair, flipping her long braid over one shoulder. The three queens gathered in Naia's tent with their mates, and only their mates. What she had to share needed to be kept among the three of them, for now at least, to avoid panic.

"Erys," Naia repeated, looking at Callan, who had donned a hard expression.

Damian's expression mirrored Calllan's, fear darkening his eyes.

Bella, the demi-goddess so loved by Lia, spoke up, her voice as calm and soft as moonlight. "She is unpredictable at best. Utterly uncontrollable by the others, but," she said thoughtfully. "I would expect her desire for self-preservation to outweigh her desire for destruction."

Damian nodded in agreement. "What would be left for her, if Kore destroys everything?"

Bella smiled. "Exactly."

"Well I don't intend to rely on that assumption," Naia snapped, patience waning.

"Of course not," Eve replied smoothly. "But it is worth noting, nonetheless."

Naia shrugged. "We have world-ending monsters and deranged goddesses invading our sleep. So what now?"

Lia shook her head, blonde hair spilling over her shoulders. "Is there anything we *can* do? Aside from what we're already doing?"

The tent fell into weighted silence.

Naia knew the answer that none of them wanted to speak aloud. They were utterly alone, abandoned by the gods who had chosen them as champions. With no guidance, they would have to make the best decisions they could and face whatever Kore threw at them next.

"We can't wait for her to come to us," Naia said, turning her attention to Damian. "Do you have any idea where she could be?"

Damian met her gaze, saying nothing for a moment as he considered. "Maybe," he said finally. "There are a couple of places we can check, but..." he sighed, shaking his head. "This is going to be dangerous for whoever goes. Her Samach will be ready and waiting."

"Their—your, powers don't work on us, if we have our artifacts," Naia began, gaze flitting to the other queens.

"Absolutely not," Damian growled, leaning closer to Naia as she jerked her attention back to him. "You are not walking into her camp. You're not even getting close."

Thunder crashed overhead. "You don't tell me what to do, Damian."

Damian opened his mouth to reply, snapping it closed when Eve spoke up.

"The shifters can do it. Their magic is also unaffected by the Samach."

Naia didn't bother to turn to look at her friend as she said, "Fine." Her gaze remained locked with Damian's, lightning flashing in hers as his went dark—a silent battle waging between them.

"Ah, well, I think we should continue this discussion in the morning," Lia said lightly.

The others murmured their agreements and shuffled out in pairs, leaving Naia and Damian alone.

"You do not get to issue orders anymore, Damian," she hissed, abruptly rising from her chair and turning away. "I am no longer your prisoner."

The sound of his chair falling to the ground had her spinning in time to come face to face with him, so close that their bodies nearly touched.

"Is that what you think that was?" he said with deadly calm, voice low. "Is that what you think I feel for you? You–"

Narrowing her eyes, she stepped closer, tilting her head to look up at him. "I what?" she challenged.

Taking her face in his hands, palms resting on her cheeks, he lowered his head to hers. "You are my very life, Naia. You are the blood in my veins, the beating of my heart. The only one held prisoner here is me. I am bound to you in every way." His eyes, swimming with emotion, remained locked on hers, pinning her in place.

Naia's heart skipped a beat. She couldn't breathe, couldn't think. "Damian–" she breathed.

"You can do anything, Thunderheart. I know you must fight in this war, and I do not doubt your strength. You can win this, you can end this for good, and we can have a life. But the thought of you putting yourself in harm's way needlessly...." He swallowed hard, voice thick with emotion. "If anything were to happen to you, I would go directly to Her, and beg Her to end my life. I will not live in a world where you do not exist."

His touch was electric against her skin. She'd known he loved her, but to hear it laid bare, to see that wall of silence he wore like armor fall. It touched her in ways she would never have thought possible. So she did the only thing she could.

"Okay," she breathed, nodding. "Okay. I'll stay away, for as long as I can."

"Thank the gods," he replied fiercely, claiming her lips with his own.

Chapter 36

"If she kills Endri," Naia whispered in the dim light of the tent. Her gaze lay on Damian's sleeping figure in their bed, lingering for a moment before shifting to the large cat on the rug near the tent opening. Shifters had been added to each of the royal tents, as well as their commanders as an added measure of security. Many had been dispersed amongst the ranks of soldiers, with the shifters working on rotation. "I wonder what that means for the world, would we all stop dreaming?"

The cat, Faline, growled in what Naia could only assume was meant to be a thoughtful sound. She resisted the urge to reach down and run her fingers through the thick, dark grey fur, only the awkwardness of knowing the cat was actually a fae woman and not truly a cat stopped her from doing so. Faline likely wouldn't appreciate it much anyway, she mused.

The tall fae woman, with long blonde hair and sparkling grey eyes, had been quiet when they'd been introduced some hours earlier, offering only a simple hello in greeting. Not in the soft way many such reserved people sometimes were; a more thoughtful, observant gleam had danced in her eyes. Watchful eyes.

Naia doubted there was much that escaped her notice.

"Do you ever use your gift to spy on people?" she asked suddenly, curiosity getting the better of her.

Faline's ears perked up, and her feline eyes shifted slightly toward Naia. If cats could smirk, she almost certainly would have been.

"You have!" Naia whispered with delight, casting a quick glance toward Damian before leaning closer to Faline. "I know you can't talk in this form, just...meow once for yes, twice for no."

Faline lifted her head and pinned Naia with a flat stare.

Big cats didn't meow. The message was clear as day, even if it hadn't been spoken aloud.

"Right, sorry." Rocking back in her chair, Naia considered what to ask first. It would be time to wake Damian soon, and there would only be time for a few questions. "Callan and Eve," Naia grinned. "Is it true she used her powers on a woman for flirting with him? I overheard some soldiers laughing about it."

The shifter sat still for a moment, not blinking. With a glance toward the tent opening and back to Naia, she blinked slowly. Just once.

Naia couldn't help the laugh that escaped her. The bed creaked slightly as Damian turned, no doubt disturbed by Naia's sudden outburst. Grinning, she shook her head. "I had no idea she had such a jealous streak."

One more question, Naia thought. "Forgive my outrageous curiosity, but have you ever...well you know, fucked in your animal form?"

Faline made what was very clearly a gagging sound before rapidly blinking twice.

Holding her hands up in surrender, Naia rose from her chair. "Okay, okay, sorry for asking."

Faline followed suit, rising from her position with a feline stretch. Her gaze turned to the tent opening, remaining there as if waiting for something.

"Your replacement?" Naia asked, striding toward the bed.

Faline chuffed quietly, casting a final glance at Naia before stepping out into the darkness with a swish of her tail. A flash of light outside let Naia know that someone, either Faline or her replacement, had shifted, and the sounds of quiet conversation drifted toward her in the darkness.

Naia turned her attention to Damian, leaning down to whisper in his ear. "Wake up." A low mumble sounded from him, and she nipped at his earlobe gently. "Wake up, darling, or I'm biting something else."

"Okay, okay," he replied groggily, rolling onto his back.

Strong hands gripped her waist without warning, pulling her close and positioning her so that she straddled his waist. His erection pressed against her core firmly, and he pulled Naia closer, drawing a gasp from her.

"Still want to bite me?" he teased darkly.

Leaning down, so close that her nose nearly grazed his, she whispered, "Unless you'd like to put on a show for the shifter that's about to walk into our tent, you'd better get up, and," she added, glancing pointedly to where their bodies met, "get down."

"Well," Damian began, chuckling as he slid his hands to grip her ass.

"Please don't," a male voice pleaded.

Rolling off of Damian, who she noted to her delight, looked positively disappointed, she turned to greet the shifter who would be sitting with Damian for the remainder of the night. "Hello."

The young man, appearing no more than early twenties, by human standards, offered her a light smile, dragging his hands through curly red hair that grazed the tips of his ears. His freckled cheeks were stained pink, no doubt embarrassed by the scene he'd walked in on.

"Hi," he replied, gaze dancing between them. "I'm Noah. I thought it less awkward if I introduced myself while I can still talk, but uh," his cheeks flushed again, and he left the rest unspoken.

"Sorry about that," Damian said smoothly. "I'm up now," he said, earning a snicker from Naia. "You can go ahead and shift whenever you'd like."

Noah nodded. "I should warn you...my preferred form is a little... different."

Naia's brow rose. "We've seen birds, bears, cats, wolves," she said. "What are you?"

The corner of Noah's mouth twitched upward in a boyish grin. "I think it's better if I show you."

Naia cast a glance toward Damian, who rose from the bed, rolling his shoulders. "Well, now you have me curious," she said, settling herself into the place Damian had vacated.

The warmth that remained from his body welcomed her like an embrace, and as her head hit the pillow, his scent surrounded her, making her heart skip a beat. As if he could hear her reaction, he turned, offering her a light smirk; one she met with narrowed eyes that warned him to keep the dirty thoughts dancing in his gaze to himself.

A flash of light drew their attention to where Noah stood...only to find a massive crocodile in his place. The knowledge that it was, in fact, the baby-faced shifter and not an actual reptile that could, and likely would, eat her did little to stop the yip of fear that escaped Naia's lips, or the bolt of fear that raced through her.

As if attempting to calm her, the crocodile Noah lay his head down on the rug floor and watched her patiently. Damian, who had gone utterly still suddenly burst into a single bark of laughter. The first time she'd heard such a sound from him.

"Fucking brilliant," he snorted. "We should send an army of you crocodile shifters into Her camp. They'd never know what to make of this."

Without acknowledging Damian's words, Noah ambled toward the tent opening and positioned himself in front. Anyone who entered would have to go through him; and if they somehow made it past that powerful set of jaws, they'd have Damian, then Naia, to contend with.

"Darling," Naia crooned, rolling onto her back. "Which of us do you think is more dangerous?"

Damian snorted before pressing a quick kiss to her lips and settling into his chair. "You are, Thunderheart, without a doubt." At her answering grin, he added, "You are utterly, and brilliantly, terrifying."

CHAPTER 37

"I still think one of us should go," Eve said, rubbing a hand along the side of her billowing emerald pants.

Naia nodded her agreement. "I agree it feels wrong for them to take this risk alone. But, if it is a trap, the only one of us going alone would be foolish." It felt wrong, allowing shifters to take on the risk alone, especially when something within her screamed it wasn't right.

Damian had marked three possible locations for Kore's forces on the map but warned that now that she was aware of his betrayal, he doubted she'd follow the patterns she had before.

"Getting one of us alone would be a dream for her," Lia reminded Eve, a shadow passing over her sunny features. "I wouldn't have lived long if she hadn't needed information from me."

Guilt washed over Naia. She'd been told of Lia's ordeal. The torture she'd endured at the hands of another Samach, another fae blessed with the same gift of silence that Damian possessed, within the temple of their god, Vidar. He had been searching for Naia, at Kore's behest, certain her disappearance had been orchestrated by the other two queens.

Had she not run with Damian, had she found her way to them sooner, perhaps Lia wouldn't have had to suffer the way that she did.

"Don't do that," Lia said softly, drawing Naia from her thoughts with a gentle touch on her arm. She could feel the warmth, the comfort flowing from Lia's touch even through the silken fabric that covered her arms. "It was not your fault."

Had Lia sensed her inner turmoil? Or had her mask of cool strength slipped enough to show the emotions that lay beneath? Naia didn't know and supposed it didn't matter now. "I know," she sighed, tossing her long braid over one shoulder.

Damian had insisted on combing and braiding her hair after she'd risen for the day with her heart heavy. The end was coming, she could feel the long-silenced voice of a woman she couldn't name screaming within her. She could make out no words, only the rage and fear, the worry.

Dreamless sleep had done little to quell her fears, had only left her feeling worn down, restless; and when she'd told him as much, he'd pulled her down to sit in front of him, and he'd taken care of her.

It was a simple gesture of intimacy, of comfort, that still left her stomach fluttering.

"Did you feel it last night?" Eve asked quietly, scanning the rest of the encampment.

Naia followed her gaze, looking out at the bustle of morning in a war camp. From their position just inside the command tent, they could see perhaps a quarter of their forces stretching far out into the sands. The might of six kingdoms united in a desperate bid to save their world.

With steel and ash, magic and rage, they would stand against the darkness that sought to end their very existence. So many would die. Perhaps even the three of them, destined to be living weapons against the greatest evil their world had known.

Would it be enough? Would the sacrifice of so many souls be the cost of survival, or would it simply be a pointless waste of what time they may have left?

"The warning?" Lia asked quietly, gentle voice wavering slightly. "It was like...someone was whispering in the darkness. Words I couldn't understand."

"Yes," Naia agreed, frowning. "Only for me, it was screaming."

"It feels like a warning," Eve remarked, expression thoughtful. "Like a warning from our past selves, right? It's a strange feeling."

"To say the least," Naia retorted.

"Isn't it odd," Eve said, turning her gaze back on the camp, "that they would warn us now, despite us being aware of what we're to face?"

A sudden chilly breeze drifted through the camp, sending goosebumps up Naia's arms.

"Like there's something we don't know," Lia whispered, taking Eve and Naia's hands in her own.

"So many secrets have been kept from us," Naia added, dropping her voice lower as the breeze turned to a whipping wind that sent Lia's blonde hair flying around her face. "Have you ever wondered," she continued, "what happened to them?"

Eve frowned, angling her body so that the three of them formed a crescent. "What do you mean?"

Naia's gaze darted toward the camp and back to Eve and Lia. "When the day was won, and whatever conflict they needed the artifact for was over, what happened to them?" Releasing Lia's hands, she crossed her arms, rubbing them to reclaim the warmth stolen by the strange wind that still whipped through the camp, now stirring the sand into small cyclones. "I know that she saved her people from a drought, but I think...I think something awful happened afterward."

"Why do you think that?" Lia asked, leaning into Eve, likely seeking comfort from the unusual chill. Though the sun still shone high above the temperature had dropped noticeably.

Only an incoming storm, Naia thought to herself, hoping it was true.

She frowned at the question. Why *did* she think that? There was no logical answer to the question. Nothing tangible had made her feel this way, only the same bone-deep instinct that guided all three of them at times.

The instinct she now attributed to the long forgotten memories of her past.

"It's hard to explain," Naia said finally. "But don't you feel it too? The feeling something is wrong, that there's something very important we don't know?"

They remained silent for a moment, sharing a glance before they both nodded.

"It's been a near-constant feeling," Lia whispered. "The last few days."

"Sure," Eve added. "I've felt it too, but why now? With all the other times our instincts, our memories, have guided us, why are we just now getting this warning?"

Truthfully, she didn't know. Perhaps something had been set in motion, or maybe their memories had been unlocked by some shared experience.

Had the gods been somehow blocking their knowledge of this? If they had, why?

There were too many possibilities to know for certain. She began to say as much as shouts sounded from the encampment, and Naia's response died on her tongue.

Aelius, with Bella at his side, ran for the tent, arms thrown up to shield their eyes from the sand that was beginning to dance on the wind.

"We need to get inside, a sandstorm is coming," Aelius all but shouted above the commotion.

As Bella reached for Lia's hand, the three queens shared a long look.

"We'll talk more about it later," Naia promised, earning a nod from them both.

With a whoosh of wind and shadow, Callan appeared at Eve's side. "We need to get back to our tent, Dove," he said, taking her hand in his.

Eve frowned at Naia, glancing around as Bella, Aelius, and Lia took off in the direction of their tents to seek shelter. "Where is Damian?"

Naia's attention turned to the landscape beyond. "I'm sure he's here somewhere. He may have fallen asleep. He didn't get much rest last night."

"We can take you," Eve offered. "We'll pace you."

"It's okay," Naia waved the offer off. "It's a short walk."

Eve frowned, unsure. "It's really no problem."

"I'll be fine," Naia assured her, stepping out before Eve could press the issue further. A rush of wind sounded from behind her, Eve and Callan pacing, or simply the desert storm, she didn't know. Thankful that the actual storm hadn't reached them just yet, Naia sprinted toward her tent, a blessedly short walk from command.

I can't believe he's sleeping through this, she thought with mild annoyance. She was far from some damsel who needed an escort but the gesture would have been nice. Sighing, she dismissed the wayward thought. He needed the rest, she knew, as had Noah, who had departed for his own camp in the early hours when she'd first woken.

As she neared their shared tent, the hairs on the back of her neck stood to attention. Two soldiers she didn't recognize were stepping inside. While it wasn't uncommon by any means to have soldiers, especially fae, coming to speak with Damian, something felt wrong.

Instinct once again warning her that something was off.

With hurried steps, she rushed inside, heart pounding.

The men stood by the bed, a slumped Damian between them, as they each gripped an arm. Rage sparked within her and thunder crashed. "You will release him," she commanded with lethal authority.

The men each looked at her then, eyes wide with manic frenzy, and grinned. "But where would the fun be in that?" they said in unison, an all too familiar female voice echoing through theirs. "I want to see what happens," Erys teased, speaking through the men; mere puppets for the deranged goddess.

"No!" she screamed, lunging forward, lightning sparking from her fingertips toward his captors. Too slow, she was too slow; by mere seconds. In a flash of blinding white they were gone, Damian with them.

And as day turned to night, sand whipping and tearing at the tents within the war camp, lighting and thunder rattled the ground with her rage.

CHAPTER 38

"Lir!" she screamed, voice booming like thunder. "If you don't get here now, I swear I will slice my throat. Good luck saving your precious fucking existence if I'm dead." Naia held the cool blade to her neck, hand steady, as unwavering as her will.

A flash of lightning announced his arrival. Appearing a few feet away, the lean god of storms met her gaze with an irritated glare, wearing only loose linen pants. "Enough with the dramatics, Bearer. I grow tired of your threats. What do you want?"

To appear so swiftly, he must have been desperate. Surely Endri's capture would have them even more on edge, less likely than before to risk coming to the mortal realm for any reason. Indeed those were shadows beneath his eyes, fear dancing within them despite his indifferent tone.

Though he was a god, it was Naia who held the power for now. She relished in it, the feeling of control. Her power had been taken from her far too many times in the last days and weeks. To reclaim it now was a high; and an opportunity she would not squander.

"Answers," she replied, still holding the blade to her throat.

"To what question," he prompted through gritted teeth.

"Where would Erys take Damian?"

Surprise flitted across his face. He hadn't known then, that Erys was playing her own game.

"That bitch," he snorted. "It depends on her game. What exactly did she say when she took him?"

"She told me that she wasn't sure whose side she was taking. That she wanted to see which would be more...interesting. When she took him she said she wanted to 'see what would happen'."

Lir rolled his eyes. It was strange to see such an utterly normal expression on a deity. Even if he was an asshole, there was typically still an air of otherworldliness about him. Right now, though, he was only giving off frustration. "There is no telling where she'd take him. Likely somewhere out in the open, perhaps close to our foe, perhaps not." Frowning as he folded his arms across his toned chest, he added, "I will ask around, but it is rather unlikely she would have shared her— I would say plans, but that would require giving her actions a single moment of rational thought. She's an unruly child, playing at being a competent adult."

"Well that's just not nice," a pouty female voice argued, moments before Erys materialized in a flash of grey smoke. "I'll tell you where he is, little queen," she said, voice rising an octave in a teasing tone. "It'll be oh so fun to see which of you gets to him first–and what she does with him if she wins."

"Erys," Naia whispered, rage flooding her veins. She took half a step forward, lowering the knife to her side and stopping only as Lir rounded on Erys, gripping her upper arms tightly. "Where the fuck is he?"

Even from where she stood, Naia could see the white knuckle grip Lir held on his fellow deity. He ignored her question entirely as he all but shouted at the goddess. "Enough with your idiocy, Erys. I don't care if you value the lives of these mortals, but do you lack such sense that you no longer care for your own existence? Why are you interfering with what *must* happen?"

Erys simply cackled, not bothering to free herself from his grasp. Ignoring his words, the goddess turned her attention to Naia. "You're asking the wrong question, little queen. There are other–"

A sharp look and a squeeze on her arm silenced Erys momentarily as he kicked at his shin. "Don't be so mean," she pouted. Returning her gaze to Naia, she went on, "The oasis where he took you. I think you know the one." Face contorting into a manic grin, wild eyes gleaming, she added, "Hurry hurry, little queen. I didn't give her as much of a hint, to make it fair, but she does have a headstart."

Lir growled, turning to Naia. "Do not let this distract you from what you must do. If she finds him first, use that rage to your advantage."

Before Naia could reply, he vanished in a flash of lightning, dragging a cackling Erys along with him. She didn't bother waiting around or giving much thought to the strange remark Erys had made about the wrong question. Finding Damian is what mattered now; and quickly.

Tapping into the same rage, the fear, that she'd felt in the moments on the dune, the moments where she'd watched him die, Naia closed her eyes.

She thought back to their time at the oasis, let her eyes see the light glinting off of the still water, the way the palm trees swayed. The feeling of washing away the sensation of Zayan's hands on her skin. Though she hadn't realized it in the moment, bathing in those waters had been symbolic of her acceptance of her new life.

The one that led her into his open arms, to the destiny laid at her feet.

Just as she prepared herself to give up, to go in search of help, a whoosh of wind whipped around her ears. Her eyes flew open as darkness surged—just in time for her to catch a glimpse of Lia's panicked face.

"What are–" she called out to Naia, rushing forward and seizing Naia's hand in her own.

The rest of her words died, swallowed by phantom wind and total darkness as Naia stepped between the folds of the world, dragging Lia along with her. Gripping Lia's hand tightly, she could do little more than pray she hadn't just killed them both.

Nausea washed over her, and within a few heartbeats, her knees collided with sand. She couldn't help it as her body heaved, and she hurled into the sand, gagging and spitting even as she jerked her gaze upward. She'd gone so much further this time, had pushed herself far harder.

Did we make it?

To her shock, she found the still water and swaying palms. The sandstorm that had begun to die down when she'd left camp had left this place untouched, it seemed, and it remained as peaceful and tranquil as it had been when she'd last been there.

"Lia?" she called out, voice hoarse from the retching.

"I'm here," Lia replied, sounding every bit as ill as Naia felt.

Scrambling to her feet, she took Lia's hand and ran, frantically scanning the area for any sign of Damian. Apologies for the mess she'd dragged her friend into would come later if they survived.

First, she needed to find Damian and get them all the fuck out of there.

Relief surged as she made out the unmistakable form of a man, standing just across the water from her. "Damian!" she cried out, only for her joy to turn to ash as the man spun.

The stranger greeted her with a cruel grin. "Hello, Bearer," the dark-haired male said. Noting Lia's presence, the man's expression shifted to one of surprise. Her stomach gave another flip as his surprise turned to joy. "Ah, and you brought another. She will be most delighted at this turn of events."

The queens jolted to a stop in unison, backing away. Heart thundering Naia began to call upon the storm raging in her veins. If he had hurt Damian in any way...

Lia squeezed her hand gently. Naia didn't dare take her eyes off of the stranger long enough to discern whether the gesture was one of support or one of warning. Regardless, they would stand together.

Reading her expression, the man chuckled. "If I was here to kill you, you would be dead already." Frowning, he added, "Pacing is rather difficult the first time, is it not?" He pressed on before she could reply, adding. "I simply bear a message for you, Bearer," he said, chuckling at his little play on words. "She will claim all that you hold dear; and when the time comes, She will devour them while you watch. All of you who have whored yourselves to gods who care nothing for you." Tutting, he sighed. "And, as a kindness, She urges you to summon your masters, if they'll come, and ask the question that is burning in all of your minds."

There was no doubt in her mind which question he referred to, though she doubted any of the gods would deign to respond now. Not even Lir. Not again.

She'd played her only hand in order to find Damian. It was unlikely the others would respond now that she had. Eve and Callan had tried in vain to call upon their own patrons, as well as Lia. Even the pretty seer Lia called lover hadn't been able to reach her own mother. Out of fear, the cowards had abandoned them to face this threat alone.

"Where is he?" Naia demanded. She would show no reaction to his threats, no matter how loudly her heart pounded, how her stomach had turned. Fear had seeped into her veins, leaving her as cold as the distant sea.

The stranger's gaze shifted to the far bank of the pond, nearly halfway between them. Damian lay still, legs half in the water. Only the steady beating of his heart in her ears told her that he lived, but whatever Erys had done to him left him utterly unconscious. Perhaps Lia could undo whatever had been done, could heal any hurts. But...

"Shall we see who can get to him first, Bearer?" the stranger teased. "I promise not to pace. Let's make it a fair fight, yes?"

Like an arrow loosed from a bow, she was off. Lia's hand left hers, and without looking to see if she followed, Naia darted across the sand. Long legs carried her swiftly, her feet pushing off of the loose sand, propelling her forward. Thunder cracked overhead, and from the corner of her eye, she caught the faintest flashes of lightning sparking from the ground as she ran.

Her heartbeat was a staccato, racing like the wind across the sea. She would get to him, she would save him. Save them all. There was no question, no room for failure. If he died, her rage, her fury, would rattle the world to its very core. She would make every one of those involved in taking him from her regret their very existence.

Damian was hers.

No one would ever lay a hand on what she called her own again.

Flashes of the past played in her mind as she moved.

Zayan's hands on her skin, the lie of a lover's touch as he plotted to betray her. Lukus' hateful eyes burning into hers as he tried to rape her, to murder her. Damian lying dead on the sands.

Even the image of things that had not yet happened.

Her sister dead in the ruins of their home. The utter destruction of Coruscis. Villages burned, people left with no shelter, no hope, as the darkness swept over all of Aestera.

Her body. Her sister. Her love. Her kingdom.

Never again.

A flash of light to her left had her stumbling. The man cried out in pain. Guttural, primal.

"My eyes!" he wailed. "You'll pay for that, bitch!"

With silent thanks for brave, thoughtful, Lia, Naia couldn't help but smirk as she pushed harder.

Nearly there now.

Damian's chest rose and fell in an even rhythm. He appeared to be sleeping. Crying out his name, a frantic prayer over and over, she fell to her knees and gripped his face between her palms. "Damian, wake up!"

He didn't move, didn't stir. She had to move, to get them out of there. But she couldn't pace them away, not without Lia. Panicked, she turned her attention to the pond. The man had begun to recover, moving toward them in a staggering jog, still holding his hands over his ruined eyes.

"Lia–"

"I'm here," Lia said, falling into place beside Naia breathlessly. "We need to go."

Lia's hand found hers once more, pulling it away from Damian's face gently.

"I'm not finished yet," she said, cool fury flowing through her veins as she fixed her gaze on the man who had tried to take what belonged to her.

His irregular gait still carried him closer, though considerable distance remained between them. Blindness slowed him, and every few steps he teetered dangerously close to the water.

"I'm going to fucking kill you, bitch," he threatened impotently.

Lia gave her hand another squeeze. "I know," she replied pointedly.

Naia's attention jerked to Lia, realization dawning. Offering a single nod in recognition of what Lia had done for her, Naia turned her attention back to him.

He had managed to get closer somehow, an impressive feat given his injury. Too bad for him his next steps would be his last.

Thunder cracked overhead, and he laughed. "She's coming for you, all three of you whores. She will rip the hearts from the chests of those you love and feast upon them. You will be little more than playthings–"

A single bolt of lightning speared straight through his skull, into the sand at his feet. His body convulsed for a moment before he fell, collapsing unceremoniously onto the ground.

"And you will be nothing," Naia said flatly. "Forgotten, rotting beneath the sun."

She'd expected to feel some sort of satisfaction from his death. Gratification in knowing she had punished one who would take what was hers. But she felt nothing. Only a cold acceptance. There would be more of this, more taking of lives. Would they feel any different? When she and the others ended this for good, would she feel relieved? Indifferent?

Sighing, she took Damian's limp hand into her own, and turned her attention to Lia.

"Are you ready?"

Lia's sky blue eyes lingered on her own for a moment before she replied. Understanding shone there. She had taken lives as well; many of them by now. Had she felt the same sort of emptiness afterward? Naia wondered, but wouldn't voice the question aloud. Not now at least.

Now, they needed to return, before any more of Her forces, or even those of Erys, found them. Reaching within the deepest depths of her strength, Naia called on the magic within and pictured the sights and smells of camp, drawing the darkness and wind around them to take them back.

CHAPTER 39

Naia collapsed onto the sand, Damian at her feet. Shouts rang out from soldiers surrounding them, as she blinked against the bright sun. Rather than her own tent, she'd paced them to the center of one of the other encampments. Fae, she judged, eyeing the nearest banner, though she couldn't recall which kingdom the white poppy on a field of silver belonged to.

Gentle hands found their way to her shoulder as Lia knelt in front of her. "You did it," Lia soothed. "We're safe."

She could manage little more than a nod, strength utterly depleted.

"I've got us from here," Lia continued. "We need to be taken to command," she called out to someone Naia couldn't see.

The edges of her vision began to fade to black as she swayed; and though exhaustion ravaged her, she never released Damian's hand.

She'd saved them. But only with Lia's help. She hadn't been strong enough, fast enough, to do it on her own.

"I couldn't–" she ground out, willing herself to stay upright.

"Naia," Lia said softly, cupping her cheeks. "You saved him. You brought us back."

Lifting her heavy eyes, she met Lia's soft blue stare. "He deserved what you did to him," she whispered fiercely.

Lia merely nodded, eyes clouding with emotion.

Someone took hold of her upper arms, as another attempted to pull Damian's hand from her grip. A female yelped as electricity shot from Naia's hand. Not enough to harm, but a warning; nobody would take him from her again.

"No," Naia snapped.

"Let them take you both to rest," Lia said, placing her hand over their joined hands. "He's safe with the healers, Naia. He's safe."

She shook her head fiercely, but spots danced in her vision and she swayed again, this time unable to keep her head above the surface of consciousness.

With Lia's hand still on hers, she fell to the sand.

~

"WHAT SHE DID WAS UNACCEPTABLE!" THE MALE VOICE boomed.

Dim lantern light greeted Naia's eyes as they opened, awoken by the shouting outside of her tent. Damian lay still beside her. Frantic, she scrambled to a sitting position and placed her hand on his bare chest. The steady rise and fall of his breathing, and the familiar beating of his heart sounded in her ears, and she relaxed, a cool wave of relief washing over her.

Safe. He's safe.

The ground rumbled gently as Eve replied calmly. "Do not raise your voice at me, Callan."

Callan's reply was soft, far more gentle as he said, "I'm sorry, Dove. But what she did put us in danger. Put *you* in danger."

"You're awake," Lia's voice drew Naia's attention from the conversation outside as she rose from her seat at the opposite side of the tent. "Damian is well," she began, easing Naia's immediate concern. "He was poisoned with something containing white ash, the fae healers say. Not enough to be fatal, but enough to render him unconscious. He should wake soon."

Naia exhaled slowly, drawing her knees to her chest beneath the thin blanket draped across both of them. "He's angry," she remarked, glancing pointedly to the tent flap.

Lia sighed. "Yes, but Eve is dealing with it."

Naia shrugged. She didn't care if he was angry with her. The only thing that mattered to her was Damian's safety, and what she had done had assured her of that. Her gaze returned to him as she fell into thoughtful silence. He had been taken by a goddess; one who was unpredictable at best and had yet to declare herself for one side of this war or another.

She would almost certainly be making an appearance again, Naia knew, but what that would mean for them, only time would tell.

"What are you thinking about?"

Naia sighed, turning to Lia. "Erys. She wanted to see what would happen, who would get to him first. Will my reclaiming him matter? Will she try again?"

Lia nodded, frowning. "I've worried about that myself."

A manic giggle sounded from the shadows in the corner, and Naia spun to find the very goddess herself emerging. Draped in gauzy strapless black gown that looked ripped and torn at irregular angles, sweeping well past her ankles while barely leaving her breasts covered. As strangely beautiful as she had been the last time.

"You won!" Erys exclaimed, delightedly clapping her hands together.

The sound of the tent flap opening and people bursting in sounded from behind her, but her focus remained on the deranged goddess as she placed a protective hand on Damian's arm.

If Erys made a single move toward them, she'd pace them away. She would regret leaving the others, but Damian was her priority.

"I'll tell you a little secret," Erys stage whispered. "I was hoping it would be you. I do think that naughty, naughty, Kore might have actually killed me." The goddess pouted. "I would have been really disappointed by that." Sighing dramatically, she waved a hand. "But you won, fair and square, so I'm yours."

As the others moved into view, Naia noted Bella protectively taking a position by Lia's side. The hand placed on Lia's forearm told Naia that

Bella likely had the same thought she'd had for Damian; and she had no doubt Callan would do the same for Eve.

They would each protect their own mates, at any cost. The realization soothed the guilt, even as Erys' words frayed her nerves.

"You're on our side now?" Naia asked through gritted teeth. Keeping a leash on her anger was difficult, but she'd learned her lesson about disrespecting this particular deity, and wouldn't repeat the mistake.

"That's what I said, silly," Erys chided, vanishing into a flash of light, only to reappear a heartbeat later. "Oh, right! I almost forgot," she laughed, tapping the side of her head. "When She whispers her lies, don't believe them. Ta-ta!"

Her heart pounded, and her head spun. She didn't dare remove her hand from Damian's arm, even as the goddess vanished once more. It wasn't until nearly a full minute later that the entire group seemed to loosen a collective breath.

Erys' warning rang in her mind. Why issue that particular warning? As if any of them would believe anything that bitch had to say. It made little sense unless–

"Does anyone else get the feeling there's something they don't want us to know?" Eve's words were low, cautious. Her tone echoed the same concern Naia had.

What if the gods were listening? They had no real sense of what powers they possessed, had no idea if they could walk amongst them unseen.

"They are never going to be entirely honest with us," Bella said, not bothering to lower her voice.

Callan made a sound of agreement, and Eve spoke once more. "So we should probably be prepared for another run in with her, if they're warning us of that as well."

"Why didn't they say anything about Endri?" Lia wondered aloud.

Naia frowned. She'd been so focused on Damian when she'd called upon Lir that she hadn't bothered to ask about Endri, and what it meant for all of them.

Lifting her gaze, she found Bella watching her thoughtfully.

If the demigoddess knew anything about what had occurred before she'd gone after Damian, she said nothing, only watching Naia for another moment before turning her attention to Lia. "They'll be in a panic, I'm sure. One of them taken...that could be disastrous. They can hide. There is a place, only one, that even Kore cannot venture." Her gaze returned to Naia briefly once more. "I doubt we'll see any of them again, now that Kore has managed to take one of their number."

"So now we do what? Wait? That seems nearly suicidal," Naia snapped.

"Speaking of suicidal," Callan said with deadly calm, stepping closer. "Let's talk about that fucking stunt you pulled."

Thunder crashed above as Naia's temper flared. "Don't raise your voice at me," she warned.

Eve stepped closer, placing a hand on his arm. "Darling," she said calmly. "We shouldn't fight amongst ourselves." Turning to Naia, she continued, emerald eyes hard as stone. "But what you did put everyone. Everyone," she repeated, for emphasis, "at risk."

"As if you would do any less for him," Naia snarled, waving a hand at Callan. "If I had to damn you all to save him, I would. In a heartbeat." Thunder crashed again, closer and louder this time.

Lia stepped in between them. "You weren't there Callan, Eve, you don't know–"

"As if that matters!" Callan shouted, turning a hard stare on Lia.

Bella positioned herself between Callan and her mate, holding a hand up in his face. "Don't. You. Dare."

Softening, Callan's gaze darted from Lia to Bella and back. "Sorry," he muttered. But when his gaze returned to Naia, it darkened, blue eyes as cold as ice. "If you ever put her in danger again, I will kill you."

Thunder crashed and boomed ahead, a symphony in the sky, the audible proof of her anger. She opened her mouth to reply, to tell him good luck with that. Before she could speak, there was a flash of movement behind her and the hand that had remained on Damian's fell to the bed; to the empty space he had occupied a heartbeat before.

In the blink of an eye, her mate, the man who had been unconscious moments before, was standing in front of Callan, the blade from beneath her pillow at his throat.

Shadows gathered around Callan, snaking around his arms, wreathing his shoulders as they wound their way toward Damian. "Damian–"

The temperature in the tent dropped noticeably and Callan's shadows guttered. "Threaten her again," he said with deadly calm. "And I will remove the tongue from your head before watching her end you herself."

"Enough!" Eve shouted, her own temper joining the fray. The ground rumbled with nearly the same intensity as the sky. "Back away from him now, Damian," she warned, the ground beneath him shaking and groaning as if a chasm were splitting. With her gift, it likely was. "Callan, you were out of line, my love. But you," she seethed, staring up at Damian intensely. "You lay a hand on him and I will see the earth swallow you whole."

Naia rose to her feet, intent on pulling Damian away. Angry as she was, she wasn't stupid. Killing each other would doom them all. They could fight it out later, if they wished, but for now, they needed to remain united.

Naia's gaze darted to Lia as bands of light wrapped around both of the men, yanking them away.

Lia's typically sunny face had gone shadowed. A cloud of anger, and a bit of sadness, dancing in her eyes. "Stop it. All of you."

The men each looked to her, then back at one another. Fury clear in their expressions, but they complied. Damian moved to Naia's side, resting his hand at the small of her back.

Eve looked to Naia, eyes softening slightly. "I understand why you did what you did. But it was reckless to do it alone."

Rolling her eyes, Naia looked away. She didn't dare let Eve see the shame in her eyes. She knew what she'd done was foolish; had realized it long before now. But she'd been so desperate to save him she hadn't wanted to risk taking the time to alert the others, to ask for help. There was no way she'd admit that, to show weakness, especially not now, so she said nothing.

"I think we should all go back to our own tents, sleep, and reconvene in the morning with cooler heads," Lia announced, pulling her light away from the men. "Now go."

With no further argument, they each obeyed, leaving Naia and Damian alone again.

"Thunderheart," he whispered, voice husky, "you saved me again..."

"There is truth in dreams, but especially in nightmares."

———*James Patterson, The Private School Murders*

CHAPTER 40

Through eyes that did not belong to her, Naia watched as sand danced and swirled on the sweep of dry wind along the narrow street, drawing delighted squeals from a group of children nearby.

Though Naia wanted to frown, the woman she had become smiled, offering them a little wave as they passed. Her actions were no longer her own, and thoughts that were not her own sprang forth in her mind; as if she had slipped into another life as easily as changing her clothes.

The city on market day was busy, a bustle of activity and chatter. She turned her head toward her destination: the temple that towered over the city, its spire reaching for the very heavens. Stretching upward toward the god who had blessed her with lightning, had gifted her the cauldron, and with it, the responsibility of keeping an entire kingdom safe.

Dread washed over Naia, even as pride swelled in the heart of the woman she'd become.

"High Priestess Cordelia," someone called from behind, and she turned, offering a smile.

"I've told you time and again, Selwyn," she said patiently, as the familiar elder approached. "You were there at my birth, heard my mother declare my name on her deathbed. I think if anyone has the right to forgo my title, it's you."

Selwyn offered a warm, familial smile in return. "I just don't believe it's proper, not in public anyway," came the expected response.

She knew better than to correct him again, he'd never change his mind, and pushing further would only offend him. "What can I do for you?" she asked instead.

"Well," he began with a heavy sigh, leaning on his cane. "You know the village of Arbela? They've been having a bit of trouble with–"

The wind rose suddenly, carrying with it the scent of baked bread from the bakery cart just beyond them, and the smell of roses from the florist, mere feet behind Selwyn. Cordelia cast a glance skyward, frowning for the first time. There had been no indications of storms today.

With her gift she would usually sense them before they arrived, allowing her to warn her people of any flooding; and be prepared to act if needed. Her command over water was nearly as strong as her command of lightning, and would allow her to redirect flood waters away from homes.

Naia blinked internally. She hadn't known Lir's gift also granted her command over water, though she remembered him being referred to as the god of storms and seas, she frankly hadn't given it much thought.

As she watched the dream, a memory she now realized, play out, she tucked the information she'd learned from this exchange away.

Still frowning, Cordelia turned her attention to the baker as he and a group of other merchants from nearby stalls approached.

"I'm sorry to interrupt, High Priestess Selwyn," the tall, broad man with a bushy beard began. "But are we to expect storms today?"

"The criers said today was a clear day," the florist, a short woman with fiery red hair and a temper to match, snapped, folding her arms across her chest. "I apologize for my rudeness, High Priestess, but it's no easy task hauling all the blooms in from Botrus, and an even harder one taking them back in the rain."

Cordelia smiled patiently, even as her mind raced. Her gift had never failed, not once, so if a storm was coming...it had been hidden from her by the only one capable, Lir.

But why?

Because he's a fucking prick, Naia replied with a snort.

"I assure you we are not," Cordelia soothed, just as a single, fat raindrop fell to the sandy street between them. A heavy silence fell over the street and Cordelia could feel dozens of pairs of eyes all fixed on her.

Rain was a rare occasion in the deserts of Coruscis, but when they did occur they were fierce enough that most didn't venture out of their homes until they had passed.

Every planned event was run by her to ensure the weather would hold. It was her responsibility to ensure their stalls, their animals, their goods would all remain dry and intact. It had been her decision to hold a market today, safe in the knowledge she had never failed.

Until now.

All at once, people sprang into action, shuttering windows, calling children indoors, and packing away their wares. More than a few pinned her with glares laced with confusion as they passed, but none dared utter a word.

Save for one.

"I suppose we all get it wrong once in a while," Selwyn said softly, patting her arm gently. A gentle lie but a lie nonetheless, and they both knew it.

The single drop turned into a downpour as Cordelia turned and made her way toward the temple. Something was wrong, and she intended to find out what, even if it meant summoning a god himself to demand answers.

Naia tensed. Lir had lied to his blessed Bearer, but why? She hadn't trusted him, but that had been based on his reluctance to help her when she needed it. He'd been a coward, more interested in hiding to save himself than helping to save them all. But this...this appeared to be a time of peace. The biggest concerns on Cordelia's mind had been flooding and protecting merchants from a few wet roses. Why bother hiding something so trivial?

"I intend to find out," Cordelia said.

Naia blinked, startled. Could Cordelia somehow hear Naia within her mind? If so, she had so many questions. Namely, where was–

"--what you are hiding from me?" Cordelia continued, glancing skyward.

Disappointment washed over Naia. *Damn.*

Cordelia continued on her path, pausing here and there to allow rain-soaked market goers to cross, as they were heading into the nearest shop or home. Anywhere to escape the torrent that now fell from the sky. The rain fell in furious waves, fat droplets carried sideways by gusting winds. In the distance, blessedly still far enough away as to not pose a danger to her people, lightning struck the sands.

But the worst of it was growing closer.

She reached out with her gift, barely breaking her stride, and attempted to calm the storm, to slow it. Lightning coursed through her veins, remaining contained within her as she called upon the magic Lir had given her. Like the intuition that should have warned her, this magic also failed her; the storm ignored her call.

Fear set her heart to a gallop, and she stifled it, forcing her features into a mask of calm. Every face she passed watched hers, looking for a sign of what was happening, why she had failed them.

"High Priestess," one woman cried out. "What is happening? Why were we not warned?"

Cordelia's eyes closed for a moment as she inhaled deeply. The scent of rain and petrichor calmed her, and she returned her gaze to the frustrated woman, slowing her pace, but not stopping entirely.

"The gods have willed it," she said patiently. "Even I dare not question the will of the gods."

The woman pressed her lips together in a thin line. It had been a non answer, but one that Cordelia knew wouldn't be questioned further. To question the gods was all but unthinkable. Not when they watched so closely, and even sometimes walked among their mortal children.

Any insult could be heard and severely punished.

Yeah, well fuck him anyway, Naia snarled inside Cordelia's mind.

Resuming her journey, Cordelia soon found herself at the base of the stairs leading to the temple. Soaring overhead, the rounded building was taller than Naia had initially assumed. Bright flowers in varying shades of blues and oranges grew wild, well cared for, but left to look natural, spilling out of large rectangular planters at even intervals along the stairs.

On either side of the structure, windows made of stained glass, set in a spiral pattern of blues and greens.

Just as she'd once seen in her mind.

The arched doorway, the remnants of which Naia had once passed through herself, bore two massive doors, thrown wide as if in invitation.

Cordelia began to ascend the stairs, only to halt as someone shouted her name, a male voice that had Cordelia's heart skipping a beat. She turned to greet him, and Naia's own heart skittered.

He bore little resemblance to Damian, save for the long black hair slicked back from his rugged features, but she knew, by some bone deep intuition that it was his soul, his past life now jogging toward them.

Something within Naia tugged at her, longing to be nearer to him, like the waves to the shore, ever destined to come together. The need to return to him, to her own time, burned within her, but she needed to see, to know what had happened; what the gods were keeping from them.

Where was Damian while she dreamt, she wondered. Was he safe, still dreaming or had he been pulled into his own nightmare of memory?

"What's happening?" he asked, concern clouding his features. Slate-colored eyes darted skyward before returning to Cordelia.

She sighed, biting her lower lip thoughtfully. "I don't know," she admitted for the first time aloud. Only with he who knew her heart and soul better than any other. Her mate, her love, her life.

Hadrian's gaze darkened. "He's keeping things from you." A statement, not a question. "That doesn't bode well. Are you going to call on him?" He glanced toward the temple, crossing his arms across his wet tunic. "I'm going with you."

Cordelia shook her head. "I wish that you could, my heart, but I need you to help here. They were caught off guard, some are still struggling to carry their wares inside and that," she said glancing behind her, beyond the city and toward the desert where the worst of the lightning, crashing bolt after bolt after bolt, approached.

No normal storm behaved that way, with so little break in between strikes.

Warnings screamed in her mind. Whatever this was, it was not good.

"We need to make sure everyone gets indoors before it's here." She sighed, turning back to him, meeting his gaze and letting the mask fall away completely. Allowing him to see the real fear behind her eyes. "Something is very wrong."

Hadrian's jaw tensed, the corded muscles of his bare forearms flexing. "I can't leave you."

Lifting a hand to his chest, resting her palm over where his heart beat only for her, she shook her head. "Okay," she relented.

Turning, she spotted a nearby temple guardian helping an elder priestess toward the temple stairs. "Adriana," she called out. "When she is safely indoors, go to the city guard, have them ensure that everyone is indoors, as soon as possible."

"At once, my lady," the guardian nodded her understanding, before resuming her trek with the elder.

Hadrian placed his hand over hers, where it still rested on his chest. "We will see things righted," he said quietly. "Together."

With a smile, she nodded, silently praying that he was right.

CHAPTER 41

The ruins had done little justice to the grandeur of this place. Naia wondered at the soaring ceilings, the mosaics that graced nearly every inch of the walls. They passed in a blur, leaving her unable to decipher what stories they told, or whom they honored.

Cordelia had seen them all countless times, and she had no time to pause to appreciate them now.

Priests and priestesses milled about, speaking quietly among themselves. A few spared curious glances at Cordelia, but none approached. Whether it was the purposeful stride carrying her toward the spiral stairs leading to her personal sanctum, where her cauldron rested, or her expression, she didn't know; but was grateful for it nonetheless.

She had no words of comfort for them. Comforting lies would do no good for the men and women who belonged to the temple; those that served Lir and knew as well as she did that something was wrong.

Minutes later, with Hadrian at her side, Cordelia stepped into the chamber, her gaze landing on the pedestal where her cauldron rested, sleeping.

Cordelia had little need to converse with it most days, and the cauldron seemed content to keep its silence. Hadrian paused by the door as she moved toward it. This was her domain alone, and he would move no further, leaving her to do what only she could.

The artifact appeared no different than it had when Naia had last laid her eyes upon the cauldron, as if the ravages of time had no effect on it. Naia watched warily as Cordelia reached out, placing her palm against the cauldron's smooth surface.

A sleepy yawn echoed through Cordelia and Naia's minds. "Mm," the cauldron hummed sleepily. "Hello, Bearer," it greeted in its eerily childlike voice. "Come to see me at last?"

Something tickled at Naia's mind, even as Cordelia spoke aloud, voicing her own greetings. Naia could barely hear them, as the now familiar voice spoke to her alone, carrying on its conversation with Cordelia in tandem.

"You've come a long way," the cauldron chirped to Naia. *"Or rather, you were brought a long way,"* it mused. *"Have you come to see the truth of the past?"*

Naia froze. Could Cordelia hear this?

"I have," she replied slowly. "Do you know what is happening?"

"She hears nothing," it replied, reading Naia's thought. *"And, if I do or do not, it is not mine to share. Watch, listen, and know that there is never only one truth,"* it said, voice fading away.

Naia blinked, and Cordelia's voice returned to a normal volume, no longer suppressed by the whispering of the cauldron. "I want to know why he lied," she ordered irritably. She must have asked at least once before, Naia judged from her tone.

"Bearer," the cauldron whined. "You are in danger, but the truth of why remains hidden, even from my gaze." Silence fell, heavy and fraught with tension. "Something has been decided, in the place where they hide. Your sisters–"

Thunder crashed overhead, so violently that the very walls of the temple trembled.

Cordelia's gaze lifted to the ceiling. "My sisters?"

Her voice remained steady, calm, even as fear coursed through her veins. Not fear for herself, but for her people, her sisters. For their world.

If something had happened to the others, then the very fate of

Aestera could be at risk. But they had earned their peace. When the empire of dragons had arrived on their shore, intent on destroying them all, the gods bestowed their gifts, to save their precious mortal children.

And yet...

"They weep," the cauldron whispered, sounding almost frightened itself. "My brothers and sisters...they weep for their Bearers." A low whine sounded from the cauldron before it fell silent again.

Nais shivered as Cordelia, shaken to her core, stepped back, dropping her hand to her side. *What have they done?*

The hairs on the back of Cordelia's neck rose, and she turned to find Hadrian behind her and met his gaze. His widened eyes met hers and for a moment, silent understanding passed between them.

Thunder boomed again, and dust rained from the ceiling above.

The deception lay deeper than she could have guessed. The cauldron's words rang in her mind. "I need to know," Cordelia said. "If they're alive."

Hadrian frowned, not understanding at first. As realization dawned, he moved to her, ignoring the laws of the sacred space. "I will not leave you."

Cordelia closed the distance between them, cupping his face in her hands. "I need to know, my heart, and you are the only one I can trust to do this. You must tell me if they live, I will wait for you here," she said, the words bitter on her tongue.

In their many years together, she had not once lied to him.

To save his life—to save him from witnessing the end of hers, she said whatever she needed to.

If he read the deception in her eyes as their gazes met, he didn't say, instead pressing a fierce kiss to her lips. "I love you," he whispered fiercely. "For a thousand lifetimes, my heart and soul are yours. I will be by your side always."

"Eternally," she whispered in return, stepping back as wind and darkness began to gather around him. She let her gaze roam his features, committing each line, each faint scar, every fleck of grey in his eyes to memory. When her time came, it would be his face she saw in her mind.

Naia's heart gave a squeeze. She wished she could tell them they would find one another again. That their souls were linked, that though they were not the same people, their promise held true.

"Let us see it done, then," Cordelia whispered, as Hadrian vanished.

Taking the cauldron from its resting place, she strode out of the room and up the spiral stairs that would carry her to her fate.

The storm had grown to such intensity that as she stepped onto the rooftop terrace, Cordelia found herself fighting against the wind, arm thrown over her face to shield her from the stinging rain. Lightning crashed all around, striking buildings as screams rang out below. Several fires had been started by the lightning, and the streets were now a deluge.

Her people, she realized with a choked sob, had nowhere left to run. No refuge from the storm.

"You took your time," a masculine voice remarked with a snort.

Naia and Cordelia startled at the same time, both pairs of eyes landing on Lir, who stood a few feet away. His long, unbound hair danced around him as if on a light breeze. His storm grey pants and bare chest, covered in a broad, branching bolt of lightning, remained dry, untouched by the rain that poured around them.

In contrast, Cordelia was left shivering, soaked to the bone, wet hair plastered to her skin as she met his gaze.

"Why?" Her spine was steel. Fear was all but forgotten now. It was fury like she had never know that fueled her. Lightning danced along her skin, her magic answering the call of her anger, but remained leashed.

It would do no good against him, the master of the very skies.

The single word hung between them, as thunder boomed once more, and another round of screams erupted below. She couldn't bear to look as bright light flashed in the corner of her eyes.

Another home ignited by Lir's lightning.

The god tilted his head to his side, slipping his hands into his pockets casually. "It's not personal," he began calmly, as if the chaos surrounding them didn't exist. As if they weren't discussing the murder of innocents, the destruction of an entire city. "One of your sisters has been very naughty, and unfortunately, you must all bear her punishment."

Surprise rocked her. "What do you mean?"

Lir shrugged. "It doesn't matter," he replied, dismissing her question entirely. "I want you to know," he added, as he began to stride toward her. "That I am truly disappointed by this turn of events."

Fuck you, Naia thought.

The sentiment was mirrored in Cordelia's mind as she lifted the cauldron, taking it in both hands.

To Naia's surprise, Lir hesitated. If only for a moment. "Brave, and foolish," he tsked, resuming his stride toward her. "It would take all four of you to do any harm to me."

"I have to try," Cordelia replied, as he reached her.

"So you do," he sighed.

Before he could strike, Cordelia screamed, rage, pain, and grief wracking her. The electricity dancing along her skin poured into the cauldron as she called upon its power. "Save us," she commanded.

Magic thickened the air. Cordelia's wet hair rose on end, and to Naia's surprise, so did Lir's. The god himself blinked, clearly not expecting her power to touch him.

With a roar Cordelia unleashed herself upon him. Bolt after bolt, lightning shot toward him, so quickly in succession that it appeared as a steady stream, directly into his chest. Lir fell to his knees as he was struck by the crackling electricity, and for a moment, Cordelia felt a hint of triumph.

Naia felt only sorrow. This would end in only one way.

Though Cordelia's imminent death laid the way for Naia to exist, for her to find Damian, she felt sorrow for the ancient woman; for the betrayal she and her sisters had faced.

Her magic spent, Cordelia stumbled back. The cauldron rattled against the terrace floor as her arms fell limp at her side. She had nothing left. Her singular hope had failed her.

Lir rose to his feet, as she struggled to remain on hers.

"Valiant effort little—"

"Cordelia!" Hadrian's voice rang out and she turned to find him racing toward them. Fire burned in his gaze as he turned to face the god.

"What have you done?" he demanded, flames sparking to life as he stepped toward the god.

"No!" Cordelia and Naia screamed in unison, in vain.

Lightning speared from Lir, who hadn't so much as raised his hand. As Hadrian crumpled to the ground, he barely spared her mate a glance. "Foolish," Lir remarked flatly.

Cordelia's chest split, something within her breaking at the sight of his lifeless body, lying between her and the god who had sworn to protect her, to guide her. Another surge of rage swept over her, and, with all the strength she had left, Cordelia launched herself at Lir.

Catching him off guard, she made contact, tackling him to the floor and landing a single blow to his face. She screamed, as tears streamed, blending with the rain that now soaked them both—the rain he had called to destroy everything she held dear.

Her heart was gone, in its place a gaping hole that was filled only with pain and fury. She would kill him with her bare hands, she would—

Something in her spine cracked as she landed on the marble. She hadn't even had time to register that he'd thrown her off of him. Pain seared the back of her head and her legs...she couldn't feel them at all.

"I am disappointed," Lir sighed, standing over her broken body.

She could do little more than stare up at him. "Fuck. You."

Naia wept silently within Cordelia. There were no words left. She hadn't known, hadn't been prepared to feel this, to witness such brutality and heartache in her quest for the truth. If she'd disliked Lir before, now there were no words in any language she knew to describe the depth of her hatred for him.

"There is no need for cruelty, brother," a female voice called out from somewhere behind him.

He didn't bother to look away from Cordelia's face as he replied. "So you've come to claim her, Macaria. She's the last?"

Macaria finally stepped into view, upper face hidden by a black veil. Her red lips turned downward in a pitying frown. "You needn't have been so brutal," she chided. "You could have made it painless."

Lir shrugged. "I had planned to, but she attacked me."

Macaria only sighed, kneeling beside Cordelia, whose breathing had become ragged.

Her ribs ached, each breath becoming more and more difficult, as if a great weight had settled over her chest.

She wanted to die.

To be with Hadrian in the Otherworld; or whatever came after this. The screams of her people below were the song that would usher her out of this life, her last regret being her inability to save them.

"Please.." she wheezed. The world around them had grown hazy. She could no longer make out Lir's face, though he still stared down at her.

"Shh," Macaria soothed, stroking her hair gently. "It's over now."

Turning her attention to the goddess, Cordelia exhaled once more, a mere whisper of a breath. Macaria lifted her veil, still stroking her hair, soothing, comforting.

Kind, soft brown eyes met Cordelia's, but the rest of her visage was a blur to Naia. She could make out no features, no age, the face of the goddess hidden beneath a sort of haze.

Cordelia let out a final shuddering breath as Macaria spoke once more, in hushed whispers. "I'm so sorry," she said, sounding far more genuine than the god who had taken Cordelia's life. "You will see him again."

As what was left of Cordelia's life faded, Naia drifted into the darkness, the voices of the gods echoing beyond.

"See that it's all gone," Macaria said sadly. "We cannot let this story be told."

"It's nearly done," Lir replied. "There will be none left to remember what happened here."

CHAPTER 42

LIA

Dark lashes fluttered open, revealing a brilliant blue sky above. A warm breeze stirred the tall grasses around her, and she rolled her head to the side, eyeing her companion with a grin.

"So, are you going to ask her to marry you or what?"

She knew the answer, probably better than he did. She'd always known his mind, nearly as well as her own. A perk of being best friends since they were in swaddles.

Rolling his brown eyes, Celio turned to meet her gaze, sighing. "You tell me."

Peering through eyes that were not her own, Lia frowned. She had never had a dream like this before, taking on the life of another, watching things play out with no control of her own. At least it was pleasant, she supposed, despite its strangeness.

The woman whose eyes she saw through, whose thoughts she heard as clearly as her own, considered it. "Yes," she replied, smiling brightly. The idea of it made her happy. To see her best friend settled, with a woman she knew would make him happy. There was little more she could ask for in this world. "And," she added, sitting up so that she rested on her elbows, face tilted upward. She relished in the warm sun on her skin, her magic practically sighing with contentment. "I think you'll do it next Saturday. After the party."

Lia's breath hitched. Her gift. A gift of sunlight. She was dreaming of another with Helie's blessing?

Celio laughed, sitting up. "Oh, and have you named our future children as well now, Luci?"

Lucienne smirked, not bothering to look at him. "Maybe," she teased. Her thoughts turned to her own love, the one she'd only so recently found. "I hope to do the same one day," she began tentatively.

"Propose to Risa?" Celio asked, metaphorical ears perking up. He'd been the one to introduce them, Luci and Risa, mere months ago.

"It's early days, but..." Sitting up straight, she turned to eye him, to judge his opinion of the matter.

Celio grinned, happiness practically radiating from his light brown eyes. "You're a hopeless romantic, and always looking toward the future." Leaning closer, he tugged one of her long, dark braids before flicking the little sun charm that had been woven into the tightly wound strands. "A little on the nose," he teased.

Lia smiled to herself, even as faint warning bells sounded in her mind. There was a reason she was being shown this. With Kore in control of Endri, and by extension dreams, she doubted the story had a happy ending.

Leaping to his feet, Celio brushed the dust and grass from his trousers before extending a hand to Luci. "Come on then, you're going to be late for the ceremony."

Sighing, Luci placed her hand in his and rose to her feet far more reluctantly than he had. "I wish I didn't have to," she said, only half seriously. "I would rather spend the day here."

"Of course you would," he shrugged, lifting his chin arrogantly. "When you get to look at this handsome face the whole day."

Lia couldn't help but feel wistful over the easy friendship. It reminded her so much of what she had with Aelius...and Bastien. Her heart ached at the reminder of that loss. She hadn't allowed herself to properly mourn him, not yet. Not with so much going on. But when the task was done, she would see to it the funeral rites were held, that the story of his life and his sacrifice was recorded in the great library.

Luci laughed. He was objectively handsome, she supposed, though she preferred women. With light brown eyes set in a strong face, a strong jaw, and firm muscles that rippled beneath his dark brown skin as he moved, he certainly drew the attention of many of the women of Iria.

Though his heart lay firmly with Sora, something she was thankful for. He needed the reasonable, level-headed priestess to keep him in line.

Her attention turned to Iria in the distance. The shining capitol of Finias. A city of gold and glass. Home of the temple of Helie. The temple she should already be arriving at, she thought with a groan.

"Enough of your preening, let's go," she teased, before wind and darkness enveloped her, and she paced to the temple.

A short time later, dressed in glittering gold that offset her light brown skin beautifully, Luci made her way to the balcony where she would host the ceremony. Midsummer was only a week away, and with it, their most important celebrations. It was Helie's time to shine, figuratively and literally, she thought with an inward chuckle.

Lia watched with interest, behind Luci's eyes. She'd never seen the likes of the temple. Soaring windows lined every wall, so massive that the entire wall was essentially made of glass. The ceilings were adorned with enormous golden chandeliers, reflected in the polished glassy floors. Every inch of the temple seemed designed to reflect Helie's light. She could only assume magic kept it from blinding those inside, and likely outside as well.

Taking a steadying breath, Luci paused as she reached the gold and glass double doors that led to the balcony. She had given countless speeches, hosted countless ceremonies, in the years since she'd been blessed by Helie. After the downfall of the dragons, she'd set to work as high priestess: healing the sick in great numbers, as many made the pilgrimage to the temple to see her, and the priests and priestesses who served under her.

Her more lethal gifts had lain dormant. Unnecessary in the years that had passed since the war. Flashes of dragons falling from the skies, seared and blinded by liquid sunlight, crossed her mind, making Luci, and Lia, wince.

She could still call upon the warmth of the sun during harsher winters, offering a boon to crops that needed a little more time before the harvest, healing the sick and injured, and other such gifts.

The small glimpse of her power Lia could see from Luci's thoughts was staggering. To call upon the sun itself in such a way, to command its appearance on a cloudy day...that was far beyond the power Lia had been able to tap into.

Lifting her chin, Luci stepped onto the balcony, offering the people below a bright smile. The sun shone brightly on her face, a gift from her goddess, as she had not called on the power herself. Gratitude and pride warmed her heart as the sun warmed her cheeks.

Cheers erupted below. Banners of white with a blazing sun were waved overhead, children pulled onto their parents' shoulders to witness the high priestess speak.

"Brothers and sisters," Luci began, tone clear and bright as a bell. "Welcome. As we near the day of Helie, we honor her by–" The light above brightened, forcing Luci to throw her arm over her face to shield her eyes. "By sharing the hope and peace that her light grants us. The healing of our hearts, our bodies."

More people were shielding their eyes now, in the crowd below as the light grew brighter. Subtle, as if a cloud that had been covering the sun had shifted, no longer dimming its light. A few uncomfortable coughs sounded as the light continued to grow brighter. The warmth that had made her feel blessed, content, now grew to an uncomfortable heat.

Lia, looking through Luci's eyes, watched as people began to fan themselves, glancing skyward as the light grew brighter by the minute. Worry began to nag at the back of her mind, ancient instinct warning her that something terrible was coming.

Luci's speech carried on, however, speaking of the blessing of the sun, the fruitfulness of their crops thanks to her light. "I.." she began, prepared to move on to the next part of the ceremony, where she would welcome those who needed healing into the temple to be seen by herself and the acolytes who served there. The light had grown so bright that it was difficult to continue looking out at the gathered masses.

Below, people had begun to shield their children, with scarves and the shirts off their very backs, from the sun's intensifying rays. Even she, one blessed with the power of the sun itself, had begun to grow too uncomfortable to remain outdoors any longer.

She needed to end this now, to speak to the only one who could give her answers.

"Welcome you all to the temple," she finished, wrapping up the ceremony earlier than intended. "Join us for refreshments and healing for those who need it."

Turning on her heel, she strode inside as the crowd began to cheer below. Celio was at her side before she reached the center of the space, where the sword of light lay resting.

"What were you doing out there?" he asked, confused. "You nearly blinded me," he added, teasing.

Luci frowned, heart pounding. "It wasn't me," she said quietly, as if whispering would keep the very gods from hearing her. "I don't know what is happening."

Celio stopped her with a hand on her arm. "What are you saying, Lucienne?"

The use of her full name had her turning to face him fully. He rarely used it, reserving it only for when he was most serious. Lifting a hand to her temple, she rubbed slow circles. "I don't know, all I know is it wasn't me, and something isn't right."

"Then let's find out what happened."

Nodding, she offered him a tight smile and returned her gaze to the sword ahead of her.

CHAPTER 43

LIA

"*H*ello again, Bearer," a small, sweet voice yawned. "*What do you require of me?*"

Gliding her thumb over the gilded hilt gently, Luci couldn't help but smile. They had served together so well, the sword and herself, had saved many, even amongst all the carnage of the dragon war. The darker memories crept into her mind, but she shoved them away. Now was not the time for that.

Lia listened intently. She couldn't help but wonder how the sword had survived the many years between whenever this had occurred and the present time. How it had ended up with her family. Her father would have–

She cut the thought short, much like Luci and her memories of war, she wouldn't allow her thoughts to turn to darker things, not now. There would be time for that, time to talk with Aelius and their mother, to work through what he had done, who he had truly been.

Hello to you too, a sweet voice whispered. This time directed at Lia.

Luci spoke aloud, a question Lia didn't quite hear above the sound of the sword speaking to her.

Have you come seeking the truth, Bearer? It cooed. *To learn?*

"I have," she whispered back. If Luci could hear the conversation she gave no indication as she loosened a frustrated growl.

Then watch, the sword replied quietly.

"You must tell me what that means," Luci ground out. Her skin heated, and she knew without a doubt that if she were to look at her reflection just now, her eyes would appear as liquid gold. "What has happened to my sisters?"

The sword whimpered in response. "I do not know, Bearer. I–I–cannot see."

With a calming breath, Luci steadied her frayed nerves and lowered the sword to hold it at her side. "Then we shall find out together."

Celio walked alongside her in silence as they descended the stairs. The lower floor was teeming with people, many whose skin had turned bright pink or red, or had taken on a more violet hue. Some had even begun to blister.

Eyes widening, she turned to the nearest priestess, carrying a basket of salves used to treat burns. "What is happening?"

The young woman shook her head. "I'm not sure, Lady, I–" she cast a glance around them, where the nearest of those gathered had begun to listen. "We were hoping you might tell us."

She inhaled deeply. Of course they'd expect her to know; she who served their goddess, who called upon the sun to heal and protect them. Turning to speak to the group as a whole, Luci lifted her chin. "I know you all must be frightened and confused. I have no explanations for you now," she began, offering a smile that she hoped would ease the worst of their fears. Despite the fear in her own heart, she would make sure they saw her as strong, unconcerned. "But know that Helie is with us and assures me that this strange occurrence will be sorted out as swiftly as possible."

While some remained skeptical, many offered words of blessing, staunch in their belief in her, in the gods. The lie left a bitter taste on her tongue, but without their faith to keep them from fear, what hope did they have?

Lia wondered if she would have made the same choice, had she been in Luci's position. Was a comforting lie better than a brutal truth? Probably, she admitted to herself. To keep hope alive, to keep them from panic, a gentle lie was worth it.

"Luci," Celio prompted, drawing her attention back to him. "We should go."

She followed his gaze to the open archway leading to the secluded courtyard that housed Helie's altar. Gripping the sword tightly, she nodded and made her way out to confront the goddess.

Stepping into the sunlight was near unbearable by now, even for Luci. Celio, for his own safety, remained in the last remnant of shade provided by the sole tree in the open space, barely enough to cover him. Even still, she could see beads of sweat forming across his forehead. Her own skin burned, and she had no choice but to lift her arm to shield her eyes.

"Hello, my child." Helie's voice rang out moments later, more somber than Luci had heard before in their many meetings. "I am so very sorry for what must be done today."

"What must be done?" Luci asked, lifting her gaze just enough to make out the goddess standing in front of her. Draped in a strapless white silk gown that pooled around her slender frame like liquid, designed, no doubt, to display the golden twin suns on either side of her collar bone.

Sun–gold eyes filled with regret met Luci's. "You, and your people, are paying for a crime that is not your own. My ever faithful Bearer. My favored child. My friend." Helie sighed, glancing to the side as another goddess appeared in a flash of white. "There is no other way?" the sun goddess asked the new arrival.

Nearly the exact opposite of Helie, the goddess of death appeared garbed in black, with her customary veil covering the upper portion of her face. Dark red lips pulled downward into a frown. "No, sister." Turning her attention to Luci, she added, "As regrettable as it is."

Celio drifted to Luci's side silently. His presence strengthened her resolve, steeling her nerves, her heart racing in her chest.

"What crime?" Her hand tightened on the hilt of the sword, and it warmed to her touch. Her skin burned beneath the blazing sun, but she ignored it, her sole focus on the two goddesses before her. "What has happened to my sisters?"

The goddesses shared a glance before Helie replied. "The eldest has had a grave lapse in judgment."

Lia frowned, tears beginning to spill. She couldn't bear this any longer. Being forced to watch all of these people, Luci, the person she had once been, die. It was too much. She had no idea who the eldest was or what they had done, but surely nothing they did deserved this response from the gods. If she saw Helie again she would–

"I cannot let you claim their lives," Luci said softly, raising the sword as she lowered her other hand. Light, as smooth and tangible as liquid, began to writhe around her free hand.

Helie's eyes closed as she sighed. "I am sorry."

Without another word, Luci raised the sword, and a blast of blinding light poured out from her outstretched palm. Celio shouted something from behind her, but she heard nothing as the light simply bounced off of the goddess, reflecting back onto Luci.

The sword fell away from her hand, forgotten as searing pain unlike anything she'd ever felt enveloped her. Brief, but unimaginable. Within the span of three heartbeats, it was over.

Lia, through Luci's eyes, stared up at the cloudless sky, nearly obscured by bright white light. As Luci turned her head, she found Celio beside her, as he always had been, nearly every day of their lives, his hand outstretched toward her. Lia's heart wrenched at the sight.

"Why?" Luci thought, a faint whisper in her mind.

Soft sobs echoed from somewhere nearby. A woman, but who?

"Rest child," Macaria soothed as the hem of her black dress came into view. Slowly, she lay beside Luci, hand outstretched, but not touching her charred skin. "It's over. Rest. You will see him again, see your sisters again. In the next life."

Lia sobbed, heartbroken and angry. How could Helie, the very goddess of healing do something so awful. How many people died on this day? How many lives were taken to pay for a crime that they, by the goddess' own admission, had not committed?

As Luci exhaled for the final time, her sight darkening, light burst from the courtyard. Screams within the temple erupted, followed by more screaming from within the city as people were burned by the unrelenting rays of sunlight.

Through heaving sobs, Helie decimated the city of Iria.

CHAPTER 44

EVE

She stood at the edge of the forest, looking over the great river rushing ever southward toward Avellon, then on to Coruscis, before meeting the southern sea. Calm and steady, the waters of the Spreva had helped bring life to Darkegrove for millenia. Much of the lush forest surrounding her, with its ancient pines and soaring oaks, owed its life to the water flowing through her kingdom, the water that began as a mere trickle northward in Gorias.

"Thinking of going for a swim?" Silas called out from behind her.

She knew without turning who was behind her. The man who had guarded her, had loved her, for so many years of their long lives as her sworn protector, and mate.

"Very funny, Silas," she replied, folding her arms across her chest. The very thought terrified her, though she could never explain why.

Eve, within the mind of her past, shuddered alongside Vivien. It had taken her mere minutes to piece together what was happening, to prepare herself for whatever lie or twisted truth Kore was trying to show her.

As Silas stepped into view, something within Eve's soul tugged at her. Recognition, longing. Here was Callan's past, and though he bore no similarities to the man she loved, she would know his soul in any lifetime.

Blond hair fell in loose waves to the delicately pointed tips of his ears. Humor lightened his pale grey eyes as he reached for Vivien, gently tugging a stray lock of chestnut hair that had fallen loose from her braid. "I know you hate that joke, I'm sorry. What are we doing here?"

His confusion was warranted, as Vivien despised being this close to water, especially moving water. Give her mountains, solid earth beneath her feet, and she was content. If it weren't for bathing, she would have no contact with water whatsoever, had she the choice.

"I wanted to speak to you, away from intrusive ears," she said, glancing to the north, to the city of Edessa.

Silas frowned. "Is something amiss?"

She hadn't yet spoken of her plans, hatched in the darkest corners of her mind. The plans that would get them all killed if discovered.

Eve inhaled sharply. The thought Vivien was afraid to speak aloud, and for good reason, was so reckless, so arrogantly foolish, that given the chance to scream, to slap sense into her past self, she would gladly take it.

"I–" she began, inhaling softly and adjusting the crown atop her brow. The Stone of Rule, resting in the center hummed against the brush of her fingertips. "I think it's time to step out from under their thumbs."

Silas' eyes widened briefly before his expression turned serious. "My heart, think of what you're saying," he whispered fiercely, casting a glance to the forest around them. If there were ever a place where the very trees could listen, it would be here. "Don't be ridiculous."

Hackles raised, Vivien lifted her chin and met his gaze evenly. "I'm not. Think of it, Silas, we could be free of their treaties, of their commands. We could have everything. We could *rule* everything."

"You would never be able to do it alone," he reminded her. She could feel his fear, his worry emanating from him. "You would need the aid of at least one of your sisters, and even then…"

"And if I could secure it?"

"How? How could you possibly?" He remained doubtful, but the intensity of his gaze softened ever so slightly.

Convinced she was winning him over, Vivien stepped closer, placing a hand on his chest.

"Leave that to me. I know them well, their strengths and weaknesses."

She felt her heart soar at the idea of what they could do with two, maybe even three of the artifacts under her command. If she could convince one, then she could likely convince two...maybe even...

"And what if your plan is discovered. How do you know it hasn't already been?" he asked, casting a pointed glance at the crown.

Lifting her hand, she caressed the stone softly. "The stone remains loyal to me, beloved. And Keithia sees me as little more than a petulant child. She has paid me little attention since the war," she reminded him. Her thoughts drifted to the battles they'd fought and won together.

She had seen what power even one or two of the artifacts commanded, but with all of them together there was no limit to what could be accomplished.

Why waste that on a quiet life of peace?

Every day of her life had been consumed by duty, responsibility. If not to the gods, then to her people, her kingdom. The mantle of queen weighed heavy on her in the early days, but now she could see the possibilities. If she must bear the weight of the crown, why not expand her reach?

She would leave her sisters in peace, out of love for them and their shared history.

So long as they did not stand in her way.

But beyond the sea, where the dragons still ruled, why not lay claim to that land? Why not seek retribution for the havoc they had wreaked when they had declared themselves conquerors and tried to lay claim to the kingdoms of Aestera?

If she wanted to claim what rightfully belonged to her, she would have to remove any obstacle in her path. Including the gods themselves.

Eve's heart pounded. Gods above, what had she done? The question raced in her mind over and over. What madness had driven her? If they had betrayed the god in the past, did that color how they viewed the bearers in this lifetime?

Because he could read every thought written on her face, Silas shook his head slowly.

"My heart, the risks," he implored, voice low. "What they will do to you if they find out–"

She narrowed her eyes at him. "Are you going to try to stop me?"

He tensed. She knew he felt the tremble of the earth beneath his feet; knew what it meant and he loved her anyway "Never," he assured her, placing a hand on her cheek. "Never. I will stand with you no matter what comes next."

Satisfied, she smiled, leaning into his touch. Arm in arm, they headed toward Edessa, to set the wheels of fate in motion.

CHAPTER 45

EVE

It had taken hours to gather her people in the square outside the castle. Minutes after their return, the city watch had been commanded to go door to door, ordering each resident to make their way to the castle grounds to hear a proclamation from their queen.

Righteousness drove her as she stepped onto the balcony. Lifting her chin, she watched the crowd below fall to their knees in deference. Silas stood to her right, the only guard she would allow at her side for this announcement. His presence comforted her, strengthened her resolve. With him at her side, there was nothing she couldn't do.

She could make out a few faces among the crowd, but those she did wore wary gazes.

Let them worry, she thought. *They will thank me for the glory I will bring to our kingdom. Our empire, when I am finished.*

"People of Edessa," she began. "I have–"

Eve silently wept for what was to come. There had been no record of this event in Falias, none of the elders seemed to know what had happened to the original bearers, and there could be only one reason for that.

There were no records because there had been no hands to record it. No memories to draw from.

A thunderous cracking sound rattled the ground as a woman appeared in the center of the crowd below. People shouted, panicked as they scrambled to get away from where Keithia had appeared. The compact earth of the courtyard splintered beneath her feet.

Vivien had the sense to pale, to take a step back from the railing, wide eyes resting on the goddess below. Fear snaked its way down her spine.

Internally, Eve shrunk back from the display of power Keithia was showing, at the fury rolling off of her, stretching and growing like the cracks on the soil at her feet.

"I–" Vivien began, mind spinning. She hadn't been prepared to be confronted, not yet. Keithia had paid such little attention to her since the war and had said matters elsewhere required her focus. She'd ignored every prayer sent by Vivien.

Perhaps it had all been a trap, she realized, to see if she could bear the weight of the stone on her brow.

A test, an ancient voice whispered in Vivien's mind. *One you've failed, Bearer.*

So you deign to speak to me now, after all these years.

I slumber, unless required, the stone replied simply.

You swore loyalty to me. Will you serve me now?

A weary sigh. *I serve you, even unto your death, Bearer.*

Aloud she said, confidence lacing her words, "I will not die today."

Keithia chuckled darkly, and vines erupted from the ground, spearing for Vivien.

The goddess hadn't even needed to raise a finger; the very earth itself answered her every call.

Vivien shouted as they wrapped around her waist, squeezing like a great python. Silas grappled her arms, fruitlessly, as she was yanked away. Pain tore through her as her shoulder struck the stone railing, then her head. Her vision blurred for a moment, and her body landed on the hard packed earth with a flat thud, leaving her breathless as the air whooshed from her lungs.

The crown dangled from her hair, barely held on with the few pins that hadn't been dislodged by either the fall or her collision with the railing. Every part of her hurt. Yet she struggled, growling with determination and will.

"Help me!" she shouted aloud. The guards who had begun pushing people back shared frightened glances, assuming she spoke to them.

A weary sigh echoed through her mind, and she felt a rush of magic in her veins as the stone boosted her powers.

It will not be enough, the stone replied.

Distantly, another thump sounded, then a pained grunt. Silas leaping from the balcony to come to her aid, she realized, as he began screaming her name.

Eve could do little more than stare at Keithia standing above Vivien, her face the very picture of rage.

"You would dare plot against *me*?" the goddess hissed. The vines gave a squeeze, and Vivien gasped, struggling to drag air into her lungs.

Vivien pulled on her power, willing the vines to release her, if only enough to allow her to breathe. As cracks continued to splinter from around them, the vines did not so much as twitch in response to her call.

Alone, you do not possess the power to fight a god, the stone said quietly.

Tears streamed, hot and wet against her cheeks. Her lungs burned, vision going dim around the edges, She needed to breathe, just one breath. The pain in her head had become a throbbing ache now, and something warm and wet pooled around her head.

"Vivien!" Silas shouted again, as he finally appeared in her line of sight, sword raised over his head as he charged at the goddess.

No! She sobbed internally. *No, no, no.*

It wasn't supposed to go this way, it wasn't–

Keithia barely spared him a glance as a boulder erupted from the earth, sending him sprawling to the ground before it landed on him with a sickening crunch.

Vivien's chest caved in. Her heart cleaving in two as surely as the ground beneath her castle. Suddenly, the vines binding her loosened enough to allow her to breathe. She gulped down air desperately, even as she was lifted from the ground by the vines, little more than a plaything for the goddess who gestured to the still crowded square.

A glance beyond told Vivien why her people hadn't fled. A great boulder now blocked the gate. Keithia had trapped them.

All of them.

Every soul in the city had been lured into a trap, by Vivien herself.

"You don't get to die just yet." Keithia's tone was low, colder than the snow-capped mountains. "You get to watch them pay for your sins first. Then you will die with the knowledge that your hubris caused this; the deaths of not only your people, but your sisters as well."

Vivien struggled anew. She hadn't known, hadn't thought...

Every decision comes with a price, the stone whispered.

Eve sobbed. Guilt surging. It hadn't been her, not really, but some part of her had made the choice that had caused countless people their lives. For what? For more power than any one person needed?

Vivien shouted wordlessly, raging against the goddess. Against what she'd wrought.

Keithia smirked, undeterred by Vivien's tears or the frightened screams of the people around, as the cracks grew and grew until they became a chasm. A chasm that swallowed them as it spread, swallowed the walls of the castle as they crumbled. The city beyond, on and on until the only remaining land as far as the still weeping Vivien could see was the small portion where Keithia stood.

"How could you?" Vivien whispered, vision hazy. She'd been bleeding, she realized, a lot. Whatever Keithia had done to slow it was no longer in effect. She could feel it dripping down her neck, her back as Keithia straightened her to a near standing position.

"No, my child," Keithia replied flatly. "You did this."

Without warning, the vines vanished, and Vivien fell into a freefall. Weightless. Too weak even to scream.

Within her dying mind, Eve covered her eyes. Unable to bear the sight of the sky growing darker, the sensation of falling into the earth.

"You will rest," a familiar female voice whispered. "And you will learn."

Eve lowered her hands, seeing through Vivien's eyes once more. As if time had slowed, so had Vivien's fall. Macaria floated above, her body parallel with Vivien's. The black veil she wore flapped in the wind ever so slightly before she raised it.

Her face, whatever Vivien saw, remained hidden from Eve, blurred as if beneath running water. But it frightened Vivien enough that her heart skittered in her chest.

"Rest," Macaria crooned again. "And learn."

A thud echoed through Eve's mind, and all went dark again.

CHAPTER 46

COLETTE

The great city spread before her. Spires of ice and glass, so seamlessly pieced together it was impossible to tell where one began and the other ended. Domed roofs, low to the ground to conserve heat, marked homes and shops. Only the royals dared build toward the heavens, only they had magic enough at their disposal to keep such towering structures warm and comfortable.

She didn't begrudge them that, as their people were well cared for, from the wealthiest merchant to the lowest commoner. From footsoldier, to herself, the commander of their great armies.

Sidra turned her gaze to where a small group of her soldiers waited, astride the great white bears that served as battle mounts. There was no war to wage today, only a simple training exercise. Something to keep their skills sharp, honed like the silver blades at each of their backs. No conflict had touched the north since the dragon war had ended; since she had been blessed by Viktoria, the goddess of victory and honor.

Within, Colette, afraid and confused, whimpered. This hadn't been part of the bargain her parents had struck. Not when she'd been forced to submit or watch them die.

"We'll ride north," Sidra said, in a voice that was foreign, yet somehow familiar to Colette's ears. "Make a pass toward Hafnia and loop back to the edge of the plains. Put the ice bears through their paces. Augustus will have a camp set up for us when we arrive. Then we'll go through hand to hand drills."

Her soldiers nodded as she met each of their gazes. Only one gave her a cheeky grin as their eyes met. Wisps of pale blonde hair danced on the breeze as Cordis' ice blue eyes met her own. Sidra's heart skipped a beat, as it always did with Cordis, her mate, her wife. But today, she would have to remain impartial and treat her no differently than any of the others under her command.

"Let's go," Sidra ordered, eyes narrowing playfully at Cordis.

Icy air stung her cheeks, the only part of her skin left bare beneath layers of fur and the balaclava wrapped around her mouth and chin. Goggles to protect her eyes kept snow from stinging them and the light bouncing off of the ice plan from blinding her.

Hours and endless scapes of blinding white passed.

Through it all, Colette watched in silent fear. Unable to understand what she was being shown, or why. Because she *was* being shown something, rather than simply having a strange dream. Instinct deep in her gut told her that much. A strange sort of knowing had passed over her the moment she'd begun to see through Sidra's eyes. The same knowing that had given her the strange woman's name to begin with, though it had remain unspoken.

By the time they reached camp, the sun had begun its descent. Soon the already frigid temperatures would grow dangerous, even for their fae bodies. They had been left little time to run through their drills before they would be forced into the shelters carved into the snow and rock.

Already, puffs of white smoke drifted from the chimneys of the handful of makeshift homes, food no doubt being prepared by the servants who had made the journey ahead of them to make the camp comfortable for this elite unit.

A nicety that Sidra had balked at. They were soldiers. They could make their own fires, cook their own meals. When she had said as much to the queen, she'd been reminded that the war was over, and there was no need to scrape and scrabble as they had in those days.

The commander snorted at the memory, turning her attention back to the soldiers. Cordis was sparring with a burly man twice her size with a bright red beard and pale face. Despite his size, Cordis had speed and dexterity on her side and had him on his ass in the packed snow in no time. Not that she hadn't taken a few blows beforehand, Sidra noted, as Cordis strode toward her.

Flexing and unflexing her small hands, Cordis offered Sidra a grin. "Still have it," she boasted.

"So you do, soldier," Sidra replied seriously. Though her tone was the same she'd use with any under her command, the spark in her eyes, the warmth that spread through her, was reserved only for her mate.

Colette watched with fading fear, and growing curiosity. This place resembled home so much. Ice and snow had been all she'd known until...the darkness had come.

Cordis opened her mouth again, no doubt to offer some witty retort, but the bell rang, warning of the swiftly approaching darkness.

With a grin for her wife, Sidra ordered everyone inside, to safety.

CHAPTER 47

____

COLETTE

Sidra sat straight up in bed. Eyes darting around the chilly room. Beside her, Cordis grumbled quietly. She had grown used to Sidra's poor sleeping years ago, and paid no mind, simply rolling away.

Colette could make little sense of the thoughts racing through Sidra's mind. Memories of a war, great dragons roaring above, shifting to a deadly quiet. Listening, it seemed for the source of the _wrongness_ she felt deep in her bones.

The commander rose from the bed, quietly pulling on her boots, and fur overcoat. She moved with utter silence as fleece-lined gloves slipped over her fingers, and she grabbed the spear leaning against the wall just beside the bed.

A sharp gasp escaped Colette and her heart began to gallop in her chest. She knew that spear. Carried that spear. The Spear of the Gods. The only weapon in existence that could kill anything, even a god.

Sidra stepped out into the moonlight, spear clutched tightly in one hand. A glance to her left, and there were the ice bears sleeping soundly. Only the faint whistle of the wind across the plains met her ears, but something still felt wrong. Dangerous.

She took four steps, eyes on the horizon, where, thanks to her keen eyesight and the lack of any obstacle, she could just make out the towering palace in the distance, glittering in the moonlight like diamonds.

"Sidra?" Cordis' sleepy voice called out, just as she decided to turn back. Perhaps there was no danger, just the nightmares of an old soldier, scarred from battle.

"Sorry, darling, it was–"

"Hello, Bearer," a strong female voice said suddenly.

Colette startled at the sudden voice, but Sidra simply turned, unafraid.

"Goddess," she said by way of greeting, dropping to a knee in the snow. A subtle crunch of snow announced Cordis' arrival just behind her.

"Rise, champion," Viktoria said. Sidra couldn't help but note the hint of emotion in her voice, unusual for the typical stoic goddess of victory.

Thoughts ran through Sidra's mind swiftly. Had a new war begun? Was her home in danger?

Seeming to sense Sidra's apprehension, Viktoria raised a hand. "There is no battle to be won today," she began, pausing. "Only..." Casting a glance to the shadow that began to form beside her, she asked, "Must I?"

The goddess of death, one whom Sidra had known well during the years that the dragon war raged. The pair of goddesses glanced to one another, something unspoken passing between them. In her grip, the spear thrummed.

The others cry out, the raspy, masculine voice of the spear whispered in her mind. *They weep, they weep.*

Colette shied away from the voice. She'd heard it many times now, calling upon her to be brave, to seek victory, rather than submission. A part of her hated it, if only for the guilt it made her feel about her own weakness.

Sidra's sharp gaze darted to the goddesses who, having finished their silent discussion, returned their attention to her. "What has happened?"

Viktoria lifted a hand to her tightly bound brown hair and smoothed it back. "A debt must be paid, for a sin not your own."

Cordis made a small sound behind her, as she rose to her feet and placed a hand on Sidra's left arm. "What does that mean?"

Macaria turned her gaze to Cordis and offered a small, sad, smile. "One of your sisters has–"

"She defied us. Tried to wage war upon us, upon the world," Viktoria cut in, speaking plainly.

Instinct took over. The danger she'd sensed now stood before her. Subtly urging Cordis behind her with her left hand, she shifted her grip on the spear. She couldn't throw it, couldn't use it on only one and then leave them both defenseless against the other. It would have to be fast though, she thought, mind racing.

Years of training and bone deep instinct sang in her blood as powerful as the magic gifted to her by Viktoria. Victory had not granted her anything showy like her sisters, but it had granted her unnatural luck and talent when it came to battle. She'd never lost. And she had no intention of doing so today.

Viktoria sighed, "You may have my gift, but I am victory, my most favored child. Lay down your arms and accept an honorable death; safe in the knowledge that you stood firm, and never betrayed what we gave you."

Sidra considered. Fighting the goddesses would certainly have collateral damage. Too close. The others were too close. She risked their lives, Cordis' life, if she fought. If they were here to claim her alone, then perhaps....

They lie, they lie, the raspy voice urged. *Ask them the real cost of the betrayal.*

"What else do you seek to claim?" Sidra whispered.

Viktoria frowned.

"My life alone?"

Viktoria glanced to Macaria, who simply nodded once.

"Your city. Your soldiers."

Colette sobbed. *No. I want to go home,* she shouted. *I don't understand. Why are you forcing me to see this? I've done everything you said. I'll be good, I swear!*

Something in Sidra's chest cracked. "No."

"It's already done," Macaria replied, regret lacing every word.

Sidra followed the goddess's outstretched hand with her eyes to the white puffs of smoke that floated out from her own shelter.

Only hers.

"No," Cordis' voice cracked as she ran for the nearest one.

Sidra knew, before her mate's cry of grief sang through the darkness, that they were all dead. Likely before she'd ever stepped out of their own shelter. Her heart ached for her mate, could feel her agony as if it were her own.

"Why take their lives? They were innocent!" she shouted. She had only ever offered Viktoria deference, as was proper, but this...this was unfathomable.

Viktoria lifted a slender hand. "A great many innocent lives have been lost to your sister's...mistake."

Cordis returned to Sidra's side, weeping. "They're all dead...all of them."

Sidra didn't respond as no words formed in her mind, only raw emotion. With a valiant roar, she launched herself at the goddess. Victory or not, she couldn't allow this, couldn't let it go unpunished.

Colette squeezed her eyes closed and screamed in terror as Sidra fell back against the snow. She hadn't seen what power had hit her, or if it had simply been Viktoria's own hand.

Sidra's grip on the spear fell slack. Something felt wrong, in her shoulder, her arm. She could no longer flex her fingers to hold it. Couldn't move either arm, she realized. Or her legs.

She turned her head, the only part of her she still had control over, in time to see Macaria drift toward a screaming Cordis.

No fear showed on her beautiful mate's face, only rage as she fought to get to Sidra's side, even as the death goddess took hold of her arms. As she whispered words Sidra couldn't hear over the rushing sound in her ears.

She could do nothing but watch as Cordis' rage turned to peace, a serene calm spreading over her face as she allowed herself to be carefully lain in the snow and took her last breath.

Sidra, beyond thought and any physical sensation, lay still, awaiting death.

Welcoming it, in her grief

Macaria, with Viktoria at her side, moved toward Sidra, both kneeling in the snow.

"It has been an honor to know you," Viktoria said sincerely. "I hope that in the next life, you are as valiant and honorable as this."

Macaria pushed back a strand of white blonde hair from Sidra's face. "Sleep now, and rest with her, until your time comes again."

As she lifted her veil, Colette squeezed her eyes tight. She knew what happened if you looked upon the face of death. And with her coward's heart...who knew what sort of monster she might see. Certainly not the face of kindness that Sidra likely saw.

"This cannot happen again," Viktoria said, something like pain in her voice.

"I know," Macaria sighed. "We will see to it that it doesn't get this far next time."

As the commander faded, their voices carried her on a phantom wind to her endless sleep.

Chapter 48

Naia

She awoke with a start. Cold sweat trickled down the back of her neck. Grief was the empty space between every heartbeat. She couldn't breathe through the emotions threatening to swallow her whole; emotions that were not her own.

Alerted by her sudden movement, Damian sat up beside her, lifting a hand to her cheek. "What's wrong?"

Naia shook her head. How could she possibly begin to explain what she'd seen? How could she tell him she'd watched him die....that the gods they had put trust in had killed him?

Had killed them all.

Even in the dim lantern light he'd be able to see her face, read the emotions there. She inhaled deeply, hiding her face with her hands. They had been so utterly betrayed. As were all the innocents who had been slain in this 'punishment' the gods had doled out. For some nameless crime committed by one of the others.

Lir hadn't even had the courtesy, or the balls, to tell the whole truth. Hadn't even so much as blinked as he slaughtered countless innocents. She had no way to know how many had been in the city that day, how many lives had simply been erased. Did they have families who would mourn them? Who would be left to wonder what had happened to them, why the city was left in little more than rubble.

Her thoughts turned back to something Cilla had said when Damian had taken her to Paradisus. Turning her gaze to Damian sharply, she asked, "Cilla said you were descendants of the Bearer from the temple?"

Damian's brow furrowed, and he nodded slowly. "Yes."

He didn't press for more, even though her sudden question clearly puzzled him. "Then she had children who weren't there." Lightning sizzled along her skin.

Again, he frowned, silently waiting for her to explain. Yet another thing to love about him, she thought, placing a hand on his thigh.

"I had a dream. More like a memory," she explained. "I saw her, the woman from the dream. Her name was Cordelia, and she was the *original* cauldron Bearer, Damian. But she was betrayed by–"

The words came out in a rush, as if a dam had burst the minute she'd opened her mouth to explain. When it came to voicing those final words however, the two that would no doubt call danger upon their head if any unseen ears happened to be listening, she snapped her mouth closed.

Damian spared a glance toward the feline shifter on guard, listening with her feline head cocked slightly to the side. "By?" he prompted.

"I can't say."

He frowned. "Okay," he said slowly, patiently. "Well, if Kore sent this dream, then you know it's likely a lie." Rubbing his beard thoughtfully, he added, "Or at least a half truth. She's got to be desperate now."

Naia shook her head. "No, Damian," she whispered. "It was true. Every moment of it. I felt it, I...it's like my soul knew it before I did. It's hard to explain. I *was* her. Seeing through her eyes, feeling what touched her skin, thinking her thoughts." Damian's eyes widened slightly, but she pressed on, seething inside at the betrayal, the utter waste of life. "I saw your past life. There was this instant knowledge that it was you, this tether in my chest pulling me toward you."

Damian's thumb slid against her cheek, rough but comforting. "I believe you," he said, voice low. His gaze shifted to Faline. "Don't utter a word of this outside this tent."

Before Faline could offer any response, Naia shook her head. "I need to talk to the others," she said, knowing he'd understand whom she meant. "I want to know if they saw the same thing."

"In the morning–" he began, only to be interrupted by a low growl from Faline, who had turned her attention to the tent flap.

Moments later, a large bear, followed by Eve and Lia dressed only in robes of green and pale blue respectively, stepped inside. All grim faced and silent. Eve's gaze met Naia's, and without words she knew what had happened, what they'd seen.

Truth or not, what Kore had shown her had rattled Naia to the bone. For someone who had prided herself on not being easily shaken, that fact alone added fuel to the fire raging inside her. Anger, as much as fear, had lightning dancing under her skin, ready to erupt at the very next sign of danger.

"Give us a moment," she said casting a glance at Damian, who nodded.

"I'll be close," he murmured, pressing a swift kiss to her lips.

It wasn't until Damian, followed by both shifters, had left them alone that Lia finally spoke, breaking the taut silence.

"You had one too," she said quietly, as both queens pulled chairs, ornate with carved roses along the backs, closer to Naia's bed. Such finery out of place within a war camp, along with the rather expensive looking rugs beneath their feet. Strange to have such luxury when the world was about to end.

"I saw the first to bear the cauldron," Naia replied, gaze flitting to the cauldron, resting on the dining table that matched the chairs. She kept her voice low, even though she knew the gods could hear even a whisper, if they chose to leave wherever they were hiding. If they chose to care about what was happening to their champions. "And you?"

"The first to bear the sword," Lia replied softly, blue eyes welling. "I watched, and felt, her die."

Both turned to Eve expectantly. The northern queen had gone still, face hard as stone. "The first to bear the stone," she said slowly, something like guilt flashing in her emerald eyes before she turned to stare at her hands, resting on her lap. "It was her fault, her doing. Mine."

Lia gasped, smoothing the loose strands of red hair that had come free from Eve's braid. "But it isn't...wasn't, you."

Naia shook her head. "No, it was." Two sets of eyes shot to Naia, who frowned. "What I mean is, it was us, once. Not that we bear responsibility for their choices." Swinging her legs, left bare by her short white nightgown, over the bed, she pressed her palms into the soft mattress on either side of her. "We were shown this for a reason."

"To be manipulated," Eve countered.

Lia made a small hum of agreement.

"Perhaps," Naia replied. "But it doesn't make it any less true, or any less useful. It needs to be addressed. But...after, agreed?"

The three shared a glance, silence a tight string lacing them together. One unit, to save or damn the world. In the dark of the night, an unspoken bond was formed, a promise made with little more than a look shared among them.

Chapter 49

Naia laid her palm flat against the table, steadying herself for the meeting about to begin. Her thoughts raced, trying to find the best way to explain what had occurred without explicitly stating anything that could very well get them all killed.

They were useful for now, tools to be wielded against the enemy. But the moment their usefulness ceased to exist, they would all die.

At the hands of those who called them champions.

She looked to each of the other six gathered around the central table in the command tent. Covered with maps and scouting reports, it had come to be a sort of symbol of their alliance. What would happen to that alliance when the war was done, she didn't know. Would the fae kingdoms retreat behind their walls once more? Would they make peace with their human neighbors, and build a more prosperous Aestera?

Or would yet another war break out as soon as this one ended?

Questions for another day, she reminded herself silently, not allowing the fear of the unknown to distract her.

"You all know we had similar dreams last night. Obviously a gift from Kore," she began, emphasizing the word with heavy sarcasm. "But there was...something...about it that is difficult to discuss openly."

"Why?" Callan asked, frowning.

It was Eve who spoke up then, explaining. "There are some," she said, gesturing vaguely toward the heavens. "Who might take offence."

"Oh," he said, tension easing from his shoulders. He and Bella looked to Damian expectantly. "That's easily solved."

Naia's attention shot to Damian as he nodded. She felt rather than saw his magic slowly ebb from him. A pulse, not quite like wind, but of power and unearthly cold.

"Done," he replied. At the confused glances of the newly turned fae queens, and Aelius, he went on, "Silence is my gift. Not just the ability to silence magic, but to literally silence a limited area around me. Unless they are paying close attention and see that I've shielded us, we'll be fine. And I'll know if it's been tampered with."

"That's useful," Lia murmured.

"And yet," Naia said, glancing toward the demi goddess at Lia's side. "We must be sure none of what is said here is repeated."

She'd heard about Bella's heritage, knew that the goddess of the moon and prophecy was her mother.

Does Bella's loyalty lie more with her lover or her mother? Naia wondered.

Lia tensed, placing a hand on Bella's lower back. "She will not say a word," she said. Though her voice remained pleasant, light as a warm summer breeze, her sky blue eyes had darkened.

Bella inclined her head. "It's likely that my mother has already seen what path we are to take anyway," she said carefully. "But I will not betray Lia. Ever."

Naia turned to Eve, who nodded once. Acceptance of Bella's assurances.

Callan turned a cold gaze on Damian. "And are we sure of his loyalty?"

Lightning flashed in Naia's veins. "Absolutely." Her tone left no room for argument, and when Damian opened his mouth to speak, she added, "He is mine, as I am his. There is no doubt where his loyalties lie."

Aelius snorted but said nothing, earning a sharp look from his twin. For a moment Callan looked as though he might reply, but a soft touch on his arm by Eve silenced whatever remark he'd been about to make.

"Now, if that's settled," Naia said, releasing a slow breath. "Here is what happened."

Naia and then Lia shared the events they'd watched unfold in their nightmares. The massacres they'd witnessed, the ultimately futile fights their past selves had put up. Even Helie's tearful reaction to her own actions. With every word spoken, the others' expressions grew more grave.

When at last it was Eve's time to speak, six pairs of eyes remained locked on her.

"I'm sorry," she said, voice low. "I–" Guilt written on her features, she shook her head. "I would never..."

"No," Naia said fiercely, leaning forward. "None of this is your fault. None of this...this history truly belongs to any of us. We may share some fragment of ourselves with these past women, but their actions, their lives, are not ours. And I for one will not meet the same fate."

Everyone nodded in agreement, save for Damian.

"While I agree," he said, tensing beside her, "simply declaring it isn't enough. We need a plan."

"Obviously," Callan replied flatly.

Naia sighed. The infighting would need to be squashed or it would tear them apart before it even came to that. "If you two would like to pull out your cocks and measure whose is largest, I certainly wouldn't object, but perhaps it can wait until we've finished saving the world, yes?"

Both men wisely kept their mouths shut.

Thoughts and ideas flowed, suggestions being offered by everyone present. While they each agreed that it would need to be faced soon after Kore, assuming they were successful, none could agree on how.

"We'll need the spear," Bella said quietly, after a while.

"Yes," Damian agreed. "But even I don't know where she keeps it."

Bella hummed thoughtfully. "Do you know who her Bearer is?"

He shook his head. "Far above my pay grade," he explained. "Only those closest to her were allowed anywhere near it. All I know is that she does have it, and whoever is wielding it remains close to her at all times."

Callan folded his arms across his broad chest. "Can we kill her without it?"

Silence fell over the tent. How did one kill an ancient monster, the very void itself? The gods certainly hadn't been forthcoming about that information.

"What if we can claim the Bearer, distract her with our gifts, while someone grabs them?"

"And face off against the person wielding a spear that can kill anyone?" Aelius snorted.

Seven sets of eyes exchanged wary glances.

"If it comes to it," Damian said. "I'll do it."

Naia spun to face him. "No."

Damian tilted his head, eyes meeting hers. "Someone will have to make that sacrifice, take the risk," he said gently. "Would you ask one of them to do it?" He gestured to the others gathered. "Or another of our allies? Besides, I know their ways, their ranks and powers, better than anyone else. If anyone has a hope of getting close enough, it'll be me."

"I doubt you'll get close enough on your own," Callan said calmly. Not an insult, simply a matter of fact. "I'll go with you."

Eve's sound of surprise and protest was mirrored by Naia's. "There has to be another way," Eve said.

Aelius, shifting from one foot to the other beside Lia, sighed. "Ah damn, count me in too."

"We're being hasty," Lia said, waving her hands. "Let's just keep the suicidal plans on hold for now. We need to figure out where she is, where and when this battle will come."

"And," Naia added, nodding in agreement. "How to wield our powers together. It's the only chance we have at surviving long enough for that to even be an option. What we did before was a start, but I doubt one blast like that will be enough to win the day."

Eve turned to Damian. "Will she be able to sense it if we use our gifts?"

He considered it a moment. "Possibly, but I cannot be sure."

"Can you create a shield like this one for us, large enough for us to have space to work, without injuring you?"

"I should be able to," he replied. "I'm willing to try anyway."

"This should be interesting," Aelius muttered, earning an elbow in the ribs from his twin. With a grunt, he said, "I'm just saying. You might kill him, or yourselves, if you're not careful."

"We'll be fine," Lia declared, chin up.

Naia wasn't quite so optimistic, but she kept the thought from showing on her face. It was a start, at least. Hone their gifts with whatever time they had left, and face Kore. Hopefully whoever served her could be swayed to their side, or at least be forced to help them....somehow. Another bridge to cross, another battle to win. As her gaze drifted around the room, to each of the others who had fallen into conversations with one another, she exhaled slowly.

Unlike their past selves, they were prepared for what the gods would likely do. Unlike the past, they stood together and remained focused on the larger, more pressing threat. Kore, no doubt, had intended for the opposite. Had sought to sow division among them, with the truth she revealed, to turn their attention to the gods.

Her attention landed on Eve, speaking quietly to Callan in hushed whispers that had her friend blushing slightly. If she'd wanted, Naia could have heard every word thanks to her newfound fae hearing, but she actively blocked it. From Damian's wry expression though, he had not. With a reproachful look for her love, she rolled her eyes.

If Kore had expected them to blame Eve for the sins of her prior life, she had sorely underestimated them, and their bond. Where an invisible string tied her to Damian, a pull in her chest that made them feel as two halves of a whole, the bond with Lia and Eve had begun to feel almost like sisters, but not in the way she felt for Maren. It was love, deep and abiding for Maren, but for Lia and Eve, it was simply a feeling of rightness.

When their hands had joined, it was like puzzle pieces clicking into place. And, she'd begun to realize, a piece was missing. She wondered if the others felt the same, if they'd noticed that their gifts, while far more powerful together, still yet felt incomplete. Only with the fourth would they feel whole.

If they could find them, and if they joined their cause.

"Where have you gone?" Damian asked quietly, stubble scratching her cheek as he leaned down to whisper to her.

"I'm thinking about the other," she replied, gaze sliding to Eve then

Lia, who each looked to her in return, briefly. "What it would do for our powers, if we can find them, get them to join us."

"I think," he replied, straightening and gently nudging her face to meet his with a light touch of his fingers along her jaw, "that the four of you would be utterly unstoppable. And they should all be terrified of you."

Something surged within her. Pride, or power, or perhaps rage. Some combination of emotions that she didn't dare look too closely at. They would be unstoppable; they could conquer the heavens themselves. The knowledge was bone deep, undeniable. But, unlike their past, they had learned the consequences of such hubris. They would rattle the heavens, but as saviors, not conquerors.

Her rage would echo across the world, and when their task was done, she would calm the raging tempest in her heart. Live a life with him on her terms, free of the shackles of fate.

CHAPTER 50

Salt air whipped Naia's hair loose from her braid. The familiar scent of the sea greeted her like a friend as she stood atop the dune, gazing out at the rolling waves. Beside her, the women she had once called sisters did much the same, contemplating their own lives, their own reasons for standing against the darkness that haunted their steps.

The shifter scouts had reported activity in this area, with entire nomadic camps simply vanishing. Their movements had followed a pattern, one set centuries ago by the earliest humans to venture into the sands of Coruscis. From oasis, to sea, to city, they traveled, never straying very far from their well-worn, well-marked, paths. But one by one, at least four had simply vanished from their route.

"What do you think she's done with them?" Naia asked no one in particular.

Eve frowned, never taking her eyes off the sea. "Nothing good."

"They could still be alive," Lia offered, ever hopeful. "Taken captive, maybe in an attempt to force your hand. She must know what our people mean to us." Leaning forward to glance at Eve, she gestured in her direction. "She took your city in an attempt to gain control over you."

"And a lot of people died," Eve reminded her gently. Her gaze shifted to Naia, who couldn't bear to meet the gaze of the one woman who perhaps knew what she felt right now. The guilt, the loss. "It's not your fault. We tried to watch over them, we sent warnings. The shifters are spread thin we–"

"I know," Naia snapped. The anger wasn't directed at Eve or even Kore, but at herself. "I know," she went on, softening her tone. "But it was my responsibility to see them safe. I should have sent my own soldiers to evacuate them to Thalassa."

"We tried that," Lia reminded her. "They refused."

And they had, she knew. Days after their discussion about the memories forced upon them, when the first reports of strangers showing up in the nearby villages; strangers with oddly pointed ears and bows of ash upon their backs, they had sent word to the various camps in the area, urging them to seek safety behind the city walls.

The villages had also been warned. A few had chosen to stay, but some had wisely moved to Thalassa or one of the other well-fortified larger towns. Some had even taken ships to the south, fleeing the oncoming storm.

It had been difficult to find the right words to explain to humans who had only ever heard legends of gods and fae that they were, in fact, real and very much returned to the world.

That a demon of the void itself now set her gaze upon them.

Even Naia had thought it madness at first.

Lia watched, awaiting a response, but she had no words to offer. The reminder that it had been their decision to remain, to refuse to abandon their homes, their lives, did little to assuage the guilt ravaging her. Had she known what was coming, she would have ordered her soldiers to force them to evacuate.

A gentle breeze brushed against her cheek, a whisper of sea air to cool the heat of her anger. No, she wouldn't have. As desperate and angry as she was, she would never take the choice from them. Even if it meant their doom.

"I heard Maren is coming," Lia said suddenly, the words ever so slightly forced, as if she was desperate for a change in topics.

Naia's head whipped to Lia. She hadn't heard anything about

Maren leaving Thalassa. As far as she'd known, her sister was to remain there, safer, she hoped, than in the war camp. Fae warriors had been sent to the city to help ensure their defenses and to send word to Naia if anything seemed amiss.

"That's not possible," Naia replied sharply.

"Aelius received word this morning, she's already on her way..." Lia trailed off, frowning.

"Maren isn't coming here. My sister is not putting herself in danger."

Eve inhaled slowly behind her, as if steeling herself. "We're all in danger already, Naia."

Naia disregarded her entirely, despite the truthfulness of her words.

"She wants to help," Lia said gently. "Aelius isn't happy about it either. He tried to send a message back, but the messenger said she left shortly after he did and will likely arrive before noon. She sounded rather determined, from what he said."

"Then I will tie her to a gods damned horse and send her back under armed guard," Naia snarled.

Lia's brow rose, but she remained silent.

"You would bind her the way you were? Take her choice away?" Eve asked quietly.

Finally Naia turned to face her. Thunder crashed in the cloudless sky. "That's not the same thing. This is for her safety."

Eve nodded. "Of course, but the loss of your right to make your own choices is still a loss, regardless of the circumstances."

Naia weighed the words carefully. Eve knew more than most what it felt like to lose your autonomy, to have the direction your life would take decided by others. And she had rebelled against it for the good of her people, and herself. The very thing Naia would have done—had done, in fact, in a similar position.

Though her own captivity had led to something good in the end, had led her to her destiny, the path to get there had been anything but gentle. "Fine," she replied through gritted teeth.

"Then we should probably go back, so that we can greet her," Lia suggested.

Naia waved them off. "Go ahead, I need a moment longer."

They hesitated, neither moving so much as a step. An agreement had been made to never be alone. "Damian is just over there," Naia added, gesturing toward the shoreline with a lift of her chin, where he was wading out into the surf. "I'll be fine."

Reluctantly, both women returned to camp, leaving Naia alone with the heavy burden of her thoughts. Dragging her gaze from Damian to the horizon beyond, she let her thoughts turn to her father, to the day he'd died.

An experienced sailor on a calm day should have been fine, but the sea was fickle, and even a man who had spent his entire life learning her ways would never know all of her secrets. Alone, he'd had no help, and there had been no witnesses to explain where he had gone or how he'd vanished from the intact vessel.

A wave of grief washed over her. Guilt for not asking to go with him that day, as she often did, thanks to her mother insisting on her attending to her lessons instead.

Would things have been different then? Or would they both have died? At least he wouldn't have been alone if she had.

Rubbing her eyes with the heel of her hands, she shook off the thought. Another salt-kissed breeze caressed her cheek, soothing the frayed edges of her nerves. As she lowered her hands, a dark spot amongst the waves caught her attention, triggering a memory she'd nearly forgotten in the recent chaos.

Shock had her rushing down the dune toward the shore. It wasn't until the surf was crashing against her knees, tangling the ends of her loose dress around her that she stopped.

"It was you." She breathed, knowing he would hear her even above the lapping waves and crying gulls overhead.

Damian, chest deep in the water watched her carefully for a moment. "What was me?"

She hazarded another few steps closer, up to her thighs now as she fought to steady herself in the shifting sands and waves. "The day on the beach," she explained, "with Zayan."

Damian's gaze darkened as he swam closer, just within arms reach. "I saw him touch you, saw the way you reacted. I didn't like it."

Her heart thundered. "You hated me then."

He shook his head, dragging a hand over his beard. "No, I never hated you. I didn't feel...anything then. Not for a long time. Not before you changed things, changed me."

"But you didn't like it?"

"No," he replied, voice low. "Even if I didn't know why, it made me angry. Nearly as much as with Lukus...when he touched you."

The thundering of her own heart was echoed in his, the sound a reminder of their bond. "You were watching me, planning how to take me."

"Yes."

Naia fell silent then. Words lost to her. There was no denying the pain and fear he'd caused her, but in the end, she'd found her freedom, and love for him. She couldn't be grateful for what he'd done, but she could recognize something good had come at the end, and that, perhaps, destiny took a dark and winding path.

"Was that the only time you watched me?"

"No," he breathed, letting the next wave push him closer. So close that their bodies nearly collided.

"What else did you see?"

The corner of his lips turned upward as his gaze shifted to hers. "I watched you stand on your balcony under the moonlight, watching the sea. I watched you swim with your sister. Argue with your mother." His eyes met hers again. "I saw him fucking you once."

"And you didn't like that very much," she guessed, breath hitching.

"No," he replied darkly, lifting a hand to the strap of her now sodden dress and fingering the material lightly. "I did not."

Her body heated, and she pressed her thighs together tightly, making her unsteady in the sand. A wave pushed her back, but his hands found her waist, steadying her. They were so exposed here, with nothing but sand and sea around them. Anyone could step over the dunes and see them. But still she said, "And you wished it was you?"

With a wordless growl, he pulled her against him, cupping her thighs as she wrapped her legs around his waist. To her delight, she found only water, and the thin material of her dress between them.

His mouth claimed hers in a bruising kiss, tongue sweeping past her parted lips. There was no tenderness, no gentle reminder of the love between them, only a fierce reminder of who and what they were to one another, bordering on ownership.

Naia's blood was fire in her veins, her need for him, for his touch on her skin, the only thing that existed. The crashing sea, the breeze that danced over her skin, the gulls, and even the nearby fae, just over the dunes, were all forgotten. Her very world, in that moment, began and ended with him. Dragging her soaked dress upward, he cupped her ass with his hands as she ground her hips against his hardened length.

"I need–" she whispered against his lips.

"I know."

Shifting himself slightly in the rolling waves, he lifted her hips briefly, before pulling her close again, sliding inside of her slowly; the water adding a new sensation that bordered on painful, but only just.

A low moan slipped past her lips, quickly silenced with a press of his.

"Quiet, Thunderheart, unless you want the guards to come over that dune and watch me fuck you."

"I may," she breathed, with a gasp as she lifted her hips and lowered them again, savoring the sensation of him filling her, "have just discovered how much I like being watched."

He growled quietly, the sound reverberating through her chest. Dragging the strap of her dress down to free her breast, he dragged a callused thumb over the peak. "You want them to see how pretty you look riding my cock?"

She moved her hips again, doing just that, with only the gulls as their audience. His hum of approval had her laughing as she wrapped her arms around his neck, sliding her teeth against the space between his collar and jaw, nipping lightly.

"Fuck," he gasped, gripping her hips.

She could feel the tension in him, the tightening of his arms beneath her hands, now sliding down his biceps as she rocked backward slightly. Her own body was as tightly wound as a coil, fire burning low in her belly.

A sudden wave propelled them closer to shore, only a step or two. Her sounds of pleasure sounded above the calls of the gulls, no doubt heard by the fae ears nearby. If anyone stepped over the dune, they would see the very picture he'd painted. Her grinding against his cock wantonly, with little more than her all but transparent dress covering her ass.

"Come undone for me, Thunderheart," he ground out gripping the back of her head and holding her close, as she moved, faster, harder.

His words were her breaking point, and the dam broke. Her inner walls pulsed around him, dragging him over the brink with her. Chest to chest, breaths heaving, they stood for a moment longer. In stark contrast to before, he kissed her slowly, gently, before lowering her to stand on her wobbly legs.

"I think," he said, slipping the top of her dress back up. "That if any man saw you like this, I might have to rip their eyes from their head."

Chapter 51

Maren had arrived by the time they returned to camp. The shirt Damian had left on shore was blessedly long enough to at least cover the curve of her ass; but only barely, she judged, from the occasional growl of warning he shot at passing soldiers.

She found her sister in Aelius' tent, to her irritation, as she had apparently made her way directly to him on her arrival. Stepping inside, she was greeted by a raise of Maren's brow and a wide-eyed Aelius, who wisely looked away.

"Why are you here?" she demanded without preamble.

Maren pinned her with a flat stare. "The same reason you are. Hello to you too, by the way."

Naia shook her head. "You can't stay. It's not safe."

"Already tried that," Aelius replied with a long suffering sigh.

Maren snorted. "And you should both know by now that I don't like being told what to do."

Damian murmured something under his breath about it running in the family, earning a light elbowing from Naia.

"Okay," Naia countered. "If you won't go back for me, then do it for Coruscis. I'm not there, so who will–"

"You forget," Maren interrupted. "That Mother was Queen long before you. She is perfectly capable of–"

Naia seethed. "Absolutely not, Maren, she hasn't been the same since Papa."

Maren folded her arms across her chest. "And you'll never let her forget that, or the fact that she's the reason you didn't go with him."

Something in Naia's chest ached at her sister's words; the well-aimed shot hitting its mark. "That's not fair."

Her sister's gaze softened as she closed the distance between them, wrapping her arms around Naia tightly. "I love you and I know you're worried." Stepping back, she added, "But you have to forgive her, and yourself. Damla Colvari is fierce, whether you choose to recognize that or not. His death wounded her, but it did not break her. Or you."

There was no argument to be made against that. Despite her issues with her mother, even Naia had to admit Maren was right. Damla had once been a force to be reckoned with. A powerhouse of a woman who ruled fairly and firmly. She would never allow Thalassa to fall, not without a hell of a fight at least, and she would give her last breath for her people.

"Fine," she conceded, "but you stay off of the front lines." Her gaze cut to Aelius. "You make sure she isn't in the thick of it," she ordered him. "She can wield a blade as well as most of our soldiers, better than some, but she isn't experienced and against a fae–"

Aelius moved to Maren's side, taking her hand in his. "I won't let anything happen to her."

Maren rolled her eyes, even as she grinned. "If you two mother hens are finished, I think Naia needs to go put some clothes on." Her pointed glance shifted between Naia and Damian. "We can talk more later. Aelius and I have things to discuss anyway."

With another brief hug between sisters, Damian and Naia set out for their tent.

"I didn't know that was possible," he remarked.

Her gaze drifted over the soldiers milling about as they saw to the various tasks their commanders had given them. Most kept their gazes averted, though a few hazarded open stares at her barely covered form. Even fewer leveled frowns at Damian, hatred in their eyes.

"What?" she asked, frowning.

"To win an argument against you."

"Ha, ha," she replied, waving a hand in his direction. "I'm not that stubborn."

He snorted. "Says the woman who tried to kill herself rather than remain a captive. The woman who paced, for the first time and with no training, to save me. The woman, who fought a god to bring me back to her." By the time he'd finished, they'd slowed to a stop in the middle of the encampment, facing one another.

Chin lifted, she met his gaze evenly. "What you call stubborn, I call determined. I don't like losing what is mine. My freedom. You."

Gripping her chin between his thumb and forefinger, he dipped his head low, pressing a swift kiss to her lips. "And I love you for it."

Halfheartedly swatting his hand away, she poked his bare chest. "Don't go getting soft on me now, big bad beastie." Glancing past him, she raised a brow at the small group of soldiers trying very hard not to get caught staring. She was acutely aware of the way Damian's tunic had ridden up her thighs, showing far more than she would have liked to half the soldiers in this camp.

He grunted in response, following her gaze and leveling an icy glare at the men. Each of them promptly turned away, suddenly very interested in the blades they'd been sharpening.

The rest of the short walk back to their tent was spent in comfortable silence. Naia had never felt the need to fill the silence with chatter, and had never really had the ability to pluck something interesting to talk about from thin air, as Maren had. A blessing then, that Damian was more comfortable, it seemed, in silence than in idle conversation.

Inside the privacy of their makeshift home, he fell into a chair to watch her as she dressed, not bothering to conceal the heat in his gaze. "If we were alone, I'd ask you to walk around naked all the time."

Naia smirked, glancing over her shoulder as she turned away to toss the tunic into a basket for the camp laundress. "You'd never get anything done," she remarked.

He snorted. "I'd get plenty done," he promised with a hungry gleam in his eye. "You, Thunderheart, would find running your kingdom rather difficult though, I think. If I spent the days with you in bed, or against the wall, or bent over your desk..." He trailed off then, leaving the statement unfinished, the unspoken question lingering in the air between them.

The breath whooshed out of her. She hadn't taken the time to consider it, what the future would hold now that she was fae. And had chosen him. The man who had been, and likely still was, viewed as a traitor, a monster, by everyone else.

Could her people ever accept a fae queen? A queen whose all but immortal life could mean unending power in her grasp.

No.

Peaceful transition from parent to worthy child was a cornerstone of their kingdom. Had been since its founding. Damla had stepped aside when Naia had reached an age and maturity that made her capable, remaining to guide her daughter if necessary, but relinquishing any right to rule. As had her mother before her, and so on.

She dressed in silence, sitting on the edge of their bed to look him over as she considered how to respond. His dark eyes, pensive, patient, rested on her. He wouldn't push for a response much less a promise, she knew. Would likely stay by her side until she tired of him.

"I don't expect you to give up your kingdom for me," he said quietly, leaning forward to rest his arms on his thighs, staring down at his upturned palms. "I don't deserve what you've already given, and I've no right to ask for more."

Of course he'd feel that way, after all that had happened. But hadn't she shown him forgiveness with her actions? She'd fought the very gods to return him to her, and he still felt as if she would abandon him. Anger, alongside hurt, lashed her.

"Shut up."

He jerked his head up, surprise etched in his rugged features as she rose from the bed and crossed the carpeted floor to him. Sinking to her knees between his, she pushed his hands to the side, taking his face in her hands.

"Naia–"

"No." Her tone was low, firm. If what she'd given him hadn't made it clear enough that she forgave him, saw him as worthy of her body, her love, then she'd speak it in a language he would understand. "I will never abandon you."

Cilla and Zale's faces flashed in her mind. Banishing a mere boy from his home, for no other crime than simply existing. Anger surged in her and lightning flashed in her eyes. "I will never leave you. You are worthy of love."

His eyes widened, and he took a slow, ragged breath.

Pressing a kiss to his lips, she whispered, "You are mine, Damian. I choose you. You are what I want, and if you ever think otherwise, I'll kick your ass for it."

"Okay," he replied slowly, quietly, as if afraid to break the spell that had fallen over them.

She raised a brow, in silent confirmation, and he nodded.

"Good." Rocking back on her heels, she sighed. "We'll figure out the rest as we go, okay?"

Damian nodded, leaning back in his seat. The corner of his mouth tipped upward slightly, the ghost of a smile gracing his features. "You're so bossy."

Naia swatted his knee before standing. "Get used to it, I'm a queen."

He grinned fully in response, but said nothing. The love and appreciation for her words shining brightly enough in his eyes to speak for him. Something had once again shifted between them, a sort of tenderness that hadn't existed amongst all the fire and passion before, and a gentleness in him that she hadn't seen before.

A gentleness that she expected had been suffocated the day he'd left Paradisus. Her gaze flitted to the tent flaps, as if she could see beyond them, beyond the many rows of tents to the one belonging to Cilla and Zale. Thunder rumbled in her mind, her heart, but she willed it to calm, to hide the signs of her ire from him. Those wounds were old and barely healed, even after all these years. Her anger at them would only rip them open once more.

For the boy he'd once been, she promised silently, she would heal those broken pieces, help him find the balance between who he'd been and who he had been forced to become.

Chapter 52

"Is it supposed to get this cold?" Eve muttered.

Naia laughed, glancing toward the northern queen with a grin. "Aren't you used to the cold? As I understand it, you spend most of your days shaded by those giant trees of yours."

Eve shrugged. "Yes, but I expected a beach to be warm."

"It is winter," Lia chimed in lightly.

Naia's gaze shifted beyond them to the roiling sea and the dark clouds on the horizon. "We shouldn't stay out here too long, a storm is coming."

Footsteps on the sand drew her attention, and she turned to find the rather delicious warrior from Eve's group approaching. Valerian, she remembered. Married to the pretty shifter named Leysa. Though they'd been introduced and had spoken a few times, she hadn't really taken the time to get to know any of the other fae Eve had brought with her.

Callan and Damian's tension certainly hadn't made visiting with the northerners very easy, and there hadn't really been much reason to do so. Not until Eve had suggested he teach them to pace.

"In case we have to run," she'd explained, the night before. "If we're separated from those who can, we should be able to do it on our own."

Naia had, twice before, and she'd pointed it out, only for it to be dismissed as luck. A remark she was still rather irritated over.

"Where do we begin?" she asked, barely giving him time to come to a stop in front of the three queens.

He blinked, but took her abruptness in his stride, crossing his well-muscled arms across his leather clad chest. "You've done it before?" he asked. At her nod, he went on. "Do it again."

Sniffing and lifting her chin, she closed her eyes, picturing herself behind him, and willed herself to be there. A phantom wind lifted her long dark hair, sending it dancing behind her and then...nothing.

A light cough from beside her had her turning a sharp glare at Eve.

"I can't," she admitted, the words bitter on her tongue.

Valerian nodded patiently. "That's okay. Sometimes our emotions make these things easier for us, or, in some cases, harder. It'll take some time to learn to control you gifts, all of them."

"Do we have time?" Lia asked, frowning.

He shrugged in response. "We'll do what we can with whatever time we have. Even a little bit of training is better than none. Now, lets go over the basics."

The basics, it seemed, were far more complicated than he had let on. He spoke about the shadows between the spaces in the world, and how with this gift you could learn to slip between them. Why only some had been blessed with the ability, only the gods knew.

Some could move barely far enough to get from one end of their house to another, and very few could move from one continent to another. He had never known any who possessed that level of skill, but Callan had once met someone who claimed to be able to do it.

An hour passed, then two, and still none of them had been able to manage it. With the storm growing ever closer, Naia grew edgy. Something nagged at the back of her mind, a tension she didn't understand growing with every passing moment.

It's only the stress of it, she told herself as she watched Eve take a step toward Valerian.

Red curls rose around her as that phantom wind that made up the dark places between the fabrics of their world swallowed her. Lia yelped as Eve vanished, only to appear a few yards away, looking a bit green, but triumphant. Practically bouncing with anticipation, Lia did the same. It took her perhaps a few seconds longer, but soon she followed Eve's lead, stumbling into the sand beside the queen of Darkegrove.

Finally, it was her turn to prove she could do it, that it hadn't been mere luck and emotion that had driven her to drag Lia and Damian both across the desert. Drawing on the well of power she'd found before, Naia exhaled, and stepped into the ether. Sand scraped her palms as she fell face first into the sandy beach and rolled to her side, grinning.

She'd done it, she'd—

Landed far, far, beyond them.

"Well," Valerian said, as he arrived beside her. "What you lacked in finesse, you made up for in sheer power," he grinned. "Well done."

Naia opened her mouth to retort, only to snap it closed as a wave of nausea swept over her. An unseen vice gripped her head, and she cried out, falling to her side in the sand. A man was shouting for help, as she screamed again, her screams echoed by Lia and Eve.

Thunder crashed and rain began to pour. A bright flash of light erupted from somewhere near Eve and Lia. Another clap of thunder, so loud and powerful that it rattled the very ground. The storm she'd been so wary of had arrived, and in force. A sudden and raging tempest that shouldn't have been there so quickly.

She couldn't think, couldn't speak. Lifting her head was an effort, but she managed to look up enough to see Damian pace onto the beach and sprint for her, followed soon after by Callan, with Bella and Aelius along with him.

Had she been able to think to feel anything beyond the pain in her head and the roiling in her gut, she might have wondered at the bear charging toward Lia.

Rough hands pulled her from the beach, and male voices shouted orders as the pressure slowly began to ebb. And when the darkness and wind overtook her, she let herself fall into a dreamless sleep.

"Aurelia and Eveline have awoken," a soft female

voice whispered above the crackling of a fire. A voice she'd never heard before. "Just a few moments ago."

It was Damian's voice she heard next. "Good," he replied, as if he'd hardly heard the woman she couldn't see.

The woman inhaled as if to speak, but paused, the silence heavy.

"Just say it," he snarled.

"If they aren't in control...we're all in danger."

The sound of wood crashing against wood erupted, and someone raced past the bed where Naia lay. She opened her eyes in time to see Damian standing toe to toe with a tall, blonde woman. Unmistakably a warrior in her own right, with toned muscled arms and a large sword strapped to her back.

She met his gaze calmly, evenly, without even an ounce of fear. Impressive, given the unearthly chill that emanated from Damian. "Don't even think about it."

The warrior held up her hands in surrender. "I'm only saying we should be prepared, and," she explained. "That we should find out what happened to them. Don't forget that Aurelia is my friend, Damian. I care about what happens to them too. Beyond the fact that they're the only hope we have of surviving this thing."

Seconds ticked by before Damian spoke again. "What did–"

"Damian," Naia croaked out, rising to her elbows. "Give the woman some space, will you?"

In the blink of an eye, he was on the bed beside her, hands roaming over her face, her shoulders, and down her arms. Checking for injuries, she realized. "You're okay," he whispered, more to himself than to her.

"I'm okay," she assured him, before shifting her attention to the woman. "Who are you and what happened?"

The woman placed a hand over her heart. "I'm Tori. I'm a friend of Aurelia's, and I guess sort of your sister's now." Waving the errant remark off, she continued. "Truthfully, we were hoping you three could tell us. You were practicing with Valerian, and he said that all of a sudden you were all screaming. Then–"

"Your powers erupted," Damian cut in. "All three of you."

A shudder ran through her. It hadn't been a storm, it had been her. Her powers. "Did I hurt anyone?"

Damian hesitated before shaking his head. "A stone hit the bear shifter, the one that watches over Lia, but the injury is minor. Valerian narrowly missed being struck by one of your bolts but he is fine, and... Aelius was burned badly, when he tried to grab his sister."

Naia winced. Lia would be devastated by that, as would Maren. "I need to see them," she said, moving to slide off the bed.

A hand on her arm stopped her. "I won't try to make you wait, but you should take care of yourself first. Whatever happened...it took a lot out of you. You've been sleeping a while."

"How long?"

"A day and a half."

Naia blinked. Her gaze shifted between the two of them. "Nobody has any idea what happened?"

"There are theories," Tori began, glancing at Damian. "But the only ones who can be sure are the three of you."

She shook her head. "I have no idea. It was like...my head was going to be crushed, and I thought I would vomit." She paused, wrinkling her nose. "I didn't, did I?"

"No," Damian replied, shaking his head with a light breath that might've been laughter.

"Good." Rising to her feet unsteadily, she found herself once again dressed only in one of Damian's tunics.

At her raised brow, he shrugged. "It suits you. If you'd been awake, I would've preferred you naked."

Tori gagged quietly.

Disregarding the warrior, Naia snatched a pair of loose pants from the wardrobe and dragged them on. "Take me to see my sister first," she demanded. "Then the others."

"I don't think–" Tori began, only to be silenced by a look from Naia.

"You will take me to see my sister."

With no room left for argument, Tori simply inclined her head and held out an arm to do as she'd been asked.

CHAPTER 53

As Naia burst into Aelius and Maren's tent, she made a mental note to thank Tori for silently pacing her there, saving Naia the precious few minutes it would have taken to walk. Lia had already arrived and had taken up a position in a chair by his bed. Behind Lia, her dark-haired mate stood still, her own attention resting solely on Lia. An older fae woman with soft brown hair and watchful grey eyes that remained fixed on Aelius, stood at the head of the bed.

Soft light, reminiscent of a summer dawn, emanated from Lia's hands as they hovered over her twin's still form. Surprised and impressed, she let her gaze linger for a moment longer before she turned her attention to the real reason she'd come: Maren, sitting on the floor by Lia's side on a small blue cushion no doubt pulled from the settee nearby. Her hand covered his, one of the few parts of his mostly uncovered form that remained unburned.

Naia's gaze slid from Maren to Aelius' badly burned torso and arm. Though her back was turned to her, Naia could see that her sister wept. Her shoulders shook softly, curved inward as she lay her head against the edge of the bed. Quiet prayers uttered in the near silence of the tent.

"Maren," she breathed, moving to her sister's side in a few quick steps before sinking onto the floor beside her.

Her sister's tear-stained face turned to hers. Maren's soft brown eyes were so bloodshot that Naia wondered if she'd stopped crying at any point in the last day. "He's going to be okay," Maren said hoarsely.

"I know," Naia assured her, sparing a brief glance at Lia, who nodded once without turning her own tear-filled eyes to her. She wouldn't ask if Maren was okay, the question ridiculous given the circumstances.

In silence, she smoothed Maren's hair, comforting her in the way she had done when they were children. When the son of a noble had shoved her in the sand, calling her a bastard and insinuating she and Naia didn't share a father. A baseless rumor that had circulated through the court during a time when Damla's power was being challenged by some of the nobility.

Maren had picked herself up, dusted the sand from her knees, and met the boy nose to nose. He'd nearly wet himself when she whispered, with utter calm despite the tears spilling down his face, "Touch me again, and you'll find an adder in your bed."

When they made it back to Maren's room, after a thorough scolding from both their governess and their mother, Maren finally broke down in tears. Naia had spent hours consoling her, reminding her that the boy's words weren't true, and even if they had been, it didn't change who she was.

Over the years Maren had honed the skill of fighting, not only with a blade but with her words. She'd learned to show others that being soft did not equate to being weak, and had gone toe to toe with some of the most difficult ambassadors known to their kingdom.

Naia knew Maren had the strength to come through this, to shoulder the pain of seeing the man she loved in such agony. To help fight this war. To rule the kingdom they both loved, when the time came.

She could sense Damian behind her, taking a place away from the others, positioning himself like the outsider he felt he was. No more, she thought, turning to look at him. He was hers, and that meant he was as much a part of this as she was, and she would never allow him to feel otherwise again.

His brow rose as she tilted her head in silent question, before stepping closer. Doubt danced in his dark eyes as he cast a glance at Lia, and then Maren. Lia gave no indication that she recognized his approach, and in truth she might not have. Her hands still moved, hovering above her brother's blistered skin, now turning a bright pink as the wounds seemed to simply fade away beneath the gentle light of Lia's magic.

Maren, however, turned to meet his eyes as his attention shifted to her. "This is a time for family," she said quietly. Her voice was level, despite the tears still welling in her eyes.

Naia tensed, hand stilling on Maren's hair. "Maren-" she hissed. She hated to argue with her sister in this moment, but she wouldn't allow him to be shut out.

Her sister ignored her entirely, as she inclined her head slightly. "You should be here with her," she continued. "You're her family now too."

Something in Naia's heart gave a lurch. Maren's acceptance of their relationship was more than she could have hoped for, given their beginning, and it made it all seem a little more real.

He didn't smile, didn't speak, only offering Maren a dip of his head in appreciation before settling onto the rug behind Naia.

"Maren," she said again, this time softly, voice thick with emotion.

Maren offered her a small smile, leaning to rest her head on Naia's shoulder. "If you're happy, then so am I."

Minutes passed in silence as Lia continued. Finally, with a heavy sigh, she sat back in her chair. The flesh of his torso and arm, once blistered and red from the burns, was now bright pink. Scarred and still healing, but whole.

Maren jumped to her feet, and Naia leaned back to let her pass, falling into Damian's broad chest. His arm came around her to steady her before he rose to his feet, holding a hand out for Naia. Hand in his, she stood, eyes locked on her sister as she lay across Aelius' chest gently.

The prince of Avellon took a long, shuddering breath. "Maren," he whispered, wrapping his arm around her. Her shoulders shook, with tears or laughter, Naia couldn't tell, but she was grateful nonetheless.

Aelius turned, his confused gaze sweeping over Naia and Damian before landing on his sister, who let out a choked sob. With one arm still wrapped around Maren, he reached for Lia with the other, giving her hand a squeeze. "I'm okay," he croaked.

Blinking back the tears that welled, Naia turned to Damian and whispered, "We should go."

Before they could step out, Lia spoke up. "Eve is with Callan," she said. "We should all talk. I'll come and find you soon."

Naia nodded, but didn't turn back to her before they stepped out into the bustling encampment.

Soldiers sat around the remnants of cookfires, on barrels and wagons. Most busied themselves with some task or another, sharpening blades or cleaning armor. A handful here and there even played cards on upturned logs, no doubt hauled with them from the north. Nearly all cast wary glares at Damian as they passed.

Naia's eyes narrowed, and she opened her mouth to rail at one such soldier they passed and sneered in his direction. Damian's hand on hers stopped her before the venom could spill from her lips.

"Don't," he said quietly. "They're restless enough as it is from all the waiting. It's making them afraid, bored. It's a dangerous time," he explained. "Their commanders should be keeping them busy, working them and training. Idleness breeds discontent, and that could spell trouble. Especially if you go around barking at them for giving me a dirty look."

She bristled, even though what he said made sense. "I don't like it."

He barked a laugh, no doubt recalling those words falling from his own lips. "They're afraid of me," he said. "Can't you smell it? The fear?" He cast a pointed glance around them as they walked, his strides long and relaxed. "I was their enemy not that long ago."

"How do they even know that?" she shot back, hurrying to keep up with him. "I certainly didn't tell any of them what happened between us. What you were."

"What I am," he corrected, slowing his pace slightly. "I'll always be Samach."

She had no reply for that and fell silent for a moment. "But how do they know?"

He shrugged. "Gossip spreads fast in a war camp. Especially one with little else to do. Most likely, one of the guards overheard and whispered it to another, and so on."

Anger whipped through her. "Then they should be found, we can't have our secrets being spread through–"

"Easy, Thunderheart," he soothed. "They've only heard what I am. Not who I served or what I did to you. Those secrets, at least, are safe."

"Still."

He laughed lightly, lifting a hand to brush a kiss across her knuckles as they neared Eve's tent. Instantly, his demeanor shifted, once again becoming the silent, deadly, warrior. Naia frowned at the easy shift, the mask he donned when anyone but her was looking.

A gift from Vidar, he'd said. One he'd learned when he'd taken his vows. A veil of silence not only of voice, but of emotion. But as her mind turned back to the abandoned teenager he'd once been, she couldn't help but wonder if it was far more than that. How long had he hidden away who he truly was, what he felt?

Would he be the man she had fallen for if he hadn't gone through it all?

Confusion broke through the mask briefly, at the pause she'd taken. "Shall we?" he asked, gesturing toward the tent where Eve waited.

"Of course," she said, donning a mask of her own.

CHAPTER 54

Naia blinked, the only visible sign of her surprise. They weren't alone. A silver haired fae with mismatched eyes, one gold, one blue, sat across from them in the little sitting area of their tent that was appointed as finely as Naia's, perhaps more so given the less rushed nature of their set up.

The stranger looked to be little more than middle aged, by human standards, but Naia knew enough by now to recognize that looks could be deceiving. For all she knew, the woman could be nearing a thousand years. She made a mental note to ask Damian about the lifespan of fae.

"Naia," Eve said in greeting, gaze sweeping over her briefly as if to check for any harm. There were shadows beneath her earth green eyes. Whatever had happened had taken a toll on her as well.

Callan, seated beside her, with his arm draped behind her chair, fingers grazing her shoulder, watched Eve closely. His eyes were clouded with worry, and from the mussed hair and circles under those eyes, she doubted he'd gotten any more sleep than Damian had since everything had happened.

"Come, sit," Eve beckoned, gesturing to a pair of chairs nearest the silver-haired fae. "I know I've been asleep," she sighed, "but I feel as though I haven't. It's like the energy has been sapped from me."

Naia nodded. "I know what you mean. It's strange."

Callan squeezed Eve's shoulder gently. "No more of these bouts of unconsciousness, Dove. You've had far too many already, and they're doing nothing for you."

Eve rolled her eyes at the jest. "We're being rude." Turning her smile to the silver-haired woman, she said, "This is Queen Lucia Chrysos of Finias." Inclining her head toward Naia and Damian, she said, "Queen Naia Colvari of Coruscis, and Damian...I'm sorry I don't know your surname." Her cheeks flushed slightly, as if embarrassed she'd forgotten to ask.

"Oh, Lord Valessos and I are acquainted," Lucia replied, smiling broadly.

Damian's brow twitched slightly, though the mask of indifference remained otherwise in place. Leaning back in his chair, he rested an ankle on the opposite knee. "Are we?"

The ancient queen's smile turned sad. "I was a great friend of your mother's. I see your Aunt Cilla failed to tell you that. It is of little surprise you don't remember. You were but a boy when last I saw you. You used to call me Aunt, once upon a time." Tapping the navy padded arm of her mahogany chair, she sighed and shook her head. "I was heartbroken when she passed."

Naia reached for Damian, placing a hand on his arm. Beneath her touch, he flinched, tensing, drawing a frown from her, but his face remained stoic, gaze locked on the fae queen.

"And yet, when her son was cast out, you did nothing."

Genuine confusion swept over the queen's features. "Cast out?" she repeated quietly.

Damian said nothing in response, and Naia wondered if her surprise had been answer enough. Turning his attention to Eve and Callan, he said flatly, "You have theories?"

Eve looked between the two fae, frowning. "Ah, yes," she said, straightening. "I apologize for not using your title, Lord–"

"I no longer recognize that title."

Damian's icy tone had Callan's gaze shooting to him, face darkening in warning.

"I see," Eve replied tightly. "Well, to answer your question, yes. Sort of."

"Sort of?" Naia interjected before Damian could speak again. The last thing they needed was another fight between the men, and though he likely appeared unbothered, cold, to everyone else in the room, she knew he must be raging inside.

To know his mother was loved by someone, had called someone friend, and that person had never known, had never been told what had happened to her only son after her death....

It had to be torture. Another injury done to an innocent boy for no worthwhile reason.

Eve visibly relaxed as she turned her attention to Naia. "We—Lucia," she corrected, "thinks that it's possible the spear was used."

A silence so heavy that a pin drop would have been as loud as thunder fell over the tent. "On who?" Naia whispered.

"There's no way to know," Lucia answered. "We could only guess. We can't even be certain that's what happened."

Naia frowned, considering. "Why do you believe it was the spear?"

Callan shifted in his seat, arm still draped over Eve's shoulders comfortably. "There are very few things in this world capable of such a... shockwave. Especially when you consider that only the three of you were affected." The shadows in his blue eyes deepened, and his fingers stilled on Eve's shoulders. "Nothing else should have been able to do what it did to you."

Eve nodded in agreement. "I assume you've been told what happened," she said, looking to Damian for confirmation. At his nod, she went on, "Our magic went haywire. It had to be something connected, and this made the most sense, to Lucia and the others."

"Okay." Naia exhaled slowly, processing. "Good to know I guess, but how does it help us?"

Silence reigned. Nobody had an answer for that it seemed, until Lucia spoke up.

"If they used it to kill Endri, then I fear things are all but over for us."

Damian tensed beside her, and Naia snorted. "Wonderful."

Eve shook her head. "It's only speculation. We will still win."

Naia opened her mouth to reply, to remind Eve that as of this moment, they still had no idea where Kore, or her army, even were. The spear had been used on some unknown person, god, or fae, or human, they had no way of knowing. Unspoken truth hung in the air between them all. The knowledge that their chances of success were slim to begin with, that every day Kore kept them waiting, stretching their resources and patience thinner and thinner, the slim chance of success was whittled away.

While the queens and their artifacts were important for defeating Kore, her army could just as easily overtake theirs and make the entire thing pointless. They had no way of knowing how Gorias would react if left standing in the wake of Kore's defeat. They could turn conquerors and simply continue what she'd started, or surrender and return to their homes in the north. With the armies of six united kingdoms standing against them, she thought the latter most likely.

"I'm sorry I was delayed," Lia's gentle voice announced her arrival as she stepped inside.

"How is he?" Eve asked, genuine concern painting her features.

Lia smiled faintly. "He'll be okay."

But would Lia? Naia wondered. The guilt Lia had to feel would be intense. As Lia took a seat near Eve, dragging another chair from around the table, Naia couldn't help but watch with a faint degree of envy. The two queens had always been close, from what Maren had reported. While they'd met a few rare times over the years of their parents' rules, Naia couldn't say the same. Truth be told the number of friendships she could count were severely limited, with the only truly meaningful one being her sister.

"I bring news," Lia said, drawing Naia from her thoughts. "The scouts are reporting an attack on a village north of here, called Tevara. Soldiers in grey arrived this morning, according to the few souls who escaped and met one of the shifters on the road to Thalassa. They appeared suddenly and just began taking prisoners. No one knew why."

Naia flinched. She knew, or at least suspected, why. As Eve's attention drifted to her, she saw confirmation of those fears echoed in her green eyes. Naia had escaped Kore's clutches, and she was retaliating, taking her people as hostages, or worse, as punishment.

"How many?" she asked.

Lia frowned, sighing. "Over a hundred, we think. It's difficult to be sure, but that's the rough estimate the survivors were able to give us."

"They didn't escape," Callan mused. "They were let go."

"Yes," Damian agreed.

"A warning then, or a taunt?" Eve asked, brow furrowed.

Callan shook his head. "A trap."

"Does it matter? We have to get them back either way." Naia said quietly, fiercely.

Eve and Lia both murmured their agreement even as the silent question passed between them.

How?

"We'll go to Tevara," Damian said, drawing everyone's attention for the first time. He'd been so quiet, Naia has assumed he was still reeling from what Lucia had revealed.

"She'll likely be close," Callan agreed. "There's no doubt she'll be waiting for us, with some nasty surprise waiting."

"Then we'll have to prepare a few of our own," Damian replied, offering a grin for the first time. "Something she won't see coming."

CHAPTER 55

Tevara was a ghost town. Utter silence greeted them as the three queens, their mates and protectors, accompanied by Callan's brother and his lovely mate, walked through the hard-packed sand street slowly. Mud brick houses with brightly colored awnings of fabric lay silent as tombs, with many of the round-topped wooden doors hanging open. Baskets of laundry, of foodstuffs no doubt being carried from the square up ahead, lay scattered on the street.

A child's doll discarded in front of a home had Naia's heart wrenching.

None of them spoke, seeming to barely breathe as they walked, surveying what was left behind. They'd nearly reached the center of town when a sudden clang from one of the empty homes had Naia nearly leaping out of her skin.

It was Damian who held up a hand, gesturing for them to wait as he slid his sword free of the scabbard at his back, and strode carefully into the dim interior of the home. Naia held her breath as she watched his shadow move past the window. But when his loud burst of laughter erupted from within, she frowned, running in after him with the others in her wake.

The home was pretty, small but well cared for. A small seating area of low cushions surrounded a pretty hearth with an empty cookpot inside. A low table with more cushions had been positioned near a window, a small clay pot with yellow flowers in the center had been knocked sideways, chipped on one side.

And the culprit, a slender grey cat with wide green eyes peered at Damian, who stood facing the little beast who stared him down.

"What did you do to her?" Naia asked, stepping forward to gently pick up the cat, who instantly began to purr.

"Me?" Damian blinked, turning to face the others, mask sliding into place again. "She's the one who hissed and swiped at me."

"Well you must have done something."

Lia moved closer, scratching the cat behind the ear. "We can't leave her here."

"We're not," Naia declared, cradling the content feline close. "She'll come with us." At Damian's raised brow, she added, "Maren would love to take care of her. If she stays here, she'll starve, or worse. When we get them back, she can be reunited with her family."

Callan made a noise that might have been disagreement, only to be silenced by a look from Eve. "It'll be fine, I'm sure."

"Well," Damian said flatly. "Let's get back to it then."

Cat still in Naia's arms, they arrived in the town square minutes later.

As expected, the square appeared empty. Buckets used to gather water from the central well lay on their sides, scattered around the brick walls of the well. More personal items lay forgotten, a scarf stuck against a fence post drifting on the breeze, a book dropped to the ground, its pages ripped as if it had been trampled on. Small reminders of the lives that had been stolen, carried away by darkness itself.

The group fanned out in silence, the only sounds in the square their footsteps on the hard-packed sand, and the occasional fluttering of the scarf. Several heartbeats passed as they waited. The scouts who had managed to fly overhead, seemingly unnoticed, had reported the presence of perhaps half a dozen soldiers milling about in the center of the town.

Where were they now?

It took only minutes for them to find out.

Naia's heart thundered, lightning lashing her veins as the words rang out across the square. Despite her rage, her strength, a tendril of fear squeezed her heart at the all too familiar voice.

"Hello again, beloved. I see death suits you," Zayan grinned, stepping out of the town's tavern.

His words must have been a signal, as soldiers stepped out of the other buildings surrounding them. The buildings they hadn't bothered to check, knowing what likely waited within. They had been prepared for this, this ambush. Each of them had arrived prepared for the confrontation. Dressed in leather armors, with swords strapped to the backs of the men, and Lia. The crown atop Eve's brow practically thrummed with power, and the pack Naia wore slung across her chest grew heavier with the weight of the cauldron.

They may have walked into an ambush, but they had done so prepared.

Without a word, Naia passed the cat to Mara, the dark-haired fae mated to Callan's brother. The two of them would remain back, once the fighting broke out, guarding them from any attacks from behind... and to offer a special surprise courtesy of Cathal's power. One that Kore had yet to see in person.

"Him," Damian growled.

"He's mine," Naia seethed, casting a glance to Damian who practically vibrated with rage.

Damian nodded, saying nothing further as he pulled the sword from its scabbard again. Each of the others followed suit. Electricity danced along Naia's forearms, left bare by the sleeveless armor she'd chosen, and the ground rumbled slightly as Eve began banking her own power.

She made it exactly one step before the rest of Kore's nasty surprise finally showed itself.

Pacing directly behind Zayan, three fae. Two men with shaved heads and unremarkable features stared flatly at the group. The third, a pale woman with short, ash blonde hair blinked at Damian before her mask of nothingness returned.

Moments later, a dozen, perhaps more, soldiers paced into the square, surrounding them.

Damian grunted at the other Samach, easily recognized by the aura of cold nothingness that now seeped from them, aimed directly for the others. Their powers may not work on the three bearers, not with their artifacts in tow, but it would certainly put a stop to the others' gifts.

Or it would have, if Damian hadn't been with them. A shield provided by him, around each of the other fae. The two Samachs should, in theory, cancel one another out, he'd explained, though he'd never seen it in action.

We will soon find out, Naia thought. She'd seen the way the woman had seemed to recognize Damian, had noted the flash of surprise in her eyes, brief as it was. Jealousy, brief but sharp, needled her.

"You look better," Zayan crooned. "Perhaps I did you a favor." His gaze never roamed from her face. "But I'm told you lay with a fae bastard," he sighed. "A pity, but I could perhaps be persuaded to accept you still. Once my goddess has finished making each of you her playthings, perhaps she'll let me taste you again. One last time."

Damian snarled and took a step forward. Naia's stomach churned, but she held her hand to the side, palm facing Damian. A plea for him to wait, to let her have this. Zayan was hers to face, her vengeance to take, for all that he'd done, and had tried to do.

Going still, Damian snorted. "You let yourselves be commanded by a human?" he taunted. "Disgraceful."

"Better than allowing a whore to break your sacred vows," one of the Samach men remarked flatly.

The other shrugged. "We answer only to she who is The Destroyer, The Darkness, The End of All Things."

"Doesn't it get tiring, listing all of those tedious titles every time?" Eve called out, drawing the attention of each of their enemies, except Zayan, who had eyes only for Naia.

"Take them," he said quietly, lips curving into a cruel smile.

Everyone moved at once. Steel met steel, and the earth groaned as the battle began. None dared go near the three bearers, focusing their attacks on their companions. Darkness erupted from Callan, snaking through the enemies, strangling some, pouring into the ears and eyes of others. Their cries of terror echoed around the square, sending a chill down Naia's spine.

Light flashed behind her in an arc as Lia unleashed herself on a soldier of Gorias, charging at her from their flank.

Damian squared off with two others, as he pushed his way toward the other Samach, who remained behind Zayan.

Fear and pride, and a little bit of lust, flashed within her as she watched him move. Despite his size, he moved with grace. The battle was a dance, and he was a master. The two he faced were not quite as skilled, it seemed, as Damian, but well trained enough to hold their own, even as he forced them back toward his goal. She watched as one fell, before a sudden movement in her direction caught her eye.

Zayan was making his way toward her, a predatory grin on the face she'd once thought handsome. Now, she saw only cruelty.

"My goddess will devour them," he threatened, as he sidestepped a falling soldier. Their ambush was faltering. Her friends cutting through them as a ship through the surf.

She didn't move for her cauldron, nor her magic. Not yet. Her vengeance would be wrought with her own hands.

"Too afraid to fight back?" he taunted. "Our last encounter was so delightful. I hope you don't cower beneath me. It's no fun if you lose your fire."

Only when he was nearly within arms reach did she move, only then did she call upon the magic gifted to her by the gods. Lifting her hand, she let the power she'd been quietly banking loose on him. Not enough to kill, but enough to stun. Lightning shot forth from her outstretched hand, hitting him directly in the chest. With a cry of surprise, or pain, he was knocked up and back, landing on the ground with a thud.

Shouts and cries of frustration and effort sounded around her. Steel against steel. Stone against bone and flesh. She heard none of it. Didn't see the fires burning brighter, wending their way through Callan's darkness to burn the lungs of the men he held with shadows. Didn't see Lia's blinding light taking down the man who charged at her back.

Only Zayan existed. Only her revenge.

Rolling to his side in the sand, he coughed and sputtered. Gasping for breath, he turned to pin a hateful stare on her. "I'll kill you," he spat. "Again. My goddess will–"

Gripping his shoulder she forced him to his back. His effort to wriggle from under her grasp fruitless against her new fae strength. Shifting the bag containing the cauldron to her back, she straddled him and leaned over him. Her fist curled into the loose sand beside his head, the other pressing against his throat. Sweat beaded at his temples, dripping into his sand-coated dark hair. The hair she'd once run her fingers through.

Rage fueled her. Lightning danced along her hands, and he hissed. Not enough power to harm him, just enough to hurt. Hurt him like he had her. Stinging like boundaries pushed, like being used...betrayal.

"Your goddess will not save you now," she said, voice as low as a lover's.

"Please," he whimpered.

How pathetic. The arrogant lordling now begging and wriggling beneath her, eyes darting from side to side searching for rescue or escape. Her grip on his throat tightened to the point of cutting the air from his lungs. As his face began to turn purple, his hands clawing and flailing against her in a desperate attempt to escape, she released him.

"Naia, please," he gasped, drawing breath into his lungs in heaving gulps. "I'll do anything–"

"You will do nothing," she snarled. "You are nothing. You will be forgotten, when this story is told, centuries from now. You. Are. Nothing."

She gave him no time to reply as she called on her lightning again, giving him only enough time for his eyes to widen in shock before she released it upon him. A powerful jolt had his body spasming, once, twice, and then his eyes went dim.

"You were nothing," she whispered, releasing her grip on him and falling sideways into the sand.

Chapter 56

As if a veil had been lifted, sight and sound returned to her. Someone was shouting. Eve, she realized, just as a wall of stone erupted from the ground to her left, was screaming her name. A heartbeat later, a thud, as a Gorian soldier crashed into it.

"Go!" Eve shouted again. "Naia, go!"

She didn't hesitate as she scrambled to her feet and took in her surroundings. Damian had finally made it to where the Samach waited. To her surprise, they had each produced weapons, though where they had hidden them in their simple linen clothes, she didn't know. The two men wielding swords, and the woman a pair of smaller blades, one in each hand.

Though she wanted to wait, to watch and assure herself that he was okay, a sound to her right had her spinning, lifting her hands and letting lightning loose at the soldier charging for her.

Flames danced across the square, followed by the screams of the men who had been immolated. It was time for her to fall back, she realized, to where Cathal and Mara stood. The safest place for her to wield only her magic.

Turning to run, her path was cleared by flame and shadow, by light and stone. Each of her friends watching over her until she reached her destination. The cat, looking concerned but strangely calm, rested in Mara's arms. Standing quietly at Cathal's side she scanned the crowd, as if waiting for something.

Flames encircled a man charging at Callan's back, spinning like a cyclone and swallowing him whole. As he cut down the one he'd faced, Callan cast a brief glance in Cathal's direction, and a slight dip of his chin in thanks. Eve, on the opposite side of Cathal called forth vines to wrap around the trio that made their way toward Damian.

More of them had arrived, she realized, while she'd been dealing with Zayan, and they were thoroughly outnumbered, though they continued to hold their own.

"How long will this last?" she asked no one in particular, launching an arc of lightning across the square at two soldiers who had turned to charge at them.

"Too long," Cathal replied. "He needs to finish it."

Damian, it seemed, had come to the same conclusion as he faced off with the trio he had once called brethren. One man had fallen, a vicious wound across his midsection. The other was flagging, but holding strong. Only the woman remained whole and unwavering, standing a few feet behind her compatriot, as if waiting her turn.

Naia narrowed her eyes, lifting a hand only for Mara to stop her with a gentle, "Wait."

She turned to blink at her, to find Mara smiling softly as a silvery mist drifted from her, toward the square.

"Oh, this will be interesting," Cathal laughed, allowing the last of his flames to fade.

Naia frowned, confusion sweeping over her. Why had he stopped? Even Eve seemed to slow her attacks, and Lia, on the other side of Eve, frowned, lowering her sword.

"What are you—"

Everywhere the mist went, men and women fell to their knees, eyes wide and silent.

While the remaining few moved away from the mist, Callan and Cathal finished them off, with shadow and flame; any who hadn't been touched by Mara's mist were soon dead.

She couldn't make sense of it, why such a simple mist could bring them to their knees, or why the Samach woman, who had eased her way to Damian's flank, now paused and turned their way with wide eyes.

"Justice," Cathal explained. "She's unleashing justice on them."

Naia frowned, watching as the Samach woman backed away from the slowly approaching mist. "What does that even mean?"

"She makes them see the worst thing they've ever done," Eve said.

Mara smiled softly. "Confess," she whispered, though the simple word seemed to echo through the mist and across the town square turned battlefield.

The kneeling soldiers each began to babble.

"I hurt her–"

"--it was an accident, we didn't see them."

"I was ordered to."

Their voices rang out, blubbered through streaming tears, or ground out through gritted teeth. And then, they screamed, or wept, or simply fell to the sand, silent and unseeing.

As the Samach woman watched in horror, gaze darting between where Callan landed a final blow against the other and where Mara stood, eyes locked on her, she dropped the blades to the ground.

"Take me," she blurted. "But I'll say nothing." Her gaze fixed on Damian. "You know that better than anyone. I won't say a word. I remain true to my vows."

Grunting, Damian shook his head. "You've already broken them, Rima. You've shown your fear."

"Fuck you, Damian," she snarled.

Ignoring her hurled insult, he turned his attention to the others, gaze landing on Naia. He went still, scanning her from head to toe and back again. For a heartbeat, she could see his shoulders sag, tension releasing. "We've got what we came for," he said finally. "Let's go back."

"What?" Rima blurted. "All of this to take a captive who will tell you nothing?" She snorted, shaking her head. "Your human whore has made you soft in the head, Damian, if you think this was worth it."

His hand shot out faster than Naia could blink, seizing Rima's slender throat in one hand. "Speak another word against her and not even your usefulness will save you," he growled.

Naia's heart skittered, and Cathal let out a low whistle. Out of the corner of her eye, she spotted Mara smirking slightly at Cathal.

"There's been enough death," Lia sighed wearily. "We should go before anyone else shows up."

Damian released Rima with a brutal shove that had her staggering backward, gasping. "Not a fucking word," he warned.

As they turned to leave, Mara leaned over and whispered conspiratorially, "That was extremely attractive."

"Shall I go around threatening lives for you my love?" Cathal teased.

"Only when necessary," Mara replied, passing the still calm cat to Naia gently.

Hugging the feline soothingly, Naia rolled her eyes and slowed her steps until Damian caught up to her, dragging Rima by the arm.

The Samach cut a glance in Naia's direction, coldly appraising her. Naia bared her teeth in response, earning a low chuckle from Damian and a scowl from Rima.

"What will you do with her?" Naia asked, not entirely sure she wanted to know the answer.

Damian's brow rose slightly, as he cast a slight glance in Rima's direction. "You'll see."

WHAT HE PLANNED TO DO, IT TURNED OUT, WAS ABSOLUTELY nothing. Once back to camp, just outside the village, he'd restrained her, dropped her to the floor of an unfurnished tent and left her there, under guard.

Once she'd been dropped to seethe and wait for whatever they planned to do next, Damian and Naia returned to their own. Exhaustion finally hit her like a wave, and without even bothering to change out of her sand-covered leathers, she collapsed into their bed with a huff.

Damian watched in silence for a moment, simply looking her over before dragging her legs sideways so that her feet hung off of the bed. With painstaking care, he unlaced her boots and pulled them off.

"You knew her, before," she said, leaning up on her elbows to watch as he tugged her socks off next.

"I did," he replied. "For a long time."

Naia frowned. "She seemed surprised to see you."

Broad hands roamed over her calves, kneading aching muscles. "She didn't know I served Kore."

Naia closed her eyes as the tension left her, sighing. "I would have expected you to work together, Samach and all."

He breathed a light laugh, sliding his hands to her hips. "We were broken up into groups, and I was...different. I was given a specific task," he reminded her, looking up from between her thighs with a raised brow.

"Oh," she replied, breath hitching at the sight of him between her legs. "Right."

His rough hands slid beneath the waist of her pants moving to the laces in the front. "Now don't get any ideas," he said quietly. "About what will happen now, or happened then." Her brow shot up and he chuckled again. "You need rest, after all you've been through today, and," he said, casting a pointed glance to the feline resting on a chair nearby. "We have an audience."

Slowly, so damn slowly, he pulled her pants down her thighs. "Rima and I were never involved, if that's what you think."

Naia sat up straight, lips curving downward. "Don't say another woman's name with your head between my thighs, Damian. Ever."

He grinned up at Naia, yanking her pants the rest of the way off and earning a surprised yelp from her. "Never again, Thunderheart," he promised.

Chapter 57

"Fuck. You." Rima ground out, spitting at Callan's feet. "Death doesn't frighten me. I've evolved beyond that."

Callan snorted. "Liar."

Damian walked a slow circle around them. Rima followed with her eyes until he moved beyond her line of sight.

"Tell us, Rima. You can be released into the sweet silence of death, or you can stay here, wishing for it."

Fire crackled in the brazier, the only light in the darkened tent, kept low to keep her in darkness. Standing in the far corner of the bare tent, Naia shivered, and it had little to do with the cold. Callan's shadows slithered across the ground like serpents, snaking their way around Rima's legs, stretched out in front of her, up her arms, bound behind her, and around her throat.

"I can make you live it," Callan said softly, the voice of death itself. "The moment the breath leaves your body. Over and over. I can make you see it, feel it. Your mind won't be able to tell reality from the lie I feed it, and you will weep for an end that will never come."

Rima had the sense to look afraid, but only for a moment before the mask of the Samach slid into place again. "I fear nothing."

Damian stepped in front of her again, dropping to a crouch with his back to Naia. "We both know that isn't true, Rima." Her gaze slid to him, eyes narrowing slightly. "Berin."

For the first time real fear broke through the facade. "You bastard. You wouldn't."

Ignoring Callan's raised brow, the silent question in his face, Damian rose to stand again. "I would, and you know it."

Shaking her head slowly, Rima's voice shook as she spoke again, tears sliding down her face. "I hope she fucking kills you all." Turning to Naia, she added, "I'll tell you what you want to know, starting with the fact that you're taking a fucking monster to your bed. Has he told you what he is? What he's willing to do for whatever master he serves?" Jerking her attention back to Damian, she added, "I thought perhaps you'd grown soft, shed the skin of the monster; now that you've been pulled into this righteous band of heroes. That maybe you'd draw the line at some point, but maybe you're more of a bastard than I realized."

Naia gave a start, gaze shooting to Damian, who didn't look away from Rima. "I haven't changed Rima," he said in a terrifyingly calm tone. "Still a monster. I'm just her monster now."

An hour later, with as many details as Rima could give recorded, and handed off to the scouts to verify, Naia and Damian walked through the camp to go back to their tent.

The energy had shifted, from restless and bored, to energetic and anticipatory. They had a lead now. With any hope, by morning they'd have a destination. The end of it all was on the horizon at long last.

Soldiers gathered around cookfires, laughing and talking animatedly, excited to finally be *doing* something. The news of Rima's capture, of the information they'd gotten from her had invigorated everyone; everyone except perhaps Naia.

"Who is Berin?" she asked, casting a sideways glance at him.

Damian groaned, stroking his beard. "Her son."

Naia froze, spinning to look at him, eyes wide. "You were threatening a child?"

He shook his head incredulously. "Not truly. I needed her to see me as the monster she knew, Naia. And the easiest way to get her to talk was through him. She wasn't lying when she said she didn't fear death. It's what we were conditioned for. Without that leverage, she never would have told us what we needed to know."

She considered his words, weighing them. "I don't like it," she said slowly. "But I do understand it. Damian," she added with a weary sigh, "are you the only one who knows about the child?"

He frowned, considering it a moment. "I don't know," he admitted. "Ask her."

"I doubt she'd tell me anything more about him," he countered.

"Then go get him, Damian," she shot back. "We can't leave an innocent child out there, not when we've taken her." She glanced sideways at the men and women around them, none paying their conversation any mind. "What do you think they'll do to him if they think she's been compromised? Do you think they'll simply leave him alone?"

"Not if they think they can use him as leverage to keep her from talking," he admitted.

"So we have to get him to safety."

He groaned, dragging a hand through his hair. "I see your point and why it matters. We'll send someone. I'll tell them what I know, and he can be taken away from Paradisus. He won't be safe there."

"Nor in Thalassa," she sighed. "He'll have to go somewhere unconnected to any of us."

Damian nodded. "I'll task one of the others with finding a place that can't be tied to any of us, and hiding him there." Grazing her cheek with his thumb, he added, "You've a good heart, Naia."

She snorted in response. "Don't tell anyone."

He chuckled, taking her by the hand and leading her back to their tent.

DAMIAN WAS SCREAMING. INKY LIQUID POURED FROM HIS eyes, his ears, his nose. His every breath was a wail of agony. Writhing on the pale stone floor, he clawed at his own bare chest, leaving trails of crimson behind.

How did they get here? How did this happen?

The questions raced through her mind. There was nothing, nothing around them but darkness. Darkness and cold grey stone beneath them, and the icy pillar she'd been bound to. No sound, no light aside from illuminated Damian.

Naia struggled against the chains that bound her to the pillar. The cold steel bit into her bare flesh as she raged, desperately calling on the lightning beneath her skin, and found nothing there. No magic. No fae strength to save them.

His eyes met hers, wide and stained with black that ran like tears. "Please," he gurgled around the black ooze that began to seep from his mouth. "Save me, Thunderheart."

Pushing with every ounce of strength she could against the chains, she screamed. The thin shift she'd been dressed in ripped and pulled as she struggled in vain.

Damian's body began to spasm, his muscular arms falling to his sides, going still, as he turned his face skyward, to the unending blackness above. He jerked once more, then went utterly, terrifyingly still.

Her throat burned with the scream that erupted from deep in her soul, only for it to be swallowed by the nothingness beyond. Sobs wracked her body, and she went limp, with only the chains to keep her upright with their bruising grip.

A sultry female laugh sounded from somewhere in the darkness, and her blood chilled. A dream, she realized. A nightmare sent by the Void herself.

"You make it too easy," Kore pouted, stepping into the light. Stepping over Damian's body as if he were nothing. Her snow white gown grazed the stone floor, pooling around her like water. Strapless, held up by an onyx serpent, its tail coiled around her neck, and the fabric of her gown in its mouth. For a moment, Naia could have sworn it blinked.

"Fuck you," Naia snapped back, despite the tears still flowing, the sheer terror and despair that had her chest aching.

"Tsk, tsk," Kore purred as she neared Naia. "That's quite rude, especially after the gift I gave you." A single, long, crimson nail slid across her cheek, scraping but not breaking the skin. "I thought you would be more appreciative."

She shivered in response, recoiling as far as the chains would allow with her back against the cold stone, which wasn't very far.

Kore chuckled in response, gripping Naia's chin like a vice and forcing her to meet the obsidian depths of her eyes. "I could kill you now, little queen. Rip that pitiful thing you call a soul from your body. Devour it. Then move on to more...exciting games," she whispered, glancing to Damian's body with a predatory grin. "Maybe I'll devour him first. Make you watch. And that sweet sister of yours–"

Realization blossomed at the back of Naia's mind, and to her own surprise, she laughed.

Kore's grip tightened on Naia's face. "What do you–"

"You can't," Naia laughed bitterly. "You can't kill me here. You would have done it already," she spat. Jerking her chin free of Kore's grasp, as surprise, and rage, lit the ancient being's face. "If you could truly harm us in our dreams, you would have done so long ago."

Rage flashed in Kore's dark eyes, but she didn't back down. "I can hurt you in ways–"

"Like that?" Naia demanded, looking to Damian's body. Ignoring the sharp pain in her chest at the sight of his still form, covered in the dark ooze that Kore commanded, she shook her head. "It isn't real. What you do to us here, it isn't real, and it can't really hurt us."

Kore's face shifted into something more terrifying than her rage, a pleased smile. "Then I suppose I'll have to resort to something more tangible. See you soon, little queen."

Every ounce of light vanished in an instant, leaving Naia in utter darkness. The cold of the chains and stone vanished a moment later. With the next blink, Naia found herself face to face with Damian, sleeping soundly.

"Damian," she blurted, shaking his shoulder. "Wake up."

In an instant he was alert, scanning her face with a frown. "What's wrong?"

"I think I messed up," she whispered in the darkness. "We need to go to Thalassa."

CHAPTER 58

Naia walked from one end to the tent to the other for the fifth time. "This is taking too long."

"Are you even sure?" Callan asked, for the second time.

Eve frowned, but said nothing.

Neither of the others had been tormented in their dreams the way Naia had. Neither had seen their loved ones murdered, had been taunted and threatened. The only reason anyone could come up with was that she had personally offended Kore.

"I'm sure," Naia snapped. "She wants to hurt me, and when I made it clear the dream she sent wasn't enough, she said she'd find something more tangible." Her gaze cut to Damian, and a chill spider walked down her spine again.

She hadn't been entirely truthful when she'd said the pain and fear of the dream hadn't been real. While the physical parts had faded the moment she'd woken, with no bruises or aches left behind by the phantom chains, the ache in her heart at watching him die had remained.

"Did you mean something to her?" Lia asked, frowning. "There must be a reason she's so focused on Naia."

Damian snorted. "She doesn't care for any of her servants like that.

Most likely," he replied, watching Naia from where he sat with the others around a small, round table, "she's angry you slipped her grasp. She wouldn't take a loss like that well."

"We have to go," Naia urged again. "The reasons why don't matter. Thalassa is guarded, yes, but they can't withstand a direct assault from that army for very long."

Callan and Aelius, seated silently at Lia's side, exchanged a glance. "What do you think?"

Aelius sighed, considering it. "I think we have to trust their instincts where this is concerned," he began, holding a hand up as Naia rushed toward them. "But, we have to be smart too. We obviously can't go charging into a trap."

"What do you suggest?" Naia snapped impatiently.

"Get us maps of the area," Callan said smoothly. "Let's see where our best approach, and best chance of victory, is. If you're right. But," he warned. "This could simply be another tactic to wear us out."

"No," Naia countered. "I saw the rage in her eyes. I could practically feel it radiating from her. She didn't expect me to fight back. I made her angry."

Callan nodded. "Then we'll go."

"Great." Naia breathed a sigh of relief. "When do we leave?"

Naia scowled at the crashing waves. Preparing a battle strategy, and then making preparations to move an army, especially one so large, was no easy task as it turned out. Impatience roiled within her. Her people could be dying right now, helpless, without her coming to their aid. She grabbed a fistfull of sand, letting it fall from one hand to the other in an attempt to soothe her nerves.

She'd considered simply pacing there herself, to do whatever she could to help. Damian had practically roared at her when she'd suggested as much. Reminding her that if she went alone, if she died, there would be no hope left for not only Thalassa, but the rest of the world.

Her life was worth more than the entirety of her kingdom.

That stark truth left a bitter taste in her mouth.

"We agreed not to go anywhere alone," Lia's gentle voice called out as she plopped into the sand next to Naia.

With her light blonde hair falling free, her light linen shirt and pants the color of a summer sky, she looked the very picture of sunny hope that she embodied. Glancing down at her own pale grey attire, in the same style as Lia's, she wondered if she looked as much like a storm-cloud as she felt.

Dropping the sand to the ground, she sighed. "I'm not alone," she replied wearily. "There are guards just over there," she explained, jerking her chin in the direction of the dunes where a pair of fae guards stood watch. None of her own soldiers had come to greet her, none had bothered to offer help with her security.

She wondered how they must see her, their queen turned fae. Did they still see her as their rightful ruler? Or as some sort of abomination? Eve had given up her throne, knowing that the people of Darkegrove would never accept a fae queen. Some had even tried to kill her for the simple fact of her being a female seeking to rule alone.

Her cousin, it seemed, would be taking up that mantle and pushing forward the change that Eve had begun.

"What will you do when this is done?" Naia asked quietly.

"What do you mean?"

Tracing swirls and circles in the sand idly, Naia didn't bother to look Lia's way. "When this is all done, if we survive–"

"When we survive," Lia corrected.

Naia smiled despite herself. "When," she acquiesced. "What will you do about Avellon? Will you remain their queen? For how long?"

Lia stretched her legs out before her, tilting her face skyward to the sun. A veritable sunflower, Naia thought. "He doesn't know it yet, but I'm giving it to Aelius."

Naia frowned. "I had planned to do the same, passing mine to Maren."

Lia laughed, light and airy. "Well, that will certainly make things complicated. I'm sure they'll sort it out though."

"I suppose," Naia snorted, unconvinced. But maybe, hope whispered in the back of her mind. If anyone could manage such a complication, her sister could. "I hope we're around to watch it unfold."

"We will be," Lia said confidently. "We'll be there to help them, if they need it."

"And their children," Naia reminded her. "Likely their grandchildren and great- grandchildren after that."

Lia hummed thoughtfully. "Does it frighten you, the long long lives we have ahead of us?"

Naia cast a glance out to the unending expanse of the sea. To the great ocean that stretched far beyond what any could see, to the distant lands to the south, where trade princes ruled. Eventually, to the east, where dragons yet roamed, and to the west, where the great unknown lay.

"Not at all," she replied, honestly. She could see the future that lay ahead as far and wide as the horizon. The many years she would have to explore, to love, to live with Damian. She would remain here, for a time, to be close to her sister. To watch her live a full and happy life.

When the time came, would they go to the east, in search of dragons? Or the west, just to see what lay beyond? Ships carried brave souls in search of riches or adventure out of the port towns near Satisse, maybe one day she and Damian would find themselves aboard such a vessel.

"The world is about to change," Lia remarked. "I think it will be rather exciting to watch, now that the fae have returned."

"Yes," Naia agreed. "Some humans won't accept it. Out of fear or prejudice."

Lia sighed softly, leaning forward. "I think you're right. But they'll have us, human queens turned fae, to help broker peace."

Naia laughed. "Maybe so." Or maybe, she added silently, they wouldn't need them at all.

CHAPTER 59

"It's time," Damian said, drawing Naia's gaze from the rising sun above the horizon.

To her surprise, she'd slept peacefully, dreamlessly. Kore, it seemed, intended to remain true to her word. A fact that frightened Naia more than a little.

"Everything is ready?"

Taking her hand in his, he squeezed gently. "They're ready. Most of the fae are being paced, in turns, by those that can. The human armies are going to march together, with a smaller group of fae soldiers to bolster their numbers, and come for help, if they run into trouble. It shouldn't take them more than a day to get to Thalassa."

Callan had pressed for the full strength of their forces to march together, wary of splitting them apart. But Naia had insisted, with Lia and Eve's backing, out of fear that Thalassa could be lost, even in so little time as an extra day.

Relief had the breath whooshing from her in a long sigh and she nodded, flipping her long braid over her shoulder. They'd dressed ready for battle in fighting leathers, and armed. Damian with his sword at his back and smaller knives strapped to either thigh, his dark hair slicked back, tied with a strand of leather.

Naia's cauldron, plant and all, had been safely tucked into a bag that she carried slung over one shoulder.

"Okay, let's–"

Her words were cut off by a quiet meow and they both turned their attention to the slender grey feline approaching them behind Damian.

"I thought she was with your sister."

"She was," Naia frowned, brushing past him and scooping up the cat. "I suppose you'll be traveling with us, little friend. I doubt Suri will approve, but you can stay at my home with Maren."

The cat, seemingly pleased by this arrangement, purring in response so loudly Naia's hands practically vibrated with the sound of it.

"If that's settled," Damian said, reaching for Naia's hand.

And as wind and darkness swept over them, she could have sworn she heard a light laugh dancing on the phantom breeze.

Naia braced herself as darkness gave way to light, and the familiar scent of the jasmine in her mother's garden greeted her. But only the sound of chatter met her ears, of her mother's cry of relief as Damla rushed toward where she and Damian had arrived. Where several of the others had also just arrived.

Maren, hand in hand with Tori, stepped toward her mother, greeting her with an outstretched hand and a smile. Brief, as Damla had her eyes fixed on Naia. The daughter she'd thought lost to her.

"Oh, thank the gods," Damla whispered in a rush as tears began to fall, taking Naia's face in her hands. "You're okay?"

Naia nodded, tears pricking her eyes.

"I'm okay, but we have a lot to do."

Damla nodded, casting only the briefest glance toward Damian, and then the cat in Naia's arms. "I've been informed. We've had the city locked down for some time now, but the fae," she said, looking utterly unfazed by what had to be a foreign word on her tongue, "are bolstering our defenses. I believe that lovely girl that turns into a bird...Oh, what was her name..."

"Leysa?"

"Yes," Damla nodded. "She and some of the others who turn into animals have taken to the skies and sands, to see what they can find out."

Naia nodded, taking it in. "Have the people been warned? Told to barricade their homes when the bells ring?"

Damla sighed, offering Naia a long suffering stare as she folded her arms across her slender chest. "I was queen long before you were born, Naia Phedora Colvari. I know what I'm doing."

"Of course," Naia replied, bristling.

"Now introduce me to your companion," her mother cut in before Naia could point out that every one of Damla's years had been spent during peace and prosperity.

Stepping to the side, Naia turned to Damian, unable to keep the smile from her face. "This is Damian Valessos. Damian, my mother, Damla Colvari."

"It's an honor," Damian said, with little emotion but lacking the coldness he typically used with strangers, before inclining his head respectfully.

"Oh," Damla laughed. "I wouldn't have expected such manners from the monster who kidnapped my child," she added, eyes turning sharp as a blade.

"Mother!" Naia chided, passing the now wriggling cat to Maren, who had approached at last.

"Mama," Maren added, shaking her head. "I told you that things are...different now."

Damian tensed beside Naia, but he said nothing.

"You told her?" Naia demanded, turning an angry stare on her sister.

For a moment, Naia could have sworn the temperature in the sunlit garden, surrounded by small fountains bubbling merrily and heady blossoms that filled the air with sweet scents, had dropped by a few degrees.

"I didn't think she'd react this way, not when I explained it all," Maren replied, cheeks flushing.

Only when it came to their mother did Maren misjudge her words.

Damla spoke up at last, snapping at Naia. "And she was right to! He may have changed his mind about hurting you, or gods only knows what else, but he kidnapped you, Naia. Dragged you from your home. Do you know what it felt like to find your office in disarray like that? To hear Suri yowling, to come running to find you gone?" Her voice rose with every shouted question.

By now everyone in the garden was either openly gaping, or desperately trying to look as though they weren't.

Naia's cheeks heated. "I don't–"

"No!" Damla interrupted. "You don't know. So while you may have forgiven him for what he did, for whatever reason you may have, I have not." Turning to stare at Damian with a coldness that could rival his own, she added, "And I hope you never expect me to do so."

CHAPTER 60

"I'll kill Maren," Naia grumbled, leading Damian down the long hall that led to her room. Mosaics lined the walls, the floors.

"She was protecting you," he replied, gaze roaming over the tiny tiles that made up the floor. "This seems impractical."

Naia shrugged, casting a glance downward. Given their current attire, leather clad and ready for battle, they'd been forced to walk on the path to the side, to preserve the artwork in the center of the hallway. The scene in this part of the hall depicted the vast desert that made up most of her kingdom. While some might have seen the expanse as a flat, uninteresting span of monotone sand, the artist who had designed the mosaic centuries ago saw it as a thing of beauty.

Shades of yellows, beiges, and whites made up the sand, with gold flecks here and there to mimic the way the light caught individual grains of sand on occasion, giving Coruscis the nickname of The Shimmering Strand. Dunes rose, reaching for the sky, depicted in shifting shades of blue with sparse white clouds.

"It wasn't meant to be practical," she replied. "According to my grandmother, these hallways were to be a reminder of the care we are to take for not only the castle, but our lands. It's about respecting the beauty of the kingdom we rule."

Damian's lips curved downward slightly but he said nothing.

Returning to the topic at hand, Naia sighed. "I know she thought she was, but my mother is...difficult sometimes. She'll latch onto this and never let it go."

"She's your mother, it isn't surprising."

Naia had no reply to that, so she led him the rest of the way in silence, stopping at an arched doorway near the end of the hall. "Did you ever watch me here?" she asked, stepping inside.

"Only on the balcony," he murmured. "It was difficult to see inside."

"Well," she replied, throwing her arms wide. "Here it is."

Fit for a queen, the chamber was large, one of the largest in the castle. Her bed, four posters with gauzy white curtains, stood on a raised platform against the wall to the left. To the right, a small sitting area with plush, turquoise colored chairs set around a low, round table. A round, pearl-covered carpet lay beneath the furniture.

A few small paintings depicting the sea graced the wall space nearest the door, but across from where they'd entered, the entire wall was nothing but open air, made of tall, pointed arches with pale gold curtains, tied back with matching sashes. Beyond, the balcony he'd watched her with Zayan.

"It suits you," he observed, striding further into the room.

"I suppose," she replied, lifting a shoulder. "My mother will insist on dinner," she said. "We'll be expected to dress."

He nodded, saying nothing, his eyes fixed on the balcony.

"As awful as it is, I hope the battle comes before that."

"Why?" he asked, turning to her with a raised brow.

Snorting, she shook her head. "Because the dinner table is my mother's battlefield, and she never loses."

Warriors, as it turned out, had no need for formal clothing. Finding something her mother would find suitable had been a near impossible task for a man his size, so they'd settled on his leather pants and a tunic. Not as formal as her mother would have wanted, but it would have to do.

As far as Naia was concerned, he could show up to dinner nude and it would be fine...though she doubted it would be food being enjoyed at dinner in that case.

For herself, she'd chosen a more simple dress in pale seafoam, trimmed with pearls, that hung low on her shoulders, tapering in at her waist before flaring out again near the bottom.

"You look like a mermaid," Damian remarked, his heated gaze sweeping over her.

"What's that?" she asked, resisting the urge to strip the dress off right then and there, and skip dinner altogether.

He laughed lightly. "Half fish, half woman. I've only seen one once, in the eastern kingdoms."

"Take me to see them, one day?"

A shadow passed over his features, and he held out his hand. "We should go, we don't want to risk making your mother hate me even more."

Naia, although puzzled by his lack of response, laughed. "I'm not sure that's possible, to be honest."

With more appropriate footwear on, they made their way down the mosaic hallway, this time through its center. "I wonder how it's held up so long," Damian remarked. "Even with the slippers, and how well your staff must maintain it."

Naia shrugged. "Family legend says that the fae used magic to help my ancestors ensure it's longevity. Nobody knows how."

He hummed thoughtfully, but remained quiet until they arrived at the dining room. Like the rest of the castle by the sea, the dining room was appointed in colors inspired by the sea, or the surrounding desert.

A jasmine and lavender bouquet stood proudly on a narrow table by a wide, open archway identical to the ones in Naia's chambers, this one leading out to a small garden. The long table that dominated the space comprised of many small pieces of driftwood, pieced together to make up the top of the table.

She'd never paid much attention to the finer details here, like the way the whorls of the wood resembled waves, or how even here, the tiniest bits of tile dotted the walls, adding a bit of shimmer to the solid sandy color. Only now, watching the way his gaze swept over the space, taking it all in, did she see past the familiarity of it all. The little things she'd taken for granted.

"Hm," her mother said by way of greeting, sweeping into the room from a side entrance. No doubt overseeing the kitchen staff's preparations.

"Hello to you too, Mother," Maren said, brushing past Naia gently to take her seat at the table, left of the head where Damla had begun to sit.

By rights, Naia, as queen, should have taken the head, but this was the one part of dinner that had slightly more lax rules of decorum. Though Naia ruled, her mother remained matriarch in this room, when not being used for state dinners.

"You look lovely, Mother," Naia said, taking a seat to Damla's right, with Damian settling into place at her other side. Unlike her daughter, Damla had dressed formally, in a gown of white and glittering with jewels.

Maren, to Naia's relief, had dressed more similarly to Naia, in a lilac dress in the same style of Naia's.

"Well," Damla replied, eyeing her daughters in turn, before shifting her focus to Damian. Her gaze swept over him, the corners of her mouth tilting downward. As if he were little more than a rodent. "Dinner is an occasion."

"As this may well be our last dinner," Naia snapped, fists curling so tightly that her knuckles turned white. "I would have expected you to treat this as a family meal, not a state dinner." Damla opened her mouth to speak again, brow raised. But Naia cut her off, adding, "Stop. Now."

Unruffled, Damla narrowed her eyes slightly, but turned her attention to the approaching servants carrying trays of food. "Well," she said calmly. "Let us enjoy it then, if it may be our last."

Platters of freshly caught seafood, lamb, and a handful of varieties of vegetables were placed around the table, as the trio waited in silence to be left in privacy once more. Nodding her thanks to the staff, Damla dismissed them with assurances that they needn't linger.

"Damian, what is your home like?" Maren asked politely, as she helped herself to a bit of fish.

Naia winced, closing her eyes briefly. She hadn't shared the details of Damian's past with Maren. Hadn't planned to ever share it, in fact. It was his story to tell, and she suspected the pitying looks the story would earn from a soft heart like her sister would do more harm than good where Damian was concerned.

Damian, however, simply continued to serve himself lamb and vegetables, as cool and collected as ever as he spoke. "I haven't had one in a long time," he began.

Damla made a sound of disgust, and Naia pinned her mother with a glare, silencing her.

Utterly unfazed, Damian continued. "I lived in Gorias, for a long time. After the fae here were sealed away. Most of us, the Samach, were there when the veil went up."

"Why?" Maren inquired, taking a bite of food as she listened with interest.

"What is a Samach?" Damla asked, tone far more blunt than her daughter's.

"Mother–" Naia began, prepared to tell her mother to be silent if she couldn't be polite, but Damian interrupted.

"One who follows the god of silence and restraint, my lady," he replied without so much as a hint of emotion. "We take vows of silence, for a time, and forsake all emotion or emotional entanglements." Turning to Maren, he replied, "Visiting the temple of another goddess, at the behest of our god."

Damla, who hadn't bothered to touch any of the food, straightened. "You certainly seem to have forsaken your vows. Unless they also command you to kidnap, and lie."

"That is enough!" Naia snapped. Appetite utterly lost, she shoved the still empty plate back and placed her hand flat on the table as she faced her mother. "While I don't expect you to be kind to him, you will be polite."

Damla stiffened, asking quietly, "Is that an order from my daughter or my queen?"

Maren, ever the peacemaker, laid her fork down and cleared her throat. "Mother, if you would–"

Damla raised her hand to silence her youngest daughter, never taking her eyes from Naia as she awaited a response.

"I would prefer it be done out of respect for your daughter," Naia said with deadly calm. "But if you are incapable of that, then obey it as an order from your queen."

Damla's chair squeaked against the floor as she rose, breaking the tense silence. She tossed her napkin onto the table and stared down her nose at her daughter. "As you wish, Majesty," she said coldly, before stalking from the room.

Maren, heaving a sigh, leaned back in her chair. "Well, that could have been worse."

Damian huffed a laugh. "Really?"

Exhausted, Naia rubbed her temples with her fingers. "We've had actual bloodshed at this table before, so yes. It could have been worse."

CHAPTER 61

"At least she didn't stab me," Damian teased, as Naia grumbled, flopping back onto her soft bed.

Waving him off, she kicked the slippers from her feet unceremoniously.

"I always wondered," he remarked, striding toward the arches leading to the balcony. "What it looked like inside this palace."

Naia sat up, twisting to watch his back as he leaned against the archway, looking out at the vast sea beyond, glittering in the moonlight, high above. The views from her room were stunning. One of the few parts of this castle she hadn't taken for granted. Watching the sun rise over the sea was worth waking early for.

"Really?"

He nodded, not looking back at her. "When he would take you out here, on the blankets beneath the stars, I looked away, at the other windows and wondered."

"You didn't like him touching me," she recalled.

He chuckled, a low and rumbling sound. "No."

"I don't like remembering it," she admitted, silk whispering as she slid off the bed. As she tugged the shoulders of her dress, letting it fall to the floor, followed by her undergarments. He didn't turn, didn't see her until she brushed past him, stepping onto the balcony, utterly nude.

His brow shot up, hunger darkening his eyes. "What are you doing, Thunderheart?"

Cool stone pressed into her lower back as she leaned against it, splaying her arms to the side, resting atop the railing. "Give me something else to think about, when I look at this balcony."

He growled, stalking toward her like a predator as he quickly removed and tossed aside his own clothing. Her gaze slid from his broad, muscled chest, over the planes of his toned abdomen, to the vee at his hip. The sight of his proud, hardened length had her core tightening, thighs damp.

Damian said nothing as he closed the distance between them, plunging his hand into her unbound hair and gripping it, making her scalp tingle. Pulling her head back so that she looked up at him, he claimed her mouth with his in a demanding kiss. Yielding herself to him completely, she parted her lips, and his tongue swept in. Every thought of Zayan vanished as his tongue met hers, as he licked the roof of her mouth. Breaking the kiss, he lowered his mouth to the space between her jawline and ear, letting his teeth graze over the sensitive skin there.

Her hands roamed over his hard chest, sliding to his back to pull him closer. Her body became little more than liquid fire, burning only for him. When his free hand found her breast, tracing the small curve of it with one finger, his calloused thumb scraping against the sensitive peak, she couldn't stop the small moan that escaped her. Goosebumps danced across her skin at his answering laugh, warm against her throat.

Without warning, he grabbed her hips, placing her on the railing. His eyes, dark and hungry, met hers. "Do you trust me, Thunderheart?" he asked, voice thick.

In answer, she slowly pulled her hands away from his back, splaying her arms to the side like a bird. Only his hands on her hips anchored her. "Always."

Pulling her closer to offer him access, he dipped one hand between them. At the first pass of his thumb against the sensitive bundle of nerves at the apex of her thighs, she moaned again, and the hand he'd placed on her back to steady her tightened. Desperate to touch him, to feel him, she placed her arms on his biceps, marveling at the strength beneath her touch.

His thumb moved in slow deliberate circles, driving her closer and closer to the edge, teasing, as he claimed her mouth again. She met him stroke for stroke, her mind a blur of color and feeling, but little thought beyond what he made her feel. The sudden absence of his hand on her core made her whimper, earning another laugh from him that rumbled through her. The broad head of his cock pressed against her entrance, and she wiggled, need for him roaring in her mind, her body.

"Hold on, Thunderheart."

He sheathed himself in her in one long, slow, stroke. Tipping her head back with a sharp gasp, she felt as though she was in free fall, tumbling right over the edge of the balcony and to the sand below.

"Fuck," Damian groaned, thrusting into her again, slow languid strokes. The hand that had driven her mad moments before sank into her hair again, gripping tight.

His sounds of pleasure drove her mad, pushing her closer and closer to the brink with every thrust. His name was a whimper on her lips, a plea for release. His grip on her hair tightened, pulling her head back to offer him access to her throat. As his teeth grazed the skin between her neck and clavicle, biting down gently, she came undone. Like a crashing wave, she broke, her inner walls tightening around his cock over and over. Lightning danced over her skin, drawing a ragged curse as he followed her over the edge, pulsing within her.

Breathless, he rested his forehead against her shoulder a moment longer before pulling away, and easing her off of the balcony railing. "I think," he said, voice husky, "that you should show me that trick more often." Grinning, he added, "That should give you something to think about when you look at this balcony".

Legs like jelly, and utterly sated, she took him by the hand and led him to the bathing chamber attached to her room. After dressing them both in her own silk robes, his comically small, barely enough to cover his cock, she called for maids to bring hot water. She felt a bit guilty, having summoned them so late to fill the massive tub, but they both desperately needed a proper bath, especially after having only oversized buckets to clean themselves with in the war camp.

"This is humiliating," Damian grumbled, as the maids finally departed, leaving them alone in the steamy room. The tub, blessedly large enough to fit them both, albeit snugly, had been filled, and fresh towels and soaps placed on the nearby table.

She waved off his complaint, shrugging the robe off and stepping into the deliciously hot water. Shuddering, she groaned with no small amount of pleasure at the wonderful heat that eased her tired muscles as she sank into the water. By the time she was settled, the frothy water was rising just above her breasts.

"Are you going to get in or just stand there in your pretty, pretty robe?" Naia taunted with a grin.

"Cruel little queen," he tossed back, dropping the robe to the floor and climbing into the tub with her.

The water sloshed gently, and after a moment, he settled in comfortably with her in front of him. "How long do you think she'll drag this out?"

She didn't need to explain what she meant. The torturous wait that Kore had been putting them through for what felt like ages now. The endless cat and mouse games. Designed, Naia assumed, to wear down their defenses; both physical and mental.

"I doubt it'll be long now," he said softly. The water sloshed with his movement, and a moment later, his hands were in her hair, fingertips gently massaging jasmine-scented shampoo through her thick locks. "Her own forces are likely growing as weary of it as we are."

"Mm," Naia hummed, as he worked the shampoo through the length of her hair. "I'm ready."

For a moment, the only sound between them was the sloshing of the water as he dipped a shell cup into the water. A gentle tug on her hair had her tipping her head backward so he could rinse the shampoo from her hair.

"I know you are," he replied calmly. "Honestly, I think you could just about rival her on your own. If not in magic, than in sheer ferocity."

Naia laughed as he put the cup to the side, and she lifted her head. The remark, as ridiculous as it had sounded, had been genuine. The battle would come soon, and after...after they would have to face the truth of what the gods had done. Of the threat they posed. Would they come to claim their artifacts and the lives of the bearers immediately? Or would they wait, allowing them a moment of peace before the end? Perhaps, she wondered, they would simply leave them alone this time.

There was no real way to know what would happen, or when, and that thought terrified her more than the battle to come.

A brush of a rough sponge across her back drew her from her thoughts. "Let it go, for tonight at least, and rest," Damian said, guessing the direction her thoughts had taken.

"I will."

Minutes passed in comfortable silence as he bathed every inch of her, and if she'd had any energy left, she would have climbed on top of him right in the tub. But exhaustion had finally settled over her like a lead blanket, her eyelids so heavy she struggled to keep them open.

Wordlessly, Damian helped her from the tub, dried her hair and skin with a gentleness she would never have thought him capable of, before scooping her into his arms and carrying her straight to bed.

She fell asleep within minutes, with him curled around her, safe and utterly content.

CHAPTER 62

Naia sat up straight in the bed, unsure what had drawn her from sleep. A glance toward the sea told her sunrise was still hours away. Her sleep had been blissfully dreamless, what little she'd had of it. No nightmares had plagued her, no memories of past lives or torment. So what had woken her?

With a sigh she dragged her hand through sleep-mussed hair, and started to lay down again. If she could fall asleep now, she should be able to have a few more hours of rest before it would be time to get up and finish the preparations for Kore. To do more waiting.

Screams rang out through the darkness.

Damian sat up straight, bolting out of the bed, followed by Naia.

The sounds of steps in the hallway had Damian yanking his sword from the scabbard, propped against the wall by the bed. Maren burst in without so much as knocking, throwing a hand over her eyes when she spotted both Naia and Damian's nudity.

"Holy gods, we're at war, sleep with clothes on!" she shouted, gagging.

"What happened?" Naia demanded.

Maren's tone was grave when she spoke again. "We're under attack. She's here."

There were no words exchanged as they hurriedly dressed and prepared themselves to go to battle. They'd had days, weeks, to prepare for this, to talk about the various possibilities. What they hadn't done, perhaps should have done as soon as they'd arrived, was familiarize Damian and some of the others with the streets of Thalassa.

"The city is essentially a ring," Naia explained, as she buckled her boots, glancing up to watch him sheath his sword. "Radiating out from the castle. It's easy to navigate if you understand that."

He nodded, silent. The mask of the Samach slid into place.

"Let me see you," she said quietly, rising from her seat and crossing to him. "Before we go, let me see you."

Dropping his gaze to meet hers, he sighed. He knew what she meant of course, and after a heartbeat, the coldness, the lack of emotion slipped away leaving behind the love and worry shining in his eyes. "Stay with the others," he said, voice low. "If I have to leave your side, stay with the others. If she got one of you alone..."

Naia nodded. "I know," she assured him, his beard scratching her palms as she took his face in her hands. "I know. If we get separated, I will find you. When it's done."

The shouts of soldiers rang out through the night. Orders for residents to take shelter in the castle if they were able, or in their homes if they were not.

"It's time."

Naia nodded, and they headed to the door. With a small amount of guil, and a silent apology to her ancestors, they ran down the center of the mosaic hallway. Hopefully they would forgive her, she thought, given the dire circumstances.

A feline yowl greeted them as they reached the main entrance, and the little grey cat they'd rescued from Tevara stepped out of a shadowed corner.

"Oh," Naia sighed. "You shouldn't be out here!" Determined to see the cat to safety, she bent to pick her up, only for the cat to sprint away into the darkness.

"Cats have an instinct for survival," Damian assured her as she rose, frowning. "She'll be fine."

"I suppose," Naia replied, frowning. "Let's go."

At the castle gates, they found the rest of the inner circle. Eve, Lia, and their closest friends and lovers, each outfitted for battle with varying expressions. Some, like Callan, Valerian, and Leysa's hardened. Prepared for what was to come. Aelius and Mara each appeared resigned, as if the entire thing was little more than a regretful duty. Bella's expression remained as unreadable as Damian's, and Cathal, he looked bored.

On Eve and Lia's faces, however, she saw her own emotions mirrored.

Determination, fear, and perhaps even the slightest hint of hope.

Hope they had what it would take to end this, to be the salvation their world needed. That they would survive this. Soldiers gathered and the gates swung open, revealing already chaotic streets outside.

People were rushed in, brushing past the group with children, pets, and whatever most valuable belongings they could carry, to seek shelter within the castle. Maren and Damla would see to their people, ensuring that everyone who was able to make it there was tended to.

While Naia and the others had prepared, the city guard and waiting armies outside of Thalassa had jumped into action. The screams they'd heard in her room, drifting in on the night wind, were merely those of fright, not any actual danger. When the fighting had begun outside the city, the sounds had frightened the residents closest to the walls, causing the commotion, a guard had explained to Callan while they'd waited for Naia and Damian. His swift explanation had come as those who could pace took the hands of those who could not.

The sounds of clashing steel and shouts echoed from beyond the city, as they paced to the city gates to meet the awaiting armies.

With only a brief hug for his sister, Aelius was off to meet with the commanders who served their armies, shouting orders and demands for a report as he ran. Naia wondered if he and Maren had taken the time for goodbyes, or, knowing her sister, for 'see you later.' Maren would have considered goodbye an ill omen on the eve of battle.

Leysa and Valerian spoke quietly with Callan and Eve, and Naia pointedly turned her attention elsewhere. Huddled close, the group exchanged swift hugs before the couple set off. The shifter taking to the skies in the form of a hawk, while her warrior husband set off to join the fray, but not before casting a long look in her direction. The others, the three queens, their mates, and the other mated pair, Cathal and Mara, would remain together for as long as possible.

The sounds and smells of battle assaulted Naia's senses as the group finally passed through the gates. Despite the unexpected onslaught by Gorias and Kore, their lines were holding. She would have thought battle to be pure chaos, having never seen it before herself, and while it certainly did have a certain madness to it, the lines were still clear enough for her to pick out individual armies among their forces.

The bright white standard of Avellon shone to the left, bolstered by the silver of Finias. In the center, the forest green clad army of Dark-egrove fought alongside the navy blue of Falias, and burgundy soldiers, human, that she could only assume answered to Eve. Far to the left, there were her own men and women. Clad in the turquoise and silver of her house, they fought beside the soldiers of Murias, in their own copper garb. Interspersed within the mass of soldiers, fae and human alike, were animals. Shifters in every imaginable form. Large cats, bears, stags, and even a wolf or two. Birds soared through the skies, dodging arrows flying at them from the opposing army. The eyes above, passing along information about the enemies numbers, their positions, she knew. How many of them would die before the day was done?

"Where is she?" Lia asked quietly as they stepped onto the small rise outside of the gates, just high enough to give them a decent vantage point of the fight below.

The tang of copper filled the air, and Naia wrinkled her nose. "What is that?" she asked, frowning.

Callan and Damian, the most experienced in battle among them, shared a glance. "Blood," Damian replied. "Before long all you'll be able to smell is blood, shit, and piss."

"The smell of death," Callan added solemnly. Turning to Lia, he said, "She'll wait, until our numbers are depleted, until they're tired, and making mistakes."

"Why?" Eve frowned. "She can't think they'll be much of an issue for her."

"No," Damian agreed, "she won't. But it will make getting to you three easier."

Naia snorted, shifting the bag slung over her shoulders lightly. The cauldron inside seemed to hum with power, only waking or banking in preparation, perhaps. "Let her come."

"We can't stay here for long," Cathal interrupted, looking at Callan. "We'll be needed down there, brother, all of us."

Callan tensed, appearing ready to argue.

"He's right," Eve said. "Stay for now, but if our armies begin to falter, they'll need you."

"I'll stay," Mara supplied. "I'll help them if they need me."

"We'll be fine," Eve said, placing a hand on Callan's arm. "We talked about this."

Silently he nodded, pressing a kiss to her lips.

Lia and Bella stepped away then, whispering words to one another that Naia deliberately tuned out. Mara and Cathal simply shared a long, silent glance. Whatever words they might have had for one another needn't be said aloud, she supposed, spoken only through long, intense looks.

Damian pulled her by the hand, drawing her attention.

"No goodbyes," she said quietly.

"No goodbyes," he agreed.

There were so many things she longed to say, so many things she wanted to ask. There would never be enough time, not in this life or the next, to tell him the things in her heart. All the many complicated feelings she had for him. She would try, when this was done, when they had the rest of their long lives, to do nothing more than share words, to explore the world, and one another.

Besides, she reminded herself, *this isn't goodbye.*

"Damian–" she began, unsure what she would even say, but something needed to be said, some words of love or luck.

"Damian!" Callan's shout had them both spinning. The far right of their line was beginning to fall apart. Callan was already pacing, vanishing into smoke and wind, his brother right behind him. Bella, with a swift kiss for Lia, ran down the dunes, heading for Lia's armies, sword in hand.

"Go," Naia urged him, stepping back. "Go."

He said nothing, meeting her gaze with his own, and nodding. As smoke and wind enveloped him, carrying him away from her, to the battle that may yet claim both of their lives, he mouthed the words she hadn't had the courage to say yet. "I love you."

CHAPTER 63

The four women stood atop the dune, watching as the battle raged below. Soldiers screamed, steel clashed, and animals roared. They said nothing as men and women fell below, said nothing as Callan and Damian bolstered the faltering line, though they had each released a sigh of relief.

As their lines began to fall back, Gorian soldiers pushing them closer and closer to the city, they began to unleash their magic, small amounts only, leaving the artifacts untouched. That power was to be reserved for Kore. The void that threatened to swallow their world.

Where soldiers began to flag, a flash of healing light enveloped them, healing and refreshing them; a beacon of hope for those around them, rallying the weary soldiers. As a group of Samach approached, they found the ground opening beneath their feet, swallowing them into the sands. The archers, taking aim at the shifters above, found themselves struck by lightning darting from a clear sky.

The sun had nearly fully risen by the time Kore made her first appearance.

Though she remained too far away to be seen, Naia could feel her. Death and doom drifted on the wind, directed, it seemed, for the three bearers. A chill ran through the battlefield, a palpable otherworldly chill that seemed to give every soldier below pause, even those fighting on the side of Gorias. Unrecognizable words spoken in a tongue she didn't understand, though the meaning was clear enough.

I am your end. Your destruction. I will swallow you whole, and this world will feel my wrath.

Still, they remained silent, sharing only a glance of understanding between the three of them. If Mara knew what they heard, what they felt, she gave no indication. Her attention remained solely on the battle below, where fire erupted from the far side of the line, lacing its way between their own soldiers before engulfing a group of Gorian warriors on the other side.

"No!" Lia screamed out of nowhere, scrambling for the battlefield.

Mara and Eve, standing closest, grabbed her arms, halting her frantic attempt to run. Light, bright and hot as the sun, erupted from her as she screamed again, wordlessly.

Like liquid, it flowed into the battle, leaving their own soldiers unharmed. Past a man who fell, speared through the chest, between the feet of a woman wearing the bright white of Avellon, sword raised above her head as she slew a Gorian soldier. All the way to the bear, lying on his side, blood seeping from a vicious wound.

The soldier clad in the grey of Gorias raised his sword again. At Lia's scream of agony and fear, he glanced up. Even from so far away, Naia could make out his grin of triumph as he realized the value of his target. Her heart ached for Lia, who struggled to pull free of Eve and Mara's grip. Stepping close, Naia put a hand on her arm, intent on comforting her friend, only to be dragged into wind and darkness without warning.

She fell to the sand, gaping, as Lia, Sword of Light in her hands, screamed in rage and swung. How she'd managed to pace them, all of them, she noted, taking in Mara and Eve's astonished stares from where they too had fallen onto their rears nearby, and gotten the sword free of its scabbard at her back, Naia had no idea.

Scrambling to her hands and knees in the loose sand, she could do little more than watch as Lia struck the stunned soldier with a vicious swipe across his midsection. Not likely a killing blow by Lia's untrained hand, and against a fae male clad in armor; if it hadn't been for the burning light that erupted from the sword.

Lia didn't bother to watch him as he fell, gaping skyward, unseeing, as the seared flesh of his open abdomen still sizzled. Sword hanging limply in her hand, she dropped to her knees by the bear. His gaze was fixed, staring somewhere far beyond any of them, his chest utterly still.

They hadn't come soon enough.

A broken sob rattled through Lia, and Naia crawled toward her. Over their heads, shouts rang out, the echo of battle still surrounding them. But nothing touched them. Naia glanced away from Lia in time to see a wall of solid earth rising around them, small but solid enough to keep them from harm.

And if any dared, Mara stood ready. The only one of them on her feet, she stood with her hands spread to the side, silvery mist winding its way around her hands, prepared to defend them as they comforted Lia, as she mourned the loss of her friend and guardian.

"Lia," Eve said gently, placing a hand on Lia's shoulder. "We can't stay."

Ignoring her entirely, Lia leaned down, resting against his side, not noticing or not caring about the blood that now coated her leathers. "I'm so sorry, I'm so sorry," she said over and over, face buried in his brown fur.

"Lia," Naia said, calm but firm. "We will see him taken care of, when the battle is won. We cannot stay."

"I'm so sorry," Lia said once more, through heaving sobs. "I'll take care of them, your girls and Leo. I promise." With a hand on his shoulder, she looked at Naia and Eve. "I will not leave him here."

"I'm here," Bella called from beyond Eve's wall of stone. She'd been closest when he'd fallen, had fought to get to him, but hadn't made it in time. "We have to take him away from here," Lia said, swiping tears from her face. "I won't leave him."

Together, Naia and Eve eased Lia up and away from her friend. Her heart ached for Lia's loss, even as she wondered how many more losses each of them would face before it was done. As Eve's wall fell the rest of the way down, she found them surrounded by soldiers in white, green, and turquoise. The human armies had come to their aid, surrounding them long enough for her to see to Amias' body. But it was the sight of shifters, in varying forms, interspersed among them that gave Naia's heart a squeeze.

The shifters had come to see him taken away to safety. The man who like so many of them, she was sure, had left his family behind in hopes of helping to save them all.

"We have to go back," Eve said, glancing to Bella.

"Sunlight," Bella soothed, wrapping her arms around Lia's neck. "I'm so sorry, my love."

Lia nodded, leaning into Bella's embrace, shoulders shaking. "I can't leave him."

A white wolf with light grey eyes stepped out of the gathered crowd, and with a flash of light transformed into a lovely, dark- haired fae woman.

"I'll take him," she said gently.

Eve heaved a breath. "Cora, I didn't know you were–"

Cora shot Eve a look and grinned. "Like I'd let my brothers have all the fun." Turning her attention to Lia her gaze softened. "I'll see him home, don't worry."

"I'm sorry, but we need to go now," Mara called out.

Outside the little space they'd carved out in the middle of the battle, the sounds of war raged. Growing ever closer.

"Go," Bella said gently, pushing Lia back into Naia and Eve's waiting arms.

"We'll have to pace alone," Eve said. "I don't know how she did it, but I can't pace all of us that far."

Lia sniffled, shaking her head as she adjusted her grip on the sword. "I can't do it again."

Naia turned her gaze toward the small rise near the city gates. The place they were meant to be. "So we pace as far as we can, and then we do it again. Until we make it back."

"And if we're separated?" Lia asked.

"Mara can't pace," Eve said at the same time. "I'll take her with me."

"Then we'll go together," Naia replied, taking Lia's hand in hers.

As she readied herself for the first leap, Bella's silver eyes met hers intently. "Don't you let anything happen to her," she ordered.

A small part of her wanted to bristle at the tone, the underlying threat in the words. But she also saw the fear shining in Bella's eyes. The love for Lia. So instead, she nodded. "I have her."

The first pace took them nearly halfway to their destination, Naia realized with triumph, as the wind and darkness ebbed away. Well within their own ranks, thankfully, and just behind a group of archers aiming skyward.

"Get down!" someone shouted.

Without questioning it, Naia ducked, dragging Lia down with her.

Unearthly screeching sounded from above. So loud that it made her ears ache, and Naia hazarded a glance skyward. Scaled beasts of pure, glistening white soared above. The ash arrows fired from the fae soldiers surrounding them mostly bouncing off harmlessly. The few that managed to pierce the beasts' skin only managed to do so near the joints of one of their four legs, each ending in great paws that sliced the air as they flew, on glittering wings. The one nearest them opened his serpentine jaw and roared, the sound rattling the ground beneath.

"Fire!" the commander shouted again, and Naia seized Lia's hand.

Naia didn't know from what hell these beasts had been summoned, as they existed in no legend or lore that she had ever heard of. Nothing like them had ever been depicted in the mosaics of her home, or in the stories told by the elders.

Dragons, maybe? They were said to be great, winged beasts who killed by fangs and claws. Vicious and deadly.

The beast roared again, and as blood fell from its wound, it sizzled in the sand, searing the arm of the archer it grazed.

Monsters with burning blood. Wonderful.

Lia gaped at the creature above, muttering a prayer to the gods before Naia dragged them both into darkness once more. Wherever Eve and Mara had ended up, she prayed they hadn't come across whatever those monsters were.

A wall of stone flew up behind them as Eve and Mara raced into the waiting arms of Brida's soldiers. The snarling of the hounds at their heels turned to yelps as the beasts collided with the wall.

"What the fuck was that?" Mara heaved, bending over to catch her breath.

They'd paced into the middle of a skirmish between a handful of Brida's human soldiers and a pair of soldiers from Gorias. Hound masters of some sort, with monstrous animals that only somewhat resembled dogs as their weapons. Eve and Mara had only had time to run, as the beasts tore into the humans so quickly that she'd had no time to save them, only to run, to reach the larger group that approached.

Now, she would fight back.

The wall of stone rose higher, higher, before toppling over, crushing anyone and anything unfortunate enough to have been on the other side.

"Whatever they were," Eve replied, catching her breath. "They're gone."

"Demons," Mara muttered.

A roar overhead drew the eyes of everyone around them, on both sides of the fight, as a massive white dragon soared over head; dwarfing even the glittering white beasts that engaged their archers, farther down the lines.

"Another beast from hell?" a soldier cried out, spitting onto the ground.

Eve shook her head, blood chilling. "No. Something much worse." Her gaze shifted to Mara. "We have to go now. She's here."

Mara seized Eve's hand, nodding. "Then let's do it."

Chapter 64

Naia's blood chilled as they arrived at the arranged meeting place, relatively safe behind their lines. A dragon's roar sounded once more, sending a chill down her spine. She would have known what monster had taken that form, even if Eve hadn't shared the details of her nightmarish encounter with Kore.

Lia tensed beside her, hand tightening around her own. "We should–"

Her words fell to silence as a cloud of darkness and wind announced Eve and Mara's arrival. Naia took in their haggard appearances. Dust covered their leathers, blood spattered across them. "Are you okay?"

"We survived," Mara replied dryly.

"We're unharmed," Eve said, more softly, gaze locked on the great white dragon that had finally settled onto the ground. In the middle of the battlefield.

Soldiers, human and fae alike, from both sides of the war, scattered from her massive form. Kore didn't bother to acknowledge any of them. Even the soldiers of her own army, squashed beneath her claws, or swept away by her tail.

Depthless black eyes fixed on where the queens stood, watching, and narrowed for a brief moment. Fear had Naia's heart thundering in her chest. Fear that Kore would incinerate them where they stood. Would destroy their friends and loved ones who still fought between the dragon and the queens.

But the dragon merely watched, baring her teeth, a predatory gleam in her eye.

Come and get me.

As clear as if she'd spoken the words aloud. And perhaps, in a way, she had. Naia could almost *feel* the taunt washing over her like a wave.

"She wants us to come to her," Eve said.

"Then let's oblige her," Naia replied, snarling.

"Together," Lia said softly.

"Together," Naia and Eve replied as one.

The sound of footsteps sounded to the right, drawing their attention as a group of four soldiers bearing the colors of Gorias approached, warily. Slowly they walked, fanning out to form a circle around the women.

Naia opened her mouth to speak, to tell them what a grave mistake they'd made, but Mara interrupted, dropping Eve's hand and stepping away from the trio.

"Go. I have them."

The sounds of screams carried them along the ethereal wind between the fabrics of their world to meet their fate.

ONLY A FEW YARDS FROM THE DRAGON, SHE APPEARED MUCH larger than she had from a distance. Despite the resolve, the bravery she felt, she couldn't help the chill of fear that coursed through her. Slipping her hand into her pocket, she grazed her thumb over the bit of tile that bore Cordelia's eye. She'd hadn't dared to touch it in days, not since the dream of their shared past.

We won't be forgotten this time.

In fact, they had already dispatched riders, sent from the last camp they'd made before departing from Coruscis, not only to the six kingdoms but to the farthest reaches of their world, sharing their story. The stories of their past selves, of the truths they'd learned in dreams.

The world would know what happened here. What they'd tried to do. More messengers waited, prepared to depart at a moment's notice when the day was won...or lost.

For good or ill, the world would know.

"Face us as a woman," Naia called out, willing herself to sound confident, unafraid. Dragging the bag slung across her chest off, she pulled the cauldron free and dropped the bag to the ground. The plant inside had grown since she'd last seen it in her office, nearly double in size now with an explosion of bright green leaves that hadn't been there before. Bolstered, perhaps, by Eve's magic.

"If you dare," Eve tacked on, lifting a hand to straighten the crown atop her brow.

Lia said nothing, but from the corner of her eye, Naia could see the gleam of sunlight flashing on steel.

The dragon huffed, perhaps a laugh in the face of their bravely spoken words, but in the span of a blink, shifted into the familiar female form of Kore. Long, dark hair hung in loose waves to the curve of her hips.

Where they had dressed for battle, she wore only a flowing gown of gossamer, bright white against her tan skin. A sharp vee cut between her breasts clear to her navel, with slits high to her hips, leaving little of her form covered. Utterly stunning in her beauty, as always.

At her side stood Endri, dressed in simple white robes, with long white hair pulled back into a simple braid. No adornments or weapons graced their figure, and though their hands remained unbound, their position as prisoner was clear enough, as they stood unmoving at her side, an unreadable expression locked on the trio.

"Such brave words spoken by little more than insects." She took a few steps forward, bare feet sinking into the shifting sand. "I tried so very hard to change your minds, to steer you to the real enemy here." Turning a light smirk at Endri, who remained stationary, she continued, "And yet, you ignore my generous warnings. How very disappointing."

Naia's grip on the cauldron tightened, lightning dancing along her palms. "We heard your warnings, and have taken them under consideration," she spat.

Kore ignored Naia, turning to Lia first. "Such a gentle, pretty, thing." Her gaze drifted to Eve. "And the earthbound queen." She grinned. "The two of you would make the most delightful pets. I would revel in breaking that stony confidence of yours, and in sharpening that gentleness into something more...entertaining." Lust and hate in equal measure danced in her eyes, the former fading entirely as she finally settled her gaze on Naia. "You. You will be nothing more than ash on the wind."

Naia's brow rose and she chuckled, low and throaty. "Yeah, fuck you too."

Darkness erupted at her words, in time with Lia's own flash of brilliant light; a shield against the eruption of power. Alone, Lia could barely halt the assault, but as their hands once more joined, the power of the sun pushed the darkness back, earning an enraged howl from Kore.

Massive boulders sprang forth from the ground, hurling themselves toward where Kore had been standing, now hidden behind a wall of utter darkness, as Naia's lightning assaulted the space. She could only hope Endri had finally moved, or had some way of shielding themself, but their safety, as much as it did matter to Naia, could not stop them from doing what needed to be done.

After several moments, they slowed their attack, falling into silence. Despite the battle that continued to rage on around them, Naia heard nothing but the roaring in her ears...until a throaty laugh sounded from the now abating darkness.

Kore, hands splayed as she recalled her magic, appeared utterly unruffled. A pile of dust, all that remained of Eve's boulders lay charred from Naia's lightning, surrounded her.

You must call on us, the childlike whisper of the cauldron echoed in her mind. *It is time.*

She could only assume the others had heard the same from their own artifacts, as they each jolted, turning to look at one another bearing intense expressions.

"Now," Naia whispered.

The lightning that had danced on her palms spread like wildfire over her form until she herself became little more than a storm in the shape of a woman. Clouds appeared overhead, cracking open and pouring rain over them all. Beside her, Eve had gone still, flowers and vines breaking free from the sands at her feet, wrapping themselves around her, and Lia —she herself glowed as bright as the sun.

In all their practicing, none had dared to call upon so much of their magic, had never allowed the artifacts to amplify their gifts to this level before.

The magic of other fae erupted around them. Ice and wind, fire and water, more magics that she couldn't see from where she stood, all aimed at the Gorian soldiers they still battled.

"Samach!" someone screamed above the din.

The magic fell silent, but only for a moment.

Kore's smirk of triumph faltered, briefly, as Damian's shield went up and their magic resumed.

"Now," Naia whispered once more, her words only for the others, as a ripple of some power she couldn't identify coursed between them.

United. Sisters in soul, bound by something that transcended friendship. They would triumph, or they would perish. Together. As they were destined.

Though she loathed the idea that she had been forced upon this path by forces beyond her control, for this, their unity, their support for another, she would forever be grateful.

Damian's face flashed in her mind.

For what she'd found with him, she would live a thousand pre-destined lifetimes. With him, she'd found her heart. Her soul. The parts of herself she'd never allowed beyond the most hidden depths of herself. To save their world, to see him again, to see her sister, her mother, she would fight with every bit of power she could call upon.

For the women she would forever be bound to, by choice and by fate, she would fight.

As one, they exploded. Life and light and rage, shoving against the darkness that threatened to devour their world.

Life and light and fury.

A whirlwind of lightning, threaded with vines and small, sharp pebbles, and waves of liquid sunlight whooshed forward, enveloping a startled Kore. Sand rose from the ground, struck by tiny bolts of lightning, sharpening the sand to miniscule shards of glass, before flying into her deceptively beautiful face.

A shriek sounded from the Void, as their magic blazed past her shield of darkness.

"Colette!" she screamed, and a flash of white blinked at her side, revealing a girl of perhaps sixteen, with short, white blonde hair and large, terrified ice blue eyes.

In the girl's hand, a tall, unremarkable spear, made of ash and tipped with a black arrowhead. Despite the distance, Naia could see the way the spear shook, wobbling in the girl's trembling grip.

"Little more than a nuisance," Kore seethed. "Even with all your power. You aren't strong enough to defeat me."

The battle around them had all but stilled, a slow wave spreading across the battlefield as both sides paused to witness the showdown between the three queens of Aestera, and the darkness itself.

"With a little help, they might just be," a familiar voice called out as a sweet-scented, phantom wind swept over the sands. Appearing in the blink of an eye, Macaria took a place just beside the trio. "You will not stand alone in these last moments," she said more quietly, lifting a hand but keeping her eyes on Kore.

A rush of power, gentle but undeniably cold, swept across the sounds, followed by shouts of surprise.

There, in the space that had reformed between the lines, when all had gone quiet to witness the end, a vast line of people had suddenly appeared.

More fae? Naia frowned. Perhaps those who served her, from some far-flung corner of the world. None stood close enough for her to tell, from their features or garb, where they hailed from, but it was the only explanation she could wrap her mind around. The mind that was still reeling, with surprise and no small amount of anger, at the goddess's sudden intervention.

Where had the gods been all this time? Hiding like cowards.

"The others?" Naia asked, voice low.

Macaria sighed. "It is only I," she replied softly, turning her veiled gaze on the three queens at last. "I will not leave you, no matter what happens next." Red lips curving into a soft smile, she added, "And, I've brought a few others who would like to make that promise as well."

A man stepped from behind Macaria then, tall, dressed in the armor of Avellon's armies, with warm brown eyes and dark hair. A crumpled sob erupted from Lia who darted from between them to envelop the man in a fierce hug.

"Who is–"

Before Naia could process what she was witnessing, a tall man, with earth brown hair and broad shoulders, dressed in deepest greens and browns, stepped out next. A man she had met before, one who couldn't be here now.

Impossible.

Eve swept forward wordlessly, embracing her father, and soon her mother, who followed from behind him moments later.

Naia's heart was thunder in her chest as she waited to see who would step out next. Every beat was agony. Half hoping he would be next, half terrified of the same. There were so many things she'd want to say, so much time they couldn't possibly have.

"Naia."

Though her view was blocked by the reunions of the others. Exactly as she'd last seen him, her father stepped out from some pocket of air behind the goddess, taking Naia's hands in his own. Slender hands took hold of hers, squeezing gently.

"My little girl," he said roughly, tears welling in dark eyes. Tall and thin, much like Naia, people had often remarked that she had favored him far more than Damla. "So brave, so strong. Like I always knew you were."

Her heart shattered in her chest. Grief, as fresh as the day he'd died, swept over her in a furious wave. So many unspoken words raced through her mind. Apologies for not being there that day. For all the cruel words spoken by a teenager rebelling against parental control. A million little things that she'd never had the chance to tell him. What would he have made of Damian, and all that had happened between them?

What would he say about her plan to relinquish the throne to Maren?

Her eyes burned with tears she didn't let fall. "Papa, I–"

A keening sound of grief sounded from Lia, and Naia turned in time to see Aldrich Vallyse step out, hovering a few steps from his daughter, as if unsure. He'd been ill, very ill she remembered, before his passing, but the version of the King of Avellon she saw now was as healthy as he'd ever been. Lia held out a hand for him, a bridge over whatever had caused the chasm that lay between them.

"As heartwarming as this little scene is," Kore called out, boredom lacing her words, "It matters little. I do hope you've had time to say your sweet little goodbyes."

In unison, the gathered crowd, living and dead, turned to face the Void once more. Along the battle lines, their soldiers did much the same, with the army of dead loved ones joining their own.

"There is yet one more farewell to be had," Macaria called out in return. Naia frowned, turning to watch the goddess, whose attention, she realized, lay not on Kore, but on the teenager at her side.

From her side, a tall, slender, teenaged boy appeared. Roughly the same age as Colette, Naia guessed, and familiar to her, judging from the way he stared intensely at her, as if he would leap across the sands to get to her if he could.

Naia's skin buzzed with electricity, anticipation, as she turned her attention to Kore. Colette had fallen to her knees in the sand at her side, spear lying in front of her. Disregarding the display entirely, Kore simply lifted a hand and signaled her forces to resume their assault.

Between inhale and exhale, all hell broke loose.

The armies clashed once more, and Kore's darkness surged for them. With near impossible speed, Lia threw a shield of light over them, as Naia and Eve hurled lightning and stone at their enemy. Soldiers swarmed them, steel clashing with that of their ghostly loved ones.

Above the din, she could hear their names, one by one, being called by familiar voices.

Bella arrived first, sword swinging, as she fought her way to Lia's side, followed soon after by Aelius, who stumbled backward: shock etched into his features as he took in the sight of the two spirits Macaria had called upon to aid Lia.

Thunder crashed overhead, lightning spearing into the soldiers of Gorias, followed by an impressive assault of sand and boulders hurled by Eve. Above it, Kore shouted words she could not understand. Something that had the corner of Macaria's lips turning upward ever so slightly.

Callan arrived next, offering a brief courteous bow to Eve's parents before joining his own magic and steel to theirs. Shadows of his own snaked through the battle, slipping into the minds of soldiers, or outright strangling them.

Between his shadows, Kore's darkness, and Naia's thunderclouds, the bright sun above had become little more than a hazy, watery speck in the sky, making it near impossible to see much of anything from a distance, and yet–

A familiar dark head appeared, just beside the spear bearer, accompanied by the teen boy with the lovelorn face, Endri vanishing from her view in the same instance.

She screamed, utter terror seizing her heart as Damian reached for Colette, who gripped the spear, raising it–and–

Naia, wracked by lightning, and love, and fear, and rage–by so many emotions she could never begin to name them all or pinpoint from which part of her they hailed, poured everything into the cauldron. Threw every part of her broken self into the attack.

If they didn't kill her now–

Kore had boasted that they lacked the strength to kill her, and deep down, Naia had suspected the three of them weren't enough. But when the blow landed, lightning laced with pebbles and vines, illuminated by burning light, she stumbled. Only a little, but it was enough.

Because the spear raised by a terrified child who had been wielded like a weapon–and, Naia suspected, who had been forced to kill her own guardian, the soul most tied to her own, hadn't been pointed at Damian.

It had been pointed at Kore.

CHAPTER 65

COLETTE

"It has to be now," the strange man said again.

"Only you," Lumi whispered, dropping to his knees beside her.

Colette stared at Lumi for a long moment. She'd seen the ghosts appear, seen what the death goddess had done, but seeing him here, now in front of her, was almost more than she could take.

Images flashed through her mind in rapid succession.

A boy and a girl, side by side, sliding down an icy hill, eight years old and just days after they'd first met.

The dark hallway two short years ago, sharing their first, clumsy kiss.

His blood spilling down his chest, the spear jutting from the wound. Only–

"Stop," he said, reading the guilt in her face. He always seemed to know exactly what she was feeling. "It wasn't your fault, Lettie, it wasn't your fault. Be strong, you have to do this."

She knew. But knowing didn't make it any easier.

Kore had lined up a dozen or so of her own people. Not even soldiers, many of them children younger than herself, and forced her to choose. A test of her loyalty and punishment for her attempt at sending some of them away, back home to safety. She hadn't understood until that moment why the Void had insisted on bringing families with the army. It had made no sense, until she saw them for the leverage they were.

The roaring of the battle, of her own blood in her ears, was deafening. Their words were ash on the wind. They wanted *her* to do it?

"But the others," she whispered, turning to look at Kore, who was so distracted by fighting the three southern queens that she hadn't yet noticed the two men.

"*Only you, Bearer,*" the now familiar, raspy voice of her Spear whispered in her mind. Clear as a bell, as if only the two of them existed. "*My siblings, they come. When she falters, only you can end it.*"

"I'm not strong enough," she whimpered, hating the truth of the words.

Barely sixteen, and hardly considered an adult. Despite the fact that she was now Queen of Gorias. Her parents sudden deaths, just before Kore's arrival, had pushed her onto the throne of her isolated kingdom. A position she'd been nowhere ready for.

"*Strength,*" the Spear returned, "*Is not reserved for adults, Bearer. The smallest of beings can be strong.*"

"What do we have here," the Void said, drawing Colette's fearful gaze. As usual, Kore didn't spare her so much as a glance as she fixed her attention on what she considered the more important matter at hand. "Damian."

The stranger, of course.

She'd witnessed enough, had overheard enough, to know who he was. The soldier who had gotten away, the one mated to the lightning queen. The one Kore hated so much.

"*Strength,*" the Spear whispered, as she tightened her grip on him.

Kore's whispered lies rang through her mind. She'd hated them all, while pouring honeyed lies into the ears of Colette's people. Gorias had been so unfairly exiled, Kore had claimed, before the veil between fae and human worlds had gone up. The other kingdoms hated them, she said.

But Colette's parents had taught her differently. When the time came, they'd said, the six kingdoms would be united. They'd spoken often of the prophecy, *'When the gods touch the crescent once more, the lost children will return and herald a new age.'*

While they'd never fully explained, or perhaps had never fully understood, they knew it meant that one day, their worlds would be united.

Once she'd claimed Gorias fully, Kore had stopped bothering to woo Colette. The war on the fae and humans was as good as won, it seemed. Attacking the southern queens, claiming their artifacts, that was the final step in her true plan. Conquering the gods.

She wouldn't need Gorias for that. Or her people. They would meet the same fate as those of the southern kingdoms. They would all die.

Trembling, she tightened her grip on the spear. Colette had no idea when she'd raised it toward Kore, or how the Void hadn't noticed.

Strength.

The word sang through her mind.

She could have sworn her mother's hand was on hers as she thrust the spear forward.

And as the world erupted into a pulse of screaming darkness, it was her father's arms around her, steadying her, as he pushed her into the callused hands of a stranger.

CHAPTER 66

A wave of absolute darkness erupted, sweeping over the battlefield and far into the distant sands, knocking many, including Naia, backward onto the sand.

If the blast of power that had rendered them unconscious days ago was a wave, then this was a tsunami. She had no idea how anyone would survive the blast of power, standing so close to it. Whether it was sheer will, a gift from the death goddess who had come to their aid, or some other unseen force, she didn't know; but somehow she managed to keep her senses.

Sounds like she had never heard rang out across the sands. As if a thousand souls screamed in unison. Throwing her hands over her ears, she tried, and failed, to block the unearthly sound that rattled her eardrums.

Scrambling to all fours, she screamed Damian's name.

But as the darkness cleared, utter shock washed over her.

Kore floated above the sands, prone, arms and legs hanging limp, as if pulled upward by an unseen tether. The spear wielded by the teenage queen remained embedded in her side, dangling. For a moment, she simply hovered. The entire battlefield seemed to hold their breath.

Another blast of power erupted from the Void, wisps and tendrils of darkness spreading from her raised abdomen before folding back into itself. All at once, her body, her entire being, imploded, erupting into one final burst of darkness; sending the spear flying free, falling to the sand. When it was over, no trace of Kore, or her power, remained.

Not a soul moved, nor dared to speak. If they had, she wouldn't have noticed. Her attention lay just below where Kore had died–or ceased to exist. Whatever one would call what had happened to her in those final moments.

There, huddled where he'd been before the blast, Damian knelt on the ground. A woman she'd never seen before draped herself over him. The hazy sheen danced around her body, the same she'd seen on the other spirits conjured by Macaria.

His mother had come to protect him in the end.

At his side, the young spear bearer lay curled on the ground, shielded by a man and woman wearing crowns of icicles, with the teen boy she'd seen with Damian beside her.

After a few moments, Damian rose, shock etched into his features as he took in the sight of his mother. The pain, and grief; the love she saw in his face made her heart ache.

She wanted to go to him, to be at his side, but the roaring of beasts drew her attention.

Kore's pets, it seemed, had remained. Unleashed now, following their mistress's demise.

Dragons took to the skies once more, fearsome and terrifying. Hound-like beasts darting for soldiers on both sides.

Still reeling from what had just happened, the soldiers of Gorias faltered. Defending themselves when necessary from the brutal monsters, but making no move to attack the soldiers they'd just been fighting. Unsure, it seemed, as to what their orders were.

Stand up. Stand up and give them orders, she silently willed the young queen across from her.

Damian, it seemed, had the same thought, as he reached for the girl, pulling her upward by her arm. A few words were exchanged, under the watchful gazes of each of the spirits, and she turned, shouting for a nearby commander, who swiftly spread the word amongst the other soldiers gathered. She could hardly breathe as she watched, the issued command rippling through the Gorian forces, almost visible.

A rough howl nearby drew her attention. One of the hounds had settled its attention on the trio. A blast of sunlight felled it easily enough, searing flesh and bone before it dropped to the sand, lifeless.

"She told them to stand down," Damian said at her side, having paced while she watched the creature's demise. "They'll help us kill what's left, and then she wishes to speak with you all."

Macaria released a thoughtful hum, saying nothing.

Dragons roared above once more. Magic from both sides; ice and fire, with blasts of lightning, burning light, and stone from the queens downed them one by one, slowly, but effectively.

After what felt like hours, Macaria sighed, as the last of the beasts perished, "It's finished."

She couldn't allow herself to feel relief. Not while they stood on the razor's edge of the next confrontation. Would they be forced to battle the gods next? Her gaze slid to Eve and Lia, the question burning in her mind. Their eyes met hers, a silent moment passing among the three of them.

Before anyone could speak what the other was thinking, a feminine voice spoke quietly.

"I want to thank you." Naia turned to face the ghostly woman at Damian's side. She had failed to notice her before, the tall, slender woman who he so strongly resembled. They had the same nose, same eyes, and the same dark hair. "I don't know how much time we have left here," she said quickly, casting a glance at Macaria. "So thank you, for taking care of my son. For bringing him out of the darkness."

Damian's dark eyes swam with emotion as he looked to his mother, saying nothing.

"I will always be there to keep him safe," Naia promised, voice raw and thick from screaming, from the storm of emotions within her.

His mother nodded once, offering Naia a smile before turning to his son and placing a hand on his cheek. "I am always with you."

At her side, her father lifted a hand to his heart, inclining his head. With no warning he and the other spirits vanished, leaving no time for final goodbyes.

Cries of surprise, pleas for more time, echoed around them.

Damian himself uttered a single cry of surprise. Naia spun to look at the death goddess, finding only the faintest wisps of darkness where she'd been standing.

Cowards, all of them.

"I think it's time we have that meeting," she said finally, turning to look at Eve and Lia. "And settle this once and for all."

CHAPTER 67

The young queen across from her shifted uncomfortably. Whether it was from Naia's direct gaze, or the spear she held, Naia didn't know. Already, the girl had changed the position of the spear from upright at her side to across her lap, at least half a dozen times. It took nearly all of Naia's remaining patience not to tell her to just choose a position already.

They had gathered in one of the receiving rooms, left empty save for a dozen or so chairs, arranged in a near circle in the center of the pale blue room. Not a word had been spoken as Naia had led them through the halls of Evertide, careful to avoid the mosaics in the center.

She couldn't help but feel pride at the way the young queen's eyes had widened as they'd walked, nearly bulging from her head, mouth falling open as they'd stepped into the room chosen by Maren. Specifically to elicit this reaction.

Sandstone floors dotted with pale shells, polished and gleaming, met walls of soft blue, with textured and painted terracotta that mimicked flowing waves. The ceiling, a dome of glass, revealed a bright, sunny winter sky above, and in the center, surrounded by their chairs, a bubbling fountain in the shape of twin dolphins.

"What is your name?" Lia asked gently.

"Colette Findari," the girl replied softly. "Queen of Gorias," she winced. "But you know that already."

It was Eve who spoke next, calmly, patiently. "Yes, we do. Do you want to tell us how this began?"

Colette shifted in her seat, spear across her lap this time. "I–it's hard to explain." Her gaze darted between the three queens, to Damian, Bella and Callan at their sides. She had no one to sit with her save an older woman with grey-blonde hair and a sour face. The commander of her armies, they'd been told.

"Try anyway," Naia said firmly. Reigning in her temper was a test of her control, but, she reminded herself, this girl was little more than a child. And despite how things had started, she had helped them in the end.

The girl nodded. "Okay," she breathed. "Um, she arrived a little after my parents died. We don't know why..." She glanced downward, and Naia couldn't but feel a twinge of sympathy at the tears she saw falling onto Colette's lap. With a deep breath, she'd composed herself by the time she looked up again. "It started slow, with promises of prosperity with her blessing. She tricked us. She tricked *me*. By the time I knew what she really was, it was too late."

Lia hummed quietly. "I'm so sorry."

"Thank you," Colette replied, voice barely above a whisper. "If I had known...well, I don't know what I would have done. I was...frightened."

Naia tensed, prepared to tell her that wasn't good enough, but Eve spoke then, perhaps to prevent Naia from speaking the harsh words on the tip of her tongue.

"We understand. I can't imagine facing that at your age."

"Which is what? Fifteen?" Naia chimed in, reigning in her temper once more.

"Sixteen," Colette replied, swiping a tear from her face and moving to hold the spear at her side as she wiggled in her seat.

Naia could hear the smile in Lia's voice as she spoke again. "You're very brave for your age."

She wanted to argue, to rail against the actions the young queen had taken. But could she say that she wouldn't have done the same? At sixteen, she'd been headstrong and sure of herself, but faced with such ultimate power, so much evil, with the safety of her kingdom threatened...

Well, she couldn't truthfully say she would have done things differently.

"Where did the god of dreams go?" Naia asked.

Colette shook her head lightly. "I don't know. They were there...and then they weren't. They vanished around the same time he appeared," she explained, jutting her chin toward Damian, who said nothing as he watched with a flat expression.

"I—" Naia began, only to be interrupted by the sudden feeling of a familiar feline jumping into her lap. The small grey cat, the one she'd thought lost for certain, purred happily as it spun in a circle before curling up in her lap. "Oh."

Colette giggled, a surprising sound that had Naia's attention returning to her.

"She reminds me of my own," the girl said softly. With the weight of six pairs of eyes on her, she shifted again. "Sorry."

Bella's voice sounded from her far right, all the way at the end of their half of the near circle, at Lia's side. "Damian, would you mind...?"

"Of course," he replied. The feeling of his power stretching and yawning washed over her, as he slid the dome of silence over them.

"The gods will not hear us now," Bella explained.

Colette frowned for a moment, glancing between them all. "Oh," she said softly. "Is this about the dream?"

"Yes," Eve replied evenly. "We had assumed...hoped, I suppose, that you were also shown a vision of the past."

"You mean that they killed us all...before?" Colette asked quietly, fear creeping into her voice.

Naia's own mind echoed that fear, but alongside it rage. After all that they had been through, all that they had given, to be punished for sins they didn't even commit...

Thunder crashed above in the cloudless sky.

Damian's hand came to rest on her forearm and the cat in her lap seemed to purr louder. Placing a hand on the grey cat's soft fur, she inhaled slowly, calming herself.

"We wish to discuss our plans for this with you," Eve explained.

"What do you mean?"

Lia tapped her nails on the arm of her wooden seat. "We wish to avoid a conflict with them," she said. "We hope that we can reason with them."

"To avoid another fight, one we might not win," Eve added.

Impatient, Naia nudged the cauldron at her feet with the toe of her boot. "We want to give these damned things back. If it'll keep them from killing us."

Colette blinked, casting a shocked glance at the spear. "That's... something we can do?"

Naia shrugged. "We don't know. It's worth a try, but we all have to agree for it to even have a hope of it working."

Silence fell, with only the merry bubbling of the fountain and the purring of the cat to break it.

"Okay," Colette said finally. "Yes."

"So then we—" Lia began.

Bright, unearthly light erupted from the center of the room, blinding Naia. Shouts of surprise and fear sounded from around her, and Damian yanked her from her seat, pulling her to his side. Where the cat had gone as she suddenly found herself standing, she didn't know.

As the light finally abated, she let her gaze slide over the room. All four queens, and their protectors, were standing. Each behind or beside their guardians.

And in the middle...surrounding the small fountain, eight gods stood waiting.

Chapter 68

"Foolish mortals," Lir remarked, straightening his storm grey tunic. "To think such minor magics can keep us from hearing your plans."

Naia narrowed her eyes at him, but remained silent.

At his side, a goddess with light brown, voluminous curly hair that fell to her waist and a tan, freckled face, rolled her grey eyes. "You wouldn't have known a thing if I hadn't been here."

Been here? Naia frowned.

"Let's focus, shall we?" the slender one with dark skin and long braids said sweetly. She could only be the sun goddess judging from the tattoos spreading across her collar bones, nearly identical to Lia's.

"Please," the brunette on her opposite side, goddess of earth her tattoo told Naia, said. Her gaze landed on Eve as she went on, "A wise decision, to relinquish the gifts we gave you all so very long ago."

Colette made a small sound from across the room, drawing the attention of the gods.

A pretty goddess beside her sighed. She bore silvery tattoos in the shape of scales on her chest, peeking above the low vee of her simple white dress; stark against the warm brown of her skin. With a shift of her head, long dark locks swaying, her grey eyes, sharp and unyielding, rested on Naia as she spoke to the earth goddess. "We are here to weigh the actions of this life, Keithia."

Keithia bristled. "I know that."

Naia tore her gaze from the sharp stare of the goddess and let herself really take in who stood before them. Aside from the ones who had spoken, Macaria, goddess of death, stood to the side, utterly still and silent as the grave. At her side, a goddess with long, wavy blonde hair staring at Colette, and a pale goddess with dark hair who Naia didn't recognize, whose eyes remained locked on Bella and Lia. Whoever she was, her tightly clasped hands and worried gaze told Naia that there was some connection among the three.

"Let's get to it then," Lir said irritably.

The brunette goddess at his side pinned Naia with a bright smile. "I'm sorry for tricking you, little queen."

Naia frowned, confused. She couldn't recall meeting the goddess, nor did she know how the goddess had been here to relay what they'd said to Lir.

"Oh," the goddess laughed. "You might have recognized me better if I were still purring."

She could do little more than blink for several heartbeats. "You were the cat?"

"Renata," Lir groused, rolling his eyes. "I still don't understand why you couldn't have chosen a more dignified form."

"What, do you think a wolf would have been welcomed in?" she shot back. To Naia, she said more gently, "I wanted to see what you three were up to. It was the easiest way. And by the way, thank you for caring so much about my safety. It says a lot about a person, the way they treat animals."

"If you're quite done, I would like to see the matter finished," the flat tone of the goddess with scales tattooed on her admonished. "I am Astraia," she said, stepping forward. "If you would be so kind as to step over here, spear bearer?"

Colette moved in wide-eyed silence, taking a place on the other side of Damian.

"As Justice, it is my duty to determine the fate of the Bearers," she began.

Renata cleared her throat, "We wish for you to weigh our words as well, sister."

"We?" Astraia questioned, raising a brow at Renata.

"Yes," Macaria said, finally moving from her place to step closer to Astraia.

Renata, mirroring her movement, came to stand between the queens and goddess of judgement. "We have had the most contact, the most opportunity to witness their deeds, their words, and wish to offer testimony."

A weighty silence fell over the room, and Naia's heart pounded. Her mind raced, thinking back to every conversation the cat, Renata apparently, had been present for. How many secrets had they let spill, thinking her little more than a pet? Would any of the fears they'd voiced about the past, the future, be weighed against them?

She stiffened, reaching for Damian's hand. A glance to her right showed the same fears mirrored in Eve and Lia's faces. Shifting her attention to Colette, she saw the same on her face, but also something that hadn't been there during their discussion with her. Hope. Her grip on the spear was tight, ready.

Astraia nodded once.

"They have given more in this lifetime than ever before," Macaria said, drawing Naia's attention. "More freely, and with no demands of their own."

Renata nodded emphatically. "I've seen little selfishness on their part–"

"I'm not sure that's entirely true," Lir remarked drily, landing a pointed stare on Damian.

Macaria waved him off. "You need someone to shout at you every once in a while."

"Besides, I think we owed her that one, after Erys," Helie added softly.

Keithia made a small noise of annoyance. "Another problem to be dealt with."

"Later," Helie agreed.

Renata waved a hand. "We're getting off topic again. I have seen their hearts, their courage," she continued. "And this one," she added, glancing at Colette. "I saw in her darkest moments, when she was most afraid, that she still carried the strength to show kindness to the smallest of creatures."

Colette squeaked. "Oh, the owl."

Renata simply nodded.

"Very well," Astraia replied, clearly finished with their testimony.

"If they are to speak," an unfamiliar masculine voice intoned as a cloud of smoke appeared, suddenly, at Lir's side. "Then we should have our say as well."

As the tall, bald man with otherworldly red-orange eyes leveled a gaze on Astraia, a pair of goddesses appeared behind him suddenly. One, utterly unknown to Naia, with flowing wavy blonde hair and a nearly perfect face. The other—all too familiar.

"Yes, yes, yes," Erys chirped. "Let us have our turn."

Astraia wrinkled her nose in distaste at Erys, turning her attention to the other two. "Aden, Hedone, what have you to say on the matter?"

"You know my feelings, Astraia," Aden drawled. "Our safety is paramount. And they," he said, turning his gaze on the queens, "are replaceable. The fact that they held meetings, attempted to keep us unaware while they plotted and planned, this alone should be enough to make a decision. We cannot allow that hubris to take root once again."

Hedone rolled her eyes. "So eloquently put, beloved." Placing a hand on his arm, she shook her head slowly. "But he speaks the truth, sister. While I pity the mortals, we must consider the potential cost of sparing their lives."

Erys giggled gleefully, bouncing on her toes. "Death or life, life or death, what will it be, dear Astraia?"

For an agonizingly long time, stretching for what felt like hours, but was likely little more than minutes, silence reigned. Over the constant drumming in her ears, Naia could barely even hear the bubbling fountain.

If it came to a fight, how quickly could she grab the cauldron? She didn't dare make a move for it now, not when it would most certainly be seen as an attack. The others, it seemed, had reached the same conclusion. Eve's crown rested on her brow, but she kept one hand in Callan's, the other at her side. The sword remained safely in its scabbard on Lia's back, and even Colette's grasp of the spear had loosened.

They would fight if they had to, wouldn't they? To save everyone who would remember them from being erased. And how many lives would that be this time, she wondered. The whole of two armies, plus countless souls spread across all six kingdoms. They would nearly have to do what Kore herself had attempted and–

"I am ready to make my decision."

CHAPTER 69

For the first time in her life, Naia thought she may faint. On one side, the end of everything stretched out before her like a gaping chasm, on the other, a future for not only herself and Damian, but the entire world. They had already defeated one impossible foe, could they defeat this one? Either through the weight of their past deeds or by force, if it came to that.

"Oh, do get on with it," Lir snapped, drawing her from her thoughts.

Unfazed, Astraia spoke again. "Forfeit the artifacts, and live long, unextraordinary lives."

A collective sigh passed through the room, as if the very castle had been holding its breath. And perhaps it had been, Naia mused. Who knew what else held magic if such simple things as a cauldron turned planter could be one of the greatest weapons ever to exist; and a cat could be a goddess in disguise.

"Does that mean we get to live?" Colette asked quietly.

The blonde goddess who had been watching the young queen finally spoke, quietly. "Yes, my chosen one. You are free."

"As soon as you hand those over," Renata added, wrinkling her nose slightly.

Colette immediately passed the spear over, as quickly as one would a burning iron.

Lia obliged next as Helie stepped forward, though far more reluctantly. Naia watched as she stared for a moment, wistfully, at the sword that had been in her family for generations.

"Thank you," Lia said softly, lifting her gaze to Helie.

The goddess simply smiled, stepping away as Keithia moved to Eve next, holding her hands out expectantly. Eve closed her eyes a moment before gently removing the crown from her head. Sympathy for her friend gave Naia's heart a squeeze as a single tear fell from Eve's green eyes, before she silently passed the crown of her kingdom to the goddess.

"If you cry, I may just vomit," Lir drawled. Jerking her gaze from Eve, she found him standing in front of her, expectantly. "I can't take it from you. It has to be freely given. So give it."

"So impatient, brother," Renata scolded.

Naia said nothing, biting back the sharp retort on her tongue. She just wanted it done. Wanted nothing more to do with any of them. But as she lifted the cauldron in her hands, the weight of the moment finally hit her. Handing it over felt like handing over a piece of herself, even if she'd only known what she had for a short time.

Lifting the cauldron from the floor, she let her hands graze the rough metal surface. The plant inside had grown, now draping over the sides in long vines with broad flat leaves, shining in the diffuse sunlight from above. So many of her ancestors had cherished this artifact, even if they hadn't known what it truly was. Returning it felt a little like betrayal.

"You were never the owners," Lir said, with slightly more patience. "Just the caretakers."

"And it's time for them to return home," Macaria said, with far more gentleness.

Naia nodded. They were right, she supposed, and even if they weren't, the safety of her people was far more valuable than holding on to an heirloom.

"What guarantee do we have that you won't just kill us?"

Lir snorted, but it was Astraia who spoke. "Little fae, if that had been what justice demanded, it would have already happened."

There was no way to respond, not any way that wouldn't have gotten her in more trouble, so she said nothing in reply. With one hand on the base between the three legs it stood on, and one on the plant within, Naia passed the cauldron over—pulling the plant free in the process, roots and all.

Surprise, and no small amount of distaste written on his face, Lir blurted, "Why did you do that?"

"Just...something to remember it by," she lied.

Seemingly satisfied with her reply, the gods shared a final glance with the queens before vanishing in a blink. Those who had blessed the four lingered a moment longer, offering smiles of farewell but saying nothing.

The queens of Aestera, forever locked into a cycle of servitude to the gods, were finally truly free.

Chapter 70

Eve

Five Years Later

"The funeral is to be held tomorrow," Mason said, strolling into the garden at her side.

It was at least his third visit to Falias in as many months, each time to deliver some important message. One that could easily have been sent by letter, but Eve knew her sister-in-law was the real reason he came so often.

"Yes," Eve replied, nodding, "in Darkgrove, but a prayer here in Falias the day after. I remember."

She offered the counselor a smile. He'd been serving Brida well these last few years and had ensured her transition to the throne had been as smooth as possible. Thankfully, the tenuous relationship between her new kingdom and her old had managed to hold steady in the years since everything had changed, thanks in no small part to Mason's efforts.

How far we've come, she mused.

"You should retire and move here," she said, not for the first time.

Mason rolled his eyes lightly. Though she remained the same as she'd been the day they had first met in the council chambers, his face was beginning to show the signs of aging. A gift from Naia, the reminder she'd kept of the war they'd won, had arrived earlier in the day. The one they hoped would grant him a long life to match that of his beloved's.

"You sound like Cora," he laughed. "But," he sighed, "I am considering it. After Eldred's passing..." He trailed off, leaving the rest unspoken.

The elder councilor's death had been painful for both Mason and Eve. Expected, but painful nonetheless.

"It's not the same," she finished for him. "I understand." Coming to a stop by a pretty ivy-covered arch, open to the rolling green lawn beyond, Eve placed a hand on her rounded belly. It wouldn't be long now. Days, a week at most.

A light breezed lifted her hair, and she turned to gaze at the forest beyond. Bright yellows and fiery oranges dotted with pale browns and dark reds stretched as far as the eye could see. Contentment had her heart swelling.

Home.

The word danced through her mind as it had the first time she'd seen this place.

Darkegrove, the kingdom she'd fought for, died for, would always have its place in her heart, but Falias was home.

"Here you two are." The sound of Callan's voice had her turning in time to see him striding across the lawn toward them. "They've finished, if you're up for the walk."

"I'm not so fat that I can't take a short walk, Callan," she teased.

"Of course not, Dove," he replied sweetly.

Mason made a sound that might have been gagging, and Eve rolled her eyes. Callan ignored him entirely. Though the two had long since moved beyond their dislike of one another, she couldn't help but worry they would never truly get along, even for Cora's sake.

Taking her hand in his, Callan led them down the stone-lined path to the western edge of the forest. In the aftermath of Kore's death, so many things had happened so quickly. Treaties renegotiated, trade and diplomacy between the now six kingdoms of Aestera debated. Some humans had seen the return of the fae as a bad omen, the true threat; others, as a thing to rejoice.

One man, the eldest of her father's advisors, had dreamed of such a thing. The return of the beauty and mystery, as he had once referred to it, of the fae. Had dreamt of seeing the great city of Falias.

She'd returned to Falias less than a week after the war had ended, and immediately had Eldred brought to the city, where he would spend the last of his remaining years doing the thing he'd dreamt of. When he passed just days ago, his remains had been returned to his family estate in Darkegrove so that their traditional funeral rites could be observed.

But here, where a part of his heart had always been, he would be remembered as well.

"Will Leysa and Valerian be back in time?" she asked, glancing at Callan.

He shrugged, one shoulder lifting as he glanced skyward. "They said they would. I've been asked to tell you not to allow their favorite baby on the planet to arrive before they return, so I assume they won't be long."

Eve rolled her eyes, laughing lightly. "Which anniversary is this again?"

Callan snorted. "They've been together too long for me to remember now."

She smiled, falling into silence again as they continued their easy pace toward the site she'd chosen.

Her heart gave a squeeze as they reached the monument at the edge of the western woods. A pillar of polished white stone, hewn from the Sgiath to the north, stood tall and proud.

"In memory of Lord Eldred Grey," Eve read aloud as she stepped closer, trailing her fingers over the words. "For his wise counsel, and years of friendship." She nodded, blinking away the tears. "He would have loved this," she said, smiling at Callan and Mason.

Mason moved to her side, placing his palm flat against the cool stone.

"He was very proud of you," Mason said quietly. "You know that, right?"

Callan moved to her side, pressing a hand to the small of her back, a simple gesture of comfort.

Mason's words had her eyes burning, and she nodded. "I know."

"He told me once," Mason said, voice cracking with emotion. "How ashamed he was, of both of us, for ever standing in your way." Eve opened her mouth to argue, to tell him that those days were long past and it didn't matter now, but he held up a hand, asking her to wait. "We were wrong, Majesty," he said, ignoring her long-standing request that he call her Eve now. "You saved Darkegrove. You saved everyone."

"We did it together," she replied, voice a hoarse whisper. "All of us."

CHAPTER 71

LIA

TWENTY YEARS LATER

"Hold still, Terra!" Eyla snapped. "You're worse than a skittish colt, I swear."

Terra rolled her brown eyes. "I'm just nervous. It's my wedding day."

"And if you keep moving," her twin, Sidra, sighed, "Eyla will stab you with that pin and there will be blood on your gown."

Terra groaned but went still, allowing Eyla to finish her task, pinning the torn hem of the white gown.

Lia sighed at the girls, smiling despite the aching in her heart. Her gaze drifted to where Bella stood by the sunny window, speaking with the twins' father.

The one who remained.

Tears burned her eyes as she dragged her attention to Terra again, who spun in a slow circle before the tall oval mirror leaned against the pretty blue wall of Terra's home in Falias.

"You're thinking about him again," Terra observed, her gaze meeting Lia's in the mirror.

"Yes," Lia admitted. "I am. He would be so incredibly proud of who you two have grown up to be, and," she went on, glancing to Amias' husband, who pressed a knuckle to the corner of his eye, "he would be so happy for you."

Terra smiled sadly. "I wish I could have known him."

Lia's heart nearly cracked in two. "Oh, Terra," she sighed.

"But I'm glad we met you," Terra said.

Sidra wrapped her arms around Lia's neck fiercely. "Me too," she whispered.

"Thank you, Aunt Lia, for helping us keep a part of him with us," Terra said, wrapping her arms around both her twin and Lia.

She had no words, none that wouldn't result in more tears for all of them, so instead, she squeezed both girls tightly before stepping back to look them over. "Now, you look perfect. But I think there are some lovely peonies in the garden out back that would complement your hair, Sidra. Why don't you three go out and find one?"

The twins nodded, chattering quietly as they made their way out of the room, followed by their father. Alone with Eyla and Bella, Lia let loose the long sigh she'd been holding back, along with more than a few tears for the man who had once been her protector and friend.

"Are you okay, mom?" Eyla asked gently, cocking her head to the side in a way that reminded her so much of the little girl she'd been when they first met.

"I'm okay. Go tell the girls it's time to go," she smiled.

BRIGHT SUMMER SUNLIGHT BEAMED DOWN ON THE CROWD gathered in the meadow, just beyond the city walls. An arch of flowers had been erected where loving promises to honor one another would be made before a blue-clad priestess of Aine, goddess of love and harmony.

A small part of Lia couldn't help but wonder which position she had taken during the debate about their lives, so many years before.

The sound of giggling drew her gaze, and she spotted a toddler with bouncing red curls being scooped up into Callan's arms. Their third daughter in a row, with perhaps another on the way, she mused, noting the way Eve's hand rested on her abdomen as they settled into their seats.

Bella's hand slipped into her own, giving a squeeze. "Our girls are all grown up," she sighed.

Lia couldn't help but smile at the woman who owned her heart. "They are."

Silver grey eyes studied her face for a long moment in silence; reading every thought, as they always did. "He won't ever be left behind, Sunlight. You make sure of that. You've kept your promise to care for his girls in the best possible way." She lifted a hand, gently wiping away a tear from Lia's cheek. "You are the light in all of our lives."

"Thank you," Lia whispered, pressing a kiss to Bella's lips.

"For what?" Bella asked.

"For making my life so beautiful," Lia whispered.

CHAPTER 72

NAIA

THIRTY YEARS LATER

The canyon rattled with the thunderous roar above. Damian's shout followed it, urging her to run. She'd been running for what felt like hours.

Her feet pounded against the rocky earth as she sprinted.

Faster. Hurry.

She couldn't see if he was still behind her, didn't dare risk the time it would take to look.

She could pace, if she wanted. Could see her destination in her mind. But getting there, the burning in her lungs, the strain in her muscles as she pushed herself harder; that was half the fun of it.

A roar sounded again, closer this time, rattling the very ground they ran on. Every breath burned, but her heart sang with the excitement of it all. Moments later she skidded to a halt, sending pebbles flying over the edge of the cliff, as Damian's hand gripped her forearm, pulling her back. She'd been in no real danger, they both knew that, but the man was a worrier, she thought, tossing him a grin.

"Did we miss–"

The roaring sounded again, this time so much closer.

Stepping back, she collided with Damian's broad chest, and looked skyward. A mass of bronze scales swept over their heads, gleaming in the spring sunlight. Wind whipped across them, forcing her to shield her eyes from the dust the dragon's flapping wings had sent flying.

They'd been tracking the stories of other travelers, sightings and rumors for years. Just to find this spot, to glimpse one of the few remaining dragons on the eastern continent.

She had remained in Coruscis long enough to see her home rebuilt, to see Maren crowned and wedded to Aelius, who had relinquished his claim to Avellon in order to be with her. A distant cousin had been crowned in Avellon sometime later, though she hadn't paid much attention to whom the choice had been.

The part of her who had cared about such things died the day Kore had.

Only once in the long years since that day had she returned, and it was to bury their mother, who passed more than a decade after the Void had been vanquished from their world.

"Maren will never believe this," she shouted above the roaring of the departing dragon, driving the twinge of guilt her sister's name brought with it from her mind. She would need to visit again, she reminded herself, and soon. Maren was nearly sixty now.

Damian's answering laugh rumbled through her. "Where to next, Thunderheart?"

"I want to see it all," she said, spinning to face him. "Show me everything there is."

Chapter 73

Colette

Fifty Years Later

"Tell us again! Tell us the one we like the most!"

Colette sighed, but smiled at her youngest. His bright green eyes, so like his father's, twinkled with mischief. "Alright, my beloved, but only once more. It is bedtime."

Lumi wiggled happily as Colette straightened the blanket over him before turning to his sister, waiting contentedly for her to do the same for her.

"Once upon a time," she began, with dramatic emphasis. "There were three beautiful queens of Aestera..."

The End

Author's Note

For a long time, writing one book seemed unattainable, but here we are with book number three. I would never have been able to make it this far without the help of amazing people who cheered me on, gave me advice, and helped me come back from the brink of burn out more than once.

To my readers: THANK YOU. THANK YOU. THANK YOU. Without your support, this trilogy would have fizzled out with book one. I am forever amazed at how incredibly supportive you all have been, and will be forever grateful.

To my amazing editor: Kathy, you have been an absolute godsend and I appreciate you helping me shape the mess I give you into something actually readable–and for taking a hatchet to 'that' for me.

B.T.B: The maps you've created for me made this world real in a way they wouldn't have been without your amazing art, thank you so much.

To my Platonic Square: I never could have done this without you three. I love you all (platonically) and appreciate you more than you know.

And to my husband, thank you for not letting me give up when things got hard, or I got tired and discouraged. Thank you for always being so supportive and for bragging about me (even when it was a little embarrassing). You are my best friend and biggest supporter, and I love you so much.

About the Author

Tricia Meyers is an avid reader and writer of fantasy romance, a collector of too many pens, a part-time coffee enthusiast, and a full-time mom. Writing has been her passion since childhood and has always been an outlet for her, creatively.

www.ingramcontent.com/pod-product-compliance
Lightning Source LLC
Chambersburg PA
CBHW022307310726
48973CB00001B/242